The Broken Daisy Chain

The Broken Daisy Chain

Best wishes x
H . L . F

Amanda Williams

A . Williams
x

Riverside Publishing Solutions

Amanda Williams asserts her moral right to be identified as the author of this book.

Published by Amanda Williams with Riverside Publishing Solutions
www.riversidepublishingsolutions.com

Copyright © 2021 Amanda Williams

ISBN: 978-1-913012-45-8 (Paperback)

For permission requests, write to the publisher, addressed
"Attention: Permissions Coordinator," at

contact@riversidepublishingsolutions.com

Printed and bound in the UK.

CONTENTS

Chapter 1	1	Chapter 18	197
Chapter 2	15	Chapter 19	215
Chapter 3	33	Chapter 20	223
Chapter 4	43	Chapter 21	231
Chapter 5	55	Chapter 22	248
Chapter 6	62	Chapter 23	258
Chapter 7	73	Chapter 24	278
Chapter 8	87	Chapter 25	295
Chapter 9	97	Chapter 26	305
Chapter 10	107	Chapter 27	317
Chapter 11	118	Chapter 28	330
Chapter 12	127	Chapter 29	346
Chapter 13	138	Chapter 30	356
Chapter 14	148	Chapter 31	370
Chapter 15	156	Chapter 32	383
Chapter 16	170	Chapter 33	395
Chapter 17	180		

CHAPTER 1

Every evening without fail I stood alone at my bedroom window discovering old childhood memories and creating what I thought were going to be perfect dreams ready for my future, but I already knew that my life was never going to be quite that simple, as life itself would prove difficult standing in my way, never allowing me to have the perfect life that I now so desired and craved, knowing that the dark, destructive storm clouds had already started to gather pace far away in the distance.

With the ambient light of the early evening now flooding through the window, lovingly casting mellow shadows throughout my bedroom, a glowing amber light seemed to bounce from wall to wall and as it did, I glimpsed at my reflection in the mirror, suddenly I was aware that I wasn't a little girl anymore as a swan like vision now graced my mirror, a very beautiful and somewhat spirited swan with a glowing dark, silky plumage complete with a delicate and unblemished porcelain face, now having and wanting to repeatedly revisit the mirror, making sure it was me that was reflecting back and not the mellow early evening light that was playing tricks with me. Looking once again at my porcelain face, touching it softly with my petit fingertips, not wanting to tarnish the stunning reflection, my long shiny jet black hair that flowed down my back in waves of pure and decadent silk cascading against my pale tender, and for now, blemish free young skin, along with my beautiful emerald-green eyes that now sparkled like frozen glass beads, my breasts full and pert, my shapely long legs complimented the new grown up Lizzy.

I could not stop gazing at the reflection that was looking back at me, disbelieving the reflection that I thought could not possibly be me. But it was me as I pinched myself sharply to make sure, my transformation was now stunning me, wanting impatiently to show off my new transformation to anyone willing to admire the new me, but I would have to wait until the morning to unleash my new-found beauty. So now, with a new day unfolding, I was once again dazzled and dazed with the attractive swan like beauty that I had become, leaving behind my adorable childhood in the shadows of my mirror, long gone now were my childish looks, my baby face features along with my childhood innocence, long gone were the innocent days when the days were endless, allowing me to cycle for miles with not a care in the world while the sun peppered warm refreshing kisses on my tender unblemished face, inhaling the stunning summers pure perfume, feeling the delicate, warm breeze rushing through my hair never again would my mirror reflect my glorious childhood that was now cast aside in the blink of an eye in a bid to embrace a future that would shake, disrupt and taint my life in bitter hatred, betrayal, endless lies, deception, grief and utter harrowing sadness, but accompanied by the most beautiful love that would be impossible to understand.

Suddenly I was brought back to reality, taking me away from my stunning reflection for now by my mother calling me relentlessly from the hallway as she waited impatiently for me at the bottom of the long twisting and creaking staircase with her arms firmly folded ready to cast her opinion on my school uniform which now with my new-found beauty would break every rule in the book.

Don't wear your skirt so short Lizzy, my mother said in a sharp and very stern voice as I wafted down the stairs. *I know, I know* I huffed as I pulled it down just to please her, rolling my eyes at her in disapproval, of her stern and unwelcome words, some of which I had heard so many times before. I huffed again my disapproval as I swept past her on my way to the kitchen, leaving her once again speechless and motionless in the hallway. Stunned and somewhat dazed by my new flirtatious appearance her objection was very clear to see as she looked over her glasses that were perched on the tip of her nose, making her scowl today all the more prominent.

I grabbed some toast and my tatty old leather school bag that had been written on, with drawn on markings and tattoos that now formed my life in one way or another, now with the new grown-up Lizzy, my bag would also carry new tattoos and blemishes that would contain stories that would shape and shake my world.

I breezily kissed my mum goodbye, who was still standing motionless in the hallway before glancing again at my new-found radiant look in the hall mirror before I slammed the door loudly behind me, smiling to myself once again in total approval.

I was loving life, absorbing it like a sponge to quench my ongoing desires, taking in the passion of the changing seasonal aromas, watching life itself flash by me, a time to embrace to the full, while still creating the many dreams that I would take into my future, a future that would test me and those in my life to the limits with not only love and laughter but with deep harrowing sadness, grief and constant torment as the storms would be relentless, tattooing my body with endless scars that would haunt me, taunt me and terrify me throughout my life.

I was just a normal teenage girl from a small, very pretty Wiltshire village where I was born and bred, attending the small intimate little school. At weekends I would play in the surrounding fields and woods, running free and untroubled by torment with not a care in the world, enjoying the company of my fellow friends, not worrying in the slightest what we looked like.

The little village shop which seemed to sell everything from milk to makeup, stamps to sausages, a shop in which we would buy sweets to eat on the way home from school an everyday ritual, when we had pocket money to spend.

And of course the village church, in which I was christened, that stood proud right next to my home, allowing me the privilege to hear the earthy tones of the church clock clanging out on the hour every hour, to hear the bells being rang on a Monday evening and on a Sunday morning calling everyone to the early service, hearing the heavy thud and chimes coming from the bell tower as the bell ringers clung on tight to the ropes that seemed at any moment would escape them, to smell the newly cut grass that surrounded the church.

But now I wore my skirts short to attract the attention of the boys, desperately trying to be the centre of attention like most girls but I was totally unaware of the consequences and the terrifying devastation that it would bring throughout my life in a bid to find my perfect dream, to have the love I now craved daily.

I drifted from one boy to the next, knowing most of them were not ready to join me on my voyage to retrieve my dreams but I still yearned so much more, still wanting to be that one special schoolboy's dream.

I imagined my life mapped out, to live every one of my many dreams, to capture the rainbows I chased daily, to find the pot of gold that was secretly hidden. But was life really going to be that simple or was I still chasing the dreams that I now thought would evade me all my life and never being able to find the end of the rainbow that remained elusive?

I now yearned to embrace the life that was about to unfold in the coming months and years, knowing my fate would take me on many journeys, some of which would be terrifyingly funny, some terrifyingly thrilling, some just terrifying and some terrifyingly sad, some that I would undoubtedly just want to forget but knowing I would never be allowed that privilege, knowing they would leave my body fragile coated in terrifying scars and tattoos that would mark my delicate skin, never allowing me the freedom to forget.

Our house was large with lots of places in which to hide away if needed and a great place to explore as a child, to play hide-and-seek, to be free to climb the apple trees that would scrape and bruise my legs, but it allowed me to be free to chase my dreams, big and small. The house was set back a little from the village church, nestled beautifully on the outskirts, away from the village itself.

My little tree house sat high in the large old oak tree that stood tall and proud in the middle of the garden, gracing the well-kept manicured lawn, commanding in its presence with its impressive stature, it was a great place to follow my constant dreams and to create memories ready to be recalled when I needed them, and on this late afternoon visit it was no different as I sat crossed legged day dreaming.

One large vista graced the garden, allowing us to have stunning views across the fields, leading to the woods where I just stood in silence, listening to the owls calling each other safely home with loud shrills, whistles and hoots. One by one I saw them soaring high above the tree tops until it was time to seek the sanctuary of the place they called home, almost floating back into the woods with their wings outstretched, feathers of snow white flecked and speckled with burnished brown, jet black and rich ruby red.

The long days of spring were here at last, I looked forward to embracing the days that would lead me to long walks alone, across the fields and into the woods, walking on a carpet of deep green velvet moss which was so soft underfoot it begged me to walk bare foot to feel its luxury between my toes. As I walked ever deeper into the woods, it became darker, even more mystifying as underfoot there was a very different carpet that was now covering this most beautiful, enchanting woodland.

I continued to walk over broken branches and discarded leaves that were old and brown having fallen from high above last autumn, now scrunching and snapping under my feet. I stood silent for a while, watching the squirrels dive for cover as I had invaded their home, interrupting them as they scurried about enjoying their daily life. The peace and tranquillity here allowed me to capture more of my future dreams and to relive the many memories that I had already made along with the many people that had graced my short life and for those who I had not yet met.

I remained totally unaware of the many heartaches that lay ahead for me in the coming months and years as my journey continued gathering speed daily, not allowing me to catch my breath. I had to ride the roller-coaster that had already started its monumental life-changing journey that would leave my body fragile, frail, tattered and very afraid of what the future would bring, knowing I had now left my childhood years in the shadow of my bedroom mirror and was now in the grip of very virginal years that would be full of surprises, some delightful, some terrifying, some funny and sad, leading me to take some very unexpected paths of darkness and of extreme light, but both would lead me astray along with the people I would meet along the way. I was a young girl waiting and wanting to be loved and to give my love in return to the right person, I knew he was out there somewhere, I just had to find him and find him I would, knowing I was already in love with him. How long would I have to wait for him to come forward? I was now convinced that it would take me on yet another terrifying roller-coaster of a journey, along with emotions that I would never have felt before, new emotions that would test my resolve daily and haunt my dreams regularly.

I stayed on after school some days to visit the cafe, all of us in the group would be there. The cafe was a great place to be with friends, the atmosphere was electric, everyone wanted to be there. The girls would all dance to the fantastic music coming from the old, battered jukebox that sat comfortably in the corner, repeatedly playing the songs we loved to dance to. The boys would just look on, feasting there gaze on the mass of beautiful girls that danced around them.

The smell of the cafe was unique, like no other place I knew, tables lined either side of the cafe and were covered with blue-check plastic clothes that seemed permanently stuck to the old tatty tables beneath. The chairs were also tatty and battered having been sat and stood on over the years, but these made the cafe what it was.

The girls were mostly my age and the boys were usually older and this, for some reason, seemed to be normal, allowing us to almost grow up quicker, relishing in the amazing and sometimes crazy time we would spend together, forming life-time friendships that would never be compromised, life-time friendships that would never fail to embrace us throughout the following months and years that lay ahead.

Lots of my friends had already started smoking the odd cigarette when they could scrounge them from the older boys who stood in groups outside the cafe shrouded in a fog of smoke that drifted silently into the cafe every time the door swung open and closed, hearing all of them coughing and spluttering as they indulged heavily in what had become a bad habit for most of them but still they encouraged me to try, however, I hated the vile smell that seemed to linger on their clothes and their breath so I hesitated, rebuffing their constant requests.

July came and the hot summer days were here at last, the school holidays were here again to thrill me, at last I was free from my stuffy uniform, free from homework and boring lessons, now free to take late evening walks with friends inhaling the heady perfume from the wild flowers that laced the hedgerows and green road-side banks with powerful vanilla undertones to compliment the floral notes, while taking our picnics into the woods being set free to unleash our growing spirits.

I managed to get a holiday job a few hours a week in a lovely big manor house, one hot mid-summer day I suddenly caught a glimpse of a young man with dark hair, he was tall, very good looking, older than me, his name was Paul. As we chatted, he made me feel very special, not like the other lads I hung around with, I suppose that was due to him being someone I didn't know, but this was different or it felt different maybe because I desperately wanted it to be real, leading me to question if it was Paul that I had given my heart to. Was it him that I craved day-by-day? Only time would tell and allow me to know if Paul, being much older than me, made it more exciting and more appealing as he would give me a certain look. I was flattered and impressed that I could attract someone like him and as the days passed we seemed to enjoy being in each other's company.

I loved the way Paul made me feel, saying all the right things at all the right times as I became blinkered and flattered by his flirtatious attention, along with his flattering words and his ability to make me feel I was special.

One particular afternoon it was scorching hot and I was asked to go to the cellar to collect items for the garden party that was to be held that weekend where lots of important people were due to visit, to enjoy a lavish party on the lawn and in the house, everyone doing something to make the grounds and the house look spectacular. The cellar was jammed pack full of stuff, old sofas, chairs, along with a massive amount of boxes that were full of unwanted, unloved stuff that at some point had been someone's beloved treasures, the cellar was cold and smelt musty, mixed with a dusty sort of smell. It was dark with very little light. As I rummaged around I was startled by an unexpected noise, I looked up from the tatty box in which I was examining the treasure that was held within, suddenly I noticed a figure standing back in the dark shadows. I was taken aback, gasping as now an ice cold shiver triggered fear inside me, I was now very scared. It was Paul, and for the first time ever he made me feel very uneasy as he just stood motionless, staring at me, his dark sapphire blue eyes burning into my skin. My gaze now firmly fixed on his, whilst my body froze to the harsh floor beneath me, not allowing me to move even my fingers. As I gasped for air that was stagnant within this cold and dark cellar, I was suddenly aware of the roar from the storm that was now casting its dark and unwelcome clouds today.

Come here, he said in a harsh demanding voice. *Come over here Lizzy.* His voice now echoing through my vulnerable body, making me tremble with a cold fear, a fear that left me feeling very alone and afraid, wanting desperately for someone to come to release me from the petrifying ordeal that was about to unfold in this dark, unwelcome, and dingy damp cellar.

I was alone with him and there was nowhere that I could run, nowhere to hide as he now had me backed into the dark and unlit corner, his voice was icy cold, harsh and demanding, which terrified me. He began forcing his body ever closer to mine, trying to kiss my delicately painted lips, touching repeatedly my delicate porcelain face, his body heavy against my young, petite and fragile frame. My fragile and vulnerable state had now started to unravel within this dark cellar, leaving me lifeless as I stood once again nailed to this very spot, still unable to gasp the air I needed desperately to breath as his heavily pungent odour filled the dark cellar, my nostrils now full of the rancid odour that I was being forced to breathe.

His hands were now all over me, touching me, repeatedly touching my virgin body, I was terrified that he would hurt me as he kept demanding

I would do as I was told. I tried desperately to rebuff his constant and vile demands on my body as I felt his rough hands creeping over my skin, leaving it blemished in evil, his lips kissing my naked arms, kisses that flowed roughly on to my neck, my body now panicked with ridged fear.

Suddenly finding the strength from somewhere I pushed him away with force as I screamed at him to get out of my way, my petrifying screams were now echoing through the cellar, bouncing repeatedly from every wall. He shouted back loudly at me, *Lizzy you're a tease, just a little fucking tease.* I was then once again panicked as I felt his rough hand brush against my arm, he tried desperately to pull me back into the corner where I was sure he would unleash his pent up sexual aggression on my virgin body.

I ran for the stairs, tripping repeatedly on the uneven concrete steps in a desperate attempt to get away from him, scraping and bruising my knees before reaching the heavy cellar door, slamming it shut behind me with such force that it seemed to shudder through the long corridor, right to the enormous wooden framed front door which at the same time seemed to vibrate through my body that was now shaking with extreme fear of what might have happened if I had allowed him to continue to violate my virgin body. His lingering stench still followed me, clinging to my clothes in a desperate bid to not let me forget my tender years.

I looked down to my knees, they were now blood stained from my trip and were stinging. I bathed them with warm water, trying hard not to cry. Suddenly I looked up into the mirror to see a frightened little girl looking back, I then knew I was still a little girl fighting hard to be someone I wasn't.

Nothing happened in the cellar with Paul and I was relieved that it didn't as I was scared for so many reasons, maybe it was because it was real and that I had allowed it somewhat willingly to happen in a bid to quench my desires, but today I heard the terrifying roar of the storm gathering pace, ready to unleash its punishing cargo over me in my quest to have the dreams I craved.

I returned to the dreary days of school life, following an almost perfect summer and fast approaching my fifteenth birthday, so with a new term unfolding I was ready to embrace every minute, to soak up the unique aromas, to listen delightfully to the sounds of life that embraced us all, waiting for life to take us on endless journeys.

Today it was the uninspiring cookery class all morning, not my strongest subject. I watched the clock that seemed to have stopped, its hands seemed frozen in time, not allowing me my freedom of the social life I craved daily. I was not at all interested in the domestic thing, so as class finished I was relieved to hear at last the heavy chiming bell that told me delightfully that it was over for another week.

I smiled to myself as I rushed through the classroom doors, not wanting to remain a minute longer, surrounded by four clinically white stark walls. I walked alone down the hard, uninspiring, and harsh concrete staircase to collect my things ready for my next lesson with my mind as always, far away from the here and now.

Suddenly I was stopped in my tracks by what seemed like an army marching all over me, a feeling that was now running riot through my body, attacking every emotion, making me shudder and shake. A boy had suddenly caught my eye as he waited to one side of the staircase after finishing his lesson in the science lab.

I knew full well he was a boy that carried with him a dark reputation, a jack-the-lad type, that I had been warned not to get involved with by so many people on so many occasions as he and his close crowd of friends carried with them a bad reputation, one that continued to follow him around like a really bad smell that would without doubt linger well into his future, just like the crowd he seemed to hang around with.

I could not take my eyes off him as he smiled such an intoxicating smile, so much so I could not help but smile back repeatedly, blushing at my actions, knowing full well he was a boy that I should not be exchanging glances with, let alone flirtatious smiles.

This boy, Charlie, had that cocky attitude and a confident beaming smile, a smile you could only describe as intoxicating, one that today unleashed within me so many new and unguarded emotions that had remained muted until now. I took my first steps on an uneasy path that would be sure to lead me astray, now with mixed emotions lashing my body as one emotion was replaced instantly by yet another, taking my breath away and leaving me gasping for air, fighting for my next breath as I remained unaware of my fellow class mates rushing past me on their way to the next boring class, encouraging me to hurry up and warning me to not be drawn in by his flirtatious advances, but I once again remained stunned, muted and breathless, glued to the step that I was stood on.

He was not the usual sort of boy I would have ever looked twice at until today, with his long unkempt hair, a light chestnut-brown colour, his eyes

9

the deepest of brown. He had a scruffy, dishevelled appearance but he had something about him, something I wanted and something I was now going to have at any cost while I stood silently embracing the power of this unexpected and very sudden silent, but very monumental moment that we were sharing, still taking my breath away and leaving me gasping for air as I stood ridged on the last cold concrete step of the staircase, frightened to take the next step in case I fell.

With our eyes now firmly gripped on each other I didn't dare take my gaze away as I was terrified that I was dreaming, but I wasn't dreaming, this was real as he nodded his approval of my ongoing smiles that had now swept across my porcelain face, smiles that were replaced by blushes that in return were replaced by beaming virginal smiles.

It was today for the first time ever that I had been seduced by a perfect smile. His smile, a smile of seduction that would undoubtedly rule my life now and in the forthcoming weeks, months and even in the years that were to follow if I continued to allow myself to be swept along on this roller-coaster, the roller-coaster that would never allow me to get my breath, that would never allow me the privilege to stop the ongoing journey that would be tainted by my own stupidity.

Was this it? Was this the boy who had already stolen my heart? Was this what I had craved for so long? Could he be the one? We continued to share each other's smiles, sharing each other's gaze, feasting on each other's bodies, but why would he be so interested in me, little Lizzy, when I felt sure his advances might have been reserved for one or more of the older girls that hung around him in small groups chewing on stale over chewed and tasteless gum, the same girls that would mend the holes in their tights with clear nail varnish in a bid to stop the holes turning into ladders, inhaling second hand nicotine drenched air that clung to their clothes for days on end, all of them wearing thick layers of makeup that seemed to be permanently stuck to their faces, all wanting to indulge and revel in his dark, secret and somewhat sexy reputation?

Suddenly a teacher shouted at me sharply whilst clapping her hands loudly, making me jump back to the here and now, her voice impatience for my approval today. *You're going to be very late for your next class Lizzy.* Startled by her command I shuffled away, annoyed that she had interrupted such a monumental moment for me, I glared at her with such frustration, how dare she spoil this important moment, a moment that I could never repeat, a moment that I had longed to experience as all I wanted was to stand and stare at this boy who had something I wanted, and something that I had to have, so with that in mind I could not wait for my next class to end.

Lunchtime came and went, the afternoon classes lasted for what seemed like forever, I could not stop thinking about him, it was torture for me. Seeing him clearly in my mind I recaptured his cocky smile, storing it away until I could experience that perfect smile again in person, hoping it would take my breath away once more, but was he just testing the water, testing my resolve? Like some sort of initiation into his world to see if I fitted in, or was I making too much of the dark circle that surrounded him, casting a dark and mysterious suspicion of my own, wondering if the girls who already surrounded him had been through such a test?

Now being jolted back to the here and now I glanced up at the huge wooden clock that hung on the plain and stark white wall that now seemed to have stopped, although I could hear it ticking loudly and with every second it felt like an hour, time seemed to be standing still, denying me the privilege to enjoy his smiles again and to be seduced heavily by his reputation.

The teacher had not even noticed that I wasn't listening, now my thoughts were far away from the maths lesson that was going on within these uninspiring dull four walls. I looked out of the window into the distance, staring at nothing. It was impossible to concentrate now, my mind was only on him, the boy with the wicked and very cocky smile that I could not wait to see again, fuelled now by an intense and somewhat terrifying need to see him again.

I could feel myself falling in love for the first time and the feeling was terrifying, but mixed with so many wonderful sensations, now rippling emotions were bombarding me from every direction, questioning over and over again... Was this the love that I had craved for? Was this boy going to change my life in the following weeks, months, even years to come, knowing full well he would turn my life upside down? But now I was ready to take all the love the bad-boy wanted to deliver.

Suddenly the afternoon bell clanged loudly, making me jump back to the here and now, classes were finally over for today, but I still could not get this boy out of my head. Who was he? Where was he? Was it him that had stolen my heart never to be retuned? The questions again were now relentless as the list continued to grow with vigour.

Exhausted from falling in love I headed to bed continuing my dreams for the future. I must have fallen into a deep sleep as I was awoken by the smell of toast that wafted throughout the house that was being burnt from the toaster in the kitchen, mum had a habit of always managing to burn my toast on a daily basis.

Now with a new day unfolding I was looking forward to seeing a glimpse of the boy I had fallen heavily in love with in such a short space of time, but as the day went on I gave up all hope in seeing him, it was a large school after all and he could be anywhere advancing his smiles, his flirtatious and dark reputation on the many girls that seemed to want his full attention and now it was my name that had been added to that list. Feeling deflated I walked into the wash-rooms to wash my hands and to find my coat amongst the mass of others that hung on the hooks patiently waiting to be collected. Suddenly I heard a noise from behind me, I turned around stunned and to my utter amazement it was him, his presence was now nailing me once again to the concrete floor, my body ridged with an overwhelming feeling of something that I knew had to be love as it couldn't be anything else.

He took my hand, holding it gently in his, whispering *my gorgeous Lizzy, my little Lizzy*. I was speechless as my heart started melting into a watery puddle that flowed across the floor and into the corridor beyond, creating yet another tidal wave of emotion to sweep over me and to allow others to witness my somewhat terrifying delight as they stood shaking their heads in total disapproval of my new found love, voices now eagerly telling me to walk away echoed loudly through the corridor, wanting to spoil this moment for me, but nothing could or ever would.

Instantly I felt like I had grown into a young woman as my nipples were now hard, rigid and standing to attention, showing through my crisp white blouse, something that Charlie had clearly noticed as he focused his smile, that trademark cocky and flirtatious smile, making me blush repeatedly. He seemed delighted at my obvious sexual arousal. I felt his hand glide gently and delicately over my breasts, I closed my eyes to embrace this most beautiful moment, my breath taken away by his intimate touch before his fingers traced the outline of my porcelain and somewhat blemished skin, all made possible by him and at that moment. I felt a tight grip embracing my body, tightening with every breath I took, a grip that had wrapped around my body squeezing it so tight, leaving me unable to breath.

His perfect smile, his perfect brown eyes left me craving more as my emotions once again were exploding inside me, taking me on a new colourful journey into the future, a future that now would involve Charlie and his thriving, seductive reputation.

Still holding my hand firmly, he leant forward, allowing our lips to meet for the first time, his lips were soft but firm on mine as we shared such tender virginal kisses, instantly fireworks burst on my lips, exploding vigorously, peppering my body with sparks that lit every emotion within my young virginal body. I felt his hand touch my long dark flowing hair, his fingers were now gently running through the waves of dark silk that flowed down my back as now my body ached from the terrifying knocking that I knew was love that seemed to now echo through the corridor like thunder, wondering to myself if it was the impending storm that was about to unleash its cargo.

Did I fall in love with that boy today? My head said I did, my heart knew I did, but it never stopped me from constantly questioning why. Why him? Why me? What was the attraction we both so obviously held for each other? Knowing only time would tell, I knew that it was him that had my heart, that it was him that I had already fallen in love with and it was him that in return had promised to cherish it, but somehow I just knew it would be smashed into thousands of splinters causing heartache and pain repeatedly, nothing would ever be the same from now on, my heart and soul stolen by a bad-boy whose reputation would seduce me endlessly, haunting my most precious dreams daily, awakening me from my nightly dreams to relive his generous kisses, his dark reputation and his commanding image as he would now continue to hold my hand, leading me to take the journey with him, which unbeknown to me at this time would leave me weak, vulnerable, afraid and terrified, but on the other hand I would know the true meaning of love, Charlie's love, a love I had to have, a love that I was not willing to be denied at any cost now or in the future.

Alone in my bedroom I stood at the window, looking out across the fields and into the woods beyond, losing myself in my thoughts, reliving the moment when our lips met for the first time. Emotions again battled through my tender body as I continued to feel the immense tightening that was now embracing me.

Again I thought of all the girls he could have chosen... Why me? Why not? Why me? Why not? Questions that only Charlie had the answers for, knowing full well he was never short of female attention, girls would follow him around in a desperate attempt to attract his attention, all of them seduced by his reputation and all of them wanting desperately to be his girl.

My head was now screaming at me, saying *forget him Lizzy, walk away.* My heart was still pounding, it was never going to allow me to do that and I knew it never would, whatever life threw at me, Charlie would overrule everything, disrupting my life, shredding it into millions of pieces, scattering our love over the landscape near and far.

I spent all day on Saturday sat in my little tree house, drifting in and out of my dreams that were taking me on a wild journey that now involved Charlie, containing emotions that terrified me, but emotions that I loved to feel, all made possible by him and his very seductive reputation, along with his cocky attitude and huge confidence that radiated in his smile. Suddenly brought back with a jolt from my dreams for now, my mum was calling me from the back door, reminding me I had homework to finish, which in return reminded me how very young and how very immature I actually was.

CHAPTER 2

Sunday was here already and I was awoken to the familiar sounds coming from the church as the bells chimed, taking me away from my dreams in which I saw Charlie's cocky confident smiles, feeling his warm, sensual kisses on my lips, wanting the seduction that only a bad-boy could give me, to rule my life daily, to haunt me in my hours of darkness, awaking me from sleep, ready to be seduced by the reputation that he carried and in return my life would be turned upside down, jolted sideways and sent spinning by him but nothing could or would prepare me for the impact that he would have on my fragile body as alarm bells had already started to ring loudly, but nothing would stop me from loving him now or in the months and years that were to follow.

Monday morning was here at last. I rushed my breakfast in a desperate hurry to indulge myself in Charlie's world once again, to see his powerful cocky smile, to feel his hand holding mine. I glanced one last time in the hall mirror before I slammed the door behind me with my mother looking on in sheer disapproval of my rebellious look that today showed all too well in my appearance.

On arrival at school, Charlie was stood leaning casually against the heavy iron rusty gates that at times made this school a fortress, but today Charlie was displaying his cocky stature surrounded by a small group of girls all wanting his attention, all wanting to be his girl, but I had taken that title, it was mine now and once again I felt that tight grip engulfing my body as I saw him looking at me with those enormous flirtatious big brown eyes that had put a spell on me. Now I was his girl and I loved it as he held my hand smiling that smile that made me melt yet again into a wet, soggy mess.

As Charlie stood embracing my perfectly delicate frame, all the other girls turned and walked away, knowing full well that it was me that Charlie had chosen to be his girl and as I looked at him I was unable to contain my smile any longer, with his shirt not tucked into his trousers, his jacket obviously a hand-me-down that appeared to be two sizes too big, his tie not done up, a very scruffy dishevelled boy with the most wicked, adorable smile that completely took my breath away every time I looked at him. I was now smitten, smiling to myself while the other girls just looked on with envy, wishing to themselves that it was them that he was calling his princess, I smiled again knowing I was that girl.

It was time to go to class, leaving me in the corridor he whispered his undying love into my long flowing hair while he held my trembling hand allowing me to fall deeper in love with him as every minute slipped by my heart filled with even deeper emotions that just wanted to be unleashed.

The day went on, I tried to concentrate but I could not get Charlie free from my mind as I continued to relive the moment when I had fallen in love with him, sparking emotions, leaving me wanting more and leaving me breathless as I recalled his very contagious cocky, reputation filled smile.

Awoken from my thoughts by the end of lesson bell, I made my way through the maze of corridors, chatting to the many amazing friends that enriched my life, now it was time for the netball match which was being held in the sports hall today. I got changed along with all the girls and as always there was lots of giggling, chatting and laughter echoing throughout the clinical changing room into the corridors beyond, girls excitedly wanting to know about Charlie and how I had become his girl, all of them seemed totally surprised by our unexpected love affair, but no more surprised than me.

Heading back to the changing rooms with the match now over, my mind still in a constant whirl of emotions, I stepped through into the little doorway in need of a shower. Then, to my complete shock, Charlie grabbed me gently by my hand, pulling me lovingly into a toilet cubical, making me gasp at his ability on having made his way into the girls only changing rooms without being detected, once again his cocky attitude and confidence ruled. Now my fragile, virginal body had been crippled by emotions that seemed to be strangling me, starving it of life, taking my breath away once again.

With my heart now in my mouth, my trembling body, he gently but firmly put his hand over my mouth so that I could not make a sound, he then kicked the door shut, locking it sharply behind us, sending a shiver of excitement ricocheting through me. I felt like a very naughty girl, I *was* a naughty girl, but this was totally beyond my wildest dreams, allowing me to experience such sensual and seductive emotions, my body being crippled by sweet emotions that I loved and that I now craved for constantly, haunting my daydreams and terrifying my night's sleep.

He whispered again into my long flowing hair as he stroked my porcelain face, running his fingertips over my lips, I nodded in approval of this unexpected daytime treat but I remained terrified that I had allowed myself to fall so deeply, so quickly in love with him as once again my body felt embraced by the tight grip I was now experiencing regularly when I was in Charlie's company.

However, I questioned why me? Little Lizzy, the virgin with no experience, or was that what Charlie wanted? An inexperienced girl to mould into being the girl that he wanted me to be, but I was being stupid… He wanted me for me, I knew that deep down.

Whispering again, *you're my girl now Lizzy*, a title that I was delighted to accept, but I knew he was going to lead me astray, taking me far away from the innocent and free spirited girl I had been right up until the day our eyes met for the first time, knowing full well it would be accompanied by heartache, anguish, betrayal and devastation, but his love for me would command my daily life as now his words seemed to vibrate through this small, cold and very clinical toilet cubical. Charlie's tongue continued dancing with mine, like some out of control sexy ritual revolving around and around my mouth sending wave after wave of cravings that would become Charlie's dirty love.

His hands were now removing my netball top as he slowly and gently pulled it over my head, allowing my long jet black hair to cascade down my back against my silky, smooth, virginal pale skin, his steamy gaze piercing into my skin, leaving permanent scars of love that I would continually ask for in the coming weeks, months and maybe even the years that lay ahead, to ask for the intense, deep cutting scars that would constantly remind me of his love but would leave my body to unravel, leaving it so very vulnerable, naked and at times petrified with nowhere to hide.

His lips were now somewhat brutally hard against mine, his desire brimming over as he undid my white lace bra, letting it drop to the floor along with my discarded sweaty netball top, my nipples suddenly bursting into bud, tingling with extreme excitement as Charlie commanded their attention. It felt right, even though I knew it was very wrong to be sharing this very sensual moment in a sterile toilet cubical surrounded by the other girls and teachers who were totally unaware of the beautiful dirty love that was being created and shared by Charlie and I on this early autumn day.

I did worry about what everyone would think, especially my parents, knowing full well that they would not approve of him and me being together, especially my mother as I could already see the finger-pointing and the tongues wagging, but this was my time to enjoy with Charlie as he began to cast his dirty love over me, seducing me with his reputation that I knew would terrify me throughout our hopefully long relationship, causing me to question my love, the love that now belonged to Charlie.

He pulled away, I whispered *don't stop Charlie*, he smiled and then replied, *I'm not going to Lizzy*, before he lovingly lifted me up and stood me on the toilet seat. Not romantic, but extremely thrilling, he suddenly unhooked my netball skirt letting it drop to the floor along with my other discarded clothes, neither of us saying a word as he slowly drew his fingers down over my virgin nipples, sending wave after wave of excitement through my body that now begged for more, he then licked his fingertips one by one letting them once again slip gently down over my full bud-like nipples, allowing me to enjoy a sensation that I had never felt before, but a sensation that I had craved for in my dreams.

My body now semi-naked from clothes as warm kisses were now being peppered over my tender skin. I started to moan with delight, suddenly he kissed his fingers, placing them over my mouth so that we would not be heard, allowing us to share this sensual moment together in total silence for a while longer whilst the mayhem continued in the changing room with laughter and continued chat, something that should have distracted us from the intense sexual ritual that was being created between us but nothing could, I wanted to scream out to let the other girls know of my continued and sudden seduction. I continued to hear him breathing hard, feeling his intense breath on my skin that was warm and deep as he seductively slipped my pretty, virginal white laced edged knickers away from me, and without any hesitation I allowed it.

I was now naked apart from my white ankle socks and plimsolls which today really did reflect my extremely young and such virginal years. Charlie stood before me, fully clothed, feasting his gorgeous dark brown eyes over the vision that stood before him. I was still shaking in anticipation of his dirty love that I hoped I would now receive throughout my life as my body demanded Charlie's full attention daily, regardless of his reputation, regardless of what people thought, knowing full well my parents disapproval and for the many who would frown at our new found love.

He stroked my tummy tenderly with his fingertips before allowing them to slip gently down to slide along my virginal lips that he now called his kitten while smiling his cocky adorable smile. I closed my eyes, wanting to relish the intimacy between his ridged fingers and my soft, velvet kitten. I wanted more, much more of what Charlie would undoubtedly deliver as our love now seemed set in stone, never to be broken or lost now we had committed to a love that would at times test us and those around us, leaving our lives torn apart, fragile, battered and bruised, tattooed with a bitter sweet love. I glanced again into Charlie's eyes while he was still engrossed in my body, I relaxed again, allowing him full control to take my innocence away from me, just as he had taken my heart, I felt it was only right to allow him my fragile, tender virgin body. Right back to the here and now and I was aware that the changing room had fallen silent from the mayhem of laughter and giggling, I wanted to indulge myself further into Charlie's world but this was not the place to take our love to the next level, not here and not today, knowing I was now already very late for my next class.

As his lips met mine I felt his tongue once again revolve around my mouth, dancing seductively with my tongue, something that I would become addicted to, I then felt the pressure build on my lips for repeated kisses, my mouth being seduced again and again.

Suddenly there was a hard fist hitting hard at the door making us both jump silently. *Come on, you're going to be late for class Lizzy, get a move on*, the teacher said sharply. I replied to her while trembling within this cold little toilet cubical as I stood naked, free from my clothes that Charlie had removed so seductively from me, allowing me to become his girl. My thoughts then turned to wonder, maybe this was my initiation into being Charlie's girl, like some sort of test, leading me to wonder if all his girls had taken the same induction into Charlie's world.

Reeling from my thoughts I brushed them aside as I kissed him with kisses that were now hard with excitement as I entered freely into Charlie's world, now leaving us both in a state of unforeseen passion that still needed to be embraced, my virginity still intact but I knew it was only a matter of time before Charlie took that from me.

I unlocked the door quietly to let him out and as I did he looked back at me with is very cocky smile, tucking his shirt partly into his trousers with not a care in the world as he mouthed silently the words of love that would rule my world not only today, but into the future. I was delighted to receive his muted words, I blushed repeatedly to be rewarded by Charlie's addictive smile that again took my breath away and not for the first time today.

I hurried to dress, all a fumble back into my netball clothes before trying to find my uniform in the main changing room. Now in a complete state of panic, I could not find my little lace knickers. I looked everywhere, turning the changing room upside down, I then suddenly realised Charlie must have taken them, taken them as a trophy of our first sexual encounter to keep for himself, I smiled uncontrollably knowing I was now totally in love with him, also fully aware that he would change my life in one way or another as I had now allowed his reputation to take me on the journey that I had longed for.

So, for the rest of the day I remained free from my knickers which made me smile as I enjoyed the freedom and something I knew would become a habit, instantly knowing that Charlie had already started to change my life, leading me astray, allowing myself to be taken his hostage along with being seduced by him, by the secret life that he lead on a regular basis, fuelled by his reputation, his dark, mysterious life that left me wanting more.

After school we met again, his cocky smile allowed me the freedom to enter again freely into his world. As he held my hand I felt the love between us gathering pace and I knew he felt it to as I could now see the hunger gathering in his eyes, ready for me to enjoy whenever I so desired, but still I questioned my love for Charlie, asking myself could it really be this easy to love someone with such a seductive and bad reputation and every time the answer was yes and that was terrifying, knowing I was so desperately in love with a bad-boy and that he was in love with me.

At last it was half term, approaching late October, the time of the year that triggered so many emotions, but now the emotions were huge, out of control emotions that never failed to deliver, some thrilling and some terrifying, I could now spend more time with Charlie to have the most amazing dirty love that seemed to have made my cravings intensify. We loved our time together as we walked in the woods and through the fields with the smell of autumn all around us, with blackberries forming in the hedgerows, the leaves turning the most amazing range of almost opulent colours from green through to amber, sandwiched in between were russet reds, gleaming golds and burnt orange, colours so vibrant, glowing in the late hazy sunshine but now and again a slight chill filled the air, you could almost smell it, a heady aroma that just filled my nostrils with all that was autumn, a heavy vanilla aroma filled the air that was laced with blackberry undertones all rounded off with the aroma of smoky bonfires that had been left to smoulder, scenting the already heavily perfumed and musty air.

It was I think the second most romantic season, but now every season would bring romance along with heartache that was sure to be mine as Charlie and I continued our journey together. Saturday afternoon was here, my emotions were running wild as we went for a walk with his hand holding mine. I felt so very proud to be his girl, happy to be his girl at any cost, but what would that cost be? I felt sure it would cost not only me dearly, but Charlie also, even the people that surrounded us daily. Suddenly it started to rain so running for shelter we ended up in an old barn, secluded away in an old farmyard overlooking the village, the vibrant aroma now lacing my senses with its fresh, clean and intoxicating smell that continued to capture my attention. Its aroma was heavy and powerful, but at least it was warm, dry and would shelter us from the heavy downpour that was imminent, the sky now heavily laden with dark threatening thunder clouds wanting to unleash its ferocious cargo.

As we sat together on the bales without a care in the world, both of us so unaware of the monumental and destructive love we would share over the coming months and years. I continued to be embraced and seduced by Charlie and his carefree and reckless reputation, now with his strong arms around me, I really did feel like a princess, his princess. He smiled at me with that cocky smile that had now captured my full attention once again, his eyes the deepest brown that alone seemed to take me on a journey of mystery, not knowing what his eyes were hiding from me, something that I may never be allowed to know, but still the mystery behind his reputation continued to seduce and tattoo my tender skin.

The rain was now falling hard, clattering onto the barn's thin tin roof with force, accompanied by lightning that crackled and popped overhead, the storm had promised a spectacular light display carried along by the dark clouds that now littered the sky.

In each other's arms once again Charlie's kisses became more passionate, more intense. I returned them all begging for more as I whispered my love for him. He smiled, then continued to kiss me, his hands holding mine, reassuring me of his ever growing determination to keep me his hostage.

I loved you from the first time I saw you Lizzy. I looked at him puzzled, my glassy green eyes questioning his strong and powerful words today that were very unexpected from a boy with a tough and rough exterior. *You gave me your heart Lizzy, don't you remember?* I nodded as I had remembered all too well that I had cast my heart far and wide for someone to love, knowing his words of love today would cast destruction and the terrifying heartache to us both as we continued on our journey, walking the wrong path on so many occasions, wondering if I should be scared of the impending love we would be creating while kissing each other with a young, fresh, and intense passion. My clothes having been removed delicately by Charlie were now hung and dripping from the bales that surrounded us, my underwear discarded in a pleasurable passion.

I desperately wanted to feel his body against mine, to experience skin-on-skin contact, and with that he moved on top of me, kissing my neck, moving seductively down my naked body, peppering his kisses on every part of my virgin skin that was now trembling with anticipation of his dirty love, my whole body tingling with an excitement that I had never felt before.

I had never allowed anyone to invade my body, my breath now being taken away as I eagerly wanted more of what Charlie could give me. Today it felt right, it felt so very right to allow Charlie to steel my virginity as he had already stolen my heart which I was delighted for him to have, a love that would test us both throughout our lives, taking us on a monumental everlasting and a destructive journey, ripping families apart, leaving me to weep alone and in silence with secrets and lies that could never be told.

Now with his body wrapped around mine, reassuringly he told me he would be gentle and with that he slipped his huge cock into my kitten for the very first time. I gasped, Charlie was about to love my delicate virgin kitten for the very first time, my kitten reacting by purring for more dirty love from Charlie. His loving was very powerful, but gentle, as our bodies were now in total togetherness, both of us moaning with the sheer beauty of it all.

Relaxing from our dirty loving for now it allowed Charlie the freedom of my body as his fingers explored my curves with ease, taking us both on yet another amazing journey of seduction, my kitten drenched with juice, my desire apparent as he moved down my body, his tongue exploring every part of me, giving me everything I could have ever wanted, allowing his tongue to revolve around my belly button, making my body go ridged with passion as I was loving the sensitivity between his tongue and my belly button, leaving tattoos of his love over my delicate skin, coating my belly in kisses.

Charlie then straddled me once again with a renewed vigour, his hands now firmly placed on my hips, thrusting lovingly his gaze firmly on mine, we were now moaning deeply together, louder it seemed than the rain that was now crashing onto the barn roof.

We lay back in each other's arms smiling with the sheer beauty of it all, listening in silence to the storm that was now overhead unleashing ferocious, booming thunder that clashed violently with the lightning as it shuddered its way across the village bringing with it heavy, driving rain that would undoubtedly turn umbrellas inside out, taking them freely from the hands of the ladies who felt it necessary to venture out down the narrow lanes, discarding them freely on the gusting and howling winds. Lightning crackled and popped above us, leaving spectacular striking white patterns against the stunningly dark blue moody background of the sky.

Now Charlie had become my first and possibly only one I felt I would ever want to make love with and to love me forever just like in my dreams that I had made for the future. But dreams were dreams and never a reality as life had promised to get not only in mine but in both of our way, taking us both on many journeys into the unknown with devastating heartache, constant pain, but Charlie's love would continue to rule my body and life on every occasion, once again leading me to question why I fell in love with him and why I would constantly crave his love knowing full well he was hiding a mysterious and very dark reputation that was sure to escalate, taking me with it while I continued to become the girl he called his Lizzy, but I remained very blinkered by love to his ongoing reputation.

We must have fallen asleep for a short time, just minutes in fact, as when we woke the rain had stopped and the sun was going down, leaving behind a beautiful rainbow that had now filled the entire sky, it was so totally perfect with its bright dazzling colours, each one absolutely perfect, reflecting in the sun, casting brightly coloured shadows over the landscape that spilled out before us. I looked again at Charlie's naked body, my love instantly hungry for more of his dirty love, needing to help myself once again and Charlie seemed delighted at my new found sexual appetite for him, so now an hour or so later we slipped back into our discarded clothes, I then naughtily slipped my knickers into his pocket smiling to myself knowing I had given him yet another trophy of another monumental time in our lives.

Charlie looked at me, smiling his amazingly warm smile with eyes that hid his secret reputation, something that I knew I would always allow to seduce me, to overpower me and overpower my ability to make the right decisions, clouding my judgement daily, leaving my world in turmoil, littering the skies in dark unwelcoming clouds, turning rainbows from glorious bright and stunning colours into rainbows that were only made up of muted monotone colours.

He walked me home, slipping his hand in mine. I was smiling to myself again, knowing I was naked from my knickers, a feeling that I was enjoying, being amazed by the start of my lifetime journey that I had just taken, committing to a lifetime of love, or was that still a dream that would eventually turn into nightmares? Many of them would unbeknown to me become nightmares of terror with nightly visitors that would become habitual and brutal with voices that would terrify and haunt me.

Now at the bottom of the road that lead to my house we kissed gently as he held my porcelain face between both his hands, squeezing my face gently, making my lips pucker up. He then thanked me for letting him be the one who took my virginity. I blushed, he smiled, I blushed again, the realisation today was that at the tender age of fifteen I had allowed Charlie to take my virginity, keeping it for himself, allowing him to take my innocence, but in return I became a little more closer to entering into the closed, somewhat dark, and mysteriously beautiful world of Charlie.

After sleeping so well with dreams that contained Charlie, the bells from the church yet again interrupted my perfect dream, but left me smiling once again in the knowledge that Charlie had taken my virginity to keep for himself and I was delighted that my dreams were now being fulfilled and all by Charlie.

At last Monday was here, my wait was now over as Charlie was here with me to quench my spiralling desires yet again, we both sat in the garden alone enjoying our time together in the little part of the garden that was my favourite place to be, with the open vista that was so stunning, and the added beauty today was that it was a beautiful warm late autumn day and so perfect for love.

We sat and talked perfectly at ease with each other, while I indulged myself a little longer in his reputation, his cocky attitude and his carefree confidence but I was intent today to make the first move, so much so, taking him by his hand nervously I led him in to the house, slipping out of my tiny cotton shorts and t-shirt, leading him to the creaking staircase and my little bedroom as I watched him cast his eyes around the walls adorned in my many pop idols, not saying a word. Charlie being Charlie had other ideas, he wanted us to explore every room in the house, he took my hand, leading me along the landing into my parents' bedroom, I gasped Charlie, he smiled, Lizzy it's fine.

I stood fixed to the floor standing in just my underwear, once again showing my tender, vulnerable years and how unprepared I actually was to the world of Charlie's love and beautiful dirty sex.

We were now stood in my parents room, this sat uneasy with me, thinking to myself, was this another one of Charlie's tests? Charlie made it seem normal and the more I thought about it, the more exciting and thrilling it was. In a strange sort of way we were going to be in their bed, making love for the second time in almost as many days. Charlie held me tight like a piece of fragile glass, supporting my petite frame with his strong hands, whispering his love for me. Suddenly he removed his clothes, wanting to love me. His clothes now lay in an untidy heap on the floor with my bra and knickers on top of them. Charlie then seemed to sense the unease reflected in my facial expression of being in my parents room, something that was not natural for me, suggesting with relief from me that we went back to my room, I nodded my relieved approval. With that, he lifted me delicately into his arms before taking me back to my room where we lay relaxed on my little bed embracing the moment together.

He straddled me, thrusting his perfect hard, long, love filled cock into my kitten and once again I begged him for more. *My beautiful princess* he moaned, *I want to love you forever and I will Lizzy, I promise you.* Charlie was more vocal today, repeating his love for me, never wanting me to forget his dirty love as I was becoming increasingly addicted to him and addicted to his most powerful love and to the dark, very secret reputation he had, that at times shrouded him in a veil of mystery, something that was hidden behind his cocky smile and behind the deepest of brown eyes.

Charlie continued to love me all afternoon, thrilling my body with a very sensual passion, commanding my nipples to stand to attention ready for his inspection. Charlie's fingertips caressed my nipples, almost pinching them, making them tingle with a sexual pleasure, before his lips gently sucked them as he whispered, *my Lizzy, my beautiful fucking Lizzy*. Suddenly I felt his warm, fresh juice drench my kitten, Charlie looked at me in that way he always did, whispering softly, *Lizzy, my forever princess*.

We lay in each other's arms for a while, enjoying our perfect time together before we knew it he had to go, fearing my parents might surprise us by coming home early but Charlie wanted more from my body, so leading me back to the garden where we climbed up into the tree house he took advantage of my body again, but I was never going to stop him. So with an afternoon that had been delightful, we kissed our goodbyes, loving and tender as normal. Charlie whispered into my long, flowing hair; *I love you Lizzy*. Smiling back at him, he instantly knew my reply.

I could smell his lingering aroma on my body and in my bed and panicked, thinking my mother might smell his aroma in her room, leaving an aroma which was unique to us, an aroma that remained a constant reminder to me and every time I thought of him his aroma would flood into my nostrils, taking me on a delightful journey of emotions, allowing me to recall the unique love we shared when needed, especially when I stood at my bedroom window that now would allow me to take any journey I craved.

I washed and changed before mum and dad got home, opening all the windows in the house to allow the clean air to filter through the house as I did not want them to know that Charlie had been here and certainly not to let them know that he and I had been in their room and in my bed making love, me knowing full well my mother's reaction, hearing her disapproving words and advice daily but I found the secret we shared so very exciting as now I constantly craved his dirty love along with being seduced by his reputation.

I didn't see Charlie for a few days, but he was never out of my thoughts as I continued to recall all our exciting memories that we had made together in recent days as I had been treated to a wild journey that had taken me from being an innocent, fun-loving, free-spirited girl to becoming a woman as I recalled again the journey standing at my bedroom window my senses being awakened. I could now hear so vividly his voice, hearing him repeat my name, whispering into my hair as I continued my sensual journey with sensations that rocketed through my body, making my cravings even stronger and more powerful as now I could smell his aroma that once again seduced and ravaged my body, having to pinch myself to not believing I really was Charlie's girl.

As we were coming to the end of our half-term holiday it was time to see Charlie again, we met this time at his house and it felt very different, his sisters and brother were all there so getting a few close, intimate moments together was almost impossible by the chaos that filled his family home, the laughter and giggling booming from every room, spilling out into the streets beyond, but I just loved being with him after, all he had stolen my virginity, my heart and he had now given me his powerful love, a love that I was not prepared to let go nor to be set free from the hostage I had become.

We went to the cafe as normal; the cafe was once again full of the old faces that we both loved, mixed with an atmosphere that made it what it was. We looked good together, everyone said so, even the ones that doubted us right from the moment I became his girl, maybe because we were so different. We knew it surprised so many people, the innocent schoolgirl and the boy that had a mysteriously dark, even sinister reputation, but that would never stop me from loving him, not now and it never would, although in the back of my mind his reputation worried me as he continued to hide it behind his beautiful brown eyes that increasingly seemed to camouflage the escalating reputation he had, the reputation that would continue to seduce me and always would.

Back to Charlie's for tea which was a family thing. We all sat together, crammed around the smallest table that was now creaking and groaning, laden with food. Charlie and I continued hiding our dirty love story for now as I continued to convince them all that I remained so innocent, but I was not the girl they saw, little did they know that we were now fucking each other at every opportunity we got, in bed and out of it. We seemed to be inseparable, sharing wild and beautiful love sessions that seemed to be taking over our lives. Charlie had put his spell on me, commanding my love for a lifetime but that now came with the terrifying roar from the storm as now I could hear the terrifying heartache knocking at my door, hearing the ripening storm gathering pace as in the back of my mind

Charlie's reputation, his cocky behaviour and his huge confidence that worried me as to what he had done to earn such an image that seemed to follow him around like a bad smell that lingered on his clothes.

Charlie's mum; a bubbly fun loving lady; his three sisters all looked so much alike, blonde hair, brown eyes, and the family trade mark smiles; he also had a younger brother Andrew, a good looking lad for his age. Nevertheless, I caught him a few times checking me out but thought nothing of it, I just stood back and enjoyed the attention.

His dad; a tall and very good looking man, slim with a mop of dark chestnut coloured hair. A very rugged man, three very handsome men in one house. Charlie's dad was old enough to be my dad, probably the same age, but he had something about him as he would look at me with an icy, cold stern stare that I found tantalisingly sexy in a strange way and just like Charlie he had an ability to seduce me with his eyes, stripping me free from clothes, my tender body allowing them both the freedom to explore my naked curves. His younger brother also, he looked so young his face certainly reflected his age, shaking my head in disbelief that I could think that way, but I enjoyed it never the less, deep down was I still that stupid immature girl that did stupid things involving the wrong men? But why, when I had everything I wanted from Charlie? I questioned myself repeatedly as I continued sliding out of control, while Charlie continued to excite me, to thrill me, treating me to his wonderful world of wild and beautiful love, which all seemed perfect, too perfect sometimes, but we had something that others would never or could never imagine existed, a love that seemed to work for us, but always lead me to question myself every day as to why I was so afraid to have fallen in love with him. I remained terrified, knowing that my love for him would rule my life every day in some way or another, to haunt my dreams by day and when night fell he would haunt those dreams, turning them into nightly terrors, but nightly terrors that would also seduce me on many occasions.

Now with Christmas fast approaching we sat watching television, Charlie's parents were out for the evening leaving us alone, the house now silent apart from the volume on the television which seemed so very loud knowing Charlie's father was always twiddling with the volume control to fix it and always failed. It seemed somewhat frustrating, but tonight suddenly and without warning, Charlie took my hand, gently leading me up the stairs to his bedroom, both of us so obviously in need of some very dirty

Christmas love, my body now demanding Charlie's undivided attention as I constantly craved all the affection and dirty love that Charlie gave me.

We stood in his bedroom kissing the kisses of my dreams, exploring each other's mouths, excitedly allowing our tongues to dance sexily together as they glided over one another leaving me trembling with pent up passion that was ready to be unleashed right here in his room tonight.

His brown eyes still heavily burdened with a secret that he was intent on keeping for himself, hiding his mystery, a mystery that I found intoxicating as his eyes were transfixed on mine, flirting with me, seducing me again.

Leading me by the hand Charlie took me along the landing towards the bathroom wanting us to share some beautiful love in the bath. I gulped back my fear, he knew instantly by my facial expression that I was a little scared, having seen that expression once before whilst stood in my parents' bedroom so holding my hand and reassuring me, he ran a bubble bath full with beautiful soft foaming bubbles that cascaded onto the floor, leaving pretty piles of iridescent bubbles that exploded one by one, sparking droplets of delicate perfume in to the air that was now heavy, so full of our love, little did we know that sharing a bath together would become so important to us both throughout the many years of our continuing love story. Locking the door firmly behind us allowed a shiver of excitement to run through me as he closed the lock sharply, not wanting us to be disturbed, not wanting this moment to be cut short.

He loved to lead the way and I was never going to object. Slowly, almost teasing me, he undid my new top to reveal my firm, bulging tits which now spilled out as Charlie released them from my tightly fitting bra, my tits that were now pulsating with a desperate need to be loved, tracing with his fingertips over the natural curves, Charlie's eyes were once again admiring my bulging round tits. I could feel his amazing cock bearing rigidly into my groin as we stood semi-naked together. He then started to suck my nipples which in return begged him for more as his tongue rolled sensually over each of them, leaving them wet from his kisses while my hands were fumbling to undo his jeans in a desperate attempt to reveal Charlie's huge cock that my kitten yearned to be loved by. Charlie's kisses peppered my neck as I fumbled to undo the belt that was fixed around Charlie's jeans, our bodies now tense like coiled springs.

I had never had a bath with anyone before and again it led me to think was it yet another test to allow me to gain exclusive access to the world of

Charlie? Now brought back to the here and now I wasn't sure If we would both fit in the small bath that was now so full of water and bubbles that at any moment would flood this little bathroom.

My body was now trembling, not only with passion but from the extreme cold on this bitterly cold winter's evening but his confidence and strong cocky attitude was filling my body with a warmth, burning my delicate porcelain face as I blushed repeatedly from his comments.

Suddenly our passionate encounter was ruined as we heard voices echoing from the front door. His sisters had returned home unexpectedly, and laughter now filled the house. We both got dressed quickly as he returned to the living room leaving me alone in the bathroom, so I pulled the plug pretending nothing had happened, but leaving both of us so in a state of frustration, both of us wanting each other so desperately and in need of some serious Christmas loving.

It was so bitterly cold as I walked out of the door, cold with shards of icy rain splashed against my face. With both of us wrapped in heavy coats, Charlie warmed my hands in his, but the cold seemed unimportant as we had unfinished love on our minds. We ended up at a little disused tumbledown wooden garden hut, the door hanging from its very rusty hinges. It was very dark, cold, dirty, and smelt like a smouldering late summers bonfire. Its lingering aroma suddenly hit the back of my nostrils making me sneeze repeatedly, much to Charlie's amusement, but it was at least dry and free from the bitterly cold easterly winds that blew across the landscape that night.

Dark heavy cobwebs hung like fine lace curtains from the ceiling which allowed the huge, ugly spiders with long spindly legs to hide behind, ready to make me squeal at their untimely appearance, knowing full well they were already watching me.

Love and passion filled the air in this little shed as we lay together huddled up under our thick winter coats watching the muted stars through the grubby little window, seeing the vast dark sky through the roof where it was broken, allowing the howling winds to rattle and shake this little hut, but I was without doubt so lucky that Charlie wanted me for his very own princess, when there were millions of girls queuing around the block for just a glimmer of his attention, each one of them wanting to indulge just like me in his confidence, his commanding stature, cheeky spirit and above all his cocky attitude and seductive reputation.

Christmas was now approaching, winter already had a tight grip on the landscape, a time of year I loved so much, my favourite season as I was treated to long walks on frosty afternoons admiring the gleaming frost that clung to every branch on every tree, trees that were baron from leaf, every blade of grass was now spiked with glistening beads of frozen dew, like pearls on a necklace.

Christmas Eve came and we were alone, this time at my house as my parents were going out for the evening, my mother having lectured me constantly about behaving, reminding me that I was still only a school girl and not to be distracted by Charlie's reputation as she wagged her finger at me making clear I knew her wishes before leaving us alone together cuddled up on the sofa, watching the pictures unfold in the fire, the logs crackled and popped with exploding sparks that burst into little shards of flames so bright that seemed to dance delicately with each other, the aroma from the scorched logs, the earthy, woody essences mixed together with the amazing perfume from the fresh Christmas tree that seemed to create a beautiful, perfect Christmas aroma, complete with the tree lights that twinkled like little stars filling the room with a fantastic mellow glow.

The Christmas kisses were flowing, and the mood was right for some delightful Christmas loving as Charlie delivered my perfect Christmas gift to love me just like the princess he called me every day, as we continued to ride the storm, dodging for now the impending clashing of the grey unwelcome clouds that were waiting for us both still far away in the distance.

We remained very much in love to the amazement of most people and the jealousy of others with the constant finger-pointing and the whispering behind our backs, but we ignored those constant remarks, the finger-pointing, the vicious rumours that were constantly spread about Charlie and his mysterious image, nothing could stop us from loving each other, but the future was now clouded by a dark forecast so it was difficult to predict what the coming months and years would hold for us both.

We made dirty love at every opportunity we got as we could not get enough of each other, the bad-boy with the reputation and the innocent girl that was slowing being drained of her innocence, to be replaced by an ongoing desire to be the only girl Charlie would ever want, which seemed to work for us regardless of the image Charlie had, but I still remained blissfully unaware of what he had done to earn such a bad reputation, a label that he would undoubtedly wear all his life, but would

I ever know why? At this moment I felt it was never going to be any of my business so I tried blocking it from my mind.

Today like many days recently I was wrapped up against the winter chill to sit in my little tree house staring out at the fields beyond, listening to nothing as it was so still, motionless. The landscape was now shrouded in a heavy blanket of snow and if you listened really hard you could hear the trees groaning and creaking as they swayed, trying to shake the snow free from their very heavily laden branches.

As I looked up from my tree house the snowflakes were free-falling once again, huge flakes that were so delicate. I tried catching them on my tongue, flakes that as I looked at them reminded me of tiny white feathers floating from side to side, as they were swept along on the icy breeze before melting into ice cold puddles.

I went for long walks alone into the snow laden woods that now had a crisp new layer of snow that had settled, creating a carpet of glistening ice coated, delicate lace peeks that had been blown in by the icy easterly breeze that swirled the snow around before crashing to the ground forming little drifts that just needed to be jumped in, sitting on old discarded logs that were now dusted with a fine dusting of snow reflecting back on how lucky I was to have Charlie in my life, to deliver all the dirty love that I now craved as I was on a mission to embrace this love and now his reputation knowing full well it would eventually drag me along with it, shedding devastating effects on both our lives.

The Christmas holidays were now over and I was studying hard, loving Charlie and socialising with my friends as well as having a loving family I had it all, or so I thought. Only the future knew what my life had in store for me, and my instincts told me it was not going to be the fairy-tale future I had promised myself as a girl sitting alone in my tree house creating my dreams that I would enjoy recalling even if they were never going to be a reality.

The grip of winter still had us firmly in its grasp and it was still extremely cold at times, but it allowed me to enjoy the winter beauty a little longer as Charlie and I would sit huddled together in my tree house, wrapped in a huge tartan blanket late into the evening listening to nothing, the stillness of the evening took over with only the moon for light setting a romantic scene on these freezing cold nights as we shared loving kisses until it was time for Charlie to leave, leaving me alone to my dreams.

CHAPTER 3

Charlie and I found ourselves a new place to be by ourselves, a palace in comparison to the wooden shed to have our precious time, a sweet tiny old stone-built shed. It was his granddad's but no longer used, very rustic in its appearance which made it quite romantic with an aroma that was so familiar, making me sneeze, just like in the old wooden garden shed with its smoky bonfire aroma that just lingered on our clothes. The shed was dusty and dark with one little grubby window for light that was piled high with old china plant pots that were now discarded and unloved.

A small tatty sofa had been pushed against one side of the shed that allowed us to have our time in some sort of comfort, but little did we know that this little shed would hold many happy and many heart-breaking emotions for us during the long days and nights in the weeks, months, even years that were to come.

One cold winter's afternoon as we sat in the little shed it was so cold, my body shivering in the icy interior and just like the old shed my eyes travelled around this little hut as I watched with intrigue the dark lace cobwebs that hung in the corners as they were wafted around on the cold draft that seemed to fill this little shed this afternoon, the window grubby and dirty having not been cleaned in years.

Today Charlie seamed very preoccupied, almost unsure of what to say as I looked at him puzzled by his pained expression. His cocky attitude now muted, his confidence diminished, his whole body seemed lifeless and limp, I had never seen him look so unhappy. His body language was confusing and so very different, his smile disappointing, his deep brown eyes shrouded by a fog that I found terrifying as I was trying so hard to avoid any eye contact that scared me for the very first time.

He sat with his head buried in his hands, the silence was deafening. As he looked up at me, his face crippled by pain that now seemed to cast a dark shadow throughout this delightful little shed, as the walls started to close in on me. *I love you princess*, I nodded somewhat casually before returning my reply, *I love you to Charlie Stevens*. He smiled back at me, that stomach churning smile that I adored but it was short-lived as instantly his smile dissolved to be replaced by a cold, lifeless expression. I felt I was not going to like what he was about to say, the tension left me trembling as I knew this was going to be a heart-breaking moment in my life, something that would challenge our relationship, changing it forever as the storm stood silent for now, holding its distrustful breath.

I need to talk to you Lizzy, I felt numb, my body frozen in time. *What, what is it Charlie?* I reached suddenly for his hand for some sort of reassurance, I was now so scared that he was going to set me free from his chains, setting me free from being his hostage, to be replaced for another. My heart now under attack and on edge at what I was about to hear as he hesitated again and now silent, just looking at me. *What is it Charlie?* I screamed at him; my voice shattered by an agonising pain as my eyes were now clouded with bitter ice-cold tears that seemed to blind my vision. I looked at him wanting and waiting for answers, his face full of sadness as he held both my hands in his, blurting out the words that today I did not want to hear... *I have to move to Wales with my family Lizzy.*

My world now crumbling into millions of pieces, shedding the contents of my heart onto the floor that was now falling away from me, sending me into free fall, he could not leave me now, not now, I needed him, I needed his dirty love, I needed his mysterious and dark reputation to continue to seduce me every day.

I was in disbelief, horrified at this devastating news, I screamed at him. I don't want you to go Charlie, please, I don't want you to go Charlie, screaming at him in a desperate bid for him not to leave me. My outburst of emotion now terrified me being that I had fallen so in love with him, knowing I could not live without his daily seduction, his confidence that had made me what I had become, his cocky attitude that made me smile every day.

My porcelain face was now engulfed by endless, cold, harsh abrasive and bloodstained tears, panicked as my heart continued to shatter bit by bit, crumbling with excruciating pain. Lost for words I stood crippled by emotion, wanting to wake up from the nightmare that was unfolding before us.

I sobbed uncontrollably, needing Charlie to tell me he would stay, but he was silent from the words I so desperately needed to hear today.

Charlie then held me in his arms allowing me to cry until I had no tears left, my body now drained of all emotions from the unexpected devastating news that had been delivered on this cold and terrifying day and once again every negative thought reared its ugly head. I was right, life would prove difficult standing in my way, denying me the happiness that I had dreamed about, but now all my dreams felt like nightmares.

Broken hearted we kissed goodnight as Charlie held me close, whispering I love you's into my long flowing hair that now was lifeless and dull, but I love you's would never stop the hurt that now peppered my body with excruciating pain, a pain that I had never experienced before, it was terrifying.

All I could hear in my head was going away, *going away*! The volume so loud I could not turn it down, just like the television in Charlie's living room as it vibrated heavily throughout my fragile tender body and with every breath I took another piece of my heart slipped away.

Wales seemed like a world away, a world that I was not going to be part of, a world in which Charlie would find another Lizzy so easily to replace me, to share with her our beautiful and unique love, our hopes for the future and all of my dreams, going away. Going away, those words played tricks with me, words that would echo in my head for the following weeks, only to be replaced by torment that would overtake my body for a lifetime, leaving my life in turmoil that was all made possible by falling in love with, Charlie the boy who had a reputation. For the first time ever, I hated him, wanting to lash out to scar him in some way just to make him feel the pain I was feeling, but maybe he did feel the same pain, knowing now we would be separated by so many heart-breaking and unbearable miles with our dirty love out of reach.

We made the best of the time we had together before the dreaded day came for him and me to say goodbye. I knew it would be hard to contemplate my life here without him, making dirty love became intense and sometimes not loving at all, sometimes it left me cold with an anger that I hated and with a pain that seemed to compliment it.

With the dreaded day fast approaching I would go for long walks alone in the woods to listen to the rush of wind blowing through the trees that at times sounded like they were whispering his name, leaving me to think I was going mad with the sound of sadness and as darkness fell it cast unwelcome shadows that once again constantly played tricks with me, taking my fragile emotions and tearing them apart, scattering them on the breeze, dropping my terrifying emotions throughout the woods and beyond into the fields that flanked the landscape. Recklessly, I tried to piece them back together only for them to be destroyed once again, knowing full well that time was never far away.

We wanted a few special days together so we made special visits to the old shed and all the other places that we called ours, just us, Charlie and I. Alone together I looked into his dark eyes once again shrouded with the ongoing mystery that still surrounded him, shrouding him in a glorious veil of darkness and intrigue, something I found so increasingly seductive, something that I would miss daily. Charlie held my hand hoping it would reassure me, whispering *you do know you will always be my Lizzy and my forever girl don't you?* I nodded fighting back the monumental tears that were now once again blurring my vision as I tried to contemplate my life without Charlie and the heartache it would bring. Charlie hardly ever called me Lizzy, so when he did it made me realise that he really meant what he said, but it was just words that could be broken and discarded without a care in the blink of an eye when something or someone better came along, my body had now been left lifeless, strangled from air, bruised, and battered by every emotion that waged war on my porcelain skin, leaving visible markings, tattoos like painted scar's that I would now carry alone all my life.

Our kisses were now a little warmer but still uneasy as we cuddled on the old but comfy sofa that had been left in the shed. We did not talk much about the move as I found it so unbearable, shutting it out of my mind was easier for now if only for a short time, before the reality was finally upon us.

Seeking the solitude of my bedroom window I tried to find so many reasons for him to stay but my mind just wandered off, recapturing memories from the snowy days of the winter that had just gone by, like trying to catch snowflakes on my tongue, wanting to inhale the ice cold winds, needing to feel Charlie warming my hands in his. I seemed to be making it harder on myself by agonising over the impending day, repeatedly telling myself our dirty love could and never would be over. Sometimes I just wish I hated him, wishing I had never fallen so deeply in love with him as it would have been so much easier to say goodbye, to be free from the chains that now shackled me to his heart. That was never an option as I had freely taken the journey, I had allowed myself to become his hostage. Why did I have to love him? Why? Why? Why when so many had warned me not to get involved? I had not listened, discarding everyone's advice, not wanting to believe what I was hearing as I was caught up in the spin of such virginal love, a love from the bad-boy that was Charlie.

Now it was approaching Easter and the signs of spring were everywhere as the delicate flowers had managed to bloom, seeking the warmth of the early spring sunshine after the hard and bitterly cold winter that had swept across the country, but now with the spring upon us it was clear to see its beauty unfold, beautiful blooming buds had now begun to form, gracing the trees far away in the woods, hedgerows bursting with renewed fresh, clean, and crisp colour.

I now seemed to spend all my free time between the tree house and my bedroom window recalling times when I thought my life was perfect and that I was going to have it all, sadly now that dream was being snatched away from me day by day. My dreams were now being shattered to allow someone else the beauty and privilege of my dreams that I had envisaged for my future with Charlie.

The day before Charlie was due to go to Wales we planned to go for a picnic in the woods not far from my house, just the two of us, but knowing full well it would bring with it heart-breaking sadness and a terrifying life sentence that I would carry alone my entire life and once again I would be left with visible scars for everyone to see and for many to admire from all those people that had told me not to get involved would now be able to say. We told you so, and for all the girls that had admired his cocky attitude from afar could now sneer at me reminding me Charlie would yet again be admired by many other girls.

I woke early to a bright sunny Sunday which came with a slight chill of the early morning that filled the air along with the toll of the bells from the church which today seemed very heavy, but somewhat muted as they rang out.

As I stood alone at my bedroom window today I saw my ghostly reflection looking back at me which was so uninviting so I pressed my nose against the glass not wanting to see the pained expression glancing back at me. My nose now frozen against the ice cold pains, but it could never leave me feeling as cold as I was feeling right now and right on queue the church bells rang out again, bells that today were so unwelcoming.

Before I left the house I stood once again at my bedroom window, taking a long look out over the fields, letting myself drift back in time to the first kiss that Charlie and I shared. We were about to share our final heart-breaking kisses and cuddles that would cripple us and our dirty love that would hold devastating consequences for us both, especially me, invading my world that would leave me frail and fragile. Now closing the door to my bedroom, knowing another chapter was about to unfold for us both, knowing I would need my bedroom window to readily give me back treasured memories in the lonely weeks that lay ahead.

Charlie found us a lovely spot secluded deep in the woods, a place that the sun had warmed so beautifully just for us in anticipation for our dirty love. Wrapped in our huge warm blanket we sat in silence, a silence that seemed to echo through the trees, every one of them standing tall with branches so heavily flooded in buds waiting to burst, branches that today were fully bowed in honour of us, fully aware of our impending sadness.

Charlie's hand held mine as I fought back the tears that now were building and gathering at an immense pace. Charlie kissed his fingers, placing them on my newly painted lips, trying desperately to silence my words that quivered undetected beneath the sadness that had now engulfed my fragile body, a sadness that was now weeping from every part of my body, sadness that was now stinging my hidden wounds and skin-torn scars.

As always, he kissed away my tears, holding my hand and looking at me with those deep brown eyes that I adored, that still held a secret life that on one hand petrified me and the other seduced me. *Lizzy I love you, you're my girl, my forever girl, the girl I fell in love with even before I met you.* Words again that took my breath away as I remained speechless, unable to find any words that could ever make him stay, I was today for the first time ever stunned by my own silence on such a monumental day, a day I just wanted to forget. As much as I wanted to remember it, Charlie's lips then met mine that were now drenched in blood stained tears, my lips quivering with terrifying sadness that rippled through my fragile body, his kisses now peppered my porcelain face in a bid to make me smile, to reassure me I was still his girl, still the girl who stole his heart, still the girl he called his Lizzy.

Our lives were going to be very different from now on and I was not sure how I would cope without him in my daily life, how I would spend my time, times that I had thought we would spend together, making and creating our future dreams to one day in the future become a reality.

As cold as it was, we felt the warmth from each other's love that now radiated through the dense trees and bushes that surrounded us, only they would know the full enormity of the love that we shared, along with the enormity of the devastation it would cause in the coming weeks, months, and years to come, but we both knew deep down this was never going to be our final goodbye, it just couldn't be, we were never going to allow that.

He lovingly and slowly removed my jeans along with my top, now sat only in my underwear allowing Charlie's eyes to have its final feast of the full beauty of my young body that he had so tenderly taken away from me, leaving it fragile once more as he wrapped me in the thick fluffy blanket to keep me warm.

His fingers then took a journey, tracing the outline of my procaine face while his eyes flirted excitedly with mine. Suddenly I started to cry, wishing this was only a dream, but sadly it wasn't as I felt Charlie's lips kissing away my tears only to be replaced by many more that were sure to burn and blister his lips as he continued to kiss away my burning tears.

Charlie then unwrapped me from the blanket that had keep me so very warm and again he was gazing at my scantily clad body, his fingers now touching the lace that edged my knickers. The touch of his fingers excited me as they edged further towards my pulsating kitten.

Charlie then kissed my tits through the fabric of my bra which made me giggle, before letting my bra fall away from my body, running his fingertips over my nipples and outlining my curves whilst his eyes continued their journey feasting on my young and tender skin.

Suddenly I felt Charlie's warm fingertips tracing the lace edge of my knickers, before slowly removing them. Now I was naked, stripped bare for his eyes only to indulge on my quivering body. *Princess you're stunning, so fucking stunning.*

Charlie had made some pretty and very delicate daisy-chains from the newly grown tiny daisy's that had just peppered the landscape over the last few days, putting one in my hair like a little crown, just like a real princess and as he led me back to admire once again what had become his, he placed the other single chain all along my kitten, peppering kisses on every daisy in the chain, whispering *she loves me, she loves me not*, kissing them one by one, spending more time teasing and pleasing my kitten with his firm tongue as I moaned with a breathless lust from this very seductive foreplay. I was now in the grip of the sheer beauty that was Charlie as he moved his tongue lovingly over my kitten, my heart pounding with a sexual desire that I found so hard to contain as I heard him whisper tenderly my name, repeating it over and over again as he moaned with a commanding pleasure that never failed to leave me demanding more, so very much more. Charlie's lips were now coated in my warm juice, something that he was yearning to share with me as his tongue travelled around my mouth for full effect.

Now having moved position we made passionate and very tender love that only we could share, a love that we had created as we led together naked on the cosy blanket our bodies covered in heavy coats, neither of us knowing what to say, the air stagnant and silent from words, not wanting the moment to come when we would have to find those devastating words of goodbye that would leave open scars on my skin that would never heal, revealing its true ugly tattoos for everyone to see and for some to admire with everyone expecting me to explain the devastating markings that now remained in my future and rule my life.

Sadly that time was now and we had to say our last goodbye. My heart was broken and in tatters but nothing he could say or do would make things right today, not even his cocky attitude or his reputation could enliven my smile. He then placed a pretty little box in to my hand, his eyes now hungry for my happiness, for my approval and reassurance that I would still be his girl in the future, a future that seemed very uncertain and very unpredictable.

I sobbed uncontrollably as bitter tears clung to my delicate porcelain face that wore not only layers of makeup but that had now started to crack under the pressure of our love while we stood holding hands, while saying our final goodbye, our last goodbyes that were again waging war on my delicate skin, leaving it blood stained and weeping.

Charlie's lips were now pressing hard on my trembling, quivering lips that were stained in bitter tears that had dissolved my pretty bubble-gum pink lipstick, the lipstick that Charlie loved. He always said it tasted of bubble-gum, which always made me smile, but there were no smiles today. Kissing our last most precious kisses that I instantly missed as our lips parted for the final time. I felt his hand leave mine, this was it, I was now alone without his love, without his kisses knowing the storm of our love was just gathering pace far away in the distance, building its relentless furry.

I went home feeling so deeply unhappy, my skin now bearing the ugly unwanted scars complete with tattoos and skin torn scars and it felt like every window in my heart had been broken as I headed to the tree house for some much needed solitude allowing me to shed all the tears that were mine.

Now less than twenty-four hours since Charlie and I had said our heart-breaking goodbyes I looked down at the little box that was Charlie's parting gift to me, telling me to open it when I was ready. My heart was beating faster and faster in anticipation of what was concealed within the box, *I love you* had been scratched delicately on the lid. I ran my fingers around and around the lid seducing every word Charlie had ingrained into it not wanting to open the pretty box. Somehow, slowly with my handshaking, a little glittering shiny glass crown appeared within the box with a note attached that had been written in pencil on a tatty scrap of paper which read *for my princess forever and always*, followed by thousands of tiny, scratched kisses, some of which had ripped through the delicate paper. I managed a smile, knowing Charlie had a soft and very sensual side that most people would never get to see as his cocky reputation being the only thing most people saw, but there was so much more, so much to the bad-boy that I had instantly fell in love with so easily, I wanted everyone to see what I saw.

I sat in my tree house with my eyes tightly closed, squeezing them so tight that my nostrils flared out and my skin around my mouth wrinkle up. I wanted to recall so many of the vivid memories that were still fresh, allowing them to delight my emotions as they tiptoed silently through my body awakening all my muted senses that now took me on a journey, a roller-coaster of a journey that lasted only a few seconds but the journey was elaborate, allowing me to recall his aroma, his voice and of course his captivating smile along with his cocky attitude and confidence. The days, weeks, and months we had spent together flashed before my eyes as the journey started again, the very vivid and colourful journey we had created together.

The tree house now burst into life, loudly hearing the laughter we created right here together, laughter that spilled out into the garden and beyond, taking with it all the love within this tree house, a love that I never knew could exist, a love that was so much ours, a love that I would treasure forever, but a love that had been marred by Charlie leaving me at such a critical time in our new found virginal love affair.

My life in some ways remained on hold as the days following rolled into one, the school days were now so very mundane, boring to the extreme as there was no Charlie to spike the day to day excitement that he and I managed to create... but it was something I had to deal with... my world blown apart, my body somewhat less alive, my sparkle was missing, my zest for life gone.

Friends rallied around trying to make me realise that I was still me, still Lizzy, still the girl who loved life, who loved being included in the most simple things, the most exciting things. Lizzy, the life and soul of the party, now diminished into not wanting to be part of anything that didn't involve Charlie.

CHAPTER 4

A couple of weeks later I had an invitation to go to Wales, I was beyond exited and as I arrived in Cardiff, Charlie was waiting for me as promised, leaning against a lamp post, his beaming smile still so powerful, accompanied by his cockiness that had not faded, his smile so inviting and his intoxicating reputation on full display. Holding my hand firmly, knowing full well I needed to feel the intense grip of his love, it felt so good to be alone with him again, to be in his company sharing our kisses repeatedly, reassuring each other of our continuing beautiful love. Charlie's tongue revolved around my mouth, over my tongue and onto my lips which tingled with that electrifying sensation, setting my lips on fire, smuggling my highly painted lips.

Charlie's hand was never far from mine on a mission to reassure me that I was his girl, his special girl, our love fully on display to his family that surrounded us. Charlie's eyes flirted with mine all the evening, needing desperately to be alone.

Charlie then leant over, sweeping my flowing hair to one side and whispered, *let me sleep with you tonight, I don't want you to sleep alone Lizzy. But what about your parents?* I gasped. *Don't worry about them Lizzy,* he then gently placed his fingertips over my quivering lips.

So we waited patiently for everyone to go to bed then wedging a chair under the door handle so that we could not be disturbed. The house was now quiet and free from the constant loud chatter and hysterical giggling from Charlie's sisters that seemed to echo through every room, but their laughter and spirits brought this somewhat dank, cold, unloved, and dreary house to life.

Charlie smiled his trade mark smile, smiling confidently as he asked me to dance for him. I swallowed hard, blushing at his request as I had never danced alone for him before or anyone else for that matter, or was this another sort of initiation into Charlie's world, had any of the others been asked this same question? I didn't want to dwell on his previous encounters knowing full well there had been many and with others who now jostled their way to be noticed by Charlie wanting to become his girl, but I was that girl now and that was all that mattered.

Charlie had obviously noticed my hesitation to dance alone, he stood up. His hands were now bracing my hips, he began to sway me gently allowing my body to enjoy the sexy routine and soon my clothes began to fall to the floor. Charlie slid his hands firmly around my tiny waist allowing us to both move slowly together, with our clothes now in an untidy heap on the floor just where they fell we continued to indulge in the sensual routine together to the rhythm of the soft background music that was playing. *I love you Lizzy*, he whispered. His breath warm against the silky, soft skin on my neck that sent wave after wave of a delightful sensation that vibrated throughout my body as his arms fully embraced my naked body.

At last I could now feel his skin on mine which I still found so exciting, that most intimate skin on skin contact, our lips met once again, immediately his tongue engaged with my mouth igniting sparks that peppered my body, his fingertips then rolled down over my nipples that instantly commanded Charlie's attention.

I let my hands delicately stroke his back as he moaned with pleasure, his breath still warm on my neck that sent icy cold shivers down my naked spine, my body was now ready to receive all the dirty love that I had missed and craved repeatedly. I heard him repeating my name over and over again. Taking my hand we laid together on the little sofa bed while Charlie was loving my very playful kitten with his tongue, I was loving his cock with my ever demanding out of control mouth, suddenly his juice filled my mouth to the limit forcing it to pepper my throat with a constant supply of warm, fresh milky juice.

His erection was still so hard and big as it left my mouth, my lips ready for Charlie's kisses, leaving his lips now smeared in my juice that made our kisses yet more seductive, more passionate and kisses that were out of control, leaving us breathless from the power that our dirty love now held for both of us. As we laid together, a silence fell within the room and once again I felt like a princess, the princess Charlie continued to call me.

Our actions and incredible love were far beyond my tender years, but then I had Charlie who knew full well how his princess needed to be loved. Wrapped in each other's arms, content for now we slept until dawn, he then quietly slipped back to his room while everyone slept on unaware of our dirty secret loving, our dirty secret safe for now, safe within these dull, dank, and dark four walls that now knew the full extent of our most precious and terrifying secret, beautiful dirty love.

The next morning as we arrived once more at the park alone together, free to be us, the sun peppered us in glorious warm kisses. We were setting ourselves free to be teenagers in love, carefree in our ability to love each other, naturally unaware of the future and the turmoil of our love that would be tested to the limits.

Charlie pushed me on the swing and as he pushed me higher it allowed the breeze to flow through my long silky smooth hair, my squeals encouraging Charlie to push me even higher. We had something that others would never understand, maybe that's why it worked for us, the bad-boy that was hiding a dark, mysterious secret along with his cocky, confident attitude and me, the sweet fun-loving immature girl who was about to be dealt the most horrific heartache in the coming months that were to come and even in the years that were to follow, never leaving me free from traumatic heartache.

We laid on the soft grass with his hand holding mine, just looking up to the huge deep blue sky that was never ending with not a cloud to mar its stunning beauty, the more I gazed up the more captivating it became, leading me to wonder where the sky ended or where it started.

Suddenly without warning Charlie sat up looking at me seriously with his deep, dark brown eyes that were filled with a look that seduced my body again and again. Charlie then straddled over me, gently pulling my hair to one side, smiling at me. *Lizzy I love you; I want you to have this.* He then handed me another box and again it had *I love you* scratched on the lid. I sat up instantly, tracing the scratched etching with my fingertips before opening the beautiful wooden box that now lay in my hands.

I was taken aback; it was the prettiest thing I had ever seen. He then took the box from me, placing the ring onto my finger, repeating thousands of I love you's over and over again. A ring for love, a plastic ring from a cracker in the shape of a daisy now graced my finger, *Lizzy this is to remind you of us.*

A huge lump sat heavily in my throat, it felt like I was choking with an emotion that was so utterly beautiful, so utterly raw it left me speechless, strangling every breath I took in a bid to control my sheer happiness.

Back at Charlie's we waited patiently once again that evening for everyone to go to bed. The house fell silent from the endless chatter and laughter from Charlie's three sisters that swept through the house like a tornado taking everyone along for the glorious ride, jolting everyone sideways as their laughter seemed to collide with everything in its path, we were now alone and spent the most amazing night together again wrapped in each other's love. I wanted to seduce him, I wanted him never to forget me, never to forget us, never to forget his Lizzy as we made glorious dirty love, beautiful dirty love complete with all the love I could have ever wanted or needed.

I slept content knowing that we had taken another step closer towards being together forever, but it would never be that simple as Charlie's reputation, cockiness and confidence would forever rule his life and now mine. I had committed to wear the badge by being Charlie's girl knowing full well I would pay the cost of loving a bad-boy and that cost would be all mine, a price that would take me to hell and back, having to bear the cost alone, but it was a price I was willing to pay, or was I?

Sadly, the morning arrived all too soon and it was time to leave and head back home, but I hated goodbyes knowing there would be many more. As I cried bitter tears Charlie held me close, outlining my porcelain face with his fingertips, then squeezing my face with the palms of his hands making my highly painted pink lips pucker up, always allowing us both to smile.

Never wanting to pull away from the intense grip that his love now had on me, tightening its grip every day, Charlie touched my hair softly as he whispered, *I love you Lizzy.*

In a muffled voice I retuned his words of love as I fought every emotion that now seemed to be spilling over, engulfing everyone who was now a witness to my distress as Charlie kissed away my tears, peppering my face with new, exciting kisses that now replaced old ones, but old ones that I could never forget or want to.

Before leaving this glorious part of the world that now contained my gorgeous Charlie, my hands shaking as my hand left his, my lips trembling as we shared a final kiss, we waved our goodbyes, blowing thousands of kisses until I could no longer see his lean, cocky and bad-boy silhouette.

The days and weeks that followed seemed to melt into one, I would often visit the woods, winding my way through the mass of brambles and fallen branches to just sit on the log next to the tree in which Charlie had carved his undying love for me and as I stared at it, I recalled the perfect afternoon that we shared together here in this very spot on that slightly chilly early spring afternoon, but it was one of the best afternoons we had shared, although it remained the most devastating.

Once again my bedroom window and my tree house proved to be my never-ending sanctuary on days when I felt low and in need of Charlie's company and today was no different, I desperately needed to feel his love, to embrace his company, his cocky attitude that always made me smile, to feel his confidence that would rub off onto me, to inhale his aroma, to hear his voice and to feel his lips on mine the list continued and remained endless.

A few weeks on and my invitation had arrived to go to Wales once more. I was excited, but nervously looking forward to being back in his arms to rekindle our love, to enjoy the journey it would once again take us on in a bid to nourish my ever demanding senses to see Charlie in my life long dreams.

Charlie was there to meet me, but today he was not alone, he was accompanied by five of his new found comrades that I had never seen or heard about before, clearly now all part of the mysterious life that Charlie continued build for himself, a lifestyle he would continue to hide behind his trade mark smile and his deep brown eyes. As I looked closer they to all seemed to be hiding something secretive behind their facial expressions along with the same cockiness that Charlie commanded which was clear to see surrounded them all.

Today there were no kisses, no loving embraces, just a cocky smile. Maybe today he was shy to show affection in front of his new circle of friends, but this was not like him, as normally he was never afraid to hold my hand, kiss my lips or embrace my tiny frame. His facial expression reflected once again the mysterious life that hid heavily behind his dark brown eyes.

He was now worrying me, after inviting me to Wales he was distant, almost invisible, although he was walking right by my side it felt like we were miles apart, his cockiness now seemed to echo a sinister tone. A chill now filled the air that we were both breathing, air that on the other hand was stifling, chocking my every breath as the dark storm clouds once again seemed to be gathering around us, spiralling out of control, ready to unleash yet another devastating storm.

Something was wrong, it did not add up. Knowing he had got in with the wrong crowd to indulge further into yet another dark, mysterious life, once again I called my thoughts into question. I had been warned about him and his image on so many occasions, but I chose to ignore it until today as reality struck, now I felt so very stupid that I had ignored everyone's advice that was now scaring me. I looked closely at his new found friends one by one, I became more terrified of the life they were all hiding, a life that now involved Charlie and his ready-made reputation. The finger pointing, the constant whispering that I felt was today justified, as his life had now started to unfold before my eyes, not knowing the full devastating impact his life, his reputation and his cockiness would have on me in the future possibly shattering every one of my ready-made dreams that Charlie had promised to grant me.

Back at Charlie's house it was silent from the normal chaos and noise that seemed to rule daily like the constant volume from the television, the continual chatter from his sisters that echoed from every room. The dark, dank and cold walls still remained the same, there was no life in this house unless Charlie's sisters were in the house to bring it warmth, so we sat in the garden alone at last, set free from his mates that seemed to cling to him like glue, not wanting to leave his side, keen to follow his every word and mirror his ongoing reputation.

I made the first move to kiss him, he kissed me back with kisses that were intense but today they left me cold, feeling alone and unwanted, kisses that were forced as he seemed distracted, miles away from the here and now. His body language diminished and as evening went on it was apparent that there was something that I would never be allowed to be a part of, however much I questioned him, which left me tired emotionally, drained today by Charlie's lack of affection and attention. I was in desperate need for Charlie to love to me, to love me like the princess he always said I was and that I always would be.

We waited once again for everyone to go to bed which seemed like forever, Charlie's sisters laughter and giggling echoed loudly throughout the house, leaving a trail of fun and freedom in its wake.

Normally we would have made beautiful love and fallen asleep in each other's arms, but tonight we talked, small talk really, it felt like we were avoiding the thing that was so obviously bothering him.

Something or someone was obviously playing on his mind, clearly he was worried about something and that yet again made me question in my mind his secret life that now seemed to over shadowed everything, putting doubts about our love into question.

On waking, my head spinning, the house was once again frantic with chatter and laughter that sent my ears ringing with the glorious laughter that was missing from my house. His sisters, mum, and dad were all preparing for work so there was a very long wait for the bathroom, but the thought of being alone all day with Charlie was a wonderful thought and as it turned out, that was all it was going to be, just a wonderful thought.

As we kissed good morning I instantly knew things were not right. Charlie was quiet, moody, and not his normal self, snapping at his sisters, his trade mark smile had vanished overnight only to be replaced by an expression that terrified me, an expression I had never encountered until yesterday, an expression that was smeared across not only his face but the faces of each one of his new bad-boy companions.

His hand held mine for some sort of reassurance that I was not to worry, as the grip of our love tightened again, reminding me once again that I was his hostage. He then pulled me into his arms looking very guilty, whispering *Lizzy I have got a few things to do today*. He did not say what, instantly apologising in a bid to silence my questions. *Sorry Lizzy, it's been arranged for a while*, his attitude now was very casual like I should accept it, like it was just one of those things and that it didn't matter, leading me to wonder if this was a regular occurrence when I wasn't here. His eyes endorsing that I would never be allowed to enter the secret world he had created for himself that today involved others, dragging them along on the crest of Charlie's wave, leaving me to hold my breath again, leaving me to wonder if he was now spreading his love further afield. He then kissed me goodbye and walked out of the door, slamming it behind him. There were no smiles today, smiles that I longed to see, smiles that would leave me breathless, but today they evaded me, leaving me cold. I needed his kisses to burn my lips, his smile to seduce every part of my body, his embrace to take me on any journey I wanted to take, to feel his hand on mine, to feel all the love Charlie had for his girl, his Lizzy.

I sat and sobbed bitter tears being on my own, or so I thought. I heard someone in the shower, of course his younger brother Andrew. Having not really took much notice of him in the past, of course I had glanced at him a few times, but nothing more, although I had caught him checking me out a few times but today as he came down the stairs semi-naked. I gasped, taken aback by the vision, so much so I took another lingering look just to satisfy my over active senses. Wearing only shorts, his upper torso on full show naked from clothing. He was very lean, tall, and very athletic looking, I found it hard to not to look again at his body, he looked so much like his dad, I could see the resemblance clearly.

He asked me why I was here alone and with that I burst into tears again; he smiled, pulling me into his arms gently, almost timidly, wrapping his arms around me. I could feel his rippling chest against my delicate frame, his skin silky smooth, reflecting his tender years as he moved my hair back from my porcelain face, looking at me, telling me repeatedly that Charlie was not worth my tears or my heartache. He continued to hold me close, but I was not ready to pull away as I was enjoying it far too much, but it was Charlie's younger brother for god's sake, he was only a boy. My feelings now totally confused; my emotions battled their way to the surface ready to battle against the impending storm.

The silence was deafening as the house this morning was empty from chatter, giggling, laughing and the normal mayhem, leaving me terrified that we were alone and in each other's arms and that I had, without thought, given into his embrace so easily and without any thought for Charlie.

He then pulled away slightly, but not freeing completely me from his arms, his head then lowered as he kissed my lips in a very boyish, virginal way. His kisses were tender and fresh. I remained still, motionless waiting again for his next kiss to delight my lips.

He then kissed me again, his kisses virginal against my pretty painted lips, lipstick that was not in the slightest smudged by his kisses. Suddenly I felt his hands moving down my back, sending wave after wave of a thrilling sensation. I must have lost all my senses at that moment, he was a young boy for god sake, a very young one at that, Charlie's kid brother. Suddenly I was brought back to reality, freeing myself from his arms, running outside to get some much needed fresh air, reeling from my appalling actions that were today all made possible by Charlie and his ability to continue to hide his mysterious life.

Damn it, damn Charlie, repeatedly cursing him, Charlie seemed not to care but today my head and heart said that I should have listened to everyone's advice and to have walked away before I had the chance to even know his name, let alone say it out loud and say it repeatedly.

Andrew and I sat in the garden most of the day, not mentioning what had happened earlier, but he soon got board of me and headed out to seek the company of his fellow companions, before pleading with me not to say anything to Charlie. He seemed terrified of him, leaving me again to wonder why he was so scared of him, I wouldn't and couldn't ever admit to him about my stupidity.

Alone in the garden I repeatedly questioned what I had done and why I felt the need to embrace the advances from Charlie's kid brother which left me feeling very guilty as these were not memories I wanted to create, only wanting to forget the stupid thing that I had allowed to happen, all due to Charlie hiding his secret life that he had made for himself here in Wales. As I reflected back thinking about it, he had already carved out that life when we were together, as everyone continued to reminded me of his spiralling reputation, especially my mother and father.

Alone again I recalled everyone's opinion of Charlie and his bad-boy image, complete with his reputation that was now becoming a constant terrifying battle that seemed to send my mind racing with so many unanswered questions that only Charlie could answer, answers I may never get or that now I may not want to hear, but his reputation intrigued me and still seduce me daily.

Charlie was back at long last, freeing me of my loneliness. Leaning over my shoulder, peppering my porcelain freshly paint face tenderly with warm kisses, kissing my newly painted pink lips, running his tongue over my lips insisting that he could taste bubble-gum. I smiled at him as he swept me into his arms allowing me to feel like his Lizzy once again, my doubts about his reputation and his secret life were now put on hold as the dark clouds had now receded, allowing the sunshine to bring its warmth into this garden this afternoon as shafts of glorious light beamed from one end of the garden to the other.

He held me close as his trade mark smile had returned, a smile that I loved so much, making everything in my world right once again for now anyway until the next storm broke. I knew for sure that there were many more that we would have to endure to have it all, but now that dream looked impossible, whichever way I looked at it, as I continued sweeping his reputation away, letting my love completely overpower it and it always would now and into the future, knowing Charlie was now leading a double life, one I would never be part of, as he would make sure of that, shielding me from the mystery that surrounded him, shielding me from the rumours, the finger pointing and from the constant whispering but nothing could shield me from the future that would torment and test not just me, but everyone that surrounded me to the limits.

With midnight fast approaching, cradled in each other's arms and very much in love once again, we must have fallen asleep. I woke with a startle nudging Charlie. *Charlie*, I whispered, *you had better go*, but before I had even said good morning Charlie's tongue was revolving around my mouth, treating my senses to yet more sensual pleasures that left me wanting more. My body craved his, I felt the grip tighten once again as we again embarked on yet another sensual journey.

Suddenly brought back to reality as the volume in the house was yet again turned up to maximum with laughter and singing from Charlie's sisters running around the house in a frenzy, he leant forward, kissing my long flowing hair, his fingertips outlining my porcelain face, smiling, *you're so beautiful Lizzy*, before leaving me alone to get my breath back.

Now with Wales behind me I was back in my bedroom, to the peace and tranquillity of the Wiltshire countryside, back to my bedroom window. As the evening light cast its long shadows, I looked into the field that once again contained the beautiful herd of black and white cattle that munched their way through mountains of grass that remained relentless in their calling, knowing they would wake me every morning from my sleep along with the church clock that never failed to chime.

As the weeks dragged by and Charlie was never far from my thoughts and never free from my dreams, my cravings were escalating daily, begging to be back in his arms, allowing me the privilege to inhale his aroma, to feel his kisses and hear him call my name and not having to just dream.

The day finally came and it had been a while, sparks flew throughout my body the minute I saw him, delighted that he was here again in the pretty Wiltshire village I called home to supply me with endless amounts of dirty love to supply my increasingly demanding kitten that now yearned for Charlie's cock constantly.

His hands now holding mine outstretched so that his eyes could feast on my body. *Lizzy, beautiful as always.* I blushed at his comments as Charlie peppered me in sweet kisses, tracing the outline of my porcelain skin with his fingertips, his touch so tender and soft. I closed my eyes to allow me the intimacy from the sensitive touch of his fingers while repeating his love for me.

We revisited the old cafe once again to soak up the atmosphere that we both still found so appealing, from the old tatty jukebox that was battered and somewhat bruised that sat content in the corner, ready to play all our favourite tunes on demand, to see all the old and much loved crowd that never changed. I was proud to be seen with him regardless of what people thought, we were together and madly in love. I didn't really care that he had a mysterious, dark reputation, a spirited past and an ongoing reputation fuelled future, he loved me and that was all that mattered, but was I blinkered by love, allowing Charlie to think that I allowed his secret life and his ongoing reputation to have my full approval as my love for him now over ruled everything.

Needing to be alone we went for a walk, his hand in mine. Suddenly we stumbled across the old tin barn in which he made me a woman, taking my innocence, and stealing my virginity away only to keep it for himself. He smiled and I just knew instantly what Charlie wanted, now sitting in the barn, I looked at him. He looked older, more grown up with his sun kissed skin, his hair glinting in the shafts of sunshine that kept creeping into the barn through the broken tin roof, his smile still so addictive, leaving me breathless once more as I was once again treated to his aroma, kissing his neck with all the Lizzy kisses he loved, my fingers running through his hair until my fingers reached the back of his neck, before pulling him forward to kiss his lips.

The smell of the barn brought back such emotional vivid memories which allowed us both to share its power with each other once again, right here in this very spot a month later, but still the raw emotion remained the same, his gaze still hungry for my love and full of passion.

His mouth now hard against mine once again, kisses that always smudged my lipstick, kissing like we had all those times before, but now this was so much more grown up, more powerful, more emotional, and very sensual. I wanted him to fuck me, fuck me like it was the very first time, when I was his Virgin, when he so lovingly took my innocence away never for it to be returned.

Charlie then looked at me with the biggest brown eyes that just smiled at me, his kisses soft on my porcelain face, his fingertips tracing my lipstick painted glossy lips. *I will marry you one day Lizzy, I promise you.* Gasping at his sudden unexpected revolution I rested my hand against his chest, feeling his heart beating as he uttered those words over again, that I would now rely on to recall in the harrowing weeks, months even in the years that were to follow as the dark thunder clouds that now ruled the sky already had my name on them in preparation of the vicious storm that was gathering pace ready to flood my life with harrowing pain drowning me in sadness.

So with Charlie now back in Wales I made regular visits to sit in my tree house which had become my every waking moment habit as it was so full of my continuing addiction to be able to recall my treasured emotions and everlasting memories, like the wildlife that surprised me daily, there was always something to capture my gaze, from the Owls to the little family of deer that always intrigued me.

I was now counting every day until we could be reunited, some days were so unbearable, some taking me on many colourful journeys, some into the past and now I took new uncharted journeys into the future which terrified me.

Suddenly the future was here, it was early June and just two weeks after Charlie had returned to Cardiff. We had written letters and kept in touch, our love still very strong and very much our future, but unbeknown to me, my world was about to be taken a devastating journey, crashing into everything in its path as the storm clouds were now above me, about to shower me in terrifying sadness, serving me the worst most devastating news.

My stomach was bloated and extremely painful, I screamed out to mum as she rushed up the stairs in a desperate bid to help me, Lizzy what's wrong. I was so scared, trembling again with fear as mum instantly called the doctor, he was on his way and now with the pain was getting worse and the need to go to the bathroom again, blood had now heavily stained my pretty pink pyjamas once again reflecting how tender my years really were.

As I reached the bathroom a massive, intense pain crippled my stomach making me scream out again and again in agony as I fell to the floor clutching my stomach in a bid to ease the escalating pain, I could feel this awful thing devouring my body, I screamed out to mum again. I was crying and shaking with the pain as I became consumed by fear that was now shredding and ripping at my heart.

CHAPTER 5

A dark grey fog had now descended over me, shrouding my body in the predicted storm that now raged again within me, a storm that was relentless, taking my body and ripping into vulnerable fragments. I remained motionless, crippled by an excruciating pain, and now accompanied by a relentless voice whispering coldly, *you are the storm Lizzy*. Dismissing the ugly voice instantly, my body was once again consumed by pain.

Mum got me up from the bathroom floor, helping me back to bed. She seemed coldly calm, as if she somehow knew what was engulfing my fragile tiny body, but said nothing. She sat on my bed holding my cold, clammy hand. I could see the look on her face, she was distraught, ashen in colour, trembling and cold.

At last the doctor was here, he looked at me and asked questions, some embarrassing, some about periods and about my sexual activity, all the time mum stood frozen in time, her pain apparent as the doctor peered over his glasses at me with an icy, cold stern stare taking a deep breath in. I started to cry as his expression was now so cold, without any feeling an expression that now terrified me.

Mum looked so sad, as if she knew what he was about to say, it was written all over her face, she was so disappointed with me, I had let her down, bringing devastating anguish into this family home.

I am sorry to tell you Lizzy, but you have had a miscarriage, you have lost a baby, his manner and his body language was one of disappointment as well as disapproval that I had allowed someone to invade my innocence at such a young and vulnerable age.

I screamed in shock, mum *I am sorry!* I sobbed terrifying tears that were blinding my vision as the storm had now broken overhead, but today there was no rainbow to admire or to chase as an ice cold sadness filled my bedroom, a haunting silence that could now be heard in every room of this house and far beyond into the woods. The storm now shaking every tree in its wake with its devastation, they too echoed my grief as every one of them knew the full extent of my love for Charlie, knowing I was pregnant, how naive I really was to the world of dirty love, to Charlie's love and how naive I actually was to the world, knowing now I was still a little girl that had chased dreams that were far beyond my tender years. Mum held my hand, squeezing it reassuringly as she smiled a smile of sadness, *get some rest Lizzy I will bring you some water*, taking in a sharp breath before closing the door firmly shut behind her, while talking to the doctor outside my room I could only hear muffled voices, my mother's voice remained petrified as I had brought shame on our family, bringing shame into our beautifully happy family home.

I cried, wanting Charlie, I cried so many tears that now consumed my body with a devastating hurt that would now never leave me, only to continue to haunt my every waking moment with bitter emotions, to disturb and disrupt my life, testing my zest for life continually, my heart broken beyond belief. This was grief on a monumental scale that today was terrifying.

I hated seeing the hurt on mum's face, disappointed that I had let her down so badly. She must have known it was Charlie's baby, knowing we had indulged ourselves in each other's bodies, that I had allowed him to take freely my innocence from me, I now felt so ashamed, all in a bid to be his girl.

I must have fallen asleep to allow my body the rest it so obviously needed, to shield my vulnerable emotions for a while. It was very late when I woke and nightfall was now here, mum must have been in to close the curtains from the outside world that today had ravaged my world, leaving it consumed in utter sadness. I could now hear dad's raised voice above mum's muffled cries, dad was angry. I could hear mum telling him to calm down, hearing him slam the back door behind him before he took himself into the garden to have some time to digest the news he had just been delivered. I had never heard my dad raise his voice so loudly, sadly I had let them both down, I continued to hear mum's ravaged tears tonight, knowing I could offer her no comfort.

I felt very uncomfortable, I needed to get out of bed, I felt so weak and as I stood up, my body seemed to have become almost floaty and light, but my heart remained bitterly heavy with a huge burden of sadness for my baby, our baby. It was ours, our baby made from pure, beautiful love… the most precious love possible and it had now been taken cruelly away from me, now thinking to myself that maybe it was a punishment, my punishment for loving Charlie.

I stood in the bathroom holding on to the tiny wash basin in a bid to steady my body that was shaking with fear and sadness, a sadness that I could never have imagined, and it terrified me, this awful thing that now engulfed my body like an ocean of sorrow that had swept over me, leaving me to drown alone in spiralling grief to once again hear the cold and almost violent echoing whispers that I was the storm, I screamed for the unwelcome voices to leave me alone.

Charlie, our baby, me, our future. All emotions that agonisingly clashed through my mind and that had now started its journey shuddering through my battered body leaving yet more terrifying scars and tattoos that painted and etched every inch of my porcelain skin.

I stayed in bed for a few days, unable to come to terms with the devastation that had ripped through my body, knowing it would haunt me every day of my life, by day and by night as the voices in my head would never let me forget, glancing over occasionally to my wicker chair seeing my freshly ironed school uniform neatly laid out ready for me on that fateful Monday morning.

Looking back, I tried to think when it had happened, when Charlie had made me pregnant, it was and had to be our last day of love that monumental day when Charlie and I enjoyed an afternoon of love, secret, beautiful love, our unique love, it had to be then he made me pregnant. I was having his baby, a parting gift of our forever lifetime commitment to love each other, but now that was gone, our beautiful love now cracking under the strain of my love for a bad-boy.

I just wanted to hide away, worried that I might break down in floods of tears allowing everyone to be witness to my devastating heart break, allowing them to know that I had brought shame into the house I called home, bringing shame to my parents.

I had a few weeks off school on the doctor's orders and I never left the house, only to walk around the garden catching up with such recent tear provoking memories of the love that Charlie and I had shared here and across the fields into the woods recapturing happy times, if only for a while before I was brought back to the stark reality that was the here and now.

I sat in the tree house for hours shedding devastating tears that never made me feel any better, they never would, as nothing could, but I managed to recall a few perfect memories that brought back a few muted smiles to my saddened face on these dark, lonely, and terrifying days.

Dark days followed; my life was in utter turmoil. Some days I didn't even get up, not even bother to wash or to eat, my life was blown apart by our loss, now with haunting reminders everywhere as they would just creep up on me taking me their prisoner, jostling my emotions, taking them on an evil ride that left my body ravished.

So as the days went by, only mum, dad and I knew about my virginal intimacy with Charlie, so we agreed to keep it that way. *Nobody needs to know*, mum said, giving me a much needed hug. *You don't need to tell anyone; we will get through this Lizzy. Have you told Charlie?* I looked at her with a questioning face. *No I can't tell him. Well Lizzy, maybe in the future if you feel the time is right.* There would never be a right time, never, it was my grief and mine alone allowing the storm to rage on inside my body.

I watched my dad going through hell being completely lost for words, his face pained by my ongoing heart-breaking agony as he continued to keep us together wanting only the best for us all. I knew this tragic time had knocked both my parents sideways, my dad especially, knowing that they were both so ashamed and disgusted with me, but neither of them saying what they truly felt.

I managed to write to Charlie, keeping it all a little light, but said nothing about our loss as I felt it unfair to tell him with him being in Cardiff and with me here, I could not bring myself to lay that burden on him, but even my writing could not hide the full devastating pain that was contained in every word I wrote as my tears dropped into puddles of despair onto the crisp white note paper leaving it stained with my harrowing grief, but not visible for anyone else to see apart from me, it was my grief and only mine. Something I had to keep to myself in the months and years that lay ahead, knowing if I allowed others to know my devastating grief it would for me bring more heartache.

As the weeks went by I changed, I lost my sparkle, my life had been turned upside down by grief and sadness, now having to sleep at night with the light on for some sort of comfort so that I didn't have to see the harrowing images that kept me awake, hearing them clearly in my mind, hearing my baby crying repeatedly far away in the distance.

One afternoon as I stood at my bedroom window it instantly let me recall the day Charlie had given me the ultimate gift by taking my virginity.

As I began the roller-coaster journey of emotion, a vivid kaleidoscope of colours dazzled before my eyes, the smell of the barn now very much apparent in my nostrils, hearing Charlie's voice echoing passionately in my head as he told me I was his girl. Then, suddenly I was back to reality, glancing at my watch, not believing that only five minutes had past but I had been on a journey that seemed like hours, recalling the torrential rain and the booming thunder that clattered above us, along with the endless rainbows that filled the skies, allowing myself the beauty of that day and the many others we had shared.

But now with haunting reminders that would invade my life every day, jolting my emotions on hearing over and over again the distant cries of a baby, my baby's torment that echoed in my head as I wept, wanting to stop the agonising pain, but sadly those reminders would never go away.

Life went on and I was back to my social life with my much loved group of friends, but it remained muted as did my smile. I put all my effort into studying hard, so when a job opportunity came along I embraced it, early September was here at last and my school days were now a thing of the past, I was offered a receptionist job in a local factory. It was only a small start, but knowing it would give me the independence I needed to embrace yet another chapter in my life with or without Charlie as we seemed to have drifted apart, following obviously different dreams, something that was always apparent but it was our love that was the bond we shared and always would be, but now I seemed to be able to see that more clearly, maybe it was having so much time to reflect, time to look into the future, a future that still looked terrifying.

My body had fully recovered from the miscarriage, but my head and heart sadly would and could never recover as I continued to hear the haunting cries from my baby and the whispering voice that kept reminding me that I was the storm that now had become a regular visitor, one that was not invited or welcome to my world.

Out of the blue I received an invitation to go to Wales yet again, having not seen Charlie for almost four long months, he was working now so time together would be precious. I jumped at the chance, how could I refuse wanting to recall the delights that surrounded him, to indulge myself again in his love, to let his reputation and cocky attitude seduce me once more.

Charlie was there to meet me, I was relieved that this time he was alone and without others to mar the beautiful moment when we rekindled our love, by our first kisses in a very long time, kisses that seemed to be endless along with his hands gently squeezing my face, making my lips pucker up, making me giggle. The more I giggled, the more Charlie squeezed my porcelain face, the tension of lost dirty love now filled the September air with emotions that were hard to hide, kisses that made me quiver as we stood on the station platform again stunned by our love, unable to say anything, motionless and still allowing our love to freely wash over us.

Holding my arms outstretched Charlie looked at me. *Lizzy my stunningly, beautiful Lizzy still as perfect as you always were.* His comments leaving me weak and vulnerable, my breath taken away once again as I was delighted to be in his company again, to be given this moment to recall when I needed.

Charlie's beautiful brown eyes and his cocky smile, the two things I loved and adored about him. These were the things I missed every day, along with hearing his voice, but still his eyes and smile hid a dark secret, a mystery that I found appealing and still so very seductive, but today his eyes were more heavy, carrying the burden of his ongoing label, the label that he had embroidered for himself years ago.

Suddenly there was no need to talk as our lips met again, lovingly out of control kissing took over and that was all that was needed as our tongues engaged in a blissful reunion, delighted once again to be recapturing all the muted emotions that had lay dormant for so long.

We slept together as normal on the little sofa bed, but tonight I didn't need to seek the comfort of the light being left on as I had Charlie for all the comfort I needed, there was no need to wedge the door closed because tonight it was different, we were not hiding anything as his parents knew and allowed us to sleep together knowing now our love was real, knowing full well that we would find a way to sleep together with or without their permission as dirty, beautiful and untamed love was fully on both our minds and neither of us were disappointed as a sensual love fuelled night came to a beautiful end.

The next morning Charlie went to work, as did his mum, his sisters. His younger brother Andrew went off to school and hardly gave me a second glance, both of us embarrassed by our stupidity on a rare visit to Cardiff all that time ago. I blushed as he said a muffled hello giving me a sideways glance, but nothing more.

Now the house was silent from the chaotic morning rush as everyone left for the day, Charlie kissed me goodbye at the front door reminding me that I was his girl, I smiled knowing full well I always would be, but I was not alone today as his dad was working from home this week. Not that it mattered as we got on really well, he was a good looking man, very rugged with an athletic build, tall and lean.

CHAPTER 6

I sat alone in the lounge watching rubbish on television with the volume that was set so loud as the volume button was broken, whilst twiddling with my hair, winding it tight around my finger. Suddenly Charlie's father walked silently in to the lounge making me jump, almost leaping from the sofa. I went to turn off the television. *No Lizzy, it's fine, leave it on*, insisting that it was not switched off with an air of stubbornness in his words, leaving me to raise an eyebrow as I had never heard that tone in his voice before, but I felt completely at ease in his company, knowing the house was empty and very quiet, apart from the television volume that made up for the silence until the girls returned home to set this house alight with laughter and mayhem.

Charlie's father looked at me with a stern, dark stare, a look I had only witnessed once before, I was a little frightened at this point. As he was sat close to me on the sofa I suddenly felt very uncomfortable, but at the same time I became rather excited as I fidgeted anxiously, pulling my skirt down, not wanting him to be able to admire my naked thighs. As I felt his burning gaze creeping over my naked thigh I suddenly found it rather thrilling and somewhat arousing knowing full well I was being seduced by a much older man, a man old enough to be my father, my mind and body now spinning, being bombarded by bitter sweet and very tempting emotions.

You're a beautiful girl Lizzy, you're too good for my son. At this point my thrills were suddenly muted to be replaced by annoyance and he knew that by my scowl and my apparent dislike to his unwelcome comments, I turned my body slightly away from him, not wanting to witness his advances.

I felt his eyes pierce through me again, scolding my already heavily scarred and battered body, forcing his unwanted gaze through my tattooed skin, but I felt very turned on and with that I felt his arm glide around me, embracing my naked shoulder. I instantly pulled away not wanting his advances. *Don't worry Lizzy, I just want to get to know you a little better* and at that moment I wasn't sure what to do or what to say, then he kissed me. His kisses were strong and powerful on my lips, his lips felt rough against mine, this was so very wrong and without any thought or hesitation I allowed him to kiss me once again, we both pulled away breathless and out of control, still staring at each other, his eyes on fire dancing over my body with a hungry lust and without any thought we started to remove each other's clothes in a frenzy. With our clothes discarded and abandoned, the tension was electric, I felt his kisses rough my neck, his breath laced with the smell of alcohol and stale cigarettes, but warm against my skin.

My neck was now being fully seduced by Charlie's father's mouth, the sensitivity from his lips that were so firm and masculine against my tender young skin as his mouth became hard on my neck, leaving blemishes that would scar and bruise my skin, but that left me wanting more, gasping unashamedly for more.

Suddenly he pulled me to the floor with force, without any thought for my tender, vulnerable and petite frame. My knees took the full impact on hitting the cold hard concrete surface that was only covered by a thread bare and tatty old carpet, I was now only in my bra and knickers. I wanted to run, but he had hold of my wrist so tight with a grip that burnt my skin making me screech as I struggled to release myself from his tight and unwelcome clutches.

My knees now bruised by the harshness of the floor, I felt powerless, my strength seemed to be dissolving away, leaving my body terrified as I gasped for breath my body ridged with intensifying panic. He was sweating and out of control, his odour was stifling my ability to breath, the acrid stench sat firmly in my throat. I could do nothing to stop him as he was too strong for me, too strong for my tiny frame as he knelt over me his tone was very demanding and so very frightening, his expression had now changed, it had become full of evil, his words so vile and crude. He kept repeating his vile unwelcome words, calling me a bitch, repeating such vile sexual commands. I felt so scared and now so very frightened I could not answer him, my mouth so dry, feeling his grip tighten around my wrists forcing them violently back against the floor. *You love this don't you? You dirty little bitch. Tell me you love it, tell me you want me Lizzy, tell me!* He wanted me to answer but I remained silent, then his grip intensified, I was so powerless.

The air now heavy with the pungent odour of stale sweat and days old cigarettes accompanied by the heavy stench of alcohol was choking me but the vile, sickening odour just lingered, sticking in my throat like a heavy thick glue that was denying me of breath.

I was disgusted with myself that I had encouraged this to happen, I had allowed it to happen. Terror now swept through my body on a collision course ready to collide with everything that stood in my way.

You want me don't you? You dirty little bitch! I have seen you looking at me. His voice now menacing, he demanded I did as I was told. The floor felt so hard and harsh against my tiny body, a body that had become instantly bruised, battered and blood stained by the hands of Charlie's father.

I was so frightened I just did as he said, he then started to drag my lacy knickers from me, tugging at the delicate lace so hard that it was now cutting deep into my thigh. I fought to keep my dignity, but he was never going to allow me that privilege at any cost. He kept on pulling with force until they were ripped free from my fragile body, they were now discarded and with no remorse I once again felt his glare inching over me, staring at my vulnerable body, wanting it for himself to indulge in taking yet more of my already tattered and frayed body. I managed to find the strength to scream at him to stop, but he wasn't listening to me, he was engrossed in my body while I remained terrified as tears now blurred my vision, my body was frozen by the terror that I was now facing. I just stared at the bare walls not being able to focus on anything.

The volume on the television was still so very loud, his reason to leave it on apparent now as it could hide his vile and threatening tone, the harshness from his comments that just keep flowing from his vile mouth all camouflaged by the volume on the television, knowing it had been his intention to abuse me today, knowing we would be alone, a cold calculated act to abuse me, to lead me into such a vile act. His hands now crawling and touching my fragile body, his hands almost brutal and vile with no intention of stopping, I wanted to lash out at him to scar his vile skin to allow him deep permanent scars that would be a constant reminder of his appalling and vile behaviour as he seemed blindingly unaware of what a cruel, evil, and vile act he was now performing.

Please stop! I mouthed, again I repeated my plea for him to stop, but still my words were silent and muted but echoed like thunder within these four bland uninteresting walls that were witness to this cruel and vile act.

He screamed at me, his voice harsh and repulsive, snarling like a dog, unleashing his destructive and vile commands, telling me he wanted to fuck me, obviously wanting to hear me beg for more, wanting me to touch him in the way his wife didn't, still I did not answer as he repeated again. *I said your loving this Lizzy!* I still did not answer him, wanting my silence to frighten him in some way, screaming at him to stop, please stop, my words now bounced from every wall in the room smashing every ornament, but he wasn't listening, determined to overrule my pleading requests while my body remained frozen to blot out this ordeal that I prayed would be over soon. I was so afraid to move, afraid to do or now say anything as I continued to let him violate my body, he was agitated by my silence which seemed to irritate him, repeating his commands over and over again, echoing vile demands that shuddered throughout the house, still with no reply from me he started to get very annoyed, pulling my long flowing hair back with force still spewing vile insults. *Tell me you love it Lizzy.* His face now level with mine, his breath warm against my skin, his face riddled with evil, still determined not to answer his vile questions as his grip now on my wrists increased, I closed my eyes shutting out the moment praying it would soon be over, his brutality was hard to comprehend.

Tell me you love it you dirty little whore, as his hands freed my wrists before twisting my hair so tight, feeling every strand would be ripped from my scalp, but I still said nothing, I was not turned on by this horrific, vile, and terrifying act that I was party to as I just wanted it to be over. Suddenly he become even more verbal, spewing vile commands at me to satisfy his own vile desires, something that I would not allow myself to respond to, wanting to deny him that satisfaction that he so obviously wanted to hear, but still I had no intention of reacting to his commands.

Tell me Lizzy you want me to fuck you, don't you! He snarled, I once again closed my eyes firmly in an effort to blot out this horrific ordeal, suddenly he seemed to regain his senses, pulling his body free from my petite frame. I was petrified by his vile actions, shaking with a fear that I had never felt before as tears rolled down my porcelain face, crippling pain now rippled through my fragile limp body as he whispered menacingly in my ear, *Lizzy you're not strong enough to withstand the storm.* I snarled back at him, *but I am the storm.*

I then stood up freeing myself from this man who claimed to be a loving husband and devoted father, but he was a monster, an evil out of control monster, trembling with disbelief at what had just happened, staggered in my ability to find the strength to even stand up let alone walk away. Scooping up my discarded and ripped clothes, I did not dare look at him, the vile, disgusting man that had forced his disgusting eyes to claim my body to allow himself the enjoyment of my tender years.

I could hear him breathing deeply as I felt his eyes once again piercing my body like hot needles that punctured my skin, leaving a permanent pictures and vile tattoos on my naked body, pictures he now never wanted me to forget.

I ran upstairs tripping over twice before locking myself in the bathroom, wedging the bathroom chair under the handle for more security relieved that at last I was free from his grip for now, but I would never be free, he had made very sure of that. He was never going to allow me to forget as I would be reminded every day by vile images, the stench of him would be forever in my nostrils.

I then heard him calling me from the stairs. *Lizzy, Lizzy*, his voice seemed now even more menacing as it echoed through the house making everything in its path freeze. While I held my breath ready for the next saga to unfold I heard his words creeping up the stairs until they met the bathroom door and then suddenly I felt the vibration and the stench of his breath as it slid under the bathroom door still determined to not let me free from his vile clutches. *I'm so sorry, I'm so sorry.* I did not answer him I was still so numb.

I stood shivering and cold, lost in fear, totally naked apart from my bra. His vile words were now crawling all over my skin in a desperate bid to never let me forget my stupidity, my gaze firmly fixed on the bathroom door, terrified that he would find a way to abuse me again. My body was now feeling the full emotional impact and distress that I had been forced to endure, forced to do as he wanted me to, the evil that I was subjected to on this early afternoon, something I would never fully understand and the massive impact it would have on my life not just today or tomorrow, my whole life now swallowed up in torment.

Suddenly I heard the door handle being tried, Charlie's vile father still on a mission to haunt me, I could hear him outside the door as the floor boards had started to creak and crack beneath his feet, I screamed loudly for him to go away, he said nothing, allowing his silence to terrify me, to haunt my fragile body. Suddenly I felt his silence slide under the door to terrorise me again. *Lizzy I'm sorry, so sorry.* His plea now so very desperate as I heard him walk away mumbling to himself, leaving me alone for now, but his vile smell, his vile words and his vile actions clung to my skin piercing and tattooing images that only I could see, blemishes that would be everlasting, tainted blemishes on my tender skin leaving in its wake an emotional nightmare to bear alone.

The water was now scolding my skin, but I didn't care, I just lay there until the water went cold, afraid to move, wanting to let myself slip into the deep water until I fell lifeless, powerless against the almighty storm that was to follow. Shaking my head, trying to make some sort of sense of what had just happened, the stern, deep and menacing voice once again brushed against my neck reminding me that I was the storm.

The storm, the impending storm that I had created by loving Charlie, the bad-boy, was this my punishment for allowing to be loved by him?

I could never visit this house again, I could not bear the thought of being alone with Charlie's father again, to feel his eyes on me, to witness his fake smile while everyone around him applauded his sense of humour, to hear his chilling voice knowing full well what evil he had cause me, the evil that I would never be allowed to forget.

Now with what seemed like hours later I knew I had to flee from this house immediately, I was too terrified to stay. Fully clothed, along with my coat, I crept out of the bathroom and walked timidly down the staircase, desperately hoping that I would go undetected. The pungent, acrid smell of alcohol now filled the hallway, holding my breath I hurried past the living room, luckily the door was firmly closed but I could hear him snoring, oblivious to what torment he had caused. He had obviously drunk himself into some sort of alcoholic coma, my nostrils were then hit with the stench of him, making my body freeze, heavy, unable to move. He was never going to let me forget so with a huge intake of breath finding renewed strength I grabbed my bag that lay in the dining room just where I had left it, packing what I could in my desperate need to escape the impending backlash from this unpleasant and vile house that now would never encourage me to visit again. I scribbled a tear stained note to Charlie, making up a lie that I had to return home urgently, my words seemed to blend into a mass of scribbles that seemed to make no sense at all.

Now having made my escape into the garden, not before I had wrestled with the lock on the kitchen door, panicking that my escape would be in vain. At last I was free, but I would never be free, my actions so vile, so utterly shameful that I had been a willing part of today's vile act, that I had eagerly encouraged without hesitation.

But how would I manage to cover my vile attack today and for the future, it terrified me that I would have to pretend, to cover every day my fake smile in layers of thick paint, to coat my lips in a glossy, silk liquid to blot out the blemishes that would now rule my world.

I knew it would be a recurring nightmare that I could never share with anyone as it would be mine to carry alone, a nightmare that would certainly haunt me forever, I prayed that in return it would be Charlie's father that also received those chilling nightmares when he lay next to his wife at night, never allowing him to sleep without pain, without guilt, hoping he would suffer the raging nightmare that I would now have to experience along with the chilling echoes of a baby's cries that I heard night after night, the harrowing and desperate cries from my baby, a baby I could not comfort.

Back home after a tormented journey I sighed in relief that I was free from the hands of my vile attacker, and again tonight I would seek the company of my bedroom light, knowing that I could never turn it off, knowing that when I fell off to sleep my dreams would leave me alone, drenched in cold, vile liquid that would stain my bedding in a vile stench that would be a constant reminder of Charlie's vile father.

My body now littered with evil blemishes, scars that were blood stained in terror and evil, more tattoos that would never let me forget how falling in love would cost more than I ever would have realised.

Being so young and naive it did not occur to me straight away that I had been sexually assaulted and violated by Charlie's father, questioning again why I had allowed it to happen so soon after my miscarriage. Now hearing the storm continue to swirl and groan, the noise was deafening, but still I questioned as to why I had encouraged it, when it was so horrifically vile and totally disgusting.

At last day light shone through the gap in the curtains of my bedroom, I was free from the nightly ritual of my bedroom light being my main source of comfort. The night had been so full of hate, trapped in torment and fear, but I was free from the vile clutches of a man that thought it was all a bit of fun, relief for me was an understatement but I needed the security of my own family now as I needed somehow to recover from the vile attack that happened to me within Charlie's family home, within those dank, dark and vile walls. Now my family home was tormented by Charlie's vile father, I had to find a way to dismiss the evil that had been tattooed over my body, to deny the evil, vile thoughts to creep into my everyday life to terrify my every waking moment. Somehow I had to sweep it away if that was possible, my head and heart engulfed with guilt, but it wasn't just my guilt, I had to keep telling myself that. It wasn't just my guilt, but I didn't know how I should feel. So many emotions, so much torment, but every day I would end up blaming myself, hating myself.

I knew I was going to find it very hard not to tell anyone, but I had to keep it to myself as I was so scared and terrified of the consequences from my appalling actions that would undoubtedly leave two families devastated, knowing my own family had already been knocked sideways because of my out of control actions, devoured by pain and I wasn't prepared to put them through it again, also fearing it would kill the love that Charlie and I continued to share.

Today my tears were of horrific guilt and of being lead into the most vile thing that could ever happen to anyone. I hated Charlie's father, but I hated myself so much more and I always would as I would continue to question myself daily, leaving a pain inside me that I could never describe to anyone as hatred now raged out of control inside me, seeing the grey explosive mist gathering pace before my eyes, leaving them pained and sore as once again out of the grey foaming mist came a galloping stampede of white horses ready to trample over my fragile, vulnerable body every day thanks to Charlie's vile father.

Now sorting through my case I found the black plastic bag that contained my discarded clothes that were stained in shameful disgust, tainted with evil, the smell repulsed me. Wanting to shred them into fragments, clothes I could never or want to wear again. With that I took the bag that contained so much evil out to the garden, tossing it onto the bonfire that dad had left smouldering away as it had been for days. Suddenly the garments were engulfed in flames that contained the vile image that was almost sneering at me, wanting to taunt me with his evil stare, I was now choking on the stench that was Charlie's vile father, a stench that stuck in my throat determined to starve me of fresh Wiltshire air. I suddenly heard the harrowing words that today I had no answers for as to why I thought I was the storm.

My thoughts then lead me to thinking about Charlie and my untimely departure, hoping he would somehow have forgiven me, my darling Charlie.

The following weeks remained torturous for me as I battled my way through the many storms that haunted me and that now ruled my life, my life would never be the same again. Charlie's father had made sure of that, allowing me the privilege of the constant nightmare to rage in my head, leaving me drenched in pools of cold unwelcome fluid night after night for weeks after I had left Cardiff, leaving me terrified that they would continue to haunt me my entire life.

I made a vow take a step back and to think hard about my life, so a visit to the garden was in order to help me through this tragic time in my life. I closed my eyes tightly, even scrunching up my nose so tight as I desperately wanted to recapture one of those special days when Charlie and I would just sit together, wrapped in each other's arms, but today I wasn't allowed that privilege however much I tried.

Sitting in my beloved tree house one afternoon alone as I thought back, the realisation hit me like a lightning bolt, sending a bright beaming flash of lightning through my body that I had indulged myself with three men from the same family which once again sent me spiralling with constant reminders never far away and today was no different as I felt the guilt that continued to consume my fragile body.

Suddenly I could once again smell Charlie's fathers vile aroma that seemed to stick in my nose and throat, denying me the glorious aromas that filled the garden as autumn was once again here, but now I was being bombarded by his menacing voice which panicked me, seeing clearly the vivid facial features that had once seduced me, his rugged features, the age lines that appeared at the corner of his eyes as he feasted on my tender body, exploring my painted, porcelain face for his evil pleasures, his thick eyebrows that seemed to frame his face, and again the vision was overwhelming, leading me back into the darkest of days, once again recalling the vile act I had been party to as the hooves of the raging wild white horses continued to trample my body, battering it, accompanied by haunting echoes.

I begged to be taken away from the here and now, but today the tree house denied me of any delightful journeys that I had taken so many times before, today it submerged me into the vile nightmare that I just wanted to forget, it felt like the tree house was today punishing me for my stupidity which was justified. Time was a great healer, but the heartache remained terrifying as I would never be free from his grasp, along with the vivid memories that were still fresh in my mind, never letting me forget what really happened between Charlie's father and me on that vile and now unforgettable morning so I put more effort into work and my life in a desperate attempt to forget, but it was never going to be that easy.

Now clinging desperately to my everlasting beautiful love of Charlie it managed to overrule most of the dark days, blocking out the vile torture that Charlie's father had put me through and still did, waging war on my fragile body. I needed to now take complete control and not those around me, so with a renewed strength born from my own stupidity I was ready to put the past to bed, to leave the storm in the distance to embrace being Lizzy again.

My birthday was just around the corner, but it was not the time to celebrate as it was laced by so many traumatic emotions that overpowered me at times and they were the times I found myself alone in the tree house desperate to recapture happier memories that Charlie and I had made here in this garden and across the fields into the woods.

Mum and dad seemed saddened by my lack of enthusiasm, by my muted zest for life. Mum constantly asked if I was OK, if I needed to talk about things, but I couldn't let her into my ongoing agony, my constant nightmares, they were mine and mine alone for not only today, but tomorrow and for the weeks, months and years that lie ahead.

As darkness now fell I headed to my bedroom looking out of the window that today took me on another wonderful journey deep into the woods once again to watch the owls that remained so perfect and graceful, elegantly gliding into the tree tops calling each other home with loud, shrieking whistles. These were the things that not even Charlie's father could take away from me, the most beautiful things that enriched my life daily.

It was now October and carnival time was fast approaching which was always busy and always a great time to socialise with some very familiar old faces and some new very exciting ones, maybe that was what just what I needed to spend time with the old crowd.

Charlie was constantly on my mind, wondering if he was thinking about me, keeping him in my thoughts was now my only link to him as

I hadn't heard from him in a while. That wasn't unusual, that was Charlie, wondering if I should write to him but knowing my words would be tainted by evil and hatred, knowing that I would shed so many tears whilst writing, tears that would stain the paper in blood stained hatred for the man he called his father, a father that at any cost felt it was his right to abuse a guest in his family home, which left me wondering if there had been other visitors that had suffered at the hands of such an evil person. The thought that he could be so calculated to line up his victims now sent me into free-fall panic, thinking that maybe I should have told someone in case his next victim was not going to be able to free themselves from his horrific actions.

CHAPTER 7

Carnival day was here at last. Now wanting to look and feel like the real Lizzy that had got a little lost along the way in a bid to seek happiness, in a desperate bid to have it all but I had nothing to show for my epic roller-coaster journey other than a tattooed body that was full of torment and despair, but I was determined that I would once again shine.

The cafe was buzzing with so many familiar faces. As the crowd grew, all of us had to sit where were could; at the tables, the floor, anywhere there was a space. The music was bouncing loudly from wall to wall. It vibrated through the café, adding to its unique interior and as the door swayed open and closed, the music spilled out into the street beyond.

The carnival was big, brash, and full of a vivid kaleidoscope of colours that captured everyone's imagination with bands playing, children dressed up as their favourite comic book characters, ladies with painted faces and clowns running in and out of the crowds treating everyone to a spectacular display. The smell of candy-floss filled the air with its pungent mouth-watering lingering aroma, along with popcorn, toffee apples and ice cream.

We all then headed off to the fair to be thrilled again by the bright lights, the thrill of the rides. The heavy perfume from the candy-floss machine was now filling my nostrils, making my mouth water once again. Suddenly the pungent heavy fumes from the engines filled the air, allowing my senses to relive the early years as a child, when I was free from the permanent heartache, free from the punishing blemishes that scarred my skin and free from vile images that now seemed to rule my life on a daily basis and now with ease, haunt my endless dreams.

The evening wore on and it was getting late when I noticed a bloke glancing over at me as if he knew who I was, but I had never seen him before. Not that I had been looking for anyone to come into my life as Charlie had filled every space I had left, leaving no room for anyone else. So obviously egged on by his companions, he walked over and stood at my side, all the while his outspoken friends stood cheering him on in a sort of ritual, hopping and whistling, complete with many more jesters of encouragement, like I was the prize that he wanted to win but I wasn't a prize or anyone's trophy. We started chatting, he was OK but nothing amazing. He asked if I was going dancing with the girls as we always did on carnival night and before I could answer he asked me out for a drink. Lost for words I said yes, stupid me, stupid me knowing instantly I had not learnt any lessons in the past few months.

My head was saying walk away but tonight I wanted and needed to feel like myself once again, the real Lizzy, to unleash my zest for life and love that seemed to have got lost in the many guilty emotions that continued to sweep through my body, masking the real fun loving, life embracing Lizzy that I really was.

God knows why him and like a fool I went, full steam ahead once again, running out of control like a car with no brakes on a collision course to yet more disaster and heartache, knowing full well that the storm was once again brewing, ready to shed its ferocious cargo.

Wondering to myself as to why was I picking up a cheap date with a man that I knew would want nothing more than my fragile body, rewarding himself with a trophy that would be without doubt engraved with my name. I remained blinkered, maybe I was trying to repay myself in some way for my stupidity, punishing myself for the evil that I had allowed, encouraging abuse to my young and fragile body but we arranged further dates to see one another, casually on my part, as love was never going to be an option with Dave, it never could or would be.

Dave was tall, slim, blond hair and a builder, but he was nothing special as I had not felt the fireworks, not even a spark triggered inside my body which left me feeling flat and deflated. Even his kisses felt cold and unloving, something I wasn't used to as I continued to crave the warm, sensual kisses that only Charlie could deliver.

We started dating and as the days followed Dave seemed hell bent on making soft demands on me and I went along with it, how stupid I was being? Lost yet again in a desperate bid to be loved, wondering if I would ever learn but I trusted his every word as he would say all the right things that seemed to make me feel a little more like the real fun-loving Lizzy I really was.

One Sunday afternoon Dave suggested we went for a walk, I knew instantly where his comments and commands were leading and I was not looking forward to it as no-one had touched me intimately since I was violated by Charlie's father, not even Charlie's hands had embraced my body intimately since I had hastily left Cardiff on that fateful Friday.

I was not sure I wanted Dave to touch me intimately, but felt I had to as he made me feel it was my duty to do as I was told. I felt cheap, dirty, ashamed of my out of control past actions, like I was betraying Charlie yet again.

It was now November, mild and sunny, autumn hanging heavily in the air, trees in a full kaleidoscope of colour, eye popping colours of russet reds, vibrant copper, and rich amber. We found a remote spot, not romantic and certainly not loving either, all I did was lay there like a limp rag, just wanting and waiting for it to be over while Dave enjoyed my body, my mind was being trampled all over by the reoccurring vile nightmare of my vile assault encountered while in the hands of Charlie's father. I wanted to cry out, cry out for the love of Charlie, to scream his name, letting it echo across the landscape but I just laid there thinking of him the entire time, the thought of Charlie got me through this very unloving, uncaring and loveless moment as Dave's kisses left me feeling flat with no feeling, no passion and without warmth, only wanting my body for his own selfish enjoyment and pleasure, a selfish trophy only he could enjoy, not wanting anyone else to have what he now called his, blatantly called his, especially when we were out with friends. It was like something he could brag about with no idea of how it made me feel, as I cringed uneasily at his repeated boastful comments.

I felt like I might never enjoy making love again as my mind would not let me forget the vile assault, the vile intrusion on my body that I had encountered with Charlie's father that had once again unleashed the devil-driven storm that hibernated inside me, waiting patiently to be unleashed when the time was right. Making love had to be with Charlie, anyone else would not do and would never be good enough. It felt like second-hand love, used, cold and very unwelcome.

I would return regularly to my tree house to escape the daily torment, which led me to wonder why Dave never appeared in any of my daydreams. Even at night in my room as darkness fell silently, he was never a visitor, it felt like my dreams were only made for Charlie to invade and my nightmares, well they were a nightly occurrence as Charlie's vile father crept silently in, trampling my dreams, crushing them menacingly to never allow me to have a full night's sleep without torment. Always rearing its unwelcome and very ugly head while telling me I would never withstand the endless storms that I would have to endure that again left me in a pool of ice cold fluid that had escaped terrified from my body.

Friday night was here again and boring, just like any other normal night that Dave and I spent together yet another that would be boringly uneventful. We never slept together in either parents' house and that was fine by me as I embraced the freedom of not having to be Intimate with him. He continued to repulse me, using my fragile, delicate body only for his selfish pleasure, but it wasn't the same for me anymore and possibly it never would be due to the monumental events that had rocked my world in the past few months that had left my body battered, bruised and very vulnerable.

I slept at the back of the house, my room looked over the back garden that with delightful views over the fields and into the woods. Dave's room was at the front of the house, tucked away out of sight from my room, flanked by my parents' bedroom.

Tonight was the same as every night, having to sleep with the light on for some sort of comfort, trying hard to find Charlie in my dreams on this chilly November night, listening to the rain beating relentlessly against my bedroom window, something that I loved to hear, especially while drifting off to sleep. Suddenly the rain was accompanied by a hard thud at the window which I chose to ignore, but it then became relentless, I heard it again and again, but now it was accompanied by a voice, a voice calling my name, *Lizzy, Lizzy,* his voice now even louder in a desperate attempt to attract my attention. I recognised it instantly, jumping out of bed I went to the window throwing it wide open to awaken my dreams. It was Charlie, he was very drunk and again in the company of a small group of people, all males that I didn't recognise, all of them soaking wet staring up at my window.

With the window now wide open allowing the wind and rain to cascade onto the windowsill for my chance to see him once again, allowing myself the pleasure of hearing his voice, to see his face and to witness his trade mark cocky smile. *Lizzy, my beautiful Lizzy, come down.* His expression still hiding a mysteriously dark secret which I still found attractive as it continually laced my tender body in mystery, seducing me during my daylight dreams but haunting me when darkness fell, along with the terrifying face of his vile father who would always remain unwelcome.

Now he was very vocal, he continued to call, *I love you, I love you so much Lizzy, come down*. I was reeling from this very welcome late night surprise, wanting to just throw my arms around him as he continued to call me from the garden. *Lizzy, I have come back for you, I said I would, I promised you Lizzy, remember.* I did remember all too well, he repeatedly told me he would come back for me. Suddenly mum and dad must have heard all the commotion that was unfolding in the back garden as my dad battled his way to the back door telling Charlie to leave and stay away in a very stern voice.

I saw the hurt on Charlie's face, pained with all the emotions of our dirty love that was still apparent. He turned and walked away down the little path. He still loved me, loved his princess and I did nothing, standing frozen to the spot at my bedroom window I let him go again, just letting him walk away in the pouring rain, into the darkness of this early winter's night.

Leaving my window now slightly ajar, beads of rain formed to what looked like necklaces of the finest shimmering silver, clinging fast to the panes of glass. I could hear every last word that Charlie continued to call back to me, his words were filled with pain and anguish tonight. I clung on to every word, not wanting it to be the last one, to embrace the luxury of him calling my name over and over again.

I could still hear Charlie shouting and calling my name as he staggered away, repeating his love for me, repeating my name. How I wished I could have returned his words tonight, wrapping my arms around him once again to never let him go, to shower him with love and all the Lizzy kisses I knew he loved, knowing full well all my love belonged to him and only to him.

Charlie's unexpected visit lead me to question why was he here? Why now? Why was he drunk? Why did he come to the house? Why was he accompanied by others? So many unanswered questions that I needed to be answered but not tonight as my parents had made sure that Charlie knew he was not welcome here at any cost and for whatever reason, leaving my world again turned upside down knowing tonight that Charlie was back in my life, wanting to rekindle our love, our dirty love that was never going to diminish.

I fell asleep thinking of him, inviting him back into my dreams once again. Now that I had a new and vivid recent vision of him I recalled his words that now filled my dreams, awakening emotions that only Charlie was capable of doing.

The next morning I woke early, the storms of last night which swept across the landscape had now been replaced by glorious sunshine, but I remained consumed by the magnitude of our love, still not believing that Charlie had kept his promise to return to collect what was so rightfully his and always would be, back to collect his trophy and I wasn't going to object.

Over breakfast mum and dad both remained steely faced, not mentioning the events of the night before. I knew they were not happy about Charlie just turning up to disrupt my life once again, the annoyance in dad's eyes and his disapproval now clear to see as it was written across his and mum's faces which told me exactly what they thought. This morning we ate breakfast in total silence, Dave seemed to have noticed the chilly atmosphere, especially from my parents as he made no attempt to make any conversation either. My eyes were fixed on the heavily patterned table cloth, scared to raise even an eyebrow. As Dave left for work I walked around the garden standing in the very spot that Charlie had stood the night before, looking up at my bedroom window, trying to understand why Charlie had just turned up out of the blue. What was he doing back in the village? So many questions, but only he held the answers that I now desperately needed to hear.

Back in my bedroom I stood at the window wishing Charlie was outside telling the world that I was still his Lizzy and the girl he so obviously loved as I instantly heard his words echoing through my bedroom filling it with love, sweeping silently around my room, taking me with it, flirting and seducing me once again until it suddenly slipped under the door, his words now echoing throughout the house ready to torment my parents yet again.

My mind was now made up, I had to find Charlie to return his love so as I looked into the hall mirror smiling in approval at my decision, knowing at long last I had something special to smile about, while my mother continued to wag her finger at me and continued to rant on about Charlie's late night visit and his intent on causing not only myself, but our family more unnecessary heartache disrupting my life once more. If only she knew the full extent of my inner unhappiness. I grabbed my coat, slamming the front door behind me with renewed vigour, making sure she and my father were now fully aware of my disappointment that they had banished him from the house, knowing full well how much I craved his love. Would I find him? Well that was not an option, I had to find him, I had to see him once more. Being selfish, I wanted just to feel his arms around me, to feel his kisses on my lips and to hear him call me his princess once more.

I arrived at the cafe, my first thought for where he might be, hoping he would at least have been there mixing with the old gang, supplying them with his endless jokes and infectious laughter, but sadly not. I asked everyone, but sadly they hadn't seen him so I left the cafe behind me, also leaving the glorious music along with the unique atmosphere, walking out on to the streets that today were so empty. I felt at a total loss, maybe he wasn't here at all, maybe he had returned to Wales? I was thinking of all the old places that we used to go but with no avail as a feeling of complete despair had started setting in. I started to think I was going to make my way home, to hide away in the solitude of my tree house forever, to be alone with my thoughts, my heart broken that I had not found him, this possibly my only chance to see him once more.

Returning to the cafe I sat alone outside, the watery sunshine felt warm on my skin, leaving warm kisses where Charlie's should have been placed. As I listened to all the fantastic music that was playing loudly from the old, battered jukebox, escaping under and over the door in a bid to entice me in, my friends eagerly invited me to join them inside, but I declined, recalling over and over the previous night's events, hearing him vividly calling my name that now echoed so loudly to the point it became louder than the music being played in the cafe. I became transported miles away, alone with my thoughts, letting very special memories invade my mind once again, one after another they never failed to awaken my emotions.

I drifted back to the here and now, to the mayhem that was happening inside the cafe. It was always such a busy and much loved place to be, normally I would have loved being inside listening to the amazing music that seemed to just bellow out from the somewhat tatty jukebox, all of us dancing just soaking up its unique atmosphere but today I was just happy to sit outside, listening to the music that faded in and out as the door swung open and slammed closed with its familiar squeaking from the rusty hinges.

Feeling very restless I walked down towards the football pitch where kids were playing football. It was a mild day considering it was November, but the season was reflected by the change in colours that adorned the trees, now fading fast from the array of vibrant red and amber tones amongst a kaleidoscope of autumn leaves that were just hanging on by a thread, waiting to fall gracefully to the ground where they would become brown and crisp as winter approached.

What a mess, my whole life had now become a bloody mess as I continued my love affair for Charlie, living my life for others, sinking back into dark days with the heavy burden of a very sad miscarriage, hearing the constant muffled echoes of my baby's cries when darkness fell and the vile sexual assault by Charlie's father that commanded my dreams, turning them into reoccurring nightmares that woke me from my sleep every night, leaving my bed linen bathed in wet, cold sweat that now contained his vile pungent aroma.

Suddenly my eye caught sight of a man sat alone on a bench with his head berried firmly in his hands, deep in thought. Glancing at him again I started staring at him, it was Charlie. I was now stunned, not able to take my gaze away from him, gasping now for air as I became breathless knowing that I had at last found him.

He looked a little older but just as sexy and still cocky in his attitude. His reputation still ripe, but his expression was empty and cold, leaving his face crippled by anguish and pain. His hair was still long and glossy, just how I remembered him. I couldn't leave now without seeing him, without indulging myself in another helping of his bad-boy reputation or hearing his voice and to hopefully put a smile back on his face, to give him back his lost trademark smile so with a deep breath I instantly smelt his aroma that filled my nostrils. Wanting more I walked around the back of him, my thoughts running wild as to what I would say when our eyes met again. My heart was now in my mouth, leaving it so dry and free from saliva that instantly allowed my tongue to stick to the roof of my mouth.

My body was shaking with terrifying trepidation, knowing that I loved him so much, this had still terrified me, the realisation that I remained Charlie's hostage, never wanting to be set free from the chains that had now become my armour against a loveless life with Dave.

I leant over his left shoulder gently. With my cold hands shaking, I put them over his eyes, hoping it would be the surprise he wanted, the present he would want to unwrap not just today, but forever.

Hello Charlie, I whispered, my voice was now low and trembling. *Lizzy, my Lizzy*. Startled, he jumped up, leaping over the wobbly wooden bench, throwing his arms around me as we held each other for what seemed like a lifetime, not wanting to release each other from the grip of love as we both indulged in the moment. My eyes tightly closed, embracing everything that was Charlie, letting his reputation seduce me once again, stripping me bare and to rip through my heart.

He suddenly pulled away, holding both my hands out stretched for his pleasure, feasting his gaze on what he had left behind. *Let me look at you Lizzy, my Lizzy, your so fucking beautiful, still my beautiful girl*. I started to cry uncontrollably, mumbling through my never-ending tears. *I can't stop loving you Charlie*, he squeezed both my hands reassuringly.

As we stood kissing I felt like I had been transported millions of miles away from reality, transported back to a time when our love was so new, so very virginal, my senses awakened again by his beautiful aroma for the second time in as many minutes. I continued my deep absorbing breaths, filling my nostrils until more passionate kisses followed, sending fireworks bursting into a kaleidoscope of coloured emotions that left me motionless and still as I embraced the moment that now devoured my body.

I was desperate to ask why he was here, but at this moment I didn't care, he was here now, allowing me to feel all the love I craved once again, bursting with a love that showed not only in my face but that now rippled throughout my quivering, young and fragile body.

We sat for a while on the bench with our arms embracing each other, wishing this beautiful moment to never end. *Lizzy lets go somewhere more private*. I looked at him, there was never going to be a refusal. *Charlie, that would be lovely*. With that, he took my hand again in his, returning some hope that we were still going to be life-time lovers that had always been his promise to me.

Today, this unexpected walk took us on a journey to the old allotment shed, our old sofa which was still as we had left it, along with the huge, dark cobwebs that seemed to have multiplied, hanging low, that today looked almost beautiful as they caught the watery mid-afternoon sunlight. My senses were treated again to the aroma of the shed which remained very much something I loved as I stood, breathing in its unique air, breathing in what was us, cocooned within these walls along with all the old memories that came flooding back like a tidal wave, sweeping me along with all the love we shared, allowing me to feel like the real Lizzy once again, something that had sadly been hidden away, muted from this almighty dirty love that I was feeling now.

Suddenly I thought I should tell him about our baby, our beautiful baby so sadly and so cruelly taken from us and about his vile, disgusting father, but I could not put him through all that agony, I had to kept it to myself as it was my agony and my guilt to carry alone all my life, secrets that I would now take to my grave that would overtime become berried along with my silence.

We lay together again, breathless from this unexpected, but delightful and very welcome reunion. It felt just like before when we loved to be in each other's arms, that powerful bond we shared and always would. Not even his vile father could snatch that away from us, but I remained terrified that the storm would cast its ugly cargo over not only me, but Charlie too, its fury seemed to have no boundary.

I stood up ready to command my ever-growing passionate dirty love, begging for the sensual feelings that I was about to experience once again so with no hesitation I took the lead, my body now desperate for Charlie's full attention.

His deep brown eyes were transfixed on mine, I could see the yearning he had, eyes that were now starving for my love, hungry for my body that were always going to be his. I undid my top to reveal my firm breasts and rock hard nipples, I then unzipped my leather skirt, letting it drop to the floor. I could see the want in his eyes as I stood in just my white lacy underwear, complete with my high heels I leant over to kiss him, kissing him hard with an intense, very grown up passion that was exclusively his, no invitation was needed, and it never would be.

Nothing had changed, our dirty love was still very much alive, still extremely passionate as I remained his life-time hostage. I would never allow myself the freedom of the chains that seemed to tighten every time I was in his company.

Charlie's breathing was now untamed, low, and extremely sexy as I seduce him. I then slipped out of my bra to reveal my huge tits, nipples that stood immediately to attention, tingling with excitement, eager for Charlie's lips to embrace them. Charlie's eyes were now bulging with delight and of course his smile, that trade mark smile as he moaned, *Lizzy my naughty little Lizzy*, I was now blushing at Charlie's comments.

I pulled him up as I began to undo his shirt, button by button I kissed each one in turn, peeling back the fabric to reveal his full and proud chest slowly allowing me to indulge once again my ever growing passion and my endless need for his love, casting his shirt aside, letting it drop to the floor while I moved around his lean, muscular body. I was now naked apart from my little white frilly knickers and high heel shoes, he could now feel my huge demanding breasts firm on his back as I felt his chest expand again, this time with absolute delight.

I then stood to face him, my gaze firmly fixed, my attention clear for him to see. Sharply pulling his leather belt undone, I let my hand slip inside his jeans to find his cock that was standing rigidly hard, long, throbbing and yearning for my attention, my full attention that was never going to be ignored.

His jeans now lay discarded on the floor, his body free from clothes and as always, he was commando, a look I loved and one that continued to delight my senses.

I slipped my fingers gently into my kitten, covering them with my fresh, warm juice that was cascading freely from my purring kitten, juice that clung to my fingers. I then offered them to Charlie's mouth for him to lick one by one, slowly and seductively. I then did it again just to tease him and to show him I meant business. Naughty Lizzy was back for good and on a mission to seduce him once again.

I kissed his chest with loving, hard and intense Lizzy kisses, I then fell to my knees, his cock standing to attention, rigidly stiff and begging to have my full undivided attention and he was going to get it, my full undivided attention. Charlie was now moaning, almost begging me to seduce his cock so I held it firmly, kissing it with beautiful Lizzy kisses, rubbing it hard to allow his juice to erupt into beautiful pearly beads that was now smeared lovingly across my tits. *Princess you're good, so fucking good*, his voice almost shaking with passion. His passion was something I never wanted him to share with anyone else apart from me, Lizzy.

Charlie pulled me on to the sofa, stripping me bare of my lace knickers, his tongue now fully engaged with my clit as I held firmly his head between my thighs, allowing his tongue to seduce my purring kitten, closing my eyes to allow the full impact of this unexpected afternoon of dirty, but beautiful love that was so tantalisingly good. He licked my juice drenched kitten, juices that were now coating his lips ready to share with me.

I then straddled him and as I did he called me his girl, his princess, his forever girl, his Lizzy. I then rode his cock like my life depended on it, never wanting him to forget this beautiful dirty love filled afternoon, something that I wished we could repeat everyday of our lives, right here in this most perfect place.

Charlie's moaning was loud, the volume now raised to maximum. *You want more Charlie?* I whispered. I teased my tongue around his mouth exploring every bit of it in a frenzy of passion, rolling it over and under his tongue.

I looked at him with my steely green eyes, intent on having a life time of love with him. Charlie then straddled me for the final stage of our dirty afternoon of love and once again Charlie never failed to deliver as suddenly I felt his tongue glide into my pussy for the ultimate love experience that we both could share as his head once again firmly braced between my thighs, my legs now wrapped around him, his lips smeared in dirty juice from my kitten, making sure I enjoyed the final moments of our love fuelled afternoon by sharing his kisses.

Laying together naked and truly satisfied, he looked at me with his deep brown eyes. *Lizzy I can't stop loving you, I won't stop loving you.* I smiled back, my eyes blurred now by tears of love as I squeezed his hand reassuring him that our love would never be over, knowing we had both committed to a lifetime of dirty love that had been stamped with approval on that very first day when we shared those first delightful smiles that contained our contagious love, a love I never thought existed, a love that would test not only us and but those around us, but today I was willing to pay the price, a price that I knew would cost me terrifying pain and more heartache.

I hesitantly ask him about the night before, his head once again cradled in his hands, he said he could not live without me and would love me forever, but it seemed that he wasn't going to reveal much about the company he was keeping, he seemed very reluctant for me to know which I found strange. Or was it really none of my business? Or was this once again part of the mysterious, secret life that I would never be part of, a life that he hid so well behind his big brown eyes, his trade mark smile complimented by his escalating cocky attitude.

We kissed our last kisses, holding each other as we said our last, very emotional, and very reluctant goodbye. Leaving me yet again, devastated and drained of a love which was only for Charlie.

Again, a small box with *princess* carved into the lid was placed in my hand. I came to give it to you last night Lizzy. God! Why were we doing this to each other, tormenting each other's hearts, when it was so obvious we loved each other so much.

So as I walked away I didn't dare turn around, but I continued to hear his whistles and calls as they echoed around me. *I love you Lizzy, you're my girl, never forget it, life won't let you princess as I will be around when you're least expecting it.* I found myself smiling at his relentless calls through my never-ending tears that today managed to splash onto my open wounds, stinging, tormenting, and irritating the vile scars that Charlie's father had brutally left on my skin.

I arrived home late and went straight to my bedroom to open my little box and on opening it I found a little scrap of crumpled paper that was torn around the edges which made me giggle and smile, his words written with a blunt pencil were beautiful, almost poetic.

Sunday morning came and I was awoken abruptly from my dreams that had been relentless, not only haunting, but beautiful, so many combinations dancing with my fertile and vulnerable emotions. As I lay in bed, my thoughts were running wild with the wonderful events of yesterday as the church bells rang out. Jumping out of my bed I stood at my bedroom window smiling uncontrollably at my unexpected and delightful reunion with Charlie, knowing it had been something we would both treasure, knowing it was our secret and that no one could ever spoil it or would they? Only time and our resilience would tell.

Wanting time alone to indulge myself in the luxury of my love for Charlie, I took myself to my beloved tree house where I could be completely alone without mum and dad's sideways looks, raised eyebrows and constant reminders that Charlie was never going to be welcome at the house.

Looking out from the tree house the woods looked enchanting today, just like every day, its beauty remained unchanged, stunning tall trees that swayed in the light breeze capturing the muted sunlight between their branches as the leaves of autumn had started to fall to the ground below, taking away the stunning colour that had once painted a vivid picture of burnt orange, rich russets, golden browns and fiery copper and as I listened it sounded like the breeze was whispering my name, beckoning me to walk again on the crisp, leafy carpet that was ready for me to feel the luxurious cushion beneath my feet. The woods always allowed me to recall emotions and memories, the majority of which contained the most pleasurable delights of Charlie that sparked a wonderful collection of my favourite memories, creating a vivid kaleidoscope that thrilled my senses, sending fireworks though my body that burst into life, sparking senses of Charlie's aroma in a bid to never let me forget the pleasure he gave me.

Dave came over on Sunday afternoon, his mood was foul, leaving the air cold and frosty between us with his constant questions that he demanded I answer, questions about my mysterious disappearance the day before. I panicked as to what I should tell him so I lied, telling him I was seeing a friend for the afternoon which seemed to calm his mood, but I was feeling tired, and I really wasn't in the mood for the constant questions that now irritated me, I found his moods increasingly hard to deal with along with his need to know my every move. Knowing he sensed that I was in no mood for him tonight, like most nights, tonight was no different as I had other things on my mind so he went home early. Relieved I was alone at last, I took myself up to my bedroom to stand at my window, looking out over the dark almost eerie landscape, thinking constantly of Charlie who would now be back in Wales leaving me alone again to cry bitter tears that only this room could understand, tonight being just like every other lonely occasion. This was not normal; how could I be in love someone so much and date another? I knew I had to either finish it with Dave or forget Charlie and I certainly would never be able to do that, what a dilemma that once again I had made possible, all for my indulgence to be the girl who wanted to be loved by a bad-boy and to be the centre of his attention.

CHAPTER 8

The day's rolled by and it was now approaching Christmas. December was a month that would bring a cold chill, reminding not only me, but everyone that winter was once again here, the season that I loved, a month that seemed to bring the real Lizzy to life, sprinkling my zest for life over everyone I knew, including mum and dad.

At last the Christmas tree was delivered. It was my job to decorate every year. It held such perfect, special memories for me, right from when I was a child growing up when my dad would have to lift me up to put the angel in her rightful place to oversee the festivities that seemed to go on for weeks of merriment and festive joy. After many years or being decorated, today the tree had been decorated once more and was taking pride of place in the lounge complete with the lights that matched its perfection. The lights twinkled, casting a wonderful glow in the lounge and once again the same angel with her angelic face graced the tree.

Christmas Eve came and I was up early having been awakened by the church bells that chimed so loudly, almost insisting I got up. I sat on the sofa in my pretty cotton pyjamas snuggled up in front of the roaring fire, wondering what Charlie would be doing today, if he was thinking of me, if he was recapturing our very own winter memories. Suddenly tears softly invaded my porcelain face as I struggled hard to try and forget him, to get on with my life without his dirty love.

I was not seeing Dave until this evening, he was going to stay the night which never inspired me as I felt trapped in his company, bored by his inability to send my heart racing, bored with what he called love as it left me cold and flat.

It was very cold outside and looked like it might snow, the sky heavily laden with snow clouds that seemed to collide with others in a desperate attempt to shed the mass of icy crystals they now carried. A white Christmas, how special that would be to once again enliven my special memories of when Charlie and I would walk for miles across the field in the snow, sitting in the freezing cold tree house wrapped in the huge multi-coloured blanket that now adorned my bed, being able to escape the constant gaze from my parents who seemed unable to understand the staggering love we shared, creating much needed memories to recall all my life when the days were tough to cope with, or if I just wanted my time alone to escape the storm.

Watching the television alone I heard the letter box rattle, it was the final post before Christmas. On gathering and sorting the mass of white envelopes that lay on the mat, one envelope caught my eye, very distinct and was addressed to My Princess written in pencil. I smiled knowing instantly it was from Charlie, and I rushed upstairs eager to open the card. I sat in my bedroom with trembling hands and with tears that trickled down my face delicately cascading on to the envelope in little droplets that seemed to bounce off the envelope back onto my already tear stained face.

A card from Charlie and it read…

To my princess, my girl, my lovely Lizzy.

I loved you 4 years ago, I love you now and I always will, you and I have made history. Our history. Our story. Our love.

So once again I stood at my bedroom window commanding memories to be recalled, to enliven my senses of Charlie, to feel him here holding me in his arms on this cold winter afternoon, to have his hands holding mine, to be treated to the kisses of my dreams, just to be together, just once more.

I was suddenly jolted back from my memories to the mouth-watering, wonderful smells wafting through the house from downstairs in the kitchen as mum was baking her famous sausage rolls, the ones with crisp, feather light pastry that just melted in your mouth and mince pies that were laced with vast amounts of brandy, ready for the onslaught of our Christmas visitors knowing the chaos that it would bring, bringing laughter and merriment that I was sure would echo through the house bringing with it colour and a vibrancy that this house seemed to lack on so many occasions.

I took one last, long and lingering look out of my bedroom window across the field into the woods just as it was just getting dark. I loved this time of the evening as the woods looked so dark and mysterious, the trees were bare and baron from leaf, some may call them uninviting and cold but I always thought it was beautiful, more so now, knowing it held the full intensity of our passionate dirty love story. Suddenly I was aware of the time and that Dave was waiting for me downstairs to bore my evening once again with his selfish comments, selfish ways and his inability to even make me smile so I had to leave my memories on hold for now but I would return to them soon without doubt, knowing I would need them more than ever in the weeks, months and even years that were to follow.

As the evening wore on, Dave and I were alone in the lounge without any form of physical contact, he didn't even attempt to hold my hand, he seemed frozen from any feelings which I always found hard to imagine why. Suddenly and without warning, he said, *can I ask you something?* I nodded, startled, and somewhat bewildered by the suddenness of his question, bringing me back from the sheer boredom of our relationship. *I love you Lizzy*, and with that he got down on one knee, a sudden ice cold chill ran through me as a deafening silence descended, filling the living room with an ice cold fog, a silence that seemed to pin me rigidly to the spot, the room now frozen in time with no response from me as I found it very hard to say the words he so wanted to hear and more importantly hear tonight, but those words of love were only for one person and that was not Dave. *Lizzy, I would love you to marry me*, again no response from me and with that a cheap gold ring laced with the smallest shiny stone was forced firmly on my finger. I did not know what to say, I hated myself for being in this situation but I hated Dave more for asking me so with nowhere to hide and my vulnerability fully on show, I stupidly said yes. For god's sake, I said *yes*! When all the time I should have said no. I didn't love him and I never ever would, how could I? My love had already been taken and tonight I heard Wales hold its breath in anticipation of the outcome of my foolish answer and my dishonest behaviour.

The champagne was flowing freely tonight with corks constantly popping but it did not make things right, it changed nothing for me, it never would, but it did help dull the emotional pain of great sadness that I was now feeling and always would for as long as I continued going along with the farce that was now going to be my life and for as long as I wore the cheap engagement ring that had been forced on my delicate finger. Tonight had already started to deny me of life.

The evening was all too overwhelming for me. Mum and dad seemed pleased but I could tell they knew I was not feeling the happiness that should have been feeling, my expression flat and empty with not the slightest feeling of love, it never would. I couldn't even raise a smile, not even a fake smile tonight graced my face.

I went to bed feeling confused as tonight it felt like my life was engulfing me, closing in on me, but now I wore his ring, a ring that now meant I would never be free from his demands, his constant moods and his inability to make me feel loved, a ring that would starve me of air and of life itself in the coming months and years that were ahead.

My life was a bloody mess and spiralling once again out of control, I would have to do some deep, heart and soul searching if I was to get my life back on track, if I was to have any chance of happiness. I fought again with the storm that was going to leave me cold, shivering, and vulnerable once more, knowing the storms would cast many violent, dark, and unruly clouds that would contain a ferocious cargo.

After a turbulent night I woke to the smell of turkey coming from the kitchen, knowing mum was up very early having to struggle again this Christmas to fit the huge bird into the oven, ready for the mass of visitors that were due to arrive today. I loved Christmas lunch, the table filled with festive food a real banquet, vibrant colours of Christmas from fiery red, the deepest of green through to gleaming golds and stunning silvers sprinkled with snowy white flecks.

Dad made his famous Christmas lunch speech that never changed from year to year, tapping his sherry glass with a spoon to attract everyone's attention, but today he started his speech by welcoming Dave to our family which again did not encourage any smiles from me. My blemished skin and open wounds fully on display as I cringed every time dad mentioned Dave's name, bringing with it images of Charlie's vile father, his vile stench then hit the back of my throat, his voice now echoing in my head. Suddenly I managed to shake the images free, bringing me back to the here and now by my aunts hooping and clapping with joy at the news they had just heard, jumping up from the table and sending the cutlery crashing onto the floor to come pepper my face in sweet kisses, squeezing my hands so tightly, smiling with joyful happiness and delight. If only they knew my full sadness as I put on a brave, highly painted face for them today. So with presents now opened and the huge lunch over our visitors began to leave, merry from the lunchtime sherry and over indulging in the heavily laced brandy mince pies, leaving the house once again free from the constant chatter and hilarious laughter from my aunts that seemed so loud it echoed in every room, filling them with a very welcome warmth but my mind was elsewhere, the only place I wanted to be was with Charlie in his arms, wrapped in so much Christmas dirty love.

At last I breathed a huge sigh of relief as Dave went home to see his family and spend time with them, knowing I was now alone where I could be me, the real Lizzy, allowing myself to drift back to Wales to the arms of the only man that made me happy, truly happy.

I must have fallen asleep on the sofa deeply unhappy at what I had committed to this Christmas. The realisation hadn't fully hit me yet, but I already knew it was never going to be a fairy-tale, it felt like only minutes into my sleep when I was awoken once more by my haunting nightmares that now contained Dave and his spiteful comments, all the while my finger being strangled by a cheap uninspiring ring as well as the image of Charlie's vile father and the distant muffled cries of my beautiful baby.

I looked out of the lounge window and I was spellbound, it had been snowing heavily overnight and it all looked so beautiful, glistening flecks reflected by a perfect moon on a blanket of light and fluffy snow that had been blown in from the east, freezing the countryside in the perfect winter scene as I continued to escape into the beautiful Wiltshire landscape that beckoned me to dance in the snow drifts that had been made by the ice cold winds which continued to blow and swirl the snow around, dropping it into perfect piles ready for my virgin foot prints.

I went to my bedroom desperate to recall warm winter memories. I stood freezing cold, shivering dressed only in my new Christmas pyjamas that mum and dad had given me, pyjamas that still seemed to reflect my tender years.

Now looking out of my bedroom window, once more I was treated to vivid winter wonderland memories that forced my thoughts deep into the woods where the trees stood laden with snow, now weighing heavily on their branches.

I should have undoubtedly been feeling so very happy, but I was not feeling it today. I would never feel and experience true happiness as long as I was with Dave and for as long as I wore his ring that was now strangling my finger denying it of life, starving it of blood and air, something that I knew Dave wanted, to slowly deny me of the real fun loving Lizzy that would be lost along the way, left in the dark, dingy and unwelcome shadows for others to sneer at and never to be admired.

I must have fallen into a deep sleep to escape my ongoing misery as when I awoke the snow was still falling, allowing a magical looking landscape to develop in front of me. Looking out from my bedroom window I was transfixed on the beauty that was laid out before me, once again I felt very lucky to have a winter wonderland all of my own to explore, to revisit little pockets of glorious winters gone by that Charlie and I had lovingly created, ready for times like these, knowing full well that we would once again walk in the snow, to jump into snow drifts and to enjoy again the winter wonderlands that we had created.

Suddenly I looked down at my freezing cold hands and at the ring that Dave requested I wore, it was cutting so deep into the skin of my frozen finger, reminding me that I had now committed my life to a man that I did not love and would never love, which had now scared my young vulnerable body. It was a lovely ring, but lovely for someone else, not me. Deep down I was not ready for the impact that engagement and marriage would have on my fragile and untamed years, there could never be a ring prettier than my plastic cracker daisy ring that Charlie had given me all that time ago. Maybe it was wrong to compare them, knowing full well I should have said no to Dave. I needed to say no, I had to say no and soon to deny him the privilege of abusing me in the coming weeks and months ahead.

The following week I was treated to further heavy snow that allowed me to enjoy fantastic walks alone in the woods, walking in pretty snow drifts that the cold, silent easterly winds had delightfully picked up and discarded leaving them in my path ready for me to discover and explore.

The woods were freezing today as the icy winds breezed through the openness, reminding me fully of the vast change in seasons that graced these woods as I enjoyed each one's beauty and grace. The winter would be cold, but stunning in its beauty that was full of a dark mystery as the woods lay dormant from colour but alive with the sound of wildlife scurrying around, going about their daily life. Spring would allow the winter to shed its heavy overcoat, allowing the trees to bud into life with birds singing high in the trees, its carpet peppered with delicate pale snowdrops, crocus, and daffodils. The summer months would see the trees fully dressed, heavy in leaf, creating a much needed umbrella for when the sun was burning high and bright. In Autumn the woods became painted in a glorious rich tapestry of colour, complete with a multitude of leaves that had already fallen to the ground, crisp underfoot, allowing the squirrels to scurry around busy collecting their winter store.

With the snow and ice now gone I was back to work, back to some sort of normality. Dave and I were still a couple but I had to admit that true love was never going to grace our relationship as now I was living a lie, living daily in the shadow of Charlie's eternal love. I knew that I should have been honest sooner, knowing our relationship was artificial and lacking any commitment from me.

We were going to spend much of the weekend together but I found it all very mundane and so very boring as there were still no fireworks in our relationship, no sparks, no passion to light my senses that seemed muted now, knowing they would continue to stay that way. I enjoyed his company but we were more like friends than anything and that was never going to change, how could it?

I was trying hard to make it work, Dave had now taken over making all plans for our wedding which at times was very heavy going for me as I became increasingly suffocated by Dave's constant demands to do as I was told, the real Lizzy had now been yet again forced to fade into the background, leaving me lacking in my zest and love for life as I continued to walk the unsavoury path to boredom and misery. I wanted to feel sparks that lit up my life, giving me that something that was so obviously missing to me anyway. Dave did love me without any doubt, but I could never return the love that he demanded, my head and heart sad, heavy with the burden of years of marriage that lay ahead for me without love, how could I marry someone I did not love, knowing the storms would undoubtedly rule my life?

Time went by and nothing changed, my feelings stayed the same as I constantly challenged my love for Charlie daily and every time I could not find a good enough reason to not love him. Was I still being led astray by the mystery of him? His reputation still intrigued me and that continued to seduce me daily, there had always been something behind his smiles that I found very appealing that continued to send ice cold shivers down my spine when I thought about him.

I wanted to be out with friends, dancing till dawn, free to let my hair down a little, free to be the Lizzy that had now been left behind in my bedroom mirror on that fateful Christmas Eve, allowing it to fade in the increasing dark shadows. I continued to drift along, jumping to Dave's demands, feeling detached from my friends, now discarded all because of Dave and his selfish behaviour.

Furious with myself that I had let this happen, I had let myself down again and on reflection it was obvious, I was on the rebound from Charlie and I would forever be guilty knowing that deep down I was going to marry the wrong man. The years that were to follow would prove that to everyone around me, testing my vulnerability, allowing a little more of Lizzy to blend into the background, to hide behind yesterday's shadows as Dave continued to command the limelight.

Was I still in love with Charlie? Yes of course I was, but I could not spend my life in love with him without a future, I had to get him out of my head and out of my heart, I had to set myself free from the chains that had shackled me to Charlie's love but I would never be able to forget him, it would be impossible as we had created so many beautiful memories, all too precious to forget.

It was now late spring and the wedding date was set, so the farcical plans had now begun. With just over a year to go I was not in any way looking forward to moving away from the sanctuary I adored, away from the surroundings that were so special, along with all the memories I had made in the garden, the tree house and far beyond.

The summer was fast approaching, and the long summer days would be here, it would be heavenly as once again I could take myself into the garden to sit and recall my dreams, none of which included Dave, not one of them, as my dreams were exclusively for Charlie. By night Dave ruled my sleep, as did Charlie's vile father with haunting visions that would wake me, leaving my body in a pool of sweat complete with all those distant echoing cries from my baby that were now fading day by day. I continued to scream, unheard, while the wild White horses came galloping again out of the foaming waves, stampeding over my vulnerable and very fragile body as I begged the nightmares to stop and allow me a perfect night's sleep.

Wanting and needing a desperate change in my life, I changed jobs hoping it would help me deal with my life. I struggled daily to forget Charlie, to rest my mind from my traumatic night's sleep and to free myself from the life I was now committed to, having to endure a catalogue of terrifying events that now ruled my life.

Today I sat having coffee, chatting, and catching up with friends. Suddenly the conversation lead to Charlie in a round-about way and his new life in Wales as they had heard he was seeing someone, a girl from Cardiff, apparently very beautiful, leaving me to almost choke on my coffee and with a heavy heart I said I was happy for him but deep down I hated the thought that he was giving his dirty love to someone else when all the time it had been promised to me, along with all the other promises he had endlessly made to me, his girl, when we were alone in the tree house or at the old shed and of course the woods, where he etched his promise on the tree for everyone to see and for everyone to know that I was his girl. Reeling from that news my friends had just delivered to me, we said our goodbyes as now I just wanted to be alone to wallow in my own sadness so I sat in the park just staring up at the huge blue sky, looking for answers to the endless questions that now formed a patient queue but questions that I may never get the answers I so needed, wondering what Charlie would be doing now. It was hard to imagine and painful to think that he was now giving his dirty love and his promises to another, seducing her with his reputation when all the time it had my name on.

The sky today was stunningly blue with no clouds to mar its unique beauty, the breeze refreshingly kind on my skin, peppering sweet kisses on my heavily painted porcelain face as I closed my eyes wanting desperately to see Charlie's smile but today it would not fill my vision, all I could see was a dark, lonely, and very long road that lay ahead with no light at the end of what now seemed like an endless tunnel that today looked even longer and darker.

Back home and totally unaware of the time I continued to recall so many delightful emotions and as I looked at my watch I realised I had been sat in the tree house for three hours, being treated to a journey of a lifetime of love, all made possible by Charlie, it was my escape to dream of a life of outstanding dirty love with the only man I ever loved, or was prepared to love.

Dave and I were going out tonight, but now I was going to be very late, knowing Dave would not be impressed by my late arrival. His annoyance would be visible, but on this occasion I did not care, as returning to my life of dirty love with Charlie was far more important and far more entertaining than being with Dave, it always would be.

The evening went surprisingly well and Dave was in good spirits for a change, despite the odd unwelcome demands and spiteful comments, we went home and I went straight to bed, Dave kissed me goodnight on the landing in the hope that tonight I would invite him into my bed, but he was never going to receive the invitation he was hoping for as that invitation had already been used, knowing full well he was totally unaware that my room held so many secrets and a passionate dirty love that Charlie and I had created in my bed on that warm autumn day, when our love was paramount, when we were inseparable, something I would always cherish, so in my bed there was only room for Charlie and I, as three would be a crowd and very unwelcome.

Sunday morning had arrived and like every Sunday I was awoken by the heavy, earthy chimes of the church bells, today was going to be a very lazy day as we just lounged around, watching television all day. I was so bored by Dave's lack of interest in me and my feelings as I yawned through every conversation, an increasing reflection of my bloody boredom. I needed to feel Dave's passion but it was non-existent, there was no fire in his blood, no desire to sweep me off my feet or to treat me like the lady I wanted to be, that I deserved to be. We talked briefly about the wedding and at that moment should have been my prompt to call it off, the perfect time, as the longer I left it the harder it would be to do but I didn't, I just seemed to go along with it like always, hesitating again and not taking control, knowing again my parents would disapprove of my sudden decision. I was such a stupid girl, I needed to find a way to get the strength from somewhere to take control, to call it off and soon, even though I knew full well the back lash it would cause, knowing Dave would hold me to ransom.

The summer days were drifting by and I spent many hours just sitting in the garden alone recalling happier times as a child, when I would climb the apple trees, run across the fields into the woods with not a care in the world and then as a teenager in love when Charlie and I would just spend endless hours alone up in the tree house enjoying each other's company as I wallowed in his cocky attitude, revelling in his reputation while enjoying our natural love, creating dreams for our future but sadly our dream future had now turned into a living nightmare for me as I was having to carry this heavy burden of marriage, the reality was now so hard to bear that I was going to be marrying the wrong man.

CHAPTER 9

Now with the months blending into one, my birthday had suddenly arrived, and it was my day out with friends so I headed for town on a mission to spoil myself as I wanted to buy lots of lovely things, pretty things, anything to blot out my misery of a loveless life I had with Dave, just to let me escape for a few hours from the prison sentence that was to be my life when judgement day arrived.

I spent a long time in town just wandering around meeting up with some friends for lunch, just being normal me, Lizzy, the girl who had a yearning for love and wanting to embrace life with every breath I took. Full from a delicious lunch and pleasant company I was ready for a spending frenzy as I was on a mission to spend every penny I could on me, it was my way of blotting out my misery and sadness so now laden with bags full of things I had no intention of buying, having been on a spending frenzy blotting out the impending misery, knowing full well Dave would object to my frivolous indulgence, all had been bought to distract my attention for a split second, allowing me a little piece of happiness even if it was short lived because I knew that once I closed the front door behind me, my life would spiral yet again into misery, a misery all made possible by Dave, but for which I had allowed.

As I arrived home, stepping through the front door I was greeted by the wonderful aromas of mum's baking, the mouth-watering aromas wafted throughout the house with most of them being captured in my bedroom, aromas that for now overpowered the misery of what my life had become. I looked at the bags now covering my bed, bags of things that could never make up for my unhappiness and the lack of love that was missing from my life.

Returning to the hallway there was a small pile of post for me, cards from family members and dear friends. The last card was now ready to open, with its unusual postmark and address written in pencil, writing that seemed so familiar. As I gazed at it, I opened it slowly, intrigued to see who the card was from, the card was pretty and glittery. Suddenly ice cold tears hit my delicate, warm, porcelain face with force, blurring my vision, stinging my vulnerable skin and smudging my perfect makeup.

Happy Birthday Princess. Charlie had not forgotten and I had not expected to receive such a beautiful card from him. I ran upstairs desperate to read the beautiful card in peace and alone in my bedroom, I sat staring at this beautiful card to absorb this unexpected birthday treat.

As I unfolded the card, the beautiful words yet again sent emotions flooding into my body, grasping every one of them, not wanting to miss the sensations that I craved.

I could never forget you on your birthday, or any other day. Have a wonderful birthday princess.

All my love, kisses, daisy chains and all. Remember princess, I'm never far away.

A million kisses followed which brought an amazing smile to my face which today burst into life as with tears that once again I shed for Charlie, my tears remained exclusively for him as I cried tears that stained my porcelain skin.

I woke on Sunday to a gorgeous warm and beautifully sunny day with the bells ringing out loudly. On days like these, the woods called me, wanting to share its glory and its enchantment but today Dave commanded we went out for a walk. I was desperately trying to avoid any physical contact with him as I was finding it increasingly difficult not to allow him any intimate moments with me, constantly struggling to hide my true feelings as there weren't any for him, all the feelings I had were only meant for Charlie and they always would be, even when Dave held my hand it left me cold, again today this would have been a perfect time to call it off, but once again I failed to say the words that desperately needed to be said.

It was nice to be with Dave, but only nice. I needed more than nice, much much more as I craved the real Lizzy to be unleashed, to be set free from the horrific life that was now going to be mine, to release her from behind the sad and ghostly like reflection that remained looking back from the mirror.

Late summer had suddenly turned rapidly to autumn in the blink of an eye and tonight my bedroom window reflected the stunning woodland in the distance, with its vivid colours that seemed to light up the sky as the sun had just started to fade, bringing the burnt ambers, autumn golds and rich russet reds to stand out, radiating a stunning glow over the garden. Suddenly I noticed the family of deer, frolicking together at the edge of the woods where it met the fields, such a glorious gathering that enhanced the already perfect picture. I was suddenly treated to the aroma of Charlie, which was an unexpected treat tonight, refreshing, and a delight knowing again tonight my sleep would be tormented once again by haunting voices and vile images.

Monday morning was here all too soon and I was back to work and some sort of normality, an invitation sat on my desk waiting for my attention. The Christmas party had been booked for a week before Christmas and I was looking forward to letting my hair down and dancing until late where I knew I could freely be me away from the watchful eyes of Dave and his escalating jealousy.

Now with only a few days to go before the party we were all in good spirits with lots of Christmas cheer and good will. Without warning, Roger from the other office brought me a huge delivery of stationary, complete with mistletoe that was delicately laid on top of the mass of boxes that had my name on them, then suddenly out of nowhere he kissed me, much to my surprise, something that was totally unexpected but very enjoyable, making my smile radiate through the office and out into the corridor beyond, making me blush knowing it was wrong not just for me, but for Roger, knowing he was also married, but the days leading up to the party Roger and I continued to flirt, allowing me to feel like I still had it as it gave me something that was missing in my life, missing from the dull life I had to endure with Dave. Roger was a few years older than me, tall, married, slim with dark hair, his outstanding looks accompanied by the stunning glasses that adorned his face making him stand out from the crowd, something that had never set my senses alight until now, he was always smiling and flirting, it seemed as if he had singled me out to be the one who deserved his attention. Maybe I did, maybe unknowingly I was encouraging him, desperately needing something or someone to brighten up my drab and dreary life in some way.

The day of the party had arrived but my joyful eagerness had been slightly marred by Dave's constant reminders that I was almost a married woman, but it was a time to let my hair down away from Dave's prying eyes, his snipping and jealous behaviour. I danced around the floor with my friends enjoying the Christmas atmosphere that now had captured the party, even Roger was up dancing and was heading in my direction doing some sort of out of control hip jerking movement that he thought was dancing. I could not help giggling at his attempts to dance as he called loudly across the dance floor. *Lizzy, Lizzy, hey Lizzy do you want to dance with me?* He swept me into his arms, wrapping them tightly around my delicate waist, sweeping me into the middle of the dance floor and I was loving the attention, Rogers attention.

We danced slowly together it was very sensual and very pleasing to all my senses, something that I did not want to end. I wanted more, much more as we continued to flirt, allowing our eyes to dance together unaware at the time of the consequences that our actions might cause. I felt his body move even closure to mine, if that was at all possible as I allowed his hands to explore my curvy body willingly, feeling his hands gliding over my spine before meeting my waist, feeling his hands exploring my thighs, inching up my silky skirt on a mission to indulge his yearning, hearing him moaning delightfully into my neck as he did. This was different somehow, being delighted sensually by a married man, but nothing like Charlie's vile father. Roger was passionate, sensual, his aroma powerfully intoxicating, everything that Charlie's father wasn't.

The naughty girl was back, allowing the real Lizzy to spring back to life, to be unleashed for now anyway for this moment just to be me and I was going to revel in it, away from Dave's prying eyes, his snipping and pathetic jealousy.

With the party finished and the dancing now over for another year, I felt deflated not wanting to return to my everyday dreary, uninspiring normal life. It was very late, squeezing my hand Roger offered me a lift home and without any hesitation I jumped at the chance to be in his company a while longer, to indulge my muted emotions and sexual fantasies, both of us obviously not wanting to let this night slip away.

As we approached my house Roger took a detour, driving up the little secluded lane close to the woods and stopped the car, dimming the lights. He thought this would be a good place to continue the party, I didn't know exactly what he meant, or did I? Deep down yes of course I did as we kissed repeatedly I knew exactly what he meant as his tongue glided further into my throat making sure I was receiving all the signals that he wanted to take our flirtatious encounter further and tonight I was not going to stop him.

He was giving me back something that was so obviously missing from my life, something that I desperately craved every day and had done so since I had walked away from Charlie on that unexpected, beautiful autumn afternoon when we shared our love for the last time.

Excitement, that was it, I needed and craved excitement, the excitement which I did not get from Dave and never would as he seemed unable to show the slightest sign of what I would call love and the excitement that it created, maybe it was because roger was married, older or was it just because I could rebel against my impending marriage that I found very exciting. It felt like I was hitting back from the drudgery of my life with Dave, hitting back from my relentless dreams and nightmares or from my never ending love for Charlie.

My lips were now reacting with intense pleasure from Rogers masculine kisses that were tantalising and passionate. As we kissed I felt his ice cold hand gently glide over my inner thigh feeling his fingers flirting with the soft lace of my stocking top before reaching the silky edge of my knickers while I was still emerged in his kisses that were intense and now slightly rough. He began to moan my name, whispering lingering comments while we continued to explore each other's bodies in a frenzy of lust, both of us knew it was wrong, he was married after all and I was engaged to Dave, but totally in love with Charlie. Suddenly I pulled away, breathless I asked him to stop immediately as I wriggled around panicked by my actions, again allowing yet another man to invade my body but not meaning it for a split second as I returned to kissing him repeatedly. He returned them all with a real intense passion that now stung and burnt my delicate lips.

He then moved his hand inside my blouse, allowing his fingers to do all the work as he gently undid every petit button on my delicate lacy blouse, casting a glance at my reaction on revealing my huge bulging tits, I was out of control. As my life continued spiralling, flashing before my eyes I was caught up in a frenzy of desire that was only meant for Charlie, once again I freely gave in to allow someone else to enjoy my body as in return I enjoyed the freedom to be me unleashing Lizzy again.

I want you Lizzy, Roger moaned, repeating his desire over and over again to fuck me, to fuck me hard tonight. I blushed uncontrollably at his comment as he made me feel alive, just like Charlie had done on every occasion, but I knew this freedom was only going to be short lived.

His fingers then slipped again past the lace edge of my knickers, fingers that were now enjoying my extremely wet kitten, feeling myself tense up, closing my eyes softly to enjoy fully the pleasure I was now receiving that in return encouraged me to rub his cock gently. We were transfixed on each other, feeling the lust between us. I could feel his fingers dancing ever deeper with my kitten, I was about to explode with the pleasure he was giving me as I continued to seduce his cock. He was very tense, uptight like a coiled spring as his juice then erupted spilling over my fingers and on to my clothes, suddenly we must have come back to reality, both of us uneasy at what had just happened, jolted back to the here and now. As I wriggled around to straighten my clothes the realisation that now, once again I had let someone violate my body. He looked at me, *Lizzy I'm so very sorry.* I snapped, *it's fine, it's fine Roger, don't worry.* I pulled again at my skirt, trying to straighten my blouse, fumbling to do up the petit buttons that I had allowed to be freely ripped open as now I was not able to even look at him, again I was so eaten up with terrifying guilt as every vivid, guilty memory came crashing down around me like the vicious storm that was building, casting its disapproval over me that would rage in my head once again, never wanting me to forget my stupidity that was all made possible, firstly by Paul who felt it was OK to terrorise me in the dark, damp and dingy cellar, wanting me to become his trophy, Charlie and his ability to keep me his lifetime prisoner and his hostage, Charlie's vile father who abused my delicate frame with intentional disregard for his own family, wanting me to never forget my out of control actions, Dave's shameful selfishness, jealousy and bitterness, wanting to control my every move and now Rogers name had been added to that list, wanting nothing more than a little bit of fun from the new girl in the office, like it was the normal thing to do and tonight and not for the first time I was blaming Charlie, reminding me that my dirty love was exclusively for one person and one person only and not for me to let my vulnerability become available to anyone other than Charlie but maybe they were all holding me prisoner in their own way, holding me to a lifetime of ransom.

I then asked Roger calmly to drive me home, we said nothing more, not a word as he drove me straight to my door in complete silence. I was relieved to be home, knowing I needed desperately to be on my own, to find the sanctuary that would allow me to try and make some sort of sense of my desperate behaviour.

I scrambled to find the car door handle to let myself out, Roger held my hand again repeatedly apologising. I froze, once again burdened by guilt and again I was so ashamed by my stupid repulsive actions. Reeling heavily from my stupidity made me realise just how vulnerable I had become, now I knew just what my terrifyingly and utterly saddened past had done to me, taking me from the fun-loving Lizzy to the now very vulnerable woman that only needed one man's love and affection but who had sadly chosen to lead a life that would never include me, giving his love freely to another.

Rebuffing Rogers words, I pushed his hand away as I stumbled out of the car, still showing my vulnerability as my fleshy, naked thighs that were still on show, that had not been covered up by my skirt with my stockings ruffled by Rogers playful hands, slamming the door hard behind me with sheer force, appalled at my behaviour. I took in a sharp intake of the bitterly cold air that hit my porcelain painted face, now completely soaked with icy tears, the air so cold it took my breath away, leaving me gasping as I choked back vile, unwanted tears of total shame. I then heard Roger drive away, roaring and screeching his way through the lanes, leaving me rigid, grounded to this very spot. As the flurries of snow were falling freely around me I remained stunned, statue like, waiting for the pain to disappear that was now rippling through my body, suddenly and from nowhere came the terrifying echoing in my head, words that sent me into free fall, startled on hearing the roar of words again tonight, another night which left me cold alone from love and terrified. Was I really the storm that had created this chaos in my life?

Shit Lizzy, get a grip! I told myself stunned by what I had yet again allowed freely to happen as all I wanted was Charlie, that's all I ever wanted, now in utter disbelief at my stupidity and once again I feeling that I had disrespected not only myself, but Dave and of course Charlie.

I rushed through the front door, slamming it so hard behind me, obviously waking my parents as I heard my mother calling from her bedroom to the empty, cold hallway wanting to know if I had enjoyed my evening. I mumbled some garbled response back, reassuring her I had enjoyed my evening and that I was tired.

I ran straight upstairs, stumbling in my wake to change out of my disgusting dirty clothes, feeling the need to scrub away my guilt but it would only be short lived as soap and water would never wash away the torment that would return again tonight to haunt my dreams in which the storm would terrify me, leaving me again like most nights, in a pool of cold bodily fluid, poisoned and laced with aromas, vile aromas that would stick in my nostrils, reminding me I was not alone and never would be.

As disgusted as I was with myself it meant nothing to me and I'm sure it meant nothing to Roger either, just a little bit of Christmas fun, if you could call it fun? I had to forget what happened tonight, but I felt used, dirty, grubby, and so guilty, feelings that I had felt all those years ago when I was violated by Charlie's vile father. With my mind once again in Wales with the only man I ever loved and could ever love, a smile was brought back to my face, I recalled his trademark smile along with his cocky attitude. Work had now finished for me due to the festive break and I was somewhat relieved that it had as I would not have to see Roger and have to answer relentless questions about him from my colleagues knowing that Roger and I would be the centre of the other girls conversation, knowing our actions on the dance floor would be brought into question with whispering and second-hand comments.

I now had time on my hands to do as I pleased as the snow continued to fall I lounged around the house, my mind constantly thinking about Charlie and when I wanted to really be alone with my thoughts I would head to the tree house to sit and reflect on all the precious unforgettable times I had shared with him and there were many to recall as they continued to invade my memory, one by one each of them no less important than the other as they lined up sparking powerful emotions that just kept my senses alive with the permanent aromas that Charlie had left for me to enjoy.

Now relieved that Dave and I were not seeing each other until Christmas Eve I had time alone to be me and be alone to enjoy my thoughts with no distractions, to revel and enjoy recalling my dirty secret love with Charlie as I tried hard to blot out everything else that was now so unimportant, like Paul, Charlie's vile father, my loveless life with Dave, my bit of Christmas fun with Roger and all the other stupid things I had let happen.

With only three days remaining before Christmas, the Christmas tree had now been delivered and awaiting my attention ready for me to decorate, I was thrilled that this year, like every year, it was my duty to make it look spectacular, to allow myself to wallow in precious winter and Christmas memories.

It was a bitterly cold day as the wind blew in from the east across the garden with such an icy blast, snow had been forecast again today, suddenly I heard a car door slam loudly. I was hoping it might be dad, but I didn't see anyone, although I heard footsteps coming up the ice coated path. I looked a mess in my tatty jeans, a big baggy jumper and boots. My hair was a mess too as I fought with the huge but beautiful tree, trying to get it into the bucket that was so obviously way too small for the gigantic spruce that dad had ordered.

Suddenly I heard someone cough, making me jump back from struggling to control the huge spruce tree. I have a delivery, it's for someone called princess, sign here he said with an abrupt tone as a pen was then forced into my hand allowing me to scribble my name, my signature illegible as my hands were now frozen from the bitter winds that engulfed the garden. Without hesitation I abandoned the beautiful Christmas tree, running into the house and up to my room, staring at the parcel that had my name on it.

There was a card attached to the box which read *Happy Christmas Lizzy, I am never far away,* followed by millions of kisses that peppered the card, an instant warm smile swept across my frozen porcelain face. I unwrapped it slowly, never wanting the wrapping to end. Inside was a little wooden box wrapped in beautiful pastel pink tissue paper and scratched in the lid was a heart and etched inside the heart was written, *my girl.*

Opening the box revealed a small delicate crown of daisy's, not real of course, but with meaning, a delightful meaning to us, adorning the box, laid on pink tissue paper. I read again the words written on the card, my tears were now flowing, smudging all the beautiful words he had once again written, reminding me that he was not the cocky bad-boy that everyone reliably told me he was.

A little note was folded so small, sat at the bottom of the box it read… *Until we make daisy chains again princess.* Daisy chains, I could not contain my smile, a smile that was now actually hurting as my ice cold rosy red cheeks glowed, but it was a smile that instantly took me back to our special day that was laced with every emotion possible, taking me once again on a roller coaster ride as I recalled them all on that perfect day of dirty love in the woods, a day that was now tainted with devastating sadness. I was now in floods of tears, my head and heart in Wales once again as I was lost in the moment, not realising mum and dad were already home. I dried my eyes for now before sweeping down the old stair case with a spring in my step, knowing today Charlie was thinking about me. Sad had lit the fire in the lounge and had put the magnificent tree into a very large bucket for me so that I could spend all the evening decorating it. It looked amazing and so very pretty as the lights twinkled in the darkness of the lounge that was now only lit by candles. The open fire casting a mellow tone, while the tiny, coloured tree lights twinkled in the muted evening light and once again the delicate faced angel was now gracing our tree again this Christmas.

As forecast, the snow had started to fall, the icy cold winds were now howling in from the east, rattling every window in the house and coating them in ice cold crystals that sparkled in the evening light, knowing that I would once again be treated to my very own winter wonderland that was all made possible by this enchanted landscape, allowing me to travel in my mind to all the places that I loved.

The evening wore on, mum and dad had gone to bed. I was still writing last minute Christmas cards in front of the roaring log fire with the television on for company, admiring the Christmas tree that I had so lovingly decorated. I glanced up at the angel that still remained so perfect, her expression captivating, wishing she had the answers to my unhappiness but she didn't need to tell me, I already knew.

Suddenly an ice cold shiver ran down my spine, it felt like someone was watching me or was it the my imagination? As I had become lost yet again in my memories, I suddenly heard a gentle tap at the window but I chose to ignore it, thinking it was the promised winter storm blowing in against the old metal framed windows that shock and rattled during the winter storms but then I heard it again and this time I went to the window to see for myself, pulling back the heavy curtains a little further. I peered into the darkness of the night; the snow was still falling heavily. It looked so very icily cold and frosty, but as I looked to see beyond the darkness to the magnificent beauty that the snow would bring to the open landscape a dark silhouette suddenly appeared from the darkness making me jump repeatedly. As I jumped back from the window, it was clear to see the face that made me smile on this very cold and dark late December night, it was Charlie, his face now pressing firmly against the ice cold window, his breath having melted the icy patches that had frozen to the glass.

CHAPTER 10

My heart was now pounding, beating so fast as I rushed to the front door throwing my arms around him, wrapping him up like a blanket. He was so cold, his face frozen by the bitter winds that were now coating everything in frosty shards, he must have been outside for ages waiting for mum and dad to go to bed.

He whispered softly, *Happy Christmas Lizzy*, while brushing firmly his cold hand across my thigh which in turn made me quiver. I quickly took him into the living room, closing the heavy front door quietly behind him, hoping it would close without its normal creaking and squeaking that would undoubtedly wake mum and dad, knowing mum was a light sleeper while dad enjoyed the beauty of sleep, snoring through the night.

We sat together by the open fire allowing him to warm up, holding hands, sharing intimate kisses that were tonight very much needed. I made him some very hot coffee and found some of the Christmas biscuits that were contained in the red and green tartan patterned tin, the tin with a thistle embossed on the top, a tin that mum had hidden away so that dad did not eat them all.

As I held Charlie's hand I noticed he was wearing a small ring on his little finger which totally surprised me as he wasn't the type to wear fancy jewellery although he did have his left ear pierced with a single black stud but this was different, it was beautiful with an intricate pattern and as I held his frozen hand I ran my fingers gently over it with intrigue. I felt the raised pattern that graced the wide band of a dark, almost red gold, wondering who had given him such a delicate ring, wishing all the time that it had been me.

We talked until the early hours, desperately holding on to each other's every word, not wanting to miss a thing, but why was he here tonight? What brought him back to this Wiltshire village on the coldest night of the year? Now his kisses, his smile, his aroma, and his cocky attitude all lined up to seduce me. I was loving it, yearning for more as yet again I just wanted the freedom to rebel against the life that had been given to me, that I had allowed and now had to accept with the deepest of sadness.

Our clothes now abandoned in a frenzy over the living room carpet, we laid together, naked, skin-on-skin on the sofa, wrapped in dirty love, a love that neither of us could never have imagined existed. I felt so content for the first time in a long time, it was beautiful, now muted emotions left my body, unleashing new ones as we lay together in silence, not needing to say anything as love once again had engulfed us both.

We must have drifted off to sleep, to sleep freely without intrusion, waking with a startle at 2am. The fire was going down and with Charlie blissfully asleep I pulled another soft blanket over us, wanting this moment to last a little longer and as I did, Charlie stirred, taking me again into his arms, straddling over me, peppering my body in soft very welcome kisses, his cock huge and firm, filled with dirty love wanting to love me so very much.

Charlie's cock loved my kitten. I moaned delightfully as he thrust so hard, wanting to love me tonight and like always for the ultimate dirty love. Charlie then buried his head firmly between my thighs freeing my kitten from the fresh, warm juice that was now smeared across his lips. His intention was clear as he cradled and seduced my firm tits before returning to love my kitten again. His kisses intensified, his thrusting hard, wanting me to know the full extent of his loving, but I was never in any doubt.

Now cradled again in each other's arms we must have fallen asleep, unaware of the time. Awoken again to watch him sleeping, saddened that he could not stay any longer, I nudged him gently, saddened that our time together was cut short all too soon. We both wanted and needed so much more time together, but my parents would object if they knew I had invited him into our home knowing full well their disapproval, hearing my mother's ongoing disappointment, seeing my dad raise his eyebrows in disbelief. Beautifully delicate kisses were replaced by very passionate kisses, Charlie then whispered, I will always love you Lizzy, you do know that don't you? I nodded eagerly as my eyes continued to follow his every word, eyes that were so scared that I would miss a split second of the mystery that still hid deep behind his cocky smile and gorgeous deep brown eyes. Lizzy, meet me later at the little shed about midday. He squeezed my hand tightly... Stay with me the night princess, say you'll come. I smiled a beaming smile that made everything right for now until the heartache returned once more, he knew I would be there without any doubt, both of us desperate to continue this dirty love affair a while longer, to indulge in our passion once again.

As I let him out the icy blast shuddered though the dark unlit hallway, sweeping up the stairs onto the landing beyond. He smiled that unforgettable smile, a smile that made me blush uncontrollably, kissing me before he walked away down the icy path once again without a care in the world, sliding his way on the ice covered path where he glided unsteadily into the huge beech hedge before composing himself.

My sides now splitting with laughter and giggles, trying hard to contain my outburst of the giggles, not wanting my parents to hear the laughter that Charlie had brought on this cold winter's night.

It was so cold outside but at least the snow had stopped falling for now. As the dawn was about to break I closed the door quietly, my beaming smile so warm it radiated through the freezing cold hallway, glancing in the hall mirror my smile was stuck, frozen by this amazing late night, very welcome visitor.

I slipped very quietly back to my bedroom for a few hours' sleep, hoping that the demons would lay dormant tonight, allowing me a perfect sleep. Suddenly, I was once again awoken by the church bells clanging on the hour, I drew back the curtains from my window to unveil the full extent of the snow storm that swept through the village last night which brought with it my unexpected but welcome midnight visitor. Over breakfast I made my excuses that seemed plausible to my parents, watching for any signs of disapproval from either of them, feeling my cheeks burning by lying to them before heading to the little shed once again, but on this occasion I was planning on a little Christmas surprise of my own, I dressed in the sexiest of underwear and my little cracker daisy ring, wrapping myself in my long fur-lined maxi-coat that now hid my Christmas surprise.

I opened the door to the little love shed, how lovely it looked. Charlie had even managed to get a tiny artificial Christmas tree, some old decorations that he had taken from his gran's house. He had made it look so beautiful and all for me. *Lizzy, I hope you like it.* Now with tears in my eyes I smiled, whispering... *It's perfect Charlie.* I fell into his arms, pulling back I undid my coat, letting it fall to the floor seductively from my shoulders, then I wished him a very Happy Christmas. *Lizzy, Lizzy, Lizzy you are the perfect present, my perfect present.* He smiled that tantalising smile that made me blush yet again. Charlie's eyes were now transfixed on my tits as they spilled out over the top of my bra, suddenly he kissed them both through the delicate lacy material that made him smile that cocky smile and made me blush uncontrollably, I stood before him adorned in just underwear and six inch heels.

He then helped me put my coat back on as I was now shivering with the extreme cold from this little old tumble down shed which now felt more like an ice bucket, the roof covered in thick snow, but our little bed now had a big padded sleeping bag on it made for two, complete with a fluffy white blanket that instantly reminded me of the snow that was fresh, crisp and newly fallen. I felt like crying, I was so overcome with emotion, my eyes blurred by the beautiful moments that we were about to share, allowing me more winter moments ready to be captured here in this little tin shed, wanting now to press the pause button, needing to cherish this very moment.

Life was good with Charlie around as I could be myself, at ease in my own skin, to talk freely without judgement. He knew me better than anyone did, better than I knew myself sometimes as Charlie's love was now shielding me from my vulnerability, a vulnerability that I would never be able to escape from, firstly Paul, then Charlie's vile, disgusting father who was to blame solely in his actions wanting me to never forget as my body wore the brutal scars left from his vile, disgusting attack, along now with Roger, wanting nothing from me, only my body and Dave in wanting to bring yet more misery upon me, taking away the little bit of life that I still had but they all had one thing in common, they all wanted me as some sort of trophy. Charlie also saw me as a trophy, but this was different, it was and always would be accompanied by love and that was the difference.

We sat and held hands like always, but as we talked I noticed his finger was now free from the ring that he had worn last night. My fingers moved over the indentation that had been made by the ring, wondering why he had today removed it, but still he said nothing as my gaze stayed firmly on his finger. Kissing my hand, Charlie brought me back to the here and now.

Charlie then opened a bottle of champagne to celebrate this unexpected Christmas surprise, letting the cork pop, hitting the tin roof with force as the bubbles cascaded over us both. Now with a champagne glass in my hand we toasted a perfect night together, the darkness was now here, and the snow was falling once again, the perfect way to spend the night before Christmas Eve. Charlie demanded nothing more than love from my body, a refreshing change from all the other men that had invaded my body, only to take what they selfishly wanted, disregarding my feelings totally.

The shed was now slightly warmer, the radio played our most favourite songs, everything was perfect for now, this moment in time, with no one to spoil its beauty as we snuggled up together, content for now until I would have to leave, to return once more to the harsh reality that was about to become my life with Dave.

As we watched the snow fall through the grubby window, muted flakes that melted on to the glass were quickly replaced by another that slid down the warm window into a freezing puddle, ready to be frozen tonight as the temperature fell.

The snow was falling hard now, it was so beautiful, the huge dark sky that was now so full of tomorrow, a day I dreaded for so many reasons as tomorrow was now laced with blood-stained tears, terrifying dreams, and endless nightmares, knowing once again I would have to look at my reflection in the mirror knowing that tomorrow would only reflect my fading and discarded shadows of yesterday.

Leaving my worries for tomorrow behind me for now, Charlie and I fell asleep, snuggled up in the big sleeping bag skin-on-skin, just what we had grown to love over the years and tonight I was free from the crazy world of my night-time terrors with no raging white horses appearing from the crashing, foaming waves, no vile visions of the men who continually ruled my life by day and who wanted to haunt and terrorise me throughout the darkness of the night, knowing it was Charlie that kept them all at bay.

Tomorrow was now here, already, and far too soon as I had not prepared myself for yet another devastating goodbye after this unexpected Christmas treat as Charlie kissed away the tears that left my heart once again broken and now beyond repair.

Straddling my legs Charlie held both my hands while taking in the full beauty of my naked, but now fragile body, smiling his cocky smile. I will be back for you, I promise you Lizzy, we have unfinished business. I smiled at him knowing exactly what he meant.

As the sun had now begun to rise over a snow covered landscape Charlie wiped a clear patch in the grubby little window to allow us both to admire the beauty that was waiting for us on this freezing cold late December morning, a time of the day that allowed once again our passion to spill over into glorious dirty love, my nipples standing full and ripe, ready for Charlie's attention, his mouth never failing to delight as he sucked them hard, making me squeal, allowing his tongue to then travel down over my curves, revolving around my belly button. His lips then peppering me in very warm sensual kisses, leaving my body quivering, wanting more.

We said our goodbyes, tears from me flowed like always, leaving my face wet with sadness and in overpowering pain that crippled my smiles today, tears that left blood stains on my terrified, porcelain skin that now reflected my mood.

So now with our loving kisses, the goodbye over, I left as I always did, being the first one to leave. I hated leaving him, I hated walking away. *I Love you Lizzy*, I heard him call loudly from the little tin doorway as he watched me walk away through the snow covered path holding on to his words for as long as I could, before looking back to indulge my senses, blowing him a thousand kisses, my breath frozen from the icy breeze that surrounded the landscape, my lips now numb with cold as I called back to him. *I love you too Charlie Stevens*, this made him smile, the smile that was so totally intoxicating.

Now back to my dark, non-dispirited life, I laid sobbing into my pillow, thumping it violently out of spite, over and over again. Beating it with my fist for some sort of comfort, my tears being soaked up by the cotton filled pillow, the pillowcase bearing the stains of my overburdened tears. Suddenly my feelings once again awoke as I fumbled in my bag, finding a little box, another box from him, the second in as many days, once again a message scratched in the lid which read, *Happy Christmas Princess.*

As I opened it I was treated to a beautiful crystal snow flake for the Christmas tree. I loved it so much, now every year it would grace our tree, bringing it to life and for me to be reminded of his love, his eternal love, and a night that we spent together shivering in the ice cold shed just before Christmas.

I stood silently at my bedroom window needing to shed my tears that were already blurring my vision as I sobbed bitter tears that just kept on flowing like a river over my entire body, over my horrific open wounds that were only visible to me as my tears splattered against my skin like frozen raindrops stinging the open wounds of our love.

I could suddenly hear my mother calling me with her stern voice from the cold hallway which encouraged her voice to echo coldly throughout the house until I replied. *Lizzy, Lizzy,* her hand now clenched and holding something, *is this yours?* She held out her hand, looking over her glasses as she seemed to do on a regular basis now while questioning me.

It was Charlie's ring; he must have left it here or it had fallen from his finger. Mum asked again if it was mine as she had never seen me wearing it before. Now having to lie to her again, twice in two days in a desperate bid to cover up the love I still carried for Charlie, I took a deep intake of breath telling her it was mine and that I had bought it, but it was too big for my tiny fingers and that I had been looking for it. *Lizzy I found it behind a cushion on the sofa.* Gulping back my guilt I thanked her, blushing at my ability to lie to her so easily, she smiled softly advising me to wear it on a chain around my neck for safe keeping so I took her advice and found a chain that complimented the mysterious ring perfectly. I would now wear something so precious adorning my neck.

Christmas came and went, leaving me delighted to have been given the most beautiful, unexpected Christmas present which allowed me to spend time with Charlie, receiving some much needed dirty love, along with the two wonderful gifts that he had given me, to treasure once again along with the mysterious ring that had adorned his finger, knowing it had been worn for some time as the indentation was deep, almost cutting into his finger.

The new year was here and it was the year in which I was getting married to a man that I didn't love and would never love, knowing the brutal storms of my stupid hesitation to call the farce of a wedding off were never far away, however, I had started to enjoy my time with Dave, but just as friends and who still remained totally unaware of my dirty love affair with Charlie, my continuing lifetime love affair, my dirty past and my sordid sex life that I still seemed not to have any control over as I seemed to search in vain for excitement.

So now with my Christmas memories stored away, it was sadly time to go back to work which meant I would have to face Roger but I had told myself it meant nothing, it was just a one-night stand and nothing more. It had not crossed my mind until now, although his vision had disrupted my sleep on several occasions it still remained unimportant and meaningless to me, and it always would.

We never mentioned it, we never spoke, it was nothing and so very unimportant, we didn't even exchange eye contact and that was fine by me as all I wanted to do was forget it ever happened, he would now share his advances with the younger, more prettier, immature girls who worked within the many offices in this department, girls that I felt sure would embrace his flirtatious and amorous advances.

Spring was now just around the corner and the beautiful warm sunshine was not far away, but still winter had its icy grip on everyone, with snow flurries never far away but that meant that my bedroom window was able to capture its stunning beauty a little longer, knowing full well that I had added more winter wonderland memories once again made possible by Charlie.

I took regular walks into the woods for some much needed time away from what was now becoming a much bigger nightmare than I had anticipated. The days and weeks had started to dissolve into a mass of wedding talk as Dave never talked about anything else, making yet more demands on my fragile, vulnerable body that would always leave me feeling cold and empty from any emotion.

Walking alone in the woods, the winter still very much keeping a hold on the landscape but it allowed me to escape, delighting my days as I took in all its beauty once again as snowdrops had begun to spring up through the carpet of snow, with glimpses of buds gathering on the trees and in the distance I could now hear the faint mellow chant of bird song in a bid to attract others.

The wedding plans were in Dave's words, taking shape, but I gave it as little thought as possible. I was board of hearing Dave's plans, my heart and soul were elsewhere, my dress and shoes had been bought without any thought, as were the rings, no flowers or invitations yet, Dave had left that chore to me but again it didn't matter as my dress was white, dull in design and very virginal so anything would go with it but I didn't really care as my heart was lost to Charlie so any wedding plans that did not involve him were unimportant and totally lost on Dave.

I had made plans to meet a close friend for lunch today, to have a much needed catch up as I had not seen her for a while, having to tell her all about my forthcoming wedding in June. My voice must have reflected my unhappiness as she asked instantly if I was happy. I nodded, before lowering my head, keeping my eyes fixed firmly on the floor which had showed my true feelings as my eyes were so full of bitter, terrifying tears that needed to be shed, but not here and not today. I would need to keep them for myself throughout my life. Suddenly, I felt her hand touch mine, *Lizzy you seem so unhappy.* I nodded my reply. *You don't love him Lizzy*, I nodded again. She sighed, the conversation was cold, there was nothing else I could say as she held my hand again, looking at me. *Lizzy, please call it off and do it soon... don't live with regrets.* I just looked at her with desperation in my eyes. We then said our goodbyes, tearful goodbyes.

I had a huge burden on my shoulders that now weighed so heavy on my mind like the house that Dave had just gone ahead and bought for us, without consulting me, which was about ten miles away from the village that I was born and bred, a small house with two poky little bedrooms. A normal everyday boring house on a normal street with no outlook and no garden.

A very different house from the lovely house that I grew up in, a home that held treasured memories from my delightful childhood right up to now, retained memories behind every door, memories that jumped all over me, sprinkling me in a cocktail of emotion.

Emotions that I would now no longer be able to recall daily as I was being forced apart from those glorious memories. My mind was now a constant sea of swaying, devastating torment that was going to be my life from now on, along with the unwelcome sea of foaming grey fog, bringing with it the stampede of pure white horses away in the distance and heading my way once again to batter my body with hooves of steel.

Suddenly I was brought back from my memories to the stark reality of the here and now, the cold realisation of what I had committed myself to as I dragged out the preparations of my forthcoming marriage for as long as I possibly could, in a bid that someone, or something, would stop the farcical ceremony from taking place.

As I walked past the florist I gazed into the window at the many floral arrangements that graced the unfolding picture, laced with glorious colours that shone from every arrangement, some very elaborate, some so simple, but all elegantly beautiful, pristine in colour and style. Suddenly I saw my reflection in the florist window, my expression clear to see, not even a smile graced my porcelain face on seeing the beautiful blooms that adorned the beautiful window.

As I opened the door, the perfume was so beautiful, it wafted throughout the shop to greet me, peppering my skin in sweet-scented kisses, sending my senses wild with so many aromas that I had never experienced before. I just stood silent and still allowing the aroma to dissolve all over me, to shroud me in a veil of perfume like no other. Then, a tall, elegant lady asked kindly if I needed help. If she only knew, feeling I was now beyond any help. She continued asking questions, most of which I had no answers for. She then kindly showed me pictures from a catalogue, they were all so very pretty. I flicked through the glossy pages with no idea other than being ordered by Dave to choose the flowers of my dreams, his words. Then out of the blue an ice cold shiver ran through me, the same ice cold shiver I had experienced many times before, but why today? I then heard a familiar voice in my head saying daisies. I must have looked stunned as my eyes filled with tears. Composing myself, I smiled, repeating my request. It has to be a posy of white delicate perfectly sweet smelling daisy's, complete with a delicate daisy ring for my hair, that was it, beautiful white daisies. My voice raised with excitement as now Charlie's cocky vision and voice had made me smile, I loved the thought of that which again sparked my memories of Charlie that came rushing back, taking my fragile body on a journey of delight. I walked away from the florist elated at my choice as it was so very perfect knowing now that ice cold shiver was Charlie standing silently at my side.

It was funny that out of this farce of a marriage it was my memories of Charlie that triggered a smile, sending ice cold shivers through my body that led me to choosing the flowers that I would now carry on the day of my life sentence, like a tribute to Charlie, a trophy of our love along with the beautiful gifts he had given me, carrying all my love for Charlie to the alter, smelling the perfect aroma from the delightful daisies as I took my life changing vows, knowing full well I was to going to live with a lifetime of regret for not walking away from Dave and the life he would now expect me to live.

I then headed to the stationers knowing Dave had given me detailed orders to follow and as I stepped inside it was silent, quiet, and peaceful, just soft whispers and echoes filled the cosy little stationers as everyone tiptoed around trying to be as quiet as mice, making me almost hold my breath so I would not make a sound that may trigger silent echoes, that would be sure to lead to the odd glance and sideways look from the many customers who seemed bemused by my somewhat casual appearance.

I looked at all the designs but nothing was inspiring me. *I need some inspiration. Why not design your own?* The lady said in a very quiet, discrete voice. *Lots of people do.* Of course, a simple daisy design, a special piece of my past to take into my future, never forgetting my only love on my wedding day, once again not wanting to ever release the chains that had always squeezed my heart so tight and that now had ripped my skin apart leaving even bigger open wounds, so every time I thought of Charlie the chains cut a little deeper, leaving me with permanent reminders of a perfect dirty love, wounds I was happy to have, happy to carry with me every day of my life.

Now I was taking all my love for Charlie into my marriage, a marriage that was not the future that I had craved or envisaged, not the future I had dreamed of as I sat in my tree house planning my dreams as a little girl, a future now that did not involve Charlie.

It was now just two weeks before the wedding, needing desperately to call it off but I was being swept along on this wave, the wedding wave that was gathering pace, a massive wave that just got bigger and bigger. I was not strong enough to swim against it, so I had to swim with it, it was out of control now and I could not turn back as the wave had become so powerful it was drowning me in a dark sea of never-ending sadness that was absolutely terrifying.

CHAPTER 11

The invitations had now been posted; the wedding cake iced. My short life now boxed up and labelled with sadness, bitterness, hate and every other awful emotion that now filled my body. Once again I felt completely vulnerable and heartbreakingly fragile as my nightmares still raged on, with haunting images of Paul wanting to take my body for his own selfish pleasures, Charlie's vile father that remained relentless, Roger's willingness to lead me astray so easily, whispering echoes of a crying baby far away in the distance and Dave's constant and overbearing commands, leaving my body to drown in a pool of vile sweat as night fell.

Dave was going out on a weekend of drunken revelling with his so-called friends. I really hated him drinking so much as I felt it was a downward spiral which I found so very unattractive and at this moment in time not knowing the full impact of what his drinking would have on our lives in the months and years to come.

My night had been planned, I was going dancing with a small intimate group of close friends where I would be free to be me, knowing it would be the last time I would be able to let my hair down if Dave had his way, and he would, forbidding and suppressing my zest and love for life, his rules were now in place. However, tonight it was all about me, Lizzy, or to use my full name, Elizabeth Jane Peters.

I was eager to get ready and as I looked into the mirror brushing my long flowing silky dark hair I did not see the swan-like Lizzy reflecting back, I saw someone who was so unhappy, leading me to question myself at that moment, was I truly this unhappy? The answer was of course I was, my body already heavily scarred and wounded by Paul, by my miscarriage, by Charlie's vile father, by Roger, by Dave and my continuing love for Charlie that was slowly being destroyed, by marrying someone else, the reflection I saw tonight had already become tomorrow's shadow as Lizzy was slipping silently away. Panicked by my reflection I screamed out for the real Lizzy to return but my pleas tonight just echoed around my bedroom, crashing into the walls, smashing my name silently and violently, splattering my blood stained grief over everything in its path as I plunged even deeper into a miserable, dark, and very lonely existence that was to be my marriage.

Desperate for reassurance I stood in complete silence looking out of my bedroom window, dressed in my underwear staring at nothing, only the darkness and the stillness of the night. My mind was wandering, wanting to capture any happy moments that wanted to invade it, but tonight my mind remained empty, numb from any precious emotions, aromas and voices as I grasped desperately for the ring on my necklace, hoping I could find something to encourage a smile.

Stepping away from the window I eagerly continued to brush my hair and to paint my porcelain face in a thick coat of makeup in a desperate attempt to mask my unhappiness once again from those around me. I lovingly removed my necklace which held Charlie's ring and as I did I saw a little more of the real Lizzy slipping away, I was now approaching the tender age of 21 and needing desperately to live life to the full, not to be bogged down in a loveless, drab, unexciting loveless marriage that lay ahead of me. As I stood in the hall, mum looked on from the kitchen. She seemed miles away, almost looking through me as she watched me tidy my hair, looking at my reflection in the hall mirror. I then squeezed her hand and kissed her goodnight before sweeping back along the hall, glancing one last time in the mirror before slamming the front door behind me, eager to enjoy my night.

As we all took to the dance floor with the bubbly flowing freely, the laughter and giggling lit up the room. Suddenly I realised I would miss my nights out and shopping with friends that would now be controlled by Dave. At that moment I felt like I was going to burst into tears so with my eyes burning and stinging with tears I headed away from the dance floor to try and compose myself, to reapply my now smudged makeup.

Just then I felt a gentle tap on my shoulder, I spun around and to my shock and total amazement it was Charlie. I stood shaking, not believing he was here tonight of all nights. My eyes were transfixed on him, dressed in his suit his stance was so imposing, he looked so handsome as he held my hands outstretched. I started to tremble, my lips quivering and my tears, well they were now of joy as tonight I was stunned into silence by Charlie's presence and not for the first time but he was not alone tonight, he was accompanied by five other males but who they were I didn't know and to be honest, I didn't care.

You look so beautiful tonight Lizzy and I wanted to be here to tell you in person. With his sexy, cocky smile, he then pulled me into the ladies' toilet, the door firmly closed, locking the door to the tiny cubicle behind us. His intentions were clear, just like when he seduced me in the girls' changing rooms all those years ago, tonight it was allowing me to rekindle memories from the past that I loved so much and remembered as if it was yesterday and how I desperately wished it was yesterday.

Yesterday was everything I ever wanted and everything I craved. To be free from torture, from torment and the crippling life that was to be mine.

Charlie's firm body forced rigidly against mine, making it clear he was never letting go of what was rightfully his while he held my wrists firmly against the sterile wall, unable to move, sending my body into a sexual frenzy and making my body react to this unexpected and sensual reunion, pleading with him to never stop as he kissed my neck, his breath warm and tantalising on my skin, whispering his love for me. My body was once again devoured by the feelings of yet more terrifying pain as the chains cut even deeper, leaving yet more blood stained scars across my heart, my open wounds were now becoming all too visible to the people that surrounded me, scars that were now becoming so hard to hide as they wept constantly, leaving behind a trail of devastating hurt.

Leaving our pent up frustration on hold for now he led me onto the dance floor, holding my hand tightly in his, his smile beaming. Suddenly I could feel everyone's eyes on us, his male entourage now standing back watching Charlie take control of what was his, allowing the finger-pointing and whispering to start once again, whispers that now could be heard across the dance floor seemed to dissolve into the gaps between the old oak floor boards, finger-pointing that now made willowy shadows on the stark walls.

We danced so close, so close that I could feel his cock boring rigidly hard into my groin, yearning to love me one last and final time, or maybe he had come to collect what was so rightfully his.

His hands were now caressing my curves in true Charlie style, I was loving all his attention as we glided around the floor we soon became blissfully unaware of the people around us, leaving the shadows to disintegrate into a foggy mass and the whispers to blend into one and to be muted as they faded into the distance.

The night was still young, and Charlie said he had to leave, wanting me to enjoy my night. I looked at him at a loss, disappointment instantly swept across my porcelain face that was now crippled in anguish that his visit was so brief, he then smiled gently, slipping a little note firmly into my hand and then he was gone, slipping away as silently as he had breezed in, leaving his entourage to seduce the girls that graced the dance floor. The note read *meet me later, you know where Lizzy, enjoy your night, I will be waiting for you.* A warm smile had now returned to my porcelain skin, but the puzzle continued, as to how he know I was going to be here tonight.

So now, an hour or so later and having made my excuses I headed to the most romantic place I knew, where Charlie was waiting for me still dressed in his suit. He looked so very handsome with his tie loosened and the top two buttons of his shirt open, his expression once again cocky. *Lizzy will this do for you?* He stood with his arms outstretched, ready for my inspection. I smiled, *Charlie its perfect, you're perfect.*

I could see something clenched in his hand as he leant forward kissing me. Taking my hand in his. *Princess I never want you to forget me.* How could I forget him? Tears once again were stinging my eye lids with such intensity as I began choking back my tears, he then placed the most gorgeous silver bracelet on my wrist covered in tiny white Daisy's, Charlie's eyes then commanded my attention, my gaze fixed on his every word, his words tonight were so powerful as they echoed delightfully from wall to wall before slipping away silently under the tin door into the midnight air to be scattered across the enchanted Wiltshire landscape.

The shed was now lit only by candles, which tonight made it look so cosy as we danced to the sexy music that was being played on the little tatty radio, exploring with ease each other's mouths allowing our tongues to entwine, I ran my fingers through his glossy hair before holding the back of his neck so tight never wanting to let him go, taking in the sensual aroma that was him, an aroma so perfect it would always entice me back for more and I always would without hesitation.

I should have felt very guilty about what I was doing, but I didn't, and I never would, Charlie was my guilty dirty secret, my dirty past, and my forever dirty pleasure to keep for now and for the future when I needed to awaken my dirty love that I hoped would be ours again in the years that were to come.

Both of us now fuelled with such a passionate love, I slowly undid his tie striping him bare to the waist kissing every button on his shirt before discarding it, throwing it to the floor in a passionate frenzy, lingering to absorb his aroma, allowing his aroma to seduce my nostrils.

His arms were still holding me tightly as he slowly unzipped my top to reveal my new delicate lacy underwear. *Lizzy your tits are so utterly beautiful*, his gaze still hungry for all my undivided attention.

He then unhooked my silky, soft lace skirt letting it fall to the floor in an unruly heap as I now stood only in my black lace bra and matching knickers, complete with very high heels, holding my arms at full stretch. *My god! You're beautiful, so fucking beautiful, my beautiful Lizzy.*

I have been a complete fool princess, can you ever forgive me? Charlie, I whispered, *not now, not tonight.* I kissed my fingers, placing them delicately on his lips. I did not want to talk about it as it was time for love, our dirty love and it was too late to be anything else, far too late for regrets, far too late to turn the clock back, and far, far too late for us to be anything other than lovers.

Now scantily clad and Charlie naked to the waist we danced together. As we danced I felt like a dirty little tart, Charlie's tart and that was fine by me as it was a label I was willing and proud to wear, to have his name tattooed across my already scarred, blood stained, battered and torn skin.

He whispered softly, *wait for me princess* as he kissed my body, starting with my mouth, delivering passionate kisses that instantly awakened my dormant spirits, moving seductively to my neck, long rolling kisses that teased my senses tonight. He then suddenly dropped to his knees, his young body tense and tight, his tongue was now revolving around my belly button, his kisses warm, leaving wet patches where his kisses had gently marked my naked and bare skin.

My kitten was now drenched with fresh juice in anticipation of receiving the beautiful attention of Charlie's dirty love. Charlie gently slipped my knickers away, leaving me naked apart from my shoes. As I stood before him he gently nudged my legs apart so that he could thrust his tongue into my ever demanding kitten with complete ease as he continued to love me with his tongue. I held his head firmly with both my hands, burying it hard into my pulsating kitten, begging his tongue to move further in. I closed my eyes, whispering *please don't stop Charlie, please never stop.* I insisted. Looking up at me, stopping for a brief moment he reassured me, sweeping his hand on to mine...

Lizzy I never intend to, not now, not ever.

Our moaning was now so loud and verbal, I found this so very exciting, lacing every emotion with a tingling sensation that rippled through my body, stripping me bare, leaving me begging for more, my breath being compromised as I struggled to allow myself the beauty of the moments we were creating, knowing I was guilty of betrayal and of lies but I didn't care and with that revelation I heard the storm's roar as it filled my body with ferocious thunder and crippling lightning.

Charlie, having witnessed my distress stood up and held me close as I kissed his face, his rugged sun kissed face. My senses were once more treated to the aroma of Charlie, sending a beautiful shrill through my entire body that was now shrouded in the violent roar of the storm.

Charlie's fingers were now coated with fresh, warm juice from my love drenched kitten that he gently worked around my mouth and across my tongue, his fingers seduced me one by one, allowing me to taste all the love that I had for him as he watched me enjoy this sensual moment. His breathing was hard as he whispered *Lizzy, my Lizzy*, continuing to repeat my name in a low, very sexy untamed voice. Charlie was now naked and tonight he was free again of underwear which allowed me instantly to glide my fingers over is full erection that was now coated with beads of pearly juice that begged for my attention. I then put my fingers to his mouth, he sucked each one of them dry from the juice, *Lizzy you naughty, naughty girl*, I blushed uncontrollably at his comment, knowing that I was always going to be the girl he desired, the girl that he would always love relentlessly, the girl whose name had been engraved on his sole, that had freely given eternal love to him from the day our eyes met for the first time.

Our bodies were now engaged in pure love, responding to each other's needs, reassuring me that I was always going to be his girl, words that were now once again crippling my body with earth shattering pain, confirming and endorsing yet again that I was marrying the wrong man.

Now it was my time to give him some much needed loving. I moved down his body, peppering him with the Lizzy kisses that I knew he loved. I placed my mouth firmly over Charlie's huge cook allowing it to slide into the back of my throat as he held my head, forcing his cock still further into my throat that was now being coated in beautiful juice that led us to share our kisses and once again his juice was smeared over my lips adding to the sensual pleasure we were both experiencing.

I then straddled him, Charlie's eyes were firmly holding my gaze, his eyes so full of emotion as he whispered, *princess I never want to love anyone else but you, I can't and I never will stop loving you, you do know that don't you Lizzy?* I nodded, unable to utter any words as I was consumed in dirty love and now in terrifying torment that clashed together knowing my dreams would never be realised.

We then laid in total silence, never needing to say anything, just to be in each other arms was enough. Loving Charlie blocked out every horrid, vile, and repulsive emotion that I had experienced in my short life. I suppose it helped me fight back from my heart-breaking miscarriage, my vile sexual assault, my one night stand and now above all a loveless relationship that was going to be my marriage, my future, and my lifetime prison sentence with Dave.

Suddenly my eyes took me on a journey around this little old shed, staring at the heavy, dark cobwebs that still hung high above us, flickering in the soft breeze that had filtered through the gaps in the grubby window frame, inhaling deeply the aroma that filled this little shed bringing back instant, cherished memories that would never fail to delight me.

We must have fallen asleep but it wasn't long before I was awoken by the nightly terrors that now ruled my life, leaving me in a pool of fluid that had drained from my body. As I laid there watching Charlie, I was overcome with a terrifying sadness, a sadness so strong that I could no longer contain my tears. I was sobbing uncontrollably, my anguish had now awoken him, he knew my pain without my explanation, pulling me gently back in to his arms where I felt safe, my hand resting on his chest feeling him breathing, feeling his heart pounding, feeling his raw emotion, knowing full well he was feeling just like me.

I could feel the tears once again burning my eyes as I softly kissed him, he then returned my kisses that now hurt so much as my heart was yet again feeling the intense grip from the chains that I never wanted to break free from, chains that had scarred my body with permanent blemishes, open wounds that would never heal, tattoos that now formed stunning patterns on my skin, patterns of anguish, pain, devastation and of love that would now protect me, shielding my vulnerability, protecting me against Dave and what was going to be my loveless prison sentence, my skin being severed every day with spiteful words and sarcasm.

Was this going to be our final goodbye, our final I love you's? My body was engulfed with huge sadness and such excruciating pain but deep down we both knew this, our dirty secret love, would never be over and I would remain his Lizzy, as we could never say a final goodbye. Now holding my arms outstretched we once again embarked on a journey, seeking each other's gaze. Charlie then whispered… *Lizzy, never forget you're my girl, you're my Lizzy.* He pulled me back into his arms, holding my delicate frame, kissing my neck repeatedly, his tongue was now seducing my mouth again, kisses that today were raw, full of raw passion that neither of us would forget.

Distraught, I left as I always did, dressed today in the same clothes I wore the night before, my hair not brushed and my teeth not cleaned, smelling Charlie's powerful aroma that now laced my delicate underwear and my lacy clothes. I could not bear to look back, it was too heart-breaking, I just wanted Charlie to pull me back into his arms and tell me to stay, to free me from yet another nightmare that was about to unfold but alas those words today were not forthcoming, leaving me to yet again question his love, his so called love for me. He now said all those familiar words like he always did, *I love you princess, you're my girl, my forever Lizzy.* But today he added a few more for good measure. I stood still, frozen to the spot, his words now running riot in my head, clashing like thunder that crackled violently as they clashed together over and over again, never letting me free from torture and torment that continued to rage whilst ravishing every part of my body. I dare not look around now as my whole world had started crumbling around me, scattering my heartache like tiny grains of sand that were being picked up and swirled around by the early morning breeze, only to be dropped at random, discarded over the open landscape. My legs felt heavy, my hands shaking and sweating, my eyes blinded by tears that once again I was not prepared to shed here in front of Charlie, he meant it, I did not have to marry Dave, I did not have to get married, but sadly I was now to scared to call it off, I was scared of Dave and his demands, his continuing vile commands and his constant bullying, knowing full well he would taunt my parents with my past history, knowing I had told him some of the stupid things I had done when on the odd occasion I had a few too many drinks while letting my hair down or on occasions when I had been left vulnerable.

So this morning, and finding the strength from out of nowhere, I walked away fearful as my life now seemed so very complicated, made even more complicated by me wanting more. Putting my selfish, out of control needs before anything, retaliating against my impending fate, my heart broken into a million pieces and not for the first time, I felt sure today it would definitely not be the last.

CHAPTER 12

I arrived home to be greeted by mother looking on in horror at my dishevelled appearance, instantly her expression told me she knew I had been with Charlie all night. I said nothing, nor did she as I rushed passed her running up the stairs before throwing myself on to my little bed sobbing uncontrollably.

I thumped the pillows hard with my fist out of pure frustration, what the hell was I doing? My mind was now so muddled, confused and totally helpless to know which emotion hurt the most as all of them melted into one, leaving me lifeless with devastation and sadness as once again I shed tears that were violently stinging my tender skin. How the hell had I let my life become so full of unhappiness and hurt? Where was the real Lizzy, the girl who had a love and zest for life, that was only allowed to be herself when surrounded by Charlie and his reputation?

I must have fallen asleep as when I woke up I was so cold, realising nothing had changed, my heart still broken and once again my body consumed with deep sadness, questioning if I would always feel like this. Would my world always be traumatised by the demons that seemed determined never to let me forget my stupidity?

I looked out from my bedroom window in need of some serious recollection of my lifetime dreams that had now failed me but it was me that had let my dreams turn to failure, allowing the violent storm to take my body and rip it to pieces. I wanted to run for miles across the fields, to hide, to hide myself away from the daily devastating life I was about to embark on but I couldn't as everyone would hate me so much, but no more than I hated myself at this moment for the mess I had created for myself, for the actions that I had stupidly taken in a bid to have it all.

So with that in mind, I just went along with the farce that was going to be my sad and sorry life, leaving me yet again to question why I had not learnt any lessons along the long roller-coaster journey I had taken, knowing I had broken every rule in the book, tripping over every page, falling apart when the words that I wanted to say had become muddled and with words that at times had become blurred by my constant tears but that was my punishment, and I had to now pay the price and that was terrifying.

All my dreams of a perfect, happy life now shattered with heartache, like glass in a mirror that had been smashed repeatedly, never to allow me the perfect reflection that once was stunning and admired by many but sadly the reflection was now only a splintered shadow of yesterday, allowing me again to feel vulnerable, fragile and frightened of the storm that was gathering monumental pace, while I watched on in horror, allowing Dave to snatch every piece of my delicate personality away to be replaced by someone I hated, making me a prisoner in a home that I would loath and in a marriage I would live to despise, complete with a husband that I would eventually detest.

I suddenly remembered the necklace which I had removed two days ago that held the mysterious ring and on closer inspection I noticed it had initials engraved inside, very faint but they were there, it looked like H L F. It was hard to make out the delicate engraving but who or what did those letters mean? Charlie obviously knew, but I remained intrigued as now the ring had begun to seduce me again as it lovingly graced my neck, feeling Charlie's breath wave over my skin, hearing him whisper my name repeatedly, feeling him hold my delicate frame like he always did, caressing my curves, holding my painted porcelain face with both his hands, all made possible by his love for me, his Lizzy.

I stood still and transfixed looking out of my bedroom window across the open landscape that went on for miles with nothing to blur its beauty that allowed me to escape to happier times and there were so many to recall at this moment, but a few stood out all of them involving Charlie, memories that we made together out in the garden or when sitting in the tree house until late into the evenings especially during the summer months when the evenings were long and mellow, both of us inhaling the seductive aromas that wafted gracefully throughout the garden.

Suddenly mum was stood at my bedroom door bringing me back from my escape to the dark and stark reality, knowing now that today there was no going back, So much for happy endings as my dreams were now crashing violently around me, leaving me with the nightmare that would wake me from my sleep, a nightmare that would rage throughout my body, never giving me peace from the haunting turmoil of seeing Charlie's fathers face, recalling his vile stare along with his repulsive smell.

What's wrong? Lizzy you look so sad. I could not tell her as I had brought her and my father so much agony, bringing a shameful disgust into this beautiful home, knowing I had brought so much shame, not just on them or this house, but on this family. I think she knew deep down that Charlie was the only one that made me truly happy, and he did.

She looked lovingly at me, her face pale, heavily pained and so obviously burdened by my sadness as she held my hand in hers. *I'm here for you Lizzy, I know mum, it's fine, I'm fine,* but I was not fine and in the coming weeks, months even years ahead nothing would change, it never would as I would continue to revel in self-pity and to wallow in perfect unhappiness, allowing the storm to shower me in ice cold rain, life changing lightning and violent thunder.

As the days grew closer to the wedding I felt totally out of control, it was as if something so powerful had taken over my body, I was not Lizzy anymore. I hadn't been the fun loving, life loving Lizzy for a very long time which now showed heavily in my porcelain face, the sparkle that had once embellished my eyes now had disappeared, taking them from a beautiful emerald green to a dull foggy grey, uninviting and lacking in colour that had once made everyone comment on how beautiful my eyes truly were. Suddenly the snarling words that were once again mine, the snarling out of control words that I had unwarily used to silence Charlie's vile father, the roar of the storm again echoed and spun in my head like a violent whirlwind, taking with it everything in its path.

The wedding now, as always, had been an expensive waste of time but it was too late to now turn back as I was so scared of the repercussions that would undoubtedly follow from Dave, creating yet more devastation on my already battered and bruised family, the consequences that would be unbearable for my parents as Dave kept for himself things that if told would bring my family nothing but heartache once again, so I would suffer in silence at Dave's hands rather than bring even more shame into this house.

The day finally came, Dave's wedding day, not mine, his! Dave's big dream being played out in full to a large audience that would allow him to play the big man but still it remained the day I had been dreading in silence since the night that the unloving ring was forced onto my finger, squeezing every last breath from me, choking me day by day as I felt a little more of Lizzy slipping away, my love and zest for life being drained away by Dave.

Needing to seek a little comfort I found my treasured box of letters, cards and beautiful wooden boxes, secured within the large red velvet box that was tattered and crumpled at the corners but contained so much love. As I read through the letters, each one inspired my face to smile once again, to be free from bitter tears, for now anyway, seeing instantly Charlie's cocky attitude shine from every letter, every card, and every piece of crumbled paper that he had written on.

I was not experiencing the feelings of what I had been told a bride should be feeling as everyone continued to tell me that it should be the happiest day of your life, well it certainly was not mine, so taking my coffee into the garden to once again be alone with my thoughts I sat in my favourite part of the garden looking up to the most perfect blue sky that was today littered prettily with chalky white fluffy clouds, letting myself drift back to much happier days when I had a lust for life, a reason to smile and a reason to love, that love was all Charlie's then as it was now. I continued to hide behind a fake, painted smile that I wore daily, having to hide my true feelings, my true love and my true desire as no one could ever know my dirty secret, my sordid past or to be able to read the label that I had given myself that had now been sown into everything I wore as they were mine to carry all my life, along with the open scars that hid a magnitude of sadness and with tattoos that painted my skin in vivid multi colours, scars that now blemished my skin by my own stupidity.

Suddenly, I was jolted back from my little journey into the past to the here and now, by someone calling very loudly in a high pitch squeal almost, it was so loud it made me jump, spilling my coffee in the process.

A lady was stood at the gate to the garden waving at me hysterically with a delivery and it was for me. I gasped as I looked into her hands, wrapped in delicate pink cellophane and tissue paper laid a single white daisy with a note attached that read…

One of many for the chain that we will make again Lizzy, H L F. Those initials, now adoring the note… what did they mean? I would have loved to make daisy chains today with him in the woods, far away from everyone, far away from the disaster that was now unfolding, to be secluded by the trees that already knew the full extent of our love. Looking down at the single daisy I was happy for a split second but that was instantly to be replaced by sadness, knowing Charlie's love was already being used to seduce another, but was meant exclusively for me.

I took the daisy and placed it in a little delicate glass vase that I managed to find at the back of the kitchen cupboard, desperately never wanting the special delivery to wilt on this scorching hot June day, thinking that I would place it in my posy to bring it to life, like putting love into it, Charlie's love.

Today I was going to wear my treasured bracelet that Charlie had given me to cherish, knowing full well that I could not get married without wearing it and of course my perfect little plastic cracker ring for our never-ending love, my glass ring for eternity, the beautiful bracelet and now there was one other special item that I was going to wear and that was the necklace that held the mysterious ring that Charlie had once worn on his finger.

So once again to satisfy my emotional senses I stood at my bedroom window in order to allow myself one more long lingering gaze across the landscape, my journey now took me back to my tree house, recalling all the dreams I had so lovingly made there of the wonderful life that I thought was going to be mine but I was now living the nightmare that was going to be my life sentence, a sentence that I had unwillingly agreed to the night a ring was forced on to my finger, that very moment the life sentence had been granted and I did nothing to stop it as I continued to plead guilty. Why had I been so stupid? I hated myself that I had not managed to find the courage to stop the farce as soon as it had begun, and at this moment I hated Charlie also for not following his passionate words and promises that I would be forever his.

Distracted again away from my thoughts my gaze now directed into the woods by the frolicking family of deer, my attention firmly focused on them as I put off the moment to adorn myself in robes that would haunt me, that would undoubtedly drown me in sorrow and utter unhappiness. Now once again I felt very vulnerable to Dave's constant demands and his ability to make me feel I had to do as I was told as he had made his commands and demands very clear.

Mum looked into my room, her face delighted by the image that stood before her, *Lizzy you look so beautiful*, and so did she as she held my hands outstretched, tears now very visible in her eyes and in mine. As she kissed me it must of been apparent to her that I was so unhappy, she whispered to me, *you don't have to marry him Lizzy*. I frowned at her, my porcelain face masked today by heavy makeup but It couldn't mask the impending sadness, knowing it was far too late to walk away as the rainbows and dreams that I once chased as a young, virginal girl had now all been claimed by someone else.

My heart and soul now diminished from all feeling, bereft from love and life itself, wanting to run away to escape the misery I had made for myself but I could not let everyone down, all the effort everyone had gone to with all the hours of planning along with the financial cost to mum and dad. Knowing I was now in the hands of Dave, I could not escape however much I wanted, the backlash would undoubtedly be catastrophic for my family.

Our tears now dried, mum went ahead to the church somewhat reluctantly, leaving dad pacing the floor in the hallway, waiting for me downstairs, so I picked up my posy, delicately placing the single most special daisy into it. Suddenly the posy came bursting into life with Charlie's love, sending a delightful aroma around my bedroom. Charlie was with me, making me smile on such a dark day in my life as I now stood lifeless in front of my mirror looking at a vision which was nothing like me. I was now only a shadow of my former self, dressed in a white non-dispirit gown, a plain, boring gown with no shape or form that hung from my body complete with a veil that couldn't mask my unhappiness today. Where was Lizzy? The girl that only wanted to be loved by the right man. I stared deeply into the mirror trying hard to find the girl who became a swan in order to find a love with a bad-boy, but today I had no permission to revisit that glorious image, thinking now I never would.

Suddenly, I could hear the bells that were now ringing out so loudly but with every toll of the bells came a cold and unwelcome tone sending my body into complete melt down. It was now all so terrifyingly real, the booming chimes that bounced from one wall to the next, leaving devastation in its wake.

Looking once more out of my bedroom window, staring into the woods beyond, staring at nothing. The landscape was now bland, naked from any form of life as I twiddled relentlessly with the ring on my necklace, winding the chain so tight it was now cutting into my skin, bringing me back to the here and now. Composing myself, before inhaling again the perfume from my posy, I walked out of my room, glancing back at my window just one more time, just to capture any picture of Charlie before I walked down the stairs to be greeted by my father's smile that today told me just how proud he was of me. *Lizzy you look beautiful,* as he took my hand that was shaking with uncontrollable fear and with a terrifying sadness, my fake smile now hiding my devastated soul.

As we walked out to the car the bells were so loud as they chimed out, sounding like they were saying *walk away Lizzy, walk away.* I screamed at dad to wait, he looked confused and stunned by my sudden and desperate request but I needed to revisit the garden, along with all the emotions that it held for me so scooping up and crumpling the pristinely ironed nondescript gown I was being forced to wear, casting my tight fitting shoes aside I stood busily absorbing a lifetime of love that was held within this garden, while all the time I stood busy silencing so many irrational thoughts, feeling inadequately prepared for what lay ahead. I stood silently telling myself I was going to be okay, but today I was too busy lying to myself, twenty-five minutes later with my emotions dealt with for now I re-joined my dad, whose face was now so pained and crippled by my obvious distress, watching my emotions splinter during the short drive to the church.

Everyone was now settled inside the church having waited so long for me to make an appearance. This was it, my sentence now set in stone, a life sentence was about to be served as I was about to commit to a lifetime of regret, a regret which I was already experiencing as it shuddered its way slowly throughout my fragile body. I knew I was about to embark on a very turbulent, roller-coaster ride that would only carry black and white menacing images as this journey would not, and never be, enriched by vivid coloured rainbows.

My heart was beating so fast, knowing that behind the huge oak doors to the church, which now would have everyone fidgeting in their seats as they sat on the hard, old oak church pews whispering and waiting for me to make a very late appearance, knowing Dave would now be so very annoyed that I had kept everyone waiting, especially him. His knuckles would now have turned white with annoyance as they so often did when he lost his temper with me.

I stalled for as long as I could before I had to walk into the cold, unwelcome church with so many people expecting the happy blushing bride, but with so many emotions bubbling away through my quivering body. I was not the happy bride they were expecting to see walk down the aisle, so with a very heavy heart I held my dad's arm tightly, clutching my posy for some sort of comfort as I walked the long and very lonely road to marriage, and to my impending life sentence that now echoed coldly throughout the church.

Standing at the steps to the alter I glanced lovingly to my left, my mother's face so apparently saddened for me, her tears now very visible as my dad clutched her hand so tightly for reassurance. I had to look away, I hated seeing them both suffering, all because of my out of control dirty love for another man.

Standing at the altar, now taking the vows that choked me, I glanced over at Dave, he didn't even give me a fleeting glance in return as he stood icily cold with his eyes focused on the altar in front of us. My heart was heavy with the burden that I would carry alone, in silence, as I fought desperately with my increasing emotions, crying muted and hidden tears throughout the service, gasping for air as I took my life changing vows, breathing in the devastation as I exhaled the almighty guilt, now with yet another band on my finger that would cause pain, suffering and anguish.

With the ceremony over, photos taken, and confetti thrown, it was time to mingle with family and friends, smiling my fake smile, a smile that would reflect in every photograph, hiding the sadness behind my heavily painted face.

Now with everyone leaving the church I held back, away from the crowd, my gaze now firmly fixed on the cobbled stones beneath my feet as I watched the delicate confetti being blown around on the soft, warm and heady summer breeze. Pale colours of pink, blue and cream spun around my feet and at that moment I wanted to stamp all over them, crushing the happiness they should hold. Suddenly I felt someone caress my hand, it was mum taking me away from my sadness with her warm smile, a smile that was intoxicating.

Today I had become Mrs Granger, I hated it! I wanted to be Mrs Stevens, sadly now that was only a dream as I was to now live this nightmare with Dave's surname, having to stand in the shadow of my new husband while my zest for life was being drained away day by day until I would become someone I did not like and a person whom I would not know. The real Lizzy was now hidden behind a mask of despair, living a life of mind-blowing devastation as the storm continued to surround and embrace me.

Staring down at my posy, little did I know that the single daisy and note would be the last time I would hear from Charlie. The single, beautifully perfect daisy was a parting gift of our eternal lifetime of dirty love, a love that could only be shared by us but now sadly it was my past and no longer my future.

So with the clock striking 11pm it seemed that it was time to leave, Dave reminded me by tugging at my arm as he took me forcefully away from the dance floor, commanding again that I danced only to his tune, to start my new life in my new home with my new and unloving husband, knowing that a shattered life lay ahead, something that I now had to bear without comment.

The days following were unbearable, I felt alone, shut away from the outside world that had once embraced me, now the cold reality had started to close in on me, making me a prisoner in a place I would never be able to call home.

My posy of daisy's now sat delightfully on the kitchen window sill so that I could admire them when I needed reassurance that tomorrow was yet another day, a day when Charlie might break me free from this prison. I kept the one special daisy that Charlie had sent me, pressing it between two pages in a book of old fairy tales that my grandmother had given me back when I was only a child.

A few months later I changed my job, I started working for the local council in the planning office but it was boring, so bloody boring like my sodding life. I had now started to resent Dave as yet again I started to sink into very dark days of hatred, bitterness, sadness and resentment which was a horrid trait, but it was how I felt as I could feel my vulnerability gathering pace once again with the constant heated demands that were made on me, especially when I had to lie next to him, to feel his breath seducing my skin, to endure his vile sexual demands that left me lifeless, frozen from any love that Dave could ever give me but I still craved love, Charlie's love was all I wanted, craved and needed daily, seeking the ongoing reassurance from the ring that still hung around my neck on a delicate chain that cut deep into my skin as I twiddled with it erratically, until it was so tight it was ready to snap.

I was now without a place to hide in this little house with no garden, there was nowhere to be alone to recall my many memories, so without hesitation at weekends I would go back home as I missed it so much. I seemed to spend hours in the garden alone as mum and dad looked on at a loss to know what to say and do, knowing I was hiding the real Lizzy away, beneath the bitter life I was leading to satisfy Dave's hunger for his constant power over me. Today was no different as I caught a glimpse of my mother looking out of the kitchen window, watching my every move, smiling to herself as I climbed again the somewhat rickety wooden ladder to the tree house to seek some solitude, but it was a welcome solitude which mum knew I needed as Dave was spending all his time in the pub, drinking with his mates. Nothing had changed, it was still all about him but I should not have been surprised as it had always been about him.

My life was now in shreds. This was not the life I wanted, needed, or craved, this was not part of the dreams I had created in the tree house, that is now just a fantasy, but still at times left me breathless as today I recalled Charlie's kisses, wanting desperately for those kisses to smudge and ruin my neatly painted lips and to feel his tongue being forced lovingly into my throat with a dirty lust.

The next few years drifted by slowly and nothing spectacular happened, nothing to be happy about in my boring life, but I thought it was normal and what I would have to endure since I agreed to taking Dave's name on that hot June afternoon, but Charlie remained a constant pleasure on my senses and that lay heavy on my emotions. I would often cry for him when I was alone, as still I felt the chains that would often bruise my already battered heart never wanting to free me from Charlie's intense grip as the wounds and scars were still very visible through my eyes.

I need something in my life apart from this house, apart from Dave and my boring office job, a more challenging job maybe. Dave seemed to be spending more and more of his time in the pub, his drinking was now becoming a major problem for us both as he would drink heavily at weekends which would lead to endless rows with vile demands on me, leading to painful and rough sex sessions enforced by him, leaving me rigid and tense as he would selfishly demand my fragile and vulnerable body to do what he commanded, using my lifeless body for his own sexual desires.

I worried, knowing that his drinking would escalate, bring yet more misery to my already spiralling life, but now fear would become my strength once again, the strength that I needed now more than ever and with many sad years behind me I needed more, much more, not having to obey Dave's constant demands that were sometimes threatening, leaving me so scared and in fear of a life of beatings that I felt were never far away, simmering away in the background, ready for the day when he served me the final unforgivable act.

CHAPTER 13

With Christmas now fast approaching I decorated the small, but delicate Christmas tree, placing my most treasured decorations on it, including my most adored snowflake that as always, took pride of place as it always had done, but today I needed more cherished winter memories so I took myself back to mum and dad's, to walk around the village, to capture once again its unique and full beauty, to visit the woods that welcomed me with a stunning winter picture with its newly frozen carpet of snow, trees that had a sprinkling of snow that now coated the branches, clumps of snow that clung fast to the small fir trees, hearing the faint sounds of the deer scurrying around, panicked somewhat by my presence here today.

With the week leading up to Christmas I managed to secure a new upmarket job, much to my astonishment, which seemed on paper very exciting. I was going to work for a large hotel chain all over England, Wales, and Scotland. My job was to oversee the updating and refurbishment of hotels, so it meant that I was going to be away a lot, but I loved the thought of being away from my drab and unexciting marriage, away from the endless rows and the excruciating pain of sex after Dave would get drunk, demanding I do as I was told, but then to be told he was so sorry and it would never happen again, but he lied. It became a vile, terrifying habit enforced by him, a vile attack on my already battered body, but he knew that and thought nothing of it other than to abuse it in his own disgusting way, but at last I was to be free from this house that had let me down in its ability to spark any happiness, not even a glimmer, as I had become its prisoner.

Now having accepted without hesitation and without any thought for Dave, I paced the kitchen floor in anticipation of the final post of the week to be delivered and today my wait was at last over as the long awaited job spec dropped on to the doormat and it all looked very exciting. I could not wait to start another new chapter in my life, never knowing what part of the country it would take me.

I stared at the assignment that was now laid out on the table for what seemed like ages, allowing my coffee to go stone cold while I just glared at the details, not wanting anything to interrupt this moment. The kitchen was now deadly silent, apart from the clock ticking and as the minutes ticked by I remained engrossed in the words that were written on the assignment as I held tightly the ring on the necklace that still hung around my neck, clinging desperately on to the past for reassurance and today it didn't let me down, it never could.

Wales now jumped off the page at me, the stark black ink clarifying my future away from this miserable life I was forced to endure daily, my heart now jolted sideways, sending it into a frenzy of excitement as well as fear of the unknown more than anything I suppose. I was going to Cardiff for 20 weeks, Cardiff! I had not been there for many years, but it remained laced with love and laughter but tainted still with such vile hatred, haunting images, and the ferocious roar of the storm, but now I felt ready to fight back against the hatred and Charlie's father's vile unwanted and unwelcome images.

I was having to now contain my sheer excitement from Dave as he seemed rather annoyed, knowing that I had secured the job, showing him that I was capable of more, so much more. I would be away from him, not having to put up with his vile moods, his drinking during the week and to be set free from the lifeless, loveless marriage I was in. I would now be able live a little and be free to find the real Lizzy again, to sleep alone without the constant nightly interruptions from Dave and his constant demands that he made on my fragile body and maybe, just maybe, to sleep without my dreams bring ruined by haunting voices and terrifying images that still seemed intent on invading my privacy, leaving my body drenched in wet, cold pools of sweat.

Maybe this would be good for both of us? Dave didn't seem to show the slightest concern or worry about me going away, his annoyance very apparent in his facial expression, but now he could live the life he wanted which revolved around the pub and his drunken mates, pleasing himself just like he had always done.

Christmas Day at last was here and lunch today was going to be a family occasion at mum and dad's, with my aunts and uncles gracing the family festivities. It was lovely to be able to relax and be myself in familiar surroundings, the lounge set alight by the enormous Christmas tree with lights that cast such a wonderful glow. The Christmas memories just kept giving, so with that I slipped up to my old bedroom for more festive memories, but that was short livid by Dave demanding I returned to the lounge for pre-lunch drinks.

So now with Christmas lunch eaten and presents exchanged, Dave suggested we went home for our own Christmas celebrations that I was not looking forward to in the slightest, but it was my duty, as a wife to do what I was told, as Dave continued to remind me.

It was now very early January and Christmas had been packed away for another year, Wednesday January 5th was here at last, a day that seemed so desperately cold and frosty, with an ice cold wind that blew in from the east. With my bags packed, I was heading to Cardiff for another chapter in my life, hoping that I could leave the turbulent storms instructed by Charlie's father behind me, the spine chilling memories that even today made my skin crawl, irritating my open wounds.

So before catching the early train there was only one place I needed to be, back at my glorious childhood home. I took a long, lingering walk in the garden, taking in its winter beauty when suddenly, out of the blue, I was treated once more to a gathering of pretty deer with their ears pricked, having startled them by wanting to say goodbye, they were shrouded by frost and snow that was glittering and twinkling in the watery early sunlight. I stood holding my breath, not wanting to blink in case I missed their delightful presence before I left to find Lizzy again.

I took a walk through the house to indulge myself in its beauty, to admire today the Christmas tree that was still in its place, with decorations that were ready to be packed away for another year, mum's tradition to keep the tree up as long as possible.

Then a trip up to my old room for more memories that had now one by one took me on a journey of hope that the future would somehow find the real Lizzy, to save her from more heartache, more impending sadness, but that was a dream, just like the others that ended in sadness.

It was now time to go and as the train pulled into to the station it suddenly felt like a huge weight had been lifted from my shoulders, relieved to be away from the clutches of Dave which felt like a breath of fresh, much needed air. I stood, inhaling the cold, crisp sharp air that filled my lungs, exhaling all of Dave's spiteful comments on to the frozen ground beneath me before I trampled all over them, smiling to myself.

At last I had arrived in Cardiff, so with time to kill, knowing I was now about to embark on something so huge in my life, also knowing I was free from Dave for ten days until I was due to return home for a weekend of misery. I took myself off to a cosy little coffee shop just around the corner from the build, my coffee came and I sat by the window looking out at all people scurrying around, going about their day to day life wondering what they were all doing and where they were all in a hurry to get to, but my mind kept me busy by all the thoughts of all the time I had spent here in Wales previously, slipping so easily back into the past, recapturing once again all the wonderful dirty love I had been given in Cardiff that never failed to make me smile every day. Sadly, it was also tarnished with such vile sadness of a vulnerable time in my life that shook my world with such crippling fear that still managed to torment me, which for the first time today crossed my mind, if he had abused any other visitors in the cold unwelcome place he was delighted to call home, but it could and never would take away the love Charlie and I created and made right here in Wales.

I sat thinking about Charlie and where he might be all these years on, if he was happy and if by any remote chance he had given me any thought. As I stared into my coffee, I twiddled unconsciously with the ring that hung frozen today from my necklace, clearly seeing Charlie's smile that brought me back to the here and now, knowing I had to get started on my paper work but I could not get to grips with it as I was finding it so hard to concentrate. Charlie was now constantly popping into my mind allowing me to raise a smile, suddenly my nostrils were awakened by the over powering and delightful aroma of the fresh bread that was being baked at the back of the coffee shop.

I ordered more coffee as it was so very cold. I thought the coffee would keep me awake and warm on this freezing cold early January afternoon, my fingers now frozen to the pen that was in my hand, it was hard to write the words that just seemed to drift of the page.

Looking out of the little window once again while twiddling endlessly with the ring that today hung proud on my necklace, it looked so cold and grey. The sky was heavily laden with the threat of snow as everyone went about their normal daily life, wrapped up in heavy coats and boots, hurrying to get out of the icy blast that was now surrounding them as the predicted storm was immanent, being blown in on the easterly winds that howled through the narrow and winding streets.

The waitress brought me yet another cup of coffee and as we started to chat. I told her that I was staying here in Cardiff on business, and I asked her if she could recommend somewhere for me to eat that evening and every other evening during my weekly stay. She then rapidly brought me over a local paper, smiling her delicate smile. *This might help*, she said, *there are lots of things to do and see in Cardiff with plenty of lovely places to eat.* Her accent was so soft, mellow, and very intoxicating. As my eyes followed her last words, I thanked her while I finished my coffee as I struggled to get on with my paperwork. All the words seemed to blur into one in front of me, nothing was making any sense as once again my past was flashing before my eyes, begging me to board once again the roller-coaster that was about to leave, that would once again jolt me sideways.

As I left for the first meeting, stepping out from the little cosy coffee shop into the icy cold air, I suddenly felt flakes of snow hit my heavily painted porcelain face with an icy sting. I hurried along with a brisk step to get to the build, out of the bitterly cold easterly wind that seemed to make my eyes water.

With the meeting about to start, I stood with the manager and site officials in front of what seemed like an army of tradesmen, knowing full well that I was being inspected from all directions. I caught a few of the builders checking me out, some of them giving me a little sideways smile, even eye contact, all in a bid to make me blush. I stood shaking, hoping desperately that I was making an impression. Thirty minutes later the meeting was over for the day and I had to admit I was looking forward to getting back to the hotel, to have a long hot bath, relax and maybe tonight I would start on my long and overdue journey to find the real Lizzy, maybe being back in Cardiff would help me to find her.

Back at the hotel after a short walk from the build I was shown to my room by a porter, very smartly dressed in a dark suit, smiling politely as he carried my heavy bags through the maze of corridors to reach what was now going to be my room, my home for the duration of my stay. There was a huge bed that graced the room that I would have all to myself, complete with fresh crisp white laundered bedding. Heavy full length curtains adorned the large windows and the bathroom was delightful, complete with soft white fluffy towels and robes so I ran myself an indulgent bubble bath as I grabbed a glass of wine and then picked up the local paper that the waitress from the cafe had so kindly given me, although now it was a little crumpled, but I managed to smooth out the pages ready for my perusal.

The bath was so warm and very relaxing as I laid in peace, enjoying the silence of the room, flicking through all the ads. The waitress was right, there was an abundance of places to eat so I would not go hungry. Flicking through the pages I caught a glimpse of an advertisement, my eyes were instantly drawn to it, my gaze firmly glued to the small box outlined in thick black ink which appeared in the centre of the page, it was from a builder, a local builder, based here in Cardiff. Suddenly I realised that the water had now gone stone cold deciding that it was time I should take my paper and wine into the bedroom to look closer at the advertisement again. *C. Stevens – local builder and carpenter.* Still my eyes were glued to the advert, wanting desperately to believe that it could be Charlie, my Charlie, shaking my head in disbelief, telling myself to forget him but how could I? He was never far from my thoughts and especially now as I was back here once again in Wales, reliving every moment of the dirty love that I had received and shared here with Charlie.

I had another glass of wine followed by another as I continued looking at the advertisement, the more I read it the more convinced I was that it was him. I closed my eyes tight, allowing me the privilege to recall the feeling of his arms around me, his strong arms that I adored so much and with that I smelt his aroma fill the room, sparking my desire for some much needed dirty love.

I was then deliberating whether I should call the contact number that completed the listing, should I or shouldn't I? I really wanted to, but my head was full of torment once again, all because of one little advertisement in a local newspaper that held for me just a smidgen of hope that it could be Charlie. I was suddenly aware of a cold, harsh chill descending around me, unaware of the impending storm that had reared its ugly head once again.

No Lizzy, I told myself, but I was not listening so with another glass of wine for courage I dialled the number and as it started ringing my heart had leapt into my mouth as again I nervously twiddled with the ring on the necklace, in need of some sort of reassurance, knowing yet again I had not thought this through enough, going in full steam ahead. Once again I was out of control in a bid to quench my desires that had been muted since my wedding day.

Before I could change my mind, I heard a voice at the other end, it was a female with a soft spoken Welsh accent. My mouth so dry now as I uttered with a muffled and very shaky voice, *can I speak to Mr Stevens please?* It was like I was being choked by saying his name aloud. *Who's calling?...* *Ah, its Daisy*. It was the first name that sprang in to my mind.

Sorry, he is still at work, can I get him to call you back? At that moment there was silence at both ends of the phone as I was now lost for words, speechless at what I had done. Looking at my watch it was almost 9pm, thinking to myself... why was he working so very late? I put the phone down immediately saddened that I hadn't been granted the pleasure to hear his voice, but I was still no wiser to if it was him behind the advertisement that now had my heart beating with a renewed desire.

I thought about Charlie all evening as I could not get him out of my mind, knowing now that the same name also appeared on the list of contractors, igniting my yearning as I so wanted it to be him, waiting desperately to hear his voice, just to hear him say my name, just one more time to have his voice play again with my senses bringing them bursting back to life, to hear him call me his girl, his princess, the list was now endless.

My mind was made up, it had to be him. I would be devastated if it wasn't as my new enlivened craving for Charlie had now started to devour my body once more, his reputation seducing me, my hunger for his love now brought to the forefront.

I must have fallen into a deep and luxurious sleep as the next thing I knew was my phone ringing loudly, I sleepily answered it, rubbing my eyes free from the nightly terrors that I was pleased to say had only visited once that I could recall. *Hello its Lizzy, can I help you?*

Good morning Lizzy. It was the building site manager. *Are you on your way?* Suited and booted I headed for the site to be greeted by an army of contractors, my stomach gurgling from skipping breakfast on my first official day on site but I had slept relatively well not having to share my bed, not having to fight off Dave's constant uncaring advances along with his demands and his vile and spiteful war of words.

I was so very nervous as this was going to be my first official brief and my first official day on-site. Thank goodness I had taken time to write the precious notes that I now relied on to make an impression. I started my brief, trying hard to concentrate while trying to also avoid any form of eye contact with the builders that were intent on attracting my attention, diverting my eyes from the builders who seemed to be intent on giving me the odd smile, even a wink, trying hard to attract my attention. I was flattered and I wanted to revel in their flirtatious advances, but my mind was kept busy by thinking constantly about Charlie and the advertisement in the local paper which now had refuelled my cravings that needed to be satisfied and only Charlie could do that. My eyes were then travelling around the army of tradesman in a bid to see a familiar face, but alas he wasn't here, my hopes dashed.

My brief went well and I was pleased that I came across as a competent planner and to be on hand if needed so we broke for breakfast thank goodness, I could now stop my tummy from rumbling as strong coffee and croissants were served a very welcome distraction on this bitterly cold day, the snow was now falling heavily, being blown in on a bitter easterly wind that was still sweeping across Wales, still determined to hold firm its grip on the landscape.

I sat and chatted with a few of the contractors and builders that seemed a lively bunch as they egged each other on with their repeated banter and crude jokes but that was a builders life, something that I knew I would have to endure daily. It was then back to work, excitedly I was looking forward to the challenge that this build would deliver and I wanted to prove to Dave I was no longer prepared to put up with the life he had commanded I lead.

With my hard hat on I headed to the site office hearing in the distance loud whistles, banter, cheering and howling that was being delivered from the builders and tradesmen, making me smile, enlivening muted spirits within me but I knew they would soon get bored as I became one of the team, in fact I was the only female on the build and that was possibly the attraction for them.

My office was now full of builders and tradesmen wanting my attention, even flirting a little with some awkward innuendos thrown in for good measure. The offer of dinner, cinema and even a cosy weekend away as I rebuffed their advances with a sideways smile, knowing I was still Lizzy, knowing full well every day would be challenging but I had to admit, it was flattering. I then handed them all my contact details complete with times of when I would be on site and including my days off only to be bombarded again with chat up lines, some of which I had heard a thousand times and some crudely new, eyebrow raising.

The day remained very busy, but it was so enjoyable, I knew I was going to love it here along with all the fun, laughter, and the constant builders jokes, but it was like a breath of fresh air that I so needed and that was so completely different from my life that I had willingly left behind in the Wiltshire countryside in a bid to find the real Lizzy.

After a busy but enjoyable day it was time to head back to the hotel for a well-deserved bath and dinner, back to resume my search for the real fun loving Lizzy who I knew was not far away from being found again. I waited patiently to be reunited with her, to resume my search for the elusive Charlie so again tonight I did my homework, checking my list of contacts and the brief time for each job. Suddenly I was staggered to see his name appear again, Charlie Stevens, with the same contact number as the local paper advert. It had to be him, it just had to be him and once again I felt the grip tighten again in response to my wishes.

Should I ring the number and make up an excuse about the build?

I had nothing to lose, I dialled the number with a trembling hand and as it was ringing, my mouth once again became so dry, my tongue sticking to the roof of it, hoping that I would be able to at least make some sort of sense from my words. I was now so very afraid that I was yet again making a devastating mistake that would eventually come back to haunt me.

Hello, Charlie Stevens, the voice so tantalising. I froze to the spot as the clocks had now stopped ticking, the time now frozen allowing my desired craving to hear his voice once more, to let the voice at the other end of the phone seduce my body. It was Charlie, his voice so recognisable. I could not speak, it all seemed too good to be true and in a shaky, timid voice. *Hello, hello it's Lizzy from the hotel site.* A long pause at the other end, I could hear him breathing hard. *Lizzy, Lizzy.* He kept repeating my name as my heart continued to miss so many beats, jolting it sideways and once again my senses were enlivened by knowing who was at the other end of the phone, repeating my name.

Yes it's Lizzy. My voice now alive and excited by hearing his voice for the first time in a very long time. *Charlie it's me.* An intense silence filled both ends of the phone. *Hold on Lizzy, let me step outside.* He sounded so calm and almost casual in his response as he repeated my name again.

With a sharp intake of breath I heard him say, *princess, my princess.* I was now a mess, a trembling, excited and a very nervous mess as he repeated my name again *Lizzy, my Lizzy*. His voice seducing me again, *I can't believe it's you my gorgeous Lizzy*.

Both of us were now silent, lost for words, dazed by hearing each other's voices again. We seemed to be lost in the vacuum of silence that had stunned us both, stunned by this glorious, unexpected reunion that for me instantly took me back to the first time we embarked on our journey of love and today I felt the same way, wanting to enjoy this monumental moment just a little longer without interruption.

After composing myself we managed a few minutes small talk, I wanted to tell him so much but time tonight was not on our side and would need to wait, but my smile was uncontrollable, it was a delight talking to him and once again my breath had been completely taken away on hearing his voice. I instantly felt in need for the reassurance from the ring that hung delicately on the necklace as his strong voice now seemed to tremble and quiver, knowing we were both fighting back emotions that had lay dormant for so long, knowing every one of them contained our names. With our call coming to an end we whispered our goodnights, hesitating to catch my breath, every bit of me wanting to tell him I still loved him, wanting to hear his I love you's in return, but he was gone, leaving me in a state of shear panic, my mind in knots thinking about where my life would now take me.

The nightly ritual came right on queue having just drifted from day into night, seeing the vile images that seemed even more sinister this night, along with the haunting cries that were slightly muted, but still so harrowing, now awoken again I laid listening to the icy rain beating heavily against the window, but tonight it was a welcome distraction from the voices that ruled my sleeping hours and suddenly tonight Cardiff took the storm from me, leaving my body to relax without being drenched in nightly ice cold fluid. The morning came at last, and the rain had stopped, I was up early eager to get myself ready. As with most days, today I was dressed to impress, I even managed to eat my breakfast, forcing it down my throat in an attempt to stop my stomach rumbling again. I headed to the build, a few contractors were on site early with smiles and cheeky laughter, even a few whistles thrown in for good measure that made me blush as I headed for my office to get my work sheets for the day and collect my hard hat.

CHAPTER 14

On opening the door I was greeted by Charlie who was sat eagerly waiting for me, comfortably in my chair. His dirty boots were hanging over the edge of my desk. Our eyes then met for the first time in a long time, instantly he leapt to his feet, sweeping me into his arms that had abandoned me seven long years ago leaving me lifeless from love, from his dirty love, something I had missed and craved for every day. He kicked my office door firmly closed behind us, *Lizzy, my darling Lizzy, it's really you.* He caressed my long flowing silky, dark hair, looking into my eyes that had now burst into life, neither of us believing this perfect and very welcome reunion. Charlie's eyes were still the deepest of brown, his smile still his trademark, his cocky attitude slightly muted, but still very apparent. *Lizzy you look, well you look fucking amazing.* He held my arms outstretched, feasting his eyes on my curvaceous body, gazing at what he had missed, his eyes today seemed desperately hungry for my love as I felt his hand glide over my thigh.

Charlie looked almost the same, although his hair was shorter and tidier, but it was that cocky smile that still remained so delightfully unforgettable.

Wrapped in each other's arms once again, it was like falling in love, I was falling in love again with him for the second time in my life, The feelings were immense as it was engulfing me just like they had done the first time. I was now engulfed by every emotion that continued to spiral through my body as tears blurred my vision, tears that once again I needed to shed. Suddenly and without warning I felt the chains that kept me his hostage tighten again, tighten around my body, but I was never going to be released as I would remain forever the hostage he wanted me to be, and the hostage I craved to be.

My phone was ringing loudly, eager to spoil this magnificent moment that had now left us both speechless, both of us not wanting to move from this very spot that had nailed not only me to the floor, but Charlie also. Overpowering emotions that took my body on a beautiful journey, suddenly jolting us away from this beautiful moment. I then felt his hand touch mine, *let it ring Lizzy*. And with that we shared the most passionate long loving kisses that exploded instantly on my pretty pastel pink painted lips with renewed sparks that had evaded my life for the last seven long and lonely years, now brought back to life like huge booming fireworks that shone in multi-colour, crackling sparks of flaming reds, glorious glittering golds, stunning sapphire blues and shining silvers, awakening every muted emotion within my body, his tongue revolving rapidly around my mouth, over and under my tongue with passion. Kisses suspended for now as Charlie was now looking down at my wrist as he smiled that perfect smile. I was still wearing his bracelet and rings that I wore every day in a bid to keep our love alive. *Lizzy you still have them. Yes Charlie of course I do*, as his cocky smile radiated through my office, sprinkling it with a warmth that was so needed on this extremely cold winter's day. Then his gorgeous brown eyes were instantly drawn away from my smile to my necklace that had caught the watery early morning sunlight that was now flooding in through the window of my office. He let his fingertips seduce the pattern that was embossed on the ring. *Lizzy my darling Lizzy.* I thought Charlie would comment on the ring, but his words were again muted, his expression stunned as his fingertips had now moved to outline my porcelain face, both of us now smiling as we both enjoyed the luxury of this moment, a moment I never expected to happen.

Suddenly I could hear him being called by the other builders, both of us now desperate not to let each other go as we seemed so unprepared for this most powerful moment to be brought to an end. As he left my office, his smile beaming, I could hear the loud whistles and banter from the builders, Charlie tried to cover his obvious delight, smiling just like a schoolboy, the cocky schoolboy I had fallen in love with all those years earlier.

Friday afternoon wore on and the paperwork was piling high. My desk was now littered with paperwork, letters, and delivery notes. Luckily I had coffee on tap as the phone was ringing every minute, not allowing me any time to recall the most powerful and monumental day this had been.

I suddenly heard a heavy knock at the office door, a smartly dressed gentleman was now stood there, letting in a blast of icy cold air that made me shiver. *I'm looking for Lizzy. Yes that's me. I have a delivery for you.* It was a most beautiful posy of sweet smelling white daisy's, wrapped

149

neatly in pink tissue and covered in pretty pink cellophane. Charlie had never forgotten what the daisy's meant to us both and on the card it read, *My Lizzy, nothing can or will keep us apart, let's make daisy chains again tomorrow, H L F.* Again, the initials that adorned the ring.

Words that sent a shiver down my spine as my smile reflected my utter delight to have Charlie back once again in my life and this time I would not be letting him go, we would be lovers once again, just as Charlie had promised all those years ago and I was back in Wales of all places to now reclaim what was rightfully mine.

This was real, I was here in Cardiff, back to the arms of the man I loved and that I had craved since I was 14 years of age when I was his virgin, now having to pinch myself repeatedly to make sure it was not a dream. My feelings were now refuelled, I once again felt the grip of Charlie's love that had kept my love alive through my dull, boring, and tiresome marriage. Not only had Lizzy been found again here in Cardiff, but Charlie too.

I lovingly placed the daisy's on my desk, they made my office glow with love and every time I looked up at them a smile swept across my face. It would have been so very hard not to smile, the perfume now triggering powerful emotions, taking me on yet another delightful journey, only to be interrupted again and again by builders and contractors as all I wanted to do was recall that kiss, the kiss I never thought we would or could ever share again.

Wales had stolen my heart all those years ago and all that went with it, now I was back to retrieve it all, it was mine, it always had been. I now wanted it all back for myself and I would do all that was needed to get it and at whatever cost, I was now willing to pay the price, any price to have Charlie in my life once more. Again, I twiddled with the mysterious ring on my necklace, retracing Charlie's own fingertips, wondering still why he had made no comment on the pretty ring when he knew full well its previous journey.

Charlie called into the office unexpectedly, his smile met mine. I blushed uncontrollably, leaving my porcelain face burning and wanting more as I was now loving the feelings that engulfed my body, sending it wild with desire, a renewed desire to be with Charlie again, to receive some very dirty and wildly out of control love. *Princess, do you fancy meeting up later? Lizzy, Lizzy my beautiful Lizzy say you will.* He sounded so very happy as he repeated my name. *Yes Charlie I would love that*, nodding my eagerness to spend time with him.

My heart and head were now thumping with every emotion possible, emotions that were just as powerful as they had always been, jolting me sideways, spinning me around and turning my world lovingly upside down yet again leaving me dazed and leaving me to wonder if Charlie would once again rock my world, but I already knew the answer that would come with a huge cost not just for me, but the people that already surrounded him.

I told him the name of the hotel where I was staying and we arranged to meet up later that evening, we had lots to catch up on as so much water had flowed under the bridge in all those long lost years, knowing it would be difficult for both of us to know where to start.

Back at the hotel I paced the bedroom floor in anticipation of seeing Charlie and being alone with him once again as it had been a very long time since we had spent any time together. Would we still have the desire, the need, and the dirty love?

As I stood at the mirror brushing my flowing hair, haunting faces were suddenly reflecting back at me, once again to disturb me, to jolt me sideways and haunt me. Reflecting back at me was Dave, Charlie's vile father Roger and Paul. I jumped back from the mirror, frightened to look again at what should have been my reflection, I glanced nervously back at the mirror, not wanting the vile and unwelcome visions to disturb me again.

So, as I waited downstairs in reception nervously fumbling with the mysterious ring, repeatedly running my fingertips over the raised pattern, winding the chain around and around knotting the chain. My hands seemed cold, so cold, my head pounding, my heart ready to explode and with my lips waiting and wanting the tender kisses only Charlie could deliver. I suddenly caught sight of him walking in through the huge glass revolving doors, looking older of course, more rugged, his hair shorter, but the same cocky smile still remained, a smile that made my heart melt once again.

I stood up nervously as we threw our arms around each other, neither of us not wanting to be the one to pull away as we had both waited a very long time to feel the desire and passion between us once again. He then hesitantly pulled away, holding me at arm's length for his maximum pleasure, feasting his eyes over my body, his gaze now fixed on my porcelain face, our eyes uncontrollably flirting with each other. Suddenly I could see his hunger, the hunger that again asked for my love, such a familiar look that I had seen so many times before.

His cocky smile took my breath away again that night. *Let me look at you princess, Lizzy you are just as beautiful, just as I remember you.* He then kissed me again. As I kissed him back, fireworks erupted and sparks exploded on my lips. I didn't want lukewarm kisses or lukewarm love, I wanted kisses that blistered my lips and love that burnt my soul, rekindling our love of the past.

His hands now cupped my porcelain face tenderly, as he continued his gaze, both of us afraid to let this moment drift by us, wanting emotions to invade my body like an ocean of foaming water. Charlie peppered me in thousands of soft kisses that I just adored, he truly was a breath of fresh Welsh winter ice cold air that I so desperately needed to breath, to inhale, to digest and embrace, his aroma still so powerful as it hit my nostrils.

Charlie ordered some very expensive champagne, after all, it was a celebration and we needed to mark this amazing occasion in style, true Charlie and Lizzy style, marking this monumental moment as we clinked the gleaming glasses, toasting yet another chapter in our ongoing lifetime of dirty love but now there was a difference, we were both grown up knowing sadly that I had been deprived of his love and affection by marrying the wrong man.

At that moment I was consumed by every emotion as one by one they all came flooding back, like a whirlwind taking me on a long roller-coaster journey that lasted just seconds, but it was multi-coloured and beautiful with vivid delights that sent my senses into free-fall. I tried to recapture them all, my body now frozen with love that sent ice cold spine tingling shivers quivering within me. We sat and talked, our fingers entwined, eager to embrace each other's touch a while longer.

The ambiance of our love just filled the room with a light that bounced from wall to wall, beaming a vast, bright light that swirled around us, cocooning us in a blanket of love as we became totally unaware of the people that surrounded us, witnessing what I could only describe as a beautiful moment.

As my fingers caressed each one of his I noticed the gold wedding band that he wore, now feeling desperately cheated I pulled my hand away, knowing it should have been my ring that adorned his finger, my love that squeezed his finger but I wasn't shocked about that, although it hurt me knowing he was married and that I hadn't been his bride, the bride he had promised that I would be but he was about to hit me with something bigger. Charlie was now sat cradling his head in his hands, a familiar sight that I had seen on a few occasions when words were tough for him, his voice quivering and somewhat muffled. *My wife is pregnant, we are expecting our first baby.* Now jolted sideways again I felt so overcome and consumed with jealousy as it brought back all those sad life changing memories for me. God I should have told him back then, there was never a day went by that I didn't think about our baby and how it would have changed our lives.

I hesitantly congratulated him, he then looked up kissing my hand nervously, clearly seeing in my expression that his words had upset me, my eyes about to burst with tears that I had patiently held back until now. *I know how hard this must be for you Lizzy.* He then quickly changed the subject, squeezing again my hand for reassurance, smiling his cocky smile which I returned a thousand times without a second thought.

Charlie seemed somewhat distracted touching my hand that was still shaking, suggesting we take our drinks somewhere more private. He seemed a little uneasy with so many people witnessing and sharing our most monumental moments, witnessing at times my distress, moments that clearly should be shared behind closed doors, somewhere more intimate and more private, alone to be us. *Yes, we can go to my room Charlie.* He nodded his head in total approval and I was not going to object as I saw again that cocky attitude that still continued to seduce me.

He held my hand gently and firmly as I led the way up to my room, all the while craving his full attention, needing to refuel my ongoing desires as once again I twisted vigorously with the necklace that held the mysterious ring.

Feeling his hand holding mine once again I felt safe, just like I had done all those years ago when we first set out on our lifetime of love and the amazing journey we took together walking in each other's footsteps.

Outside my room I put the key into the lock and suddenly I stopped as I looked into his big brown eyes. *Charlie is this OK?* Desperately wanting his approval. *Princess you know it is.* He squeezed my hand again for all the reassurance I needed tonight. *Lizzy we have got history, a powerful past and lots of unfinished business.* He then smiled that sexy, cocky smile, I blushed at his comment knowing exactly what he meant.

Now in my room Charlie seemed to relax, as did I, it was easier to talk here, to be us without the glare of others, feeling their eyes disapproving of our apparent dirty love affair. Charlie then poured more champagne as we sat on the bed talking until very late. He seemed slightly distracted and tense as he kept looking at his watch. *Do you have to go Charlie? I should princess, but I don't want to leave, I want to stay Lizzy, I want to say with you.* I wanted him to stay, I wanted to seduce him, I wanted him to seduce me, as seduction seemed to be on both our minds, but for now it would have to wait but the desire to be together was still very much alive and very much on each other's minds.

We laid back on the freshly made bed wrapped in each other's arms, relaxed once again in each other's company, sharing kisses, the kisses that I had never forgotten and that I remembered so well as we continued to flirt, our body language on fire. Charlie then straddled my fully clothed body, his fingertips were now tracing the outline of my porcelain face again, his eyes still starving for my love. *It's so good to see you Lizzy, so very good.* His eyes engaged with mine, locking into each other's gaze as we continued flirting and seducing each other. *I can't believe your here in Cardiff, here with me again and still looking so fucking adorable, so fucking beautiful, so fucking gorgeous.* His fingers then gently traced the outline of my painted porcelain face, I blushed again knowing that Charlie still wanted to seduce me and to make dirty love to me.

Time was not going to allow us the full impact of our very welcome reunion on that night, to allow us time to reflect on the past and what had happened in those fearful years, to express the monumental feelings that we had obviously bottled up. There was so much I wanted to tell him and so much I couldn't, wishing desperately I could have told him about our baby, the baby that was made by absolute love for each other, trying hard not to mention his vile fathers name, hoping that Charlie would not mention his name. Charlie then kissed my hand, his phone now ringing loudly which he dismissed and did not answer, making no comment as to who the call was from but I could only guess it was Charlie's wife, keeping tabs on his whereabouts.

I will have to go soon Lizzy. Tears now welled up in my eyes knowing yet another goodbye was immanent, another goodbye that tonight would haunt my sleep, knowing it would not be me that he seduced tonight as it wasn't going to be me that slept in his arms, but I wanted him, he wanted me, we both knew it was so wrong or was it? It was going to be unavoidable as far as I was concerned.

We stood at the door embracing our love as one kiss followed another, not wanting the last one to end so it was instantly replaced by another, each one a little more beautiful than the last, his fingers entwined with mine until my hand was set free from his as he turned and walked away through the maze of corridors back to his unsuspecting wife, leaving me to crave his body again tonight but leaving me with a feeling that once again embraced my body with the chains that held me hostage to Charlie's love, the chains that were always meant for me.

I closed the door reluctantly, leaving my body to slide heavily down the solid door into a crumpled heap on the floor, sobbing uncontrollably, wanting more, desperately wanting to rekindle our dirty love on that night as the hunger was still very much alive and needing to be unleashed, knowing that night was going to leave me restless, lonely, and so very confused.

The weekend was now here and I had been in Wales only a few days, but it felt right, so very right to have been reunited with my gorgeous Charlie.

I hardly slept all night tossing and turning, not only by the haunting dreams of vile images and taunting voices, but by a haunting excitement, as now I yearned once again everything that was Charlie.

Today being Saturday I had a late start so I indulged myself in the luxury of a very late breakfast, suddenly the waiter appeared carrying a small delicate vase containing a single daisy, accompanied by a note which read, *see you at 6.30 and bring an overnight bag*. My face lit up the cosy dining room with such a welcome warmth on that bitterly cold January morning, Charlie had never forgotten how to make me smile but I couldn't help wonder, what was he telling his wife and how would he hide what I hoped would now become an extension of our on/off lifetime love affair? The reality of this was that Dave and Helen may have to encounter this at some point, having to face the backlash of our selfish dirty love or would it be me, yet again that would suffer the recurring consequences of my eternal love for Charlie which would yet again encourage the storm to batter, bruise and jolt me sideways, turning my world upside down, a world in which Charlie and I would undoubtedly have to make life-changing decisions.

CHAPTER 15

Returning to the hotel after a very brief visit to site I hurried to look my best, ready to seduce him and in return to be seduced by him. 6.30 arrived and I was ready, my heart leaping into my mouth and back again as I raced down the stairs to meet Charlie with great excitement and sheer delight. Charlie was waiting outside in an immaculate, very expensive, sleek, and shiny sports car. It looked very impressive and I was sure it held a huge, impressive price tag.

Charlie greeted me with the biggest, most seductive and cocky smile and on that night, as I looked at him I had to look again as I could not believe he was mine once more, that I had been given another chance to have him in my life but knowing full well that it was never going to be easy, as life had already given me a terrifying dress rehearsal.

Having driven for about an hour or so through heavy snow we turned up a deserted little lane. I was stunned into silence as I was greeted by such a cute log cabin, isolated away from the main road, secluded by snow-capped trees, the front door adorned by an old fashioned carriage lamp that glowed almost amber in colour to welcome us. I gasped, *Charlie it's beautiful. I'm pleased with it Lizzy, I built it a few years ago, it's my escape when I need to get away for some peace and quiet where I could do some deep thinking.* He sighed before glancing over, his expression somewhat sad. *I have thought about you endlessly Lizzy.* He then squeezed my hand for reassurance, letting me know our love was forever.

Taking my hand, he opened the tiny but heavy wooden door for me. I was instantly seduced by the charm of this cosy, warm and so very romantic little hideaway, my eyes followed the candles that were scattered all around the room casting a mellow romantic light everywhere. My gaze was then drawn unexpectedly to a rustic tin vase containing daisy's that adorned the large oak table, he really had thought of everything. Locking the door behind us Charlie's eyes were desperate to set my soul on fire and I was never going to object.

Exploring each other's mouths once more in a frenzy, his tongue revolving seductively around my mouth, I could feel him tensing up as I kissed him hard, he moaned. *I've missed you so much princess.* We then stood motionless and still, Charlie's eyes once again drawn to the ring that was hanging delicately from my necklace. I then felt his fingers gently trace the outline of the ring. I stood holding my breath in the hope he might make some comment, but again his words were muted, something I found mysteriously odd, suddenly I remembered one of the initials engraved inside was an H, his wife was called Helen…

Was it hers? Had he bought it for her? Was he dating her during that special Christmas my mother had found the ring? Now with that thought I wanted to rip the ring free from the necklace, shattering all the hope that it was meant for me.

Distracted from my annoyance I felt his fingertips exploring the curves of my tits through the material of my blouse as he moaned with delight, *Lizzy, Lizzy, my beautiful Lizzy.* Suddenly I felt his lips kissing my neck, his breath delicate against my skin, *I love you.* I pulled back from the sensual position that we were embracing, looking at him somewhat bemused, panicked on hearing his much longed for words, my expression clearly asking for an answer. *Yes, I love you Lizzy, I always have.* Now engulfed with a tidal wave of lost love I continued to hear his words echoing around the room, words that emotional, raw and very welcome, knowing his love for me had never been forgotten or lost all these years on.

Brought back to the here and now. *Lizzy I have a present for you, go slip them on.* Wrapped in beautiful soft pink tissue paper was the most sexy, seductive underwear I had ever seen, I hurriedly slipped them on and excitedly walked back into the lounge, complete with my six inch heels and a smile. Charlie looked stunned by my appearance as I was now dressed in only underwear and heels, my long flowing jet black hair completed the seductive look. *Lizzy, you look fucking amazing.* Charlie's eyes were now feasting on every inch of my curvy body, his eyes hungry once again to seduce my body, a body that had always belonged to him.

He pulled me back into his arms kissing me again and again, the love between us was now electric and full of a refuelled fire that was now burning out of control with flames that continued to spark and pop with a new enlivened excitement as I felt his fingertips tracing my spine until he reached the soft lacy top of the silky, soft seductive knickers.

With the champagne flowing we sat together on the sofa, me in my beautiful undies and Charlie in his jeans and shirt. I felt his arm slide around me, kissing my naked shoulder as he gently slipped the strap of my bra down over my upper arm to deliver yet more soft kisses on to my naked skin, stroking my arm gently and softly just like he did all those years ago.

We both looked at each other, about to say something, almost stumbling over our words nervously. *You go first princess. No, you Charlie.* We were normally not lost for any words but tonight words were not necessary as he then led me by the hand to the bedroom. A large wooden bed commanded the centre of the room that was laden with fluffy white blankets and snow soft cushions along with another delightful little fire that sat in the corner of the room, how romantic. Charlie had done all this, making it perfect for me, bringing back some old memories of the past like the cushions and candles that now graced yet another special place lovingly created by Charlie.

His kisses were now hard on my mouth, delivering intense passion to my lips, knowing he was getting aroused as I undid his shirt with my trembling fingers, leaving it open for my pleasure to admire once again, his lean torso begged for my kisses, the Lizzy kisses I knew that he loved. It had been a very long time since we had seduced each other, apart from when I seduced him in my nightly dreams, but tonight I was taking control, Lizzy was back, so I stripped him naked ready for my inspection.

His cock stood rock solid, commanding my undivided attention but tonight I needed no encouragement, my moaning was intense. We were now exploring each other's bodies, his hands caressing my tits, sucking them hard, making my nipples stand to attention. His commanding fingertips outlined my curvy body, allowing my senses to once again relive such sensual moments that we had shared many times before.

He then reached for the ice cold champagne, letting it drizzle delicately down over my nipples before licking and sucking it all away, tracing again with his fingertips the outline of my curvaceous tits as I whispered, *I want you to fuck me Charlie.* He looked at me with those deep brown eyes that just tantalised me, his gaze fixed on mine, allowing again the hunger to explode in both our eyes as he whispered, *Lizzy the party has only just started.*

I was now tensed up like a coiled spring as I begged him to let me be his bitch, his whore, his tart, my words loud and untamed, wanting to be everything and anything he wanted me to be, ready to be his girl in whatever way he wanted, my body his once again.

His body felt firm against mine with his arms and legs now taught with tension as we were once again loving the skin on skin contact, something we still found very sensual and seductive as I continued to inhale Charlie's aroma.

I screamed at him that I wanted rough love tonight as I began digging my nails into the skin on his back with pent up lust. He then held my arms at full stretch, firmly, not allowing me to escape the raging passion that now filled the room, echoing throughout the tiny cabin escaping through the tiny windows, carried on the breeze into the dark and silent forest beyond.

Charlie continued peppering kisses down my body, his kisses now rougher and untamed, reacting to my somewhat out of control needs as his tongue rolled over my naked skin, stopping to revolve around my belly button before continuing to invade the rest of my naked body.

He then rolled me on to my tummy, kissing my back with very seductive long rolling kisses that slipped gently down my spine, again and again I felt his tongue work its way up and down my spine, his tongue was now in free fall, gliding down over my curves, peppering me with rough passionate kisses.

As I turned to face him, once again he held my porcelain face, whispering his love for me repeatedly as the hunger in his eyes had gathered immense pace, drawing me in, taking my body on an epic journey that lasted just seconds.

I then sat on his legs with my fingertips slowly teasing the huge, wet helmet of his cock that was begging for my mouth, tonight to be seduced by my lips. Suddenly I felt his ridged fingers enter my juice drenched pussy that made my pulse race. I closed my eyes to allow myself to get lost in the sensual love that I was receiving from Charlie's fingers, my breath being taken away once again knowing I was being loved by the right man.

With his fingers now wet with my juice he rubbed them gently over my lips and into my mouth, coating my tongue, making sure I received the beautiful taste. He then kissed me hard to share my fresh, warm juice, which we still found so amazing.

He was now in full control as he made his intentions clear, both verbally and now with actions that my body craved, moving down my body, smothering it in champagne drenched kisses until his head was firmly braced between my thighs, allowing his lips to lock firmly onto my clit as I tensed up with pleasure, a pleasure that sent me wild with passion, a passion that I had not felt since I had last slept with Charlie. His tongue was now coated with juice that was escaping freely from my pussy, I felt his tongue flicking my clit with a firmness that sent my body spiralling with desires that were now allowed to be set free.

I straddled him once again, allowing all my craving to be fulfilled, as his stiff cock glided into my pussy for the first time in so many long and lonely years, both of us now feeling the rekindled dirty sex driven love that was ours once again. I begged repeatedly for Charlie to fuck me harder, making sure he was fully aware of my ongoing cravings that now only could be nourished by him.

We were back, lovers with a past, a history, and now with renewed grown-up desire that was never going to disappoint either of us. He then pulled my legs up, letting them relax over his strong arms. God he was so strong. He began to thrust gently, allowing the rhythm to build, becoming so overwhelmingly powerful with both of us ready to explode as my juice clung to the massive cock that now had my full and intense attention.

He rode me hard and at times rough, neither of us ever wanting it to end, thrusting again and again as I screeched delightedly for more while he continued his gaze on my porcelain face, wanting to watch me enjoy the sensual love we were making together and I was never going to deny him that pleasure.

Charlie's moaning was deep and very sexy, *Lizzy, I'm going to love you being my dirty little secret.* Suddenly his juice filled my pussy as my juice continued to cling to his huge, powerful cock. Silence then filled the room as powerful memories had been rekindled, our dirty love now filled us both to the limits as we laid side by side, enjoying the skin on skin contact that left us both totally breathless, totally lost in love once again. There was no need for any other conversation on that night as we fell asleep in each other's arms, we were now cradled in a renewed grown up love.

Waking to a new day that had been born while we were sleeping, bringing with it a beautiful crisp winter sunrise that was visible from every window in the cabin, crisp white frosty shards clinging to every branch on the trees that surrounded us, enriching this beautiful Welsh landscape.

Charlie and I stood at the bedroom window, both of us wrapped in just a big fluffy white blanket, my skin against his, our bodies naked and now as one, his arms now firmly around my waist just gazing at the glorious surroundings, never wanting to move from this wonderful spot, wanting to enjoy it a while longer, selfishly wanting to indulge my senses, rewarding myself in yet more glorious emotions. Suddenly the roar of the storm reared its ugly head. The dark, cold reality reminded me that a very turbulent road lies ahead of us but we would never be able to stop at whatever cost, but that was our love, on one hand it was unpredictable, dark, stormy and mysterious and on the other hand it was passionate, beautiful, natural and very seductive as both continued to take my breath away, leaving me gasping for air.

Charlie then took my hand smiling at me. *You're one beautiful lady Lizzy, I love you, I love you being my everything, just like you always have been.* I blushed at his heart-felt words, squeezing his hand, my gaze once again firmly on his.

We both knew that him calling me his tart, his whore and his bitch was not said to be disrespectful, but said with passionate love and affection, once again a label I was going to love and be proud to wear, along with the label that had been sown in to every piece of my clothes all those years ago.

Charlie made coffee as I collected all my things, packing them back into my bag, now having to leave this adorable love nest. Charlie's hand then brushed against mine. *Princess, leave some things here for next time.* I gasped, *next time Charlie? Yes Lizzy.* He smiled his cocky smile. *You know there will always be a next time.* I nodded in approval that there would be a next time. We really were lovers again and this little cabin unbeknown to me at this moment would become my retreat in the months and maybe even years that were to follow.

Cardiff was now on the horizon, clearly visible with its sprawling outline shrouded in frost on this freezing cold, very early morning, looking so bleak without the warmth of sunlight but it seemed strangely romantic as overnight the bitter winds had blown in again from the east, chilling the landscape that was now covered by a thick unforgiving layer of snow, the first display of early spring flowers were now masked again by winter, shivering to keep warm, but the landscape looked spectacular, making it look like a magical scene straight from a frosted Christmas card.

Charlie then dropped me at the hotel and I rushed to change and get ready for the day ahead, knowing full well I would be distracted all day recalling the events of the night before, at the love we had once again committed to and what a love we still shared, still beautifully passionate, still so natural and so needed by us both, but a love that seemed to always carry endless devastation if the past was anything to go by.

Working on a Sunday was strange for me but at least I was away from Dave's evil clutches, today was a mixture of paperwork and planning, also a time when every time I thought of Charlie I fell in love a little more with the married man that he was, the married man and me, a married woman that now made me his mistress which seduced me enriching my growing, intense and demanding cravings, allowing my mind to wander off to the cute log cabin and how it made me smile on this extremely cold winter's day, but I was committing a betrayal, cheating on my husband when I knew full well that my actions would enrage the ongoing storm that was brewing again far away in the distance, but it was only a matter of time until the storm broke, clouding my world in agonising decision.

Six o'clock came and I was still working, my desk piled high with delivery notes still needing to be filed away, my diary and planner needing updating, all the contractors were leaving now so it gave me a chance to catch up on the ever-growing mountain of paperwork, wondering where to start on the paper mountain as I twiddled somewhat nervously with the ring on my necklace, I had now reminded myself that the storm would cast its dark and unwelcome shadows again.

Suddenly a hard knock at the door made me jump as I was not expecting anyone at this time, with everyone eager to get home on this very cold Sunday January night. *It's open* I called. It was Charlie, his smile still very much his distinct trade mark, infectious, cocky and ready to seduce me again. *You off soon Lizzy? No not yet Charlie.* His eyes once again hungry for my love, begging me to be his tart, his whore, but still the virgin girl he had fallen in love, his eyes dancing with mine eager to please and satisfy my cravings which were now on fire with burning amber flames, both of us seemed uneasy tonight as we battled to find a conversation. The tension remained high between us knowing that all we really wanted to do was to rip each other's clothes of and fuck each other passionately here, right here, right now.

You doing much tonight Charlie? No, no plans, you Lizzy? No nothing. I am just going to have a long hot bath and relax. I glanced over at him to see his reaction, he was looking at me with dirty love in his eyes, something that was clearly on both our minds. *Would you like some company Lizzy?* He then held my hand across the desk, squeezing my fingers while awaiting my response, how could I refuse a long bath and bed with Charlie? I jumped at the chance as we wanted and needed to seize every opportunity we had now our dirty love had been refuelled once again, but this time it was with grown up dirty love, both of us knowing full well the consequences of what our love entailed, both of us willing to risk everything in a bid to have it all to battle again with the storm, I was now on a mission to claim back what was rightfully mine.

For the second night in a row we were together, but my thoughts lead me to Helen once again, she must have wondered where he was and what he was doing surely. I found it hard to imagine her life with Charlie and what life they shared, if she had been my replacement, if she looked like me, so many questions were now entering my head, bombarding me in somewhat negative and unwelcome thoughts as once again I reached for the reassurance from the ring that hung around my neck.

Brought back to the here and now Charlie ran a bath, complete with soft foaming bubbles and as I stepped into the bathroom the candles flickered, delicate rose petals floated on the water in amongst the soft, sweet smelling bubbles that now had cascaded onto the bathroom floor forming soft iridescent piles that made me smile.

Tonight, once again I was needing some serious dirty loving, so abandoning the bath we made ourselves comfortable on my big bed, wrapped up in each other's arms again, remembering the good times and there were so many to recall along with the sad times that we had shared, but now our love and our long separation was being rewarded in full.

Charlie leant over gently stroking my long silky hair, his chocolate brown eyes meeting mine, flirting once again with each other, never wanting to be distracted from each other's gaze as we both boarded the same roller-coaster journey once again in a bid to be together as the future now was hurtling towards us, both of us capturing a snap shot of the future, but it was once again shrouded in a grey mist and ghostly shadows that for me contained some familiar images and haunting voices, some that I had never encountered before standing back taking their place in the queue ready to haunt my life and my nightly dreams, voices that echoed from afar.

And now there were new voices, so loud they left my body shuddering, voices that were not familiar, voices that I had never encountered until tonight knowing the minute I closed my eyes those images and terrifying voice would leave me to wake drenched in vile pools of fluid.

Lizzy I can't stay tonight you do understand don't you. Yes of course I do Charlie. We snuggled down again, lost in our moment until he had to leave to return to the arms of his pregnant wife. We must have fallen asleep briefly, content to be in each other's company. *Lizzy it's midnight I have to go.* His phone was now constantly ringing, I guessed from his expression that it was his wife, I did not ask, and he did not attempt to tell me.

His kisses peppered my porcelain face as we said goodnight, his smile still so warm and inviting. *Lizzy I still can't believe your here with me it's wonderful.* He held my porcelain face cupped in both of his hands for all the reassurance that I needed, kissing me once again as we struggled to say a final goodnight.

It was Monday before I knew it and I had meetings planned most of the day. Charlie popped in to the office to say hello, he was eager to know what I was doing at the weekend, reluctantly I answered him. *I'm off home on Friday evening why? I just wondered Lizzy.* His expression now muted by my words, what Charlie, have dinner with me tomorrow tonight? I smiled at him, the answer so clear to see by my expression. *That sounds lovely Charlie.* Seven o'clock and as always punctual Charlie was waiting outside for me in his expensive sports car dressed to thrill. He opened the car door for me, touching my hand, grasping my wrist, and pulling me into his arms. *Lizzy you look stunning, so bloody stunning and still so fucking adorable.* He rewarded me not only with his comments, but with those endless cocky smiles.

Now having arrived at the very posh restaurant we were seated and comfortable, both of us remained stunned and overwhelmed by the enormity of our love that was still so fresh and now refuelled again. *Charlie, you wanted to ask me something earlier, what was it? I wondered if you fancied a weekend away with me something special? I can't this weekend Charlie, I'm so sorry.* I lowered my head at my disappointment, Charlie touched my hand for reassurance. *Well what about next weekend? Please Lizzy, a whole weekend together princess, you and me, away from everyone with no phones, no work. Alone, just us, a romantic weekend to relax and unwind together.* It sounded so delightful so how could I refuse?

Charlie then leant over the table and whispered; *I love you Lizzy.* I smiled back as tears now welled up in my eyes, the feeling of overwhelming sadness had now entered my body, sadness knowing that I would never totally be Charlie's as I would always have to share him with Helen. Charlie's hand now once again on mine as I tried desperately to hold back my lonely tears. Charlie questioned my home life, I hesitated, looking away, chocking back the tears I so needed to shed. He looked at me with a questioning expression. *You're not happy at home then?* I hesitated again as I did not want to reveal my unhappy life of being Dave's wife who did what she was told, obeying his constant commands as it seemed like I was a failure allowing Dave to trample all over me.

Lizzy, talk to me. My hesitation obviously worried him. *No not really Charlie, my marriage is, well it's not and I hate it.* It was the first time he had asked, Charlie's face now pained by my comments. *Lizzy, my darling Lizzy. I'm fine Charlie.* I hid my growing distress and hatred of Dave behind my fake smile and heavily painted face but now it seemed like my fake smile was starting to crack, more than ever I was now unsure if I could continue living in yesterday's shadows, just where Dave wanted me to be, as again my hand instantly sought the reassuring comfort from the ring that still remained a mystery.

My mind once again led me to think about his wife. Where did she think he was and with who? So many things that just did not add up… the cabin, his very expensive sports car, his expensive clothes. He seemed to have lots of money. The nights away, evenings out and now a weekend away, maybe it was not my business to know his private life, a life that I would never be fully a part of, knowing he still led a life that was dark, mysterious and fuelled with a reputation that he was never going to escape from, but it continued seducing my body by day, walking silently by my side and at night when darkness fell, Charlie's reputation would haunt my dreams, riding my soul, seducing my vulnerable emotions and kissing my heavily tattooed scarred skin, leaving me gasping for air.

I began to think back to all those years ago, not knowing why the reputation that surrounded him existed. Maybe it was easier to ignore, storing it away, not wanting to know, but once again I questioned myself about his mysterious reputation that now was without doubt a secret that I would never be allowed to know.

But where did his wife fit in to the secret life that Charlie was so obviously living? Did she not know or even care? The mystery deepened and would undoubtedly continue to challenge my thinking over the coming weeks, months and into the future, questions that would challenge both of us, testing our love to the bitter end in a bid to have it all.

The week dragged on, not having seen much of Charlie since Tuesday night and it was now Friday morning, I was on site early, as I had lots of things to clear up before I went home for the weekend, using the word home loosely, I had not been in the office very long before Charlie appeared, wearing his hard hat which I found so very sexy, Lizzy what time you off home, about 6 Charlie why, do you fancy having lunch with me, I nodded eagerly yes Charlie, we can eat here in my office, he smiled and as he walked out of the door I smiled back at him, waving my finger at him attracting his attention, oh and wear your hard hat, he smiled back with that cocky smile that made me blush, as he knew full well it was not only going to be just lunch.

Midday had arrived and on the dot, Charlie was stood in the doorway complete with the lunch he said he would deliver, lunch that had been lovingly prepared by the little cafe around the corner from the build, complete with a single Daisy that lay proud and delicate on top of the cardboard box that contained our lunch.

He looked so sexy in his white hard hat, I then excitedly gave him the keys to lock the door, Charlie then kicked the door closed, as I then heard the key turn in the lock which sent a cold, but loving shiver through me in anticipation for some special dirty Friday lunch time love.

I had put a note on the door saying out for a long lunch, underlining the long lunch, along with a message written in dark ink, as I did not want to be disturbed on this freezing cold January afternoon, so with my phone now off, door locked, peace and quiet now ruled my office complete with Charlie and his very sexy hard hat.

Lunch was delicious and sadly over, having dragged it out for as long as I could. Charlie was now sat in my leather chair looking at me with those eyes I loved that seemed to take me once again on a journey. *Come here Lizzy.* Clutching at my hand. *Princess your stunning, still so very fucking stunning.* With that he kissed me gently, stroking and caressing my long flowing jet black hair, his fingertips then traced repeatedly the pattern on the ring once more that hung around my neck on the fine gold chain, but he still made no comment and once again I was stunned by his silence, his reluctance to even acknowledge something that he once wore on his finger.

I stood up ready to take command, but Charlie had other ideas, he was taking full control, we were alone without any distractions, his hands now making their way inside my delicate cream silk blouse gliding around my huge tits, exploring with his fingertips that made my nipples stand to attention before undoing every petit silk covered button on my blouse, letting it drop to the floor to reveal the beautiful underwear that he had bought me. *Lizzy you look amazing, let me look at you.* His hungry eyes now feasting on my huge tits, pulling me into his arms I felt his fingers gliding down the contour of my spine before meeting with the zip on my skin tight skirt that fell away with ease to the floor along with my blouse. I could feel is eyes exploring my body, gently outlining my silhouette just like he always did, allowing his eyes to cast their gaze over my curvy body and back again to dance with my eyes that were now gleaming and sparkling with renewed vitality.

I tugged excitedly at his t-shirt, pulling it over his head, dropping it on top of my clothes that had now been discarded, laid untidily on my office floor. I undid his jeans, he was of course commando today, a look he knew I loved, we stood in my office admiring each other's body's, transfixed, now lost in the beautiful moment that we had created here in my office on this cold Friday lunchtime, hidden away from the outside world, allowing me to escape the torture that awaited me at home, a distraction that was so seductively naughty.

As he sat in my leather chair once again in just his hard hat, completely naked, he pulled me towards him allowing me to straddle over him, intent on seduction as our lips met, allowing our tongues to dance together the dance of love, a ritual that was made by us way back, all those years ago, and now today for us both to embrace.

I allowed my hips to gyrate slowly as I held the back of the chair with Charlie holding my hips firmly, going with the passionate motion that allowed us both to moan with pure delight, his cock was now penetrating and loving my demanding pussy. *Ride me you beautiful bitch, ride me,* Charlie moaned repeatedly, but I needed no encouragement.

Both of us were now moaning to the rhythm of our love making. As our passion grew, my office was alive with the sound of sexual moaning, untamed groaning and a frenzy of passion that was out of control from both of us, rippling from the four walls that blanketed us from the outside world.

He was now playing frantically with my nipples, almost pinching them but I loved it, my nipples now felt like they were burning from the roughness of Charlie's fingers, making sure I never received cold tepid or lukewarm love, it was always a love that burnt and set my sole on fire.

Holding my hips again we were loving it, loving the sheer pleasure of being together, fully fuelled with dirty, out-of-control love, right here in my office, both of us married, both of us unable to stop this love affair that started all those years ago that had now become our dirty secret once again and I loved it, I loved the secrecy, the seduction and the excitement that was always made possible by Charlie.

Come on Lizzy, you dirty bitch, you dirty whore, fuck me! So with a few more very penetrating thrusts our juices met, our kisses were now frantic with desire as Charlie moaned, *I want to fuck you again Lizzy*. I had no intention of making him stop, wanting all the dirty love I could take from him daily, so with that we moved to my desk in a dirty frenzy, the neat pile of paperwork now scattered, discarded on to the office floor in one huge sweeping movement, but I didn't care, I was in control, it was my office, my dirty love making, my dirty, horny little secret.

I laid on my desk, my legs now draped lovingly around Charlie's neck, both of us completely naked and fully aroused as he was about to fuck me again. Charlie's moaning was very loud as he slowly allowed his cock to go all the way, I could feel his full balls brushing against my very wet juice filled pussy, he thrust so hard allowing both of us to climax again as he continued working his juice around my pussy for maximum effect.

My gaze, now fixed on Charlie's rugged face. *Make love to me forever, say you will Charlie*, I moaned. He was now silent and seemed somewhat stunned by my words as I waited for him to return the words I craved to hear him say, wishing now I had not said anything in the moment of pure dirty love driven passion.

His cock now relaxed from my ever demanding pussy, he lowered his head forcing with ease his tongue deep inside my pussy as I clenched his head between my thighs wanting more as his tongue revolved over my clit that again today begged for more.

168

Relaxed again and in each other's arms, now holding each other's naked, love soaked bodies, we composed our breathing, taking in the full beauty of our dirty love that had ridden the twelve-year very-turbulent storm to bring us together once more. Charlie smiled. *Oh Lizzy, before I forget the answer to your question.* He hesitated again as I waited patiently for his answer. *Yes Lizzy, forever.* His cocky smile now told me just how much he meant his words, his smile the only endorsement I needed.

Loving at lunchtime was now over sadly, and it was time to get back to work after enjoying an extremely delicious lunch that has lasted for well over two hours, but I was still hungry for more. Charlie went back to site as if it were all normal, his smile was incredible as he left my office after having some much needed dirty afternoon delights while I dressed and composed myself before reinstating my neat pile of paperwork.

Nearing the station with my stomach in knots, tears were now spilling onto my skin as my vision became blurred once again, but I was supposed to be the strong, independent, and now the powerful woman with a job that commanded respect which I got from everyone involved at the build, but I was still the fragile Lizzy with seams that were unravelling daily as the past would keep pulling any visible thread, leaving my body tattered, torn, and worn.

Stood on the station platform which tonight was so cold, uninviting and dimly lit, Charlie was desperately holding on to my hand, not wanting me to board the train, showering me in kisses that I didn't want to leave for him to share with Helen this weekend and at that moment the ring on my necklace became my reassurance as I twiddled with it franticly, my distress was now clear to see. I boarded the train that was now ready to leave. *See you on Sunday Lizzy and never forget I love you.* We blew millions of loving kisses, leaving our silhouettes to fade into the cold darkness of the evening.

The weekend at home was much the same, but I was kept busy by seeing family and visiting friends, everyone wanting to know about my new and exciting job, everyone except Dave that was as he was more concerned about not having an ironed shirt to wear to the pub or his dinner prepared for him.

CHAPTER 16

As I glanced across the open landscape the woods looked so beautifully stunning dressed in its winter coat that sparkled in the watery sunshine with snow still carpeting the fields that surrounded us, a glorious picture that never failed to delight me. I also walked around the garden taking in the glorious colours of winter, the holly with its deep green leaves complimenting the fire red berries and mistletoe that still hung low in the trees far in the distance ready for secret kisses, all now coated in a dusting of snow.

Dave was drunk most of the weekend, enjoying his time with his drunken loud mouthed mates, commanding orders that I was too afraid to dismiss, so I jumped to his demands rather than cause more arguments, but my mind drifted to Wales every so often over the weekend which made me smile, feeling the burn from the fire of dirty love that Charlie and I had once again had reignited.

Sunday afternoon was here at long last, and my bags were packed again, thrilled to be going back to Cardiff ready for another two glorious weeks away, but thoughts of Charlie and his wife just kept entering my mind, wondering if they had been intimate, sharing what was always rightfully mine, but I had no rights, I was just his tart, his whore, his dirty little secret and now his mistress, needing reassurance I reached for my beloved ring.

I was so desperate to hear his voice so I rang Charlie excitedly just to let him know I was on my way as I could not wait to see him again, sadly there was no reply which worried me and when he didn't bother to return my calls the ring on my necklace became once again my reassurance, but today I wanted much more than anything the ring could give me.

It seemed colder than ever as snow had fallen hard again across Wales over the weekend with a change from the easterly winds to the northerly wind that felt bitterly cold against my skin as I shivered the whole way back to Cardiff, the carriage of the train free from heating. I sat on my hands to stop them from freezing, winter really had taken a severe grip on the landscape as a bitter blast of wind and snow had swept silently across Wales, leaving it shivering under a fluffy blanket of fresh ice white snow. Arriving at the station I could not see Charlie so I rang him again, still no reply. I was now becoming very worried, knowing there had to be a good reason why he was not waiting for me as he had promised, but promises could be broken in the blink of an eye as I would find out to my cost in the coming weeks and months that were ahead.

As I looked out of the taxi window snow now covered every pavement in every street, houses topped with a sprinkling of snow just like icing on a cake. The blanket of snow had left everything in its path shivering silently, desperately waiting patiently for spring to arrive, but it made everything look so mystical, enticingly beautiful.

Back at the hotel I unpacked, wondering why Charlie had let me down, but I should have not been that surprised as it was not the first time and I knew deep down it would not be the last, as once again the old Charlie with his rouge and cocky ways along with his reputation were now invading my memory, reminding me he was still a bad-boy, a boy I should never have exchanged glances with all those years ago.

I rang again as I told myself that this would be his final chance to answer my calls. *Hello Charlie Stevens, Charlie it's me Lizzy*, I snapped. I heard him gasp, taking a sharp intake of breath. *Shit Lizzy, sorry, I'm so sorry Lizzy*. He sounded very preoccupied, something I had witnessed many times before, but now my mind was in overdrive. Did he not want me in his life? Was he bored of me already? Was I just a pleasurable distraction for a few days away from his life with Helen?

It's Helen, she's in hospital, we lost our baby yesterday. I gasped at his heart-breaking news. *Charlie I am so sorry*. I instantly felt their grief, a cold silence now filled the air between us as I heard Charlie trying to compose himself. *I Love you Lizzy, promise me you will never forget it*. Holding back my tears I promised him his love would never be forgotten, it never had and never would.

The phone then went silent, leaving me to relive my own miscarriage, my own agony. He must be heart-broken, they must be totally devastated. I knew exactly what they were going through but he could never know. I knew the hurt and loss they were both feeling once again at this present time as it was still all to vivid in my memory, it always would be, the raw, terrifying pain that I was sure would cripple them both.

I tried to sleep but I tossed and turned all night, I just kept thinking of them, all the bitter emotions and sadness they must have been feeling as I recalled again my own devastating loss that would forever leave me feeling cheated.

I woke early, unable to evade the menacing and haunting voice along with a procession of lingering, vile faces that I wanted to ignore, tonight like every night, images that never allowed me to comfort my own baby's muffled cries, Charlie's vile father as always the first image I saw, followed closely by Dave, Paul and then Roger... none of them welcome in my world day or night.

The sun hadn't even started to rise over Wales as I stood staring out at the darkness of the city with just a sprinkling of lights for company, taking my thoughts away from the harrowing dark cloud that was hanging over Charlie and Helen.

My walk to the build this morning was certainly a cold one, so hot strong coffee was ordered as I sorted through the ongoing mountain of paperwork. I got started on the planner, my head splitting as once again I had boarded the roller-coaster, taking me on a journey of emotions from sadness, right through to happiness, a journey that was now out of control. It was hard to sort out which emotion was the most frightening as the past few years flashed before my eyes, dreams sparked a multi-coloured kaleidoscope taking me from a little girl that had made dreams in the tree house that I thought were going to form my future, but alas the future was so uncertain.

I was now stood in this lonely office, my hands wrapped around the hot mug of coffee for some warmth. The office was silent from voices as I continued to listen to negative echoes that invaded my mind from every direction, maybe I should have never dialled the number from the advert in the local paper, maybe I should not have returned to Wales. So many maybes, so many things now praying on my thoughts and all of them involved Charlie once again.

Brought back to reality and it was 8am already. The contractors were all arriving on site in and out of the office, all I wanted was some peace and quiet today but I was not going to be allowed that privilege as deliveries were due which meant a huge amount of paperwork to add to what was already a paper mountain, it was now toppling under the strain.

Charlie rang, we managed a little light chat but I knew and could tell from his voice that he was hurting and once again I was helpless to help him, helpless to allow him my very own experience, but I was not going to allow myself to cry for them.

Princess I love you, he mumbled and with that we both said a tearful goodbye and then he was gone, leaving me with my very own painful memories to dwell on while twiddling once again with the mysterious ring tracing the raised pattern that was so delicate.

I sat watching the minutes tick by on the clock that was hung on the office wall, the ticking seemed so loud as it echoed throughout my office which was now silent from the frenzy of the daily activity, willing 6pm to be here, wanting to escape these four walls for the sanctuary of my hotel bedroom which tonight would remain cold and again without love.

A warm bath and my bed were calling me as I needed to get a good night's sleep after having had a very draining day mentally. I was desperate to take the torture away, even if only for a while and how I wished I could be stood in my old bedroom looking out of my window that would transport me back to a time when I was free from torment, free from so many emotions to a time when everything was so beautiful and new.

Tuesday morning was here before I knew it, a night that left my body drained, leaving me to sleep in a pool of vile images while having to listen to the distant cries of my baby, a harrowing sound that left me limp, just like a rag doll.

I had meetings booked most of the day and I had not heard from Charlie, I did not want to call him as I knew things were difficult, but it did not stop me from thinking about him constantly, knowing how they were grieving and how much it would be hurting them, draining them of emotions and the devastation it would have on their lives.

As the day wore on I felt tired and stressed. I went back to the hotel wanting a long hot bath, soft music, a glass of wine and above all, peace and quiet, away from the constant questions from the builders and tradesmen that seemed to still echo in my head, long after I had locked the office door behind me.

I picked up my key from reception and headed to my room which was now my sanctuary. I knew as the weeks went by these four walls would be hard at times to cope with and tonight was one of them. As I shut the door behind me I felt the walls closing in on me as the pressure was now so heavy to comprehend.

I ran myself a bath, desperate to soak away the day as my soft chanting music played and the wine was consumed. Well, it was almost perfect, all I needed was the comforting arms of Charlie, then my world would be complete. I now needed nothing more, I never had.

The evening wore on and I was alone, snuggled up on the bed, wrapped in clean white laundered sheets watching junk on the television for company while eating my cold takeaway, but I didn't care, I was away from Dave and my lifeless, loveless marriage. However, I was terrified that I had fallen so easily back into Charlie's arms, falling totally in love with him again, knowing he was married, knowing full well he was still wearing the label that he had carried all his life with the mysterious reputation that still surrounded him all these years on.

I laid in the darkness of this sterile room, the silence was deafening as I thought about Charlie and his wife. I really felt for her, knowing I had been sleeping with her husband which made me feel uncomfortable, knowing that I had overnight become Charlie's mistress, his tart, his whore, but once again I selfishly didn't care, instantly hating myself for thinking that, but he was mine, he always had been and again I grabbed the ring that was still hanging patiently from the chain around my neck in a bid for some comfort which was now becoming my best friend as I demanded answers from the ring that I knew would never be granted unless Charlie was willing to let me walk in his dark shadow.

I must have fallen asleep as I awoke about midnight, blurry eyed, remembering that I had to be on site for 6am so I brushed my teeth and climbed back into my lonely bed, setting the alarm for an eye-watering 5am, wanting the world to stop revolving for a while so that I could have a little peace from the roller-coaster I had once again just boarded, jolting me sideways, spinning me around, turning me upside down, leaving me breathless as I continued to question every day my ongoing dirty love for Charlie.

I managed to get myself ready and in on time, it felt like I had not slept at all, having relived Charlie's and Helen's heartache, visiting again my own nightmare that still remained so vivid in my mind from my own miscarriage that never failed to haunt my life daily and invading my nightly dreams with harrowing cries of a baby that remained out of my reach.

The contractors were due in today for a briefing so I needed to be alert and looking my very best, so I dressed in my black suit, high heels, and crisp white shirt. I looked good, even if I said so myself, my confidence was back with my zest for love and life. I waited for them all to arrive while writing my notes, going over my brief making to be sure it was all correct and that everyone knew what was expected of them.

One by one, in they came. *Morning, morning, morning Lizzy.* I was still so busy sat writing more notes that I did not see Charlie walk into my office, but as I looked up from my brief I was greeted by his huge seductive smile, a smile that yet again radiated throughout my office, a smile that was for my eyes only. *Morning Lizzy. Morning Charlie.* We could not take our eyes off each other. I glanced over, his gaze fully on my thighs, my skirt having ridden up. I blushed uncontrollably, my face burning with desire, you could feel the wanting and the need between us, feeling it bounce from every wall in the office which must of been so easy to see by everyone in the room as it was now impossible to hide our dirty love, but today I knew he possibly just needed a shoulder to lean on, complete with a loving hug to express his feelings without interruption, without questions.

His eyes today were the most beautiful dark chocolate brown, god he was so very good looking, so very handsome, and still he managed to attract lots of female attention which on this day left me fragile so once again I reached for the comfort of my necklace, outlining with my fingertips, seducing the delicate pattern on the ring.

The briefing started, I could feel his hungry eyes on me while I delivered my brief and every time I looked up from my notes he was giving me that famous trademark cocky smile that just added to my constant blushing, now so obvious to everyone in the room as I fought to hide my blushes, hurrying through my brief to avoid any further embarrassment to myself.

I felt hot, flustered, frustrated and he knew how I was feeling as his cocky smile told me so. He really did know me so well, knowing what made me blush, what made me cry, even my favourite foods, the list was endless but I still keep huge secrets from him, secrets that would be devastating if he ever knew.

Breaking from the brief for coffee, relieved that my part of the brief was over and everyone seemed to know what I was expecting of them, Charlie and I managed to speak for a while and I knew all too well what he was feeling, but he remained hungry, wanting my attention, and wanting my love.

He held my hand discreetly as he whispered his love for me, asking for another night away from the everyday stress and pain. I nodded eagerly to grant his wishes, but I knew it was wrong, but he needed me, we both knew we could depend on each other for the solitude we both needed, replacing what neither of us had found in the last few years of our lives.

Charlie as promised was waiting for me, leaning against his car. We kissed our hellos over and over again, not daring our lips to be parted from these most delightful intense kisses that were being delivered and received. Charlie's tongue was now seducing my mouth, leaving my lips once again craving his love as I felt the fire again tarnish and burn my lips.

You look stunning Lizzy. He held my hands outstretched in a bid to feast his eyes once again over my curvy body. I was wearing tight figure hugging jeans, a crisp white shirt and soft leather jacket, completely commando from underwear, all for Charlie's pleasure.

As we drove into the countryside we talked, but only small talk, skirting around the sadness that was so obvious as once again I twiddled nervously with the ring on the necklace, again wondering about the mystery that surrounded it and if I would ever know its true and rightful owner.

We sat and talked over a drink, holding each other's hands. Charlie seemed distracted by any conversation tonight and rightfully so, so I changed the subject, not wanting to dwell on his pain that was clearly visible and I was unsure what to say or do to ease the apparent grief he was feeling. Back at the hotel we talked, still sat in Charlie's car. I took a deep breath. *Charlie, why don't you come in for a coffee?* Being selfish I wanted his attention a little longer, wanting to just feel his love a while longer, wanting his company for as long as I could.

Taking our coffee Charlie and I laid on my bed as we so often did, we just laid there in total silence, but tonight we seemed to accept our silence, it was almost like Charlie needed time out from the constant questions to allow him some peace, if only for a while, knowing his thoughts would be shrouded in pain. Once again my thoughts lead me to Helen, her sadness must be terrifying. I felt for her, knowing full well what she was going through, but why wasn't Charlie at home comforting her, sharing their grief together? This was something else that puzzled me, along with everything else that still did not make any sense.

More kisses and more cuddles followed until it was time for Charlie to go back to his wife and to the sadness that surrounded them both, the heart-breaking sadness that filled their world right now.

Awoken to the new day by the sound of the alarm which interrupted the most powerful dream and the most perfect sleep, a sleep that for once had not been interrupted by haunting visions and vile words that had become my frequent visitors.

Arriving on site the build was buzzing with contractors, full of bloke jokes along with endless invitations for dates that I instantly rejected, hysterical laughing, the odd whistles and the jokes that were far from clean at the best of times. Suddenly I could see Charlie heading towards my office, his face still pained by grief and emotional loss. *I was just coming to see you Lizzy.* He held my hand, looking at me with those come-to-bed eyes, hungry for my gaze while his body remained hungry for my love.

I squeezed his hand for reassurance while he poured his heart out, knowing they were hard words for him to deal with, but as hard as it was he was right and time would be a great healer, but the loss something they would never forget, I could sympathise with that, knowing exactly what he was going through, but more so what Helen was feeling and how terrifying it must be for her, but I still questioned silently to myself why was Charlie not at home with her, to comfort her needs, to be sharing their tragic loss together.

Let's have that weekend away soon Lizzy. I looked at him, I questioned him. *Is that OK with you Charlie? Yes, I want something special for you Lizzy, so very special for my girl.* He touched my silky hair, pulling it away gently from my porcelain face before peppering sweet kisses onto my neck and as he did I felt him kiss the ring that hung on the chain around my neck for safe keeping. I remained still, not reacting to his sudden kisses and he once again remained silent, but why? I remained totally baffled by his actions and his inability to comment.

The next few weeks merged into one and was pretty much mundane as I waited patiently for Charlie to whisk me away for some serious dirty love, needing my slice of Charlie that had been lacking for a few weeks. I understood why, but I was starving for his love, his dirty love, craving his dirty, untamed love, I was ravenous.

Friday was here and I was travelling home that weekend which filled me with absolute terrifying sadness, knowing I would have to face a weekend of verbal abuse, cold, vile, and unwelcome comments, but not before Charlie and I had spent a much needed night together.

I would catch the early train on Saturday morning, allowing us to have a few hours of us time, to experience a renewed, much more grown up love affair which had become more intense, more passionate than before, but now came with the added heartache and a hefty lifetime price tag which once again terrified me. Both of us were so very guilty, but we had a history, a past and a spark that was never allowed to fade and a passion that would forever over ride our guilt.

I still had that niggle at the back of my mind about Charlie's wife, did she wonder where he was? Who he was with? Did she not care, or did they not get on? Now with only a few weeks since the loss of their baby and he was with me, loving me, giving me all his dirty love.

My mind was now totally baffled by Charlie's mysterious, secret and very private life, but it was none of my business and possibly it never would be as it had been a mystery from the moment my eyes met his, on that wonderful and unexpected early September morning. His labelled life still seduced me, still that bad-boy intrigued me and would do for the next twelve hours, twelve hours of us, just the perfect time before it would be time to say yet another goodbye but not before we had checked into the beautiful, charming little log cabin deep in the Welsh hillside, a perfect retreat that now was transformed into our very own winter wonderland with trees laden in snow, frosty shards hanging precariously from the branches, virgin snow drifts that were just begging to be jumped in. Once again I was captivated by its charm, by its surroundings, standing ankle deep in snow just soaking in the glorious gift that just kept giving.

As I stepped through the door the warmth once again greeted me, this little cabin delighted my senses, taking me on a journey, one of a mystical, enchanted winter tale with every page now laced with a captivating charm all of its own. The warmth created by the tiny fire that filled this cosy cabin with a wonderful aroma, seductive and powerful, sent my senses into free-fall. Hearing the crackle and pop as it sent amber shards of sparks onto the hearth, the ambient light now being bounced from wall to wall. On the bed was a wicker picnic hamper full of lovely food, complete with a picnic rug. I gasped wanting to cry, this was so like Charlie, always wanting to please me, always wanting the best for me.

Daisy's adorned the large old oak table in the old rustic tin vase that had to my delight a winter snow scene painted on it that once again captured my gaze. It was so beautiful I lost myself in the somewhat rustic painted snow scene as it reminded me of when I was a child when the winters went on forever, snowing heavily from late November until March, even longer sometimes if we were lucky.

Now the candle light filtered throughout the log cabin, candlelight bounced from every wall in every room, it was so beautiful, making a very calming atmosphere that allowed us to relax and to have our time. The champagne was opened and now poured, the candle light flickered in every room, making a beautiful ambiance as at last we were alone with our personal problems tucked away in the background, but only for now as they could never be forgotten, mine as they constantly tormented me and Charlie's as they were so precious and still so very raw.

Charlie then led me into the bedroom holding my hand, his eyes hungry for my love. He kicked the door closed behind us, his body now firm against mine as he held me hostage against the heavy oak door, kissing me with wild passionate kisses, long awaited kisses, allowing his tongue to revolve around my mouth, rolling his kisses onto my neck then back to my mouth in a frenzy of longing to love me as dirty passion filled the air tonight, my body wanting everything Charlie could give me, wanting him to take what was rightfully his, knowing again that I was being loved by the right man, the man who knew exactly how to love me.

Having moved to the bed we laid drinking champagne, both of us half naked from our passionate outburst, our clothes scattered unruly over the floor where they fell. Now relaxing, Charlie stroked my flowing silky hair as he so often did, he then squeezed my hand in recognition of our continuing love as he smiled his cocky, trademark smile that always managed to make me blush, just like the schoolgirl he fell in love with.

His seduction was so powerful tonight as his fingers caressed my body, fingers that danced their way over my silky shoulders before tantalising my most intimate curves that just needed to be embraced tonight and every night. Suddenly I felt his kisses strong against the skin on my neck, his kisses then moved to the ring on the chain, his tongue caressing the ring before returning to kiss my neck, firm, seductive kisses that left me wanting more.

His arms now firmly gripped around my delicate frame, holding me like a fragile piece of glass, the fragile piece of splintered glass I had become at the hands of the men who had crossed my path, only wanting to abuse my body for their own selfish pleasures, to abuse me in a way that was evil, vile and without justification, but maybe that was my fault to allow them to treat me in that way.

CHAPTER 17

Suddenly we were both jolted away from our passionate embrace by my phone ringing loudly. Annoyed with myself, thinking I had switched it off, knowing I wanted complete relaxation away from work and the outside world tonight, a world that seemed determined to invade my precious time with Charlie. I hesitated to answer it, hoping they had the wrong number, Charlie then suggested I should.

Hello! I snapped, the annoyance clearly reflected in my voice, my annoyance at being so rudely interrupted on a night that was so precious, a night that we had snatched away from the ongoing misery and pain that surrounded our lives on a daily basis.

I did not recognise the demure, very soft spoken ladies voice. *Lizzy is that you? Yes it's Lizzy*, I grumbled. *Lizzy, it's staff nurse brown.* I blurted out, *staff nurse brown from St James hospital?* Now with my mind completely muddled and confused, I replied abruptly. *Can I help?, Lizzy it's your mum... Mum what?* I screamed.

I'm so sorry Lizzy, her hesitance now scared me, afraid as to where the conversation was leading. *Lizzy.* I held my breath. *Lizzy your mother died an hour ago, your father needs you.* Charlie was now sensing that it was bad news, his face white with concern as he held my violently shaking hand. I dropped the phone onto the bed, not wanting to hear anymore. *What is it Lizzy? Lizzy your scaring me.* I slumped onto the bed in a quivering heap, grasping at the necklace, scrabbling to find comfort from the ring that tonight I knew felt my grief. The cabin suddenly fell silent as a cold unwelcome chill descended around us, the cabin now shuddering with the pain that I was now feeling, a pain so terrifying it left me motionless.

I screamed out ... *It's mum!* I stood up, frozen in time, my body although frozen felt limp like my life was being drained away from me. *Lizzy, I'm so sorry princess.* Charlie held me close, propping up my lifeless and limp body as I sobbed into his chest.

The nurse was still on the other end of the phone… *Are you still there Lizzy?* Reluctantly I picked up the phone again, bitter tears now streamed down my porcelain face that were stinging the already open deep scars on my fragile skin, scars that still remained visible to me, my voice low and trembling, my mum, my beautiful mum. *Lizzy can you get home? Your needed.* My voice was now silenced by the devastating news I had just received, words that were now chocking me.

I have to go home Charlie, dad needs me. I slumped on the bed once again, sobbing uncontrollably, wanting answers, so many questions echoing through my head, nothing at this petrifying moment made any sense. Charlie held my shaking hand throughout, allowing me to express my feelings of this sudden devastating news. *Princess, I will drive you tonight, I will take you home. No Charlie, I can't expect you to do that. Lizzy, you can't go alone, I won't let you.*

What do you need to do princess? I sobbed uncontrollably. *I don't know, I don't know Charlie.* My screams were now echoing from room to room, ricocheting of every wall with nowhere to hide, my lonely cries dissolving within the cosy cabin that now felt icily cold, the candle light was now grey in its colour as the flames flickered low. Suddenly shadows appeared in front of me, shadows of mum were now everywhere I looked, shadows that were spinning me around uncontrollably, suddenly her shadows were replaced by a thick descending fog that slithered down the walls and the windows, not allowing me to see out as grief now ruled my body.

My head and heart were destroyed by the tragic news that had been delivered on this icily cold winter night, but Charlie took complete control as he packed up my things. He then held me close until I was ready to make the long terrifying journey home.

Taking a deep breath and finding some strength from somewhere, Charlie drove me to the hotel in complete silence, both of us not knowing what to say. I was completely confused, my emotions blown apart, my fragile state now so visible to Charlie, my vulnerability now on show. Charlie packed everything he thought I would need while back at home. *Princess, give me your office keys, I will take care of things.*

I had not given the site and build a thought, but then why should I? I had been once again hit with the most tragic news, my life once again in meltdown on receiving yet more devastating news. How much more could my fragile body take? How much more would I have to endure to have a life that was normal and the life I craved?

Life seemed so very cruel that night. Twisting its knife a little more, hearing the roar of the storm that once again petrified me as it always had, but this was the final impact, my darling mum taken away from me. Suddenly I thought of dad, my poor dad, it was heart-breaking to imagine what his life would be like without mum to prop him up.

We were now almost home having driven through heavy snow, blizzards, and thick ice that had been scattered on every road in our path and now as we neared the village the realisation was so hard to digest, just what impact mum's sudden death would have on not only me, but the extended family, my dad, my aunts, my sister and of course everyone else that loved her.

Crying once again into my cupped hands, tears that had turned into frozen droplets, shattering on impact as they hit my terrified frozen palms, little splinters that dissolved into thousands of puddles all of them with my mum's name on.

How would I cope without mum? I didn't dare think, mum was the family's rock, the person who kept everyone together, there would now be no one to replace her as no one ever could, she always had a calming influence on most every situation and was without doubt an inspiration to everyone that was lucky enough to know her.

Charlie would be my only support now, apart from dad, I knew that, but with Charlie back in Wales and me back home it would be hard, but I had to face it alone, to walk the path of grief again and to find a strength from somewhere, knowing that my strength would be Charlie's love.

Home was now in sight, and I felt sick, my heart heavy with grief as I nervously twiddled again with the necklace, seeking some sort of comfort, but tonight the ring was icily cold from comfort and any reassurance. Charlie stopped the car and leant over to give me some much needed loving kisses, wrapping his arms around me in a desperate bid to take away my agony. *Lizzy, would you like me to drive around for a little bit or would you like me to stay? No Charlie, I have to face it alone and Helen needs you…* He nodded knowing full well we were both hiding our grief and guilt for now behind our love. He kissed away the tears that had blurred my vision for the entire journey home that had now left watery stains on my clothes, but sadly he could not kiss away the pain and grief that I was feeling as yet another piece of my heart had been destroyed tonight in the blink of an eye.

We kissed goodnight as he held me tight whispering his undying love for me. *Lizzy, never forget I love you princess, you're my girl, my forever girl, call me when you can, day or night if you want to chat, cry or even if you just want me at the other end of the phone, I will be there for you.* He then smiled his cocky trade mark smile that said I love you.

Leaving the comfort and warmth of Charlie's car behind me, I walked up the road hardly able to put one foot in front of the other as my body was totally numb, heavy, and now devoured from the earth shattering news I had received. I looked back at Charlie who was still sat in his car at the bottom of the road watching me get safely back as the street was so dimly lit with no welcoming lights to guide me, with no warmth from this cold and miserable street, but then there never had been, tonight the snow was still falling heavily over this unwelcoming village that I had been forced to call home for so many long years.

I stood at the front door wrestling to find the keys that were at the bottom of my bag, my hands were shaking violently, cold and clammy, making it almost impossible to get the key into the lock, forcing it backwards and forwards, fighting with it to open, kicking the bottom of the door repeatedly out of frustration as all my attempts seemed in vain, suddenly I heard the roar of Charlie's car, as he sped away though the Wiltshire countryside knowing I had at last reached the dingy, dark uninviting front door. I felt that I was about to collapse with the grip of grief that had completely taken over my fragile body with such evil force, shaking me, suffocating me and now petrifying me, knowing mum was gone, leaving us all alone with what was now a huge hole in our lives that would never be filled.

The house was dark, empty of life and cold from the lack of heating, something that was not unusual. I almost expected it, as soon as I switched on the lights I switched them off again not wanting to cast my gaze around this bleak little house, wanting to blot out from light the misery of grief, devastating heartache, and sadness.

I sat in the darkness wondering what I was supposed to do now so I called my dad only to be greeted by him sobbing down the phone inconsolably, leaving my heart breaking for him as his was so obviously breaking for me.

I wanted to curl up into a ball away from the ongoing pain that just kept inviting and forcing itself on me, wanting to fall asleep, awakening to finding it had been the most terrible dream and the most horrific nightmare, but sadly this was terrifyingly real.

My mum had been stolen away from me, stealing her at such a young age, something that was so very hard to deal with and now sadly there was no one here to kiss away my sadness or hold me until I fell asleep the only one that could do that was on his way back to Wales, fighting his way back through the snow storms that had been forecast on this extremely cold mid-winter night and to our little love nest that would now feel so empty, cold. I was fully aware of not only my sadness, but Charlie's too.

I did not know where Dave was, my guess was the pub as that was his second home or maybe now it had become his first home. As I stood here drained of life it really did seem like my life had tonight spiralled to its lowest ebb, wondering if I would ever be able to rewind the downward desperately sad spiral.

I continued to sit in the darkness of the lounge alone, wrapped in my coat for some warmth, alone with my thoughts and with my sadness, the heartache was totally beyond my belief, my head in utter turmoil, going over and over it in my mind, trying to make some sense of the terrifying last few hours, seeking again any form of reassurance from the ring that was almost frozen, an icily cold ring of intrigue that hung safely from the chain around my neck.

I must have fallen asleep, I awakened with a startle to my phone ringing. It was Charlie, thank god it was him; it was almost 3am, I had been home for hours and Charlie would be almost back in Cardiff having travelled through the worst weather conditions from heavy snow to frozen roads.

As I answered, his voice gave me a much needed loving hug as I was completely chocked with grief trying to fight back the emotional tears that now swept across my porcelain and tear stained face, leaving me crippled as I managed to tell him, I loved him.

Suddenly, I heard the front door slam with a shudder, Dave was home. *I have to go Charlie.* So with no goodbyes or loving kisses the phone fell silent as I cut the call short in anticipation of the full and unwelcome war of words that would for sure be mine tonight as I heard the storm breeze under the door bringing with it clouds that were so dark and tonight so unforgiving.

Dave stumbled into the dark living room drunk like normal, switching on the light looking stunned to see me. *What are you doing home Lizzy? Have you got fed up with Wales, no one to have fun with? Or did you think it would be nice to have some fun with me instead, your husband, or had you forgot Lizzy?* He pointed and waved his finger erratically at me ready to shower me in a war of words, his eyes were on fire with a spiteful rage, bloodshot from his constant drinking.

I glanced at my watch and Dave had noticed. *Yes Lizzy its very late once again.* Dave was showing his true colours but he was right, he didn't care, he never really did as all I ever was to him was a trophy, like something he had won, not wanting anyone else to have me. He stank of beer and stale cigarettes and continued with his never ending stupid comments that just spewed from his vile mouth which he thought were so funny, but unbeknown to him it made him look so totally stupid and a complete bumbling idiot.

After holding my temper for so long and biting my tongue I screamed at Dave, telling him that mum had died, leaving me consumed with tears of grief, tears and words that choked me, suddenly with my words of distress Dave seemed to sober up. *I'm sorry Lizzy what can I do?* I glared at him; how dare he be so fucking casual in his choice of words. *Nothing tonight, nothing ever Dave, I don't need your help!* I snapped as I slammed the living room door behind me with utter force.

I was repulsed by Dave and his capability to be so bloody insensitive, even with my strong and tragic words he did not comment or look in the slightest concerned, leaving me cold yet again from his lack of feelings.

After a very sleepless, turbulent night that left me weeping, waking up in a cold pool of fluid, I tried hiding from the vile images that crawled over my skin, trying to blot out the harrowing voices that were so familiar, but a new voice had been added to the list, my mum, hearing her fading echoes far away in the distance, telling me to be strong.

Dave was still asleep as bloody normal, having slept without any concern for me at this devastating time in my life. He was a total mess, his drinking had become his priority, nothing else seemed to matter in his life that was now cocooned in a blanket of drinking, smoking and being one of the boys to satisfy his escalating out of control image.

The slightest thing or vile comment from Dave and I knew I might crack, but then maybe I should get everything out into the open, to tell the world about Charlie, our dirty love, our dirty sex secret, to tell everyone that I was now Charlie's tart, his whore, his bitch and that I always had been and that I was proud to wear the label that I had always secretly worn, to tell everyone about my past, our baby, my vile assault, my one night stand and Charlie being my on/off lover for years. Maybe if everyone knew the full story I would at least be emotionally free from a painful past that still consumed me daily.

I wanted to scream at Dave, to tell him I had been sleeping with Charlie during the time before we were married, to tell him now that I was sleeping with him again, being delighted to be his whore, his tart, his bitch and mistress, but I was thinking unreasonably at the time with my emotions that were at an all-time high as I didn't know what to think or do, my mind now over crowded with so many emotions that were jostling, pushing to the forefront of my mind with terrifying pain that I just wanted to blot out, to be allowed to forget just for a minute.

Now at the start of a new day, terrified I walked alone through the front door of my much loved family home and instantly I smelt death the stench overpowering the ice cold reality that was now staring at me. As I closed the door behind me I could feel mum's presence everywhere, her perfume suddenly invading my nostrils, her calm voice echoing from upstairs calling me to join her, knowing instantly she was in my bedroom looking in my mirror, trying to find images that once reflected back, but I was to scared to take that lonely walk, not knowing what might lay behind my bedroom door, if I would once again see a harrowing vision that would today terrify me, worried that her vision might haunt my dreams along with the others who continued to disrupt my life by night.

Suddenly a cold unwelcome shiver hit my spine as I remained frozen to the spot, bringing me back to the here and now, back to the stench of death that was now clinging desperately to my clothes, not wanting me to forget the day when my life had been ripped apart beyond belief.

The minute I saw dad my heart was once again broken with grief, ripped apart. He looked so lost, his face riddled with the devastating pain that was all too clear to see, but to be expected, nothing I could say or do would make things any better for any of us.

Suddenly my eyes were drawn to the crumpled blankets that lay unloved on the sofa, it was apparent now that dad had not been to bed and had slept on the sofa last night, he must have been so absolutely devastated to know mum was never coming home, how could this be happening?

We sat and cried together, aware that we had some heart breaking decisions to make concerning the funeral and what mum would have wanted, knowing we had to carry out her final wishes to the letter.

I watched my dad struggle to make all the appointments that needed to be made, wishing I could ease his apparent pain, his face haunted by mum's death, today being ashen and free from any warmth.

It was now late on Saturday afternoon, I could not now do much until Monday, so with dad exhausted from pain and fast asleep in the chair I took myself off for a walk up to the snow cover woods in search of some well-kept memories.

The trees seemed to echo my sadness which reflected throughout the dense woodland, they were barren from leaf, frozen by the snow that had once again fallen overnight leaving everything blanketed in a frost that glinted in the tepid sunshine, nothing had escaped the storm that had blown in, casting its icy grip not only here but all over the country, leaving us all to shiver within its tight grip.

But the scene was stunning, pockets of snow that had created little drifts, sweeping snow up the trunk of the trees, odd little snow drifts had been left in my path ready for my footprints so that today I could call them mine.

As I sat on a log I let myself drift away, thinking of mum and how beautiful she was. My head was in a frenzy, a torrent of grief that just kept washing over me, mixed emotions filled my body as when I thought of her I smiled, but with my smile came a terrifying pain.

Today my emotions were like a double-edged sword, smiling at her grace and beauty, knowing we had a great mother-daughter gift as we shared the same kind of caring and love, something I would miss so much. I never knew just how much I would miss her, she was my mum, and nothing could prepare me for the loss and the impact her death would have on me now and in the years to come.

My mind was now miles away, drifting back to happier times, disturbed at this moment by my phone ringing making me jump back to reality, to the here and now. It was Charlie, we managed a few minutes of light chat, skirting around my mother's sudden death as I fought to hold back my tears that my body so needed to shed. *Lizzy, talk to me.* My words were muted.

Please don't cry. He said. *Charlie, I'm not much company at the moment… Lizzy, you don't have to say anything.* I didn't, I just clung to his words as he repeated his love for me while my numb fingers clung to the ring once more for some sort of comfort on this bitterly cold afternoon, unaware it was starting to get dark, and I was freezing cold. I had not noticed until now that I was not wearing a coat so I wrapped my thick woolly cardigan even tighter around me, we said our goodbyes with lots of kisses and I love you's.

I needed now to grieve for mum, be a support for dad, to be some sort of a wife to Dave, if only in name, a lover to Charlie and a supportive sister. It all seemed simple when I said it aloud, but it wasn't as I knew a very rough and very turbulent road lay ahead for all of us.

I was reminded that I would never be, or want to be, a proper wife to Dave as we did not have that sort of relationship. It was a relationship that I didn't want or need, I had never wanted it and I never would.

The funeral was now arranged, knowing it was going to be a very hard day, a heart breaking day for me. There would be no one to hold my trembling hand, to kiss away my tears or to hold me close, having to walk the long and painful journey alone and in silence.

Dave was his normal unhelpful self, going about doing his normal thing, drinking the pub dry most nights and spewing his constant vile unfunny comments even at this devastating time. I asked myself constantly why the hell was he so bloody uncaring and why did he seem totally unaware of my grief?

I didn't sleep properly for many nights. Tossing and turning, waking up cold and in pools of skin drenching liquid, my dreams haunted still by vile images, the haunting echoes and now the turmoil of not having mum in my life. This led me to make an appointment with the family doctor and after many tears, outbursts of emotion and desperate plea's he looked sternly over the top of his glasses, a look I had seen only once before. He relented and gave me something to help me rest, knowing full well my torment, and whilst looking through my notes having had an emotional and frank conversation, he advised me to consider a different form of contraception rather than the one that I had taken for so many years.

Walking away from the surgery I was now contraception free and now would have to use condoms for protection, this would be much to

Dave's annoyance, knowing he would hate the fact that it would be his responsibility to supply the new form of contraception if he was still intent on forcing himself on me for the continual chore of painful, dull, and unexciting sex that still managed to leave me cold, fighting the vile demands that he made on my already battered body.

I had also made up my mind to not tell Charlie just yet, knowing he had gone through hell over the last couple of months. I knew it was wrong, so very wrong, but it was now part of my long term plan to have him in my life permanently, to have his baby, a baby that I selfishly craved, that I had always craved, but this was my chance to prove my lifetime dreams, a very selfish dream but they were my dreams, and mine to at last be realised, bringing me some much needed long term happiness, or would it? Time would tell and possibly be my downfall in the long-term quest to have it all.

Maybe Charlie would feel trapped if I got pregnant? Maybe he wouldn't? Maybe grief was not allowing me to think rationally as once again I was going full-steam ahead and not thinking it through, proving once again that I had not learnt any lessons along my roller-coaster journey, but now I was willing to take the risk once again to for fill my long-term dreams.

After some very turbulent, sorrowful nights, and dark days, there was the stark realisation that it was here, the day I had been dreading, the day we had all been dreading was finally here, the day of mum's funeral. The cars waited outside to drive us the short journey to the church, to say a final goodbye to mum. My fragile body was once again consumed with overwhelming grief and sadness, I did not know how I would get through this, the most devastating day of my life, without Charlie to hold my hand or to hear him whisper his love for me.

I returned to my old bedroom for some much needed time alone to just stand silently in the window again twiddling uncomfortably with the ring on my necklace, asking to be transported back to my childhood to embrace memories of mum and once again I was not disappointed as I was taken on a kaleidoscope of a vividly coloured journey. One memory lead to another, allowing me to recall my childhood spent in this house and in the garden that I adored.

Suddenly there was a knock at my bedroom door awakening me from my journey, my aunt was stood pale faced, her petit features ashen in colour against her jet black hair, she was holding flowers delicately wrapped in pale pink cellophane, caressed in pink tissue paper, I knew instantly they were for me and who they were from. The card read a simple message... *Thinking of you today Lizzy, H L F...* Those initials again adorned the message. They were from Charlie, a beautiful bunch of the sweetest smelling white daisies, looking at them and knowing who they were from made me smile on such a sad day. He always made everything a little better, a little brighter on the most darkest of days, knowing he was thinking about me was a great comfort. I left the flowers in my old bedroom for now on the window sill as I would then have to return to be able to enliven my senses of Charlie and to recapture more memories that were now queuing up in a bid to bring a little comfort on this cold, unbearably sad winter's day.

Time to go, dad said as he squeezed both my sister's hand and mine. Instantly I recalled the last time he said that to me, it was the day he walked me down the aisle, that to was a devastating day for me, but not so earth shattering as this day.

As we all walked out to the cars that were waiting for us it was worse than I could have ever imagined as tears streamed down my ice cold face, my heart terrified by the grief that was invading my body. Just walking to the cars was more difficult than I could have imagined. Dad remained so calm so I held onto him for all the support that I needed right now, Dave was nowhere to be seen having gone on ahead to visit the pub that stood opposite the church.

I was a wreck, shaking violently with the most frightening sadness I had ever felt. All I wanted to do was run away, to escape this torture as now I could not breath, my heart was being wrecked by grief, slowly and powerfully leaving my body to splinter into thousands of pieces that were now covering the cold pavement on which we were walking. It was difficult to say what emotion was worse as they were all so terrifying, the slow paced journey took for what seemed like hours as I stared out of the window seeing nothing but fear, again the dark shadows slithered its way down the windows, not allowing me any day light.

As the vicar greeted us at the door, he remained steely faced. I instantly felt the unwelcome chill brush against my delicate porcelain face from the interior of the church that was lacking in any warmth on this bitterly cold afternoon, forcing me to shiver my way throughout the service, my feet now numb from the cold concrete floor that we were all stood on, my focus never fading far away from the oak coffin that was adorned in fresh spring flowers. The perfume was so delicate, so intoxicating, feeding my senses to a vibrant aroma as I continued to shed so many tears that seemed to freeze like icicles to my porcelain face, melting onto the hymn book, staining every word, words that were now smudged by grief, words that were smudged in horrifying sorrow, standing alone frozen in grief this was the true realisation for me that I would now walk my life time journey alone.

The service was delightful, carrying out mum's wishes right through to her choice of flowers that now adored this pretty church. The perfume was delicate and fresh, the hymns were perfect for mum, my dad then read a poem that he had written straight from the heart that had everyone reaching for tissues, everyone now in tears it was so utterly beautiful as he spoke about mum, his love for her so apparent which once again terrified me, wondering if he would cope without her.

Now with the service over we had to say the final, terrifyingly sad, goodbye. Standing in the churchyard with the snow once again falling around us, I suddenly felt very alone with my thoughts, frozen to the spot and still unable to come to terms with mum's unexpected death. Looking around me I felt cocooned in grief, stunned into a petrifying sadness. Suddenly I felt dad's arm around me, bringing me back to reality, to the stark darkness that now shrouded this unfriendly churchyard, but I wanted to linger a little longer. I watched the snowflakes fall onto the mass of pretty spring flowers that were now covering mum's grave, the colours were glorious, from stunning pink, vibrant white, spring yellow, right through to beautiful pastel blues.

Thirty minutes later dad was now by my side, once again having returned to the churchyard after leaving me to say my silent goodbye to mum. *Lizzy, your freezing let's get you home.* Dad took my freezing cold hand, squeezing it reassuringly, not wanting me to dwell on my own grief any longer, my distress so visible for everyone to see.

Returning to dad's and Dave was already drinking heavily, once again everyone having to hear his pathetic voice, having to listen to his vile unwelcome comments, leaving me to apologise to everyone that he seemed happy to offend. My aunts were now all rallying around me, fussing over me, but that was normal and now very welcome, wanting to feel their arms around me giving me their gentle support, propping me up in case I stumbled, shielding me somewhat from the impending storm.

The evening wore on and I could not wait to be alone with my thoughts, to possibly call Charlie for a chat, a much needed chat which again led me to thinking about getting pregnant. It did seem rather reckless, but I had to have his baby at any cost, my mind was now firmly made up knowing that I would undoubtedly pay the price.

As I looked at my bunch of daisies that sat delightful and patiently on the window sill and as they reflected back through the mirror on my dressing table, suddenly my old bedroom came alive with Charlie's dirty, intense love which triggered a much needed smile on such a terrifying day.

Everyone was now leaving and suddenly the house fell silent from the muffled chatter. It felt so very lonely but I could feel mum's presence everywhere, her things still in place where she had left them on that fateful day, her makeup bag still sat on the shelf in her bathroom along with her hair brush. Her hair was her pride and joy, immaculate always, her photos standing joyful in pride of place of the family which were such nice reminders of her and the love she held for all of us.

I could smell her perfume wafting through the house. Her perfume was so distinctive as she always wore the same one and had done for years and now, as I walked freely around the house touching her things it brought back so many vivid memories of happier times, behind every door there was now a list of memories just waiting for me, all to enliven my emotions, taking me once again on a journey, hearing mum telling me to not wear my skirt so short, to not be led astray by Charlie, along with all the other things that today rang loud and clear in my head. I heard her words so clearly and as I walked down the stairs I heard her again, telling me not to wear so much makeup, these were just memories, but ones that I would always treasure.

Once again I found myself stood in my old bedroom looking out of the window for the third time today, but now darkness had fallen. I looked out across the open landscape, there were so many memories I had of this house from growing up as a child, a teenager and now here today a woman. This house, this village, it was a perfect place for a child to grow up. I felt privileged that I had been so lucky to have a loving family and great childhood friends that allowed me a perfect childhood, these were memories that not even grief could take away on this day.

We would always have mum with us, as her soul and legacy would live on in this house, bringing happy memories to everyone who loved it here. Suddenly cold shivers took over my motionless body once again as I realised it was so cold in the house. Returning to the lounge I found the fire had burnt down very low, but I managed to get the fire going again without any help from Dave as he staggered around mumbling, helping himself to yet another drink.

We then left for home but not before I had walked around the garden in the darkness, knowing it was the right thing to do somehow. I stood at the open vista just listening to nothing, staring into nothing but darkness, a calmness had now descended, shrouding the garden, once again terrifying me, the garden now in mourning for mum as the trees stood frozen, laden with snow, even the old owl was silent from his constant whistles and calls.

We made our way home, silent all the way, the silence was deafening between Dave and myself as he offered no words of comfort or support on this grief filled day. I continued to seek reassurance from the ring that was once again frozen against my skin. Once home I headed for bed while Dave headed for the pub, leaving me to wonder if he had any idea of how I was feeling, I had just said goodbye to my mum for god's sake!

A night of punishing sleep followed, with images and voices that were relentless but tonight was different, the images and voices were only of mum, her harrowing cries that begged me to help her as I felt her hands slip through mine. Her voice echoed as she faded away into the distance allowing her willowy shadow to slip silently into the darkness on this bitterly cold winter's night.

The light of a new day unfolded and it looked just as bleak as yesterday. Nothing had changed, grief still hung pungently in the cold light of day, my heart had been broken into a thousand pieces like tiny shards of glass that had managed to pierce every part of my fragile skin, leaving small blood stained wounds that would never heal. My body was now visible, with scars and open wounds left behind, born out of hatred, sadness, and now extreme grief.

I took another walk to the woods before going to the churchyard to be completely alone with my thoughts, taking with me the flowers that Charlie had sent me, ready to place on mum's already heavily flower laden grave. It felt so good to be back in a familiar place surrounded by a love that Charlie and I had created right here. The heavy snow-laden trees looked spectacular today, shimmering in watery March sunshine, groaning as the breeze swept through, shaking all the branches free from snow knowing that tonight the snow would come once again as forecast, to dust the branches again as the winter was still relentless, showering its ice cold cargo over the already frozen landscape. I was now surrounded by an enchantment that only these woods could deliver. As I sat alone, still and motionless, I was treated to a familiar sight as the little family of innocent deer played happily, scurrying around, finding what food they could in amongst the fluffy carpet of fresh virgin snow.

Then before I knew it I was stood alone once again in the freezing cold, staring at the vast amount of flowers that graced mum's grave. I added the flowers that Charlie had sent me, now saying a final goodbye to my mum, my beautiful mum. My tears falling again in droplets that splashed onto the delicate blooms that adorned her grave, her final resting place.

Suddenly I felt a firm hand on my arm and as I looked around it was Charlie. I squealed with excitement on seeing his face, a face that I had missed so much, that constantly reminded me of our first encounter all those years ago, now having his arms wrapped around me, my sexy, handsome Charlie. Suddenly my body seemed very light, almost limp as I fell into his arms. I cried and sobbed so many bitter sweet tears, this was what I needed, someone who understood, someone that would let me cry without explanation, knowing how I felt and why. *Charlie, how did you know I was here? I was coming to see the flowers anyway and I saw you walk into the churchyard Lizzy, so I thought I would give you some time alone with your mum before coming to find you.*

I have come to take you back to Cardiff Lizzy. He held my porcelain face tenderly between both his hands just to make sure my tears were gone for now. *I have missed you so much Lizzy.* I smiled back at him letting him know that I felt the same way.

I glanced back at the heavily flower laden grave, blowing a kiss to mum as Charlie and I walked out of the churchyard with our arms wrapped around each other, not caring at this moment if we were seen together, if people stood and stared or pointed fingers at us. The grip tightened once more, knowing I would remain his forever hostage, never wanting to be released from the chains that so obviously embraced my body, shackling me to him and to his mysterious life, a life that continued to seduce me daily and now that had started to invade my dreams and to seduce my nightly terrors.

Charlie kissed me, kissed me so tenderly, holding my porcelain face once more with both his hands for reassurance. *See you in the morning princess, we will have a wonderful weekend, I think you need it my beautiful girl.* I had to agree it was going to be lovely and I was looking forward to being back in his arms, to have his dirty love, his dirty kisses and to be back in Wales being his tart, his bitch, his whore and now the woman who wanted his baby, who was now on a mission to have the baby I today so foolishly and selfishly craved. But was it foolish? Was it selfish? Was grief over taking me, not allowing me to think straight?

Friday morning was here at last and how relieved I was to be once again leaving this bloody prison cell with its cold, dark walls that continued to close in on me as it seemed to strangle every last breath out of me, leaving me gasping for some fresh, clean and exciting Welsh air. Dave had already left for work, leaving me a really loving note, the note read, *See you next week.* That was all he thought of me but the feeling was mutual. I slammed the door with force behind me wishing I would never have to return to this unwelcoming and unloving house again.

The air that day was laden with ice crystals that dropped randomly onto the pavement forming icy puddles that now reflected my miserable life here in this street, a street that held nothing for me, I could not find one thing that I liked about it.

Before I left I needed desperately to revisit the garden of my childhood that was now shrouded in frost which looked enchanting on this March morning as the sun had cast a cold, watery light over the garden, allowing me to share the delights of a winter wonderland that was now laid out before me that never failed to impress on my senses. I took a last lingering look and as I looked further deeper into the woods the family of deer were all looking back at me, looking startled to see me with their ears pricked rigidly as they all stood motionless and still, waiting for me to exit the garden.

I could now see Charlie's car parked down the road from dad's house, it was not hard to miss as it shone brightly in the early spring sunshine. On opening the door the aroma was staggeringly seductive. The smell of Italian leather filled the air, a pungent, seductive, and very sexy heavy aroma and I nestled into Charlie's butter soft Italian leather jacket.

As we kissed our hello's, Charlie instantly slid his tongue into my mouth gently, but firmly, before sliding it even further into my throat. God I had missed him, missed his dirty loving. With his tongue still engaged in my mouth I was very turned on by his actions, I pulled back wanting to see his cocky smile, that sexy smile that I had grown to love over the years.

Charlie was holding my freezing cold hands in his. *It's not too soon for you is it Lizzy?* I shook my head. *No, I just want to be with you.* But my grief still remained so very raw and from time to time I found it very difficult to deal with, leaving me cold and frightened in a world without my mum, without her our family would undoubtedly fall apart, leaving us all very fragile.

We drove for about four hours talking all the way. Charlie was amazing company and just what I needed right now, he was like the breath of fresh air that I needed, having been choked with the stale, second-hand and rancid air that had filled my prison cell for the last two weeks that I had been forced to endure, having to breath the same rancid air as Dave which continued to repulse me.

CHAPTER 18

With March now firmly here, I looked back at what the last couple of months had been for both of us, months full of sadness that had managed to cripple us in the grip of grief and utter turmoil, but today, knowing spring was almost here lifted our somewhat muted spirits but it remained extremely cold with the winter not wanting to release us from its grip. Looking out of the window as we travelled through the Welsh countryside I was treated to a mysterious, hidden beauty all of its own as the trees groaned under the heavy snow that now clung to every branch, bushes that were wrapped in snow like big balls of cotton wool. The Welsh frozen landscape on full show for everyone to admire and it was absolutely stunning, captivating my full attention.

Having now found a very remote open landscape, Charlie stopped the car wanting us to share the beauty that surrounded us on this beautiful, cold, crisp afternoon. An open vista sprawled out before us with an icily cold blast of air that brushed against our faces making my eyes water, but it managed to hide the vast amount of tears and painful grief that still remained to be shed. We sat in silence, admiring the scenery that we loved, the snow-capped hills, the sprawling untamed beauty of Wales. I looked at Charlie as his hand was now firmly on mine. *Princess, I love you so much.* As I looked back at him, he knew I felt the same.

The watery late winter sun had now began setting over the rugged Welsh countryside, it was a perfect start to what I desperately hoped would be an unspoilt weekend. Charlie then opened the ice cold champagne, pouring it seductively into glass flutes that were so delicate. Once again he had thought of everything, we clinked and raised our glasses to the love of each other.

Suddenly after a very short dive Charlie stopped the engine and took my trembling hand, leading me to a place where I was transported back in time to something from a fairy tale. I blinked, not believing my eyes as before me was a huge fairy-tale castle with large turrets on either side, huge stone walls with the tinniest of windows, a massive heavy wooden oak door that was hiding the charming interior that was waiting to greet us, that would leave me speechless as it looked so very enchanting, hidden deep within the Welsh remote countryside that wrapped itself around us. Snow covered the long driveway with what looked like a long silky blanket, the extensive lawns now buried beneath a thick layer of snow as the delicate flowers of spring were trying so hard to make an appearance through the chill of the ice blanket that covered them, little snowdrops, crocuses and primroses all wanting to feel a little warmth from what little sunshine there was.

Charlie smiled as I squeezed his hand tightly with excitement. I still had many thoughts in the back of my mind about his wife and who she thought he was with and what he was doing, it remained a massive dark void that seemed to swallow me, spinning me around in different directions, not allowing me to make any sense of Charlie's life like the huge amount of money that Charlie always seemed to have to lavish on me, like this weekend, the presents, the flowers and his lavish car and a lifestyle that went with it.

Charlie held my hand as we checked in as Mr and Mrs Stevens, my heart was beating faster and faster in anticipation for the dirty love I was about to give and to receive from Charlie as we excitedly walked up the old wooden winding stair case that creaked and groaned under foot. Old and uneven floor boards added to the beauty along with the old windows that allowed the freezing cold wind to echo around the room, followed by a howling chill that ran the length of the landing, carpeted in glorious rich red velvet which felt like we were walking on air.

Charlie then unlocked the huge heavy wooden door to our room that would be our dirty love nest for the next couple of days, scooping me into his arms and with the biggest, cockiest smile, whispering *welcome to us Lizzy*. I gasped at the wonderful room as I inhaled its beauty. A huge wooden four-poster bed stood commanding the middle of the room, complete with its heavy full length drapes, soft lighting lit the room and the pretty fireplace emitted a warm, cosy glow to complement its surroundings. The furnishings were lavish, decadent and opulent, glimmering golds, rich regal reds, plush Greens and a very majestic blues graced the walls. Luxury bedding and pillows complimented the plush interior.

I put my bag down. Charlie once again pulled me in to his arms and at that moment I never wanted him to let me go. It was a spine chilling feeling that I had never experienced with anyone except Charlie as the shackles of our love gripped my body a little tighter on that day.

We were still holding each other lovingly, never wanting to be the first one to pull away. Charlie then stood with his arms outstretched, holding mine, wanting to feast his eyes that were today full of hunger. *Lizzy you look stunningly beautiful.* His fingertips caressed the outline of my porcelain face, slipping down onto my neck, caressing again the ring on my necklace. Again he was silent from any acceptance that the ring was his as he lingered a little longer, tracing again the raised pattern that seemed to seduce him as I watched him close his eyes for a split second while the ring seduced him. He whispered softly. *How could I have ever let you marry someone else? I must have been mad Lizzy.* I silenced his words by placing my fingertips over his lips, not wanting to hear the words that reflected my painful and bitter life by marrying the wrong man.

Our kisses were now intense, passionate, and so very full of dirty love as seduction was bubbling away throughout my body, bubbling with pent up passion, waiting to be unleashed on Charlie.

Our tongues were now exploring each other's mouths and once again his arms were so strong around my body, holding me so gently, just like a fragile piece of glass. I then felt his hand glide gently over mine as he reached into his luxurious soft brown Italian leather weekend bag. *Lizzy I have presents for you. Charlie you spoil me.*

Charlie was always showering me with lavish expensive gifts, treating me to a luxury lifestyle I had never encountered before, but I was not complaining and never would as it was a lifestyle that I would readily embrace.

Open it princess. I thought you could slip into them later. He smiled a cocky smile that melted the ice that filled our champagne bucket. Charlie had been shopping to a very expensive and exclusive lingerie boutique in Cardiff for some very sexy underwear. Knickers, a bra, stockings, and suspenders, it was all so beautiful, silky soft and very seductive. I leant over to kiss him as he pulled me onto the bed for some much needed us time, a time in which to reflect on both our losses.

We lay together, embraced in each other arms, silent and still for me to recall special moments of mum that would never remain far away, ready to recall when needed and for Charlie to morn his baby. He then straddled over me. We were both fully clothed, his fingertips gently stroked my porcelain face, his eyes exploring every bit of me, hungry for my love as he whispered. *You're so very, very very beautiful Lizzy.* Making my skin tingle and burn.

His fingers then ran through my long flowing hair onto the silky pale skin of my neck as he peppered his kisses onto the ring that hung on the chain around my neck. I took a sharp intake of breath, hoping tonight he might reveal its true mystery but alas I was not granted that wish as his fingers then delicately met my blouse. He lovingly undid my buttons one by one, kissing each one and revealing my underwear that I was wearing in order to seduce him. *Princess, your tits look fucking amazing.* They spilled out over the silky fabric of my bra.

His fingers danced delightfully over my nipples, commanding their attention as they reacted naughtily, encouraged by his actions, bursting into firm buds that yearned to be loved by Charlie's lips. He gazed at my open blouse with eyes that were now on fire, he then sat me up to remove my blouse, along with my bra, my tits spilling out firm and full. Charlie then dropped my bra onto the floor along with my blouse that now laid in a crumpled and discarded heap.

He then led me back on the bed, his lips covered my nipples firmly and as he did I held his head, gently forcing him to suck them harder, to suck them roughly, allowing me to feel the extreme sensual feelings I had constantly craved. My nipples were now hurting from Charlie's rough sucking, but I loved it.

I undid his shirt to reveal his chest which was so firm, solid, smooth, and so damn sexy. I grabbed his hair, pulling him gently towards me to kiss him again, making sure he knew my intentions as I forced my champagne drenched ice cold lips against his.

Suddenly and without warning he pulled me up from the bed leading me to the bathroom, locking the door hard behind us, pushing me gently, but with a passionate force against the door, kissing me hard and again with the roughness I loved. *Seduce me Charlie, fucking seduce me,* I demanded. He then covered my mouth with his fingers and whispered, *Lizzy you bitch, my whore, my beautiful dirty secret.*

The bathroom was romantically lit with candles that flickered, sending beautiful dancing shadows which bounced across the walls creating patterns of seduction that embraced us both, setting the scene for a night of passion. Charlie kissed my neck passionately, moving down towards my tits, now avoiding any contact with the ring that hung on my necklace that I had lovingly worn for eight years. He moaned loudly, his voice untamed, moaning repeatedly, *you fucking turn me on Lizzy.*

Both of us now semi-naked, Charlie suddenly lifted me on to the toilet seat as he had done on our first sensual encounter all those years ago, bringing back such sweet innocent memories, allowing me to once again become his virgin.

He unzipped my jeans, letting them fall. I now stood in just my knickers and high heels. *Wow princess.* He feasted his eyes over my curvy body, taking him on an erotic journey, leaving my body quivering as still Charlie continued his journey, outlining my curves with his fingertips, indulging his hunger a while longer by feasting on what had now become his once again.

As he kissed my belly button I felt his tongue revolve around it, leaving wet and soggy kisses. *Lizzy you have a beautiful belly.* I giggled, blushing again at his comments while Charlie enjoyed my blushes, smiling his very cocky smile which endorsed his love for me once again and not for the first time.

He then licked all his fingers and suddenly with gentle force, slid past the soft lace edge of my knickers into my pussy. I screamed out with lust as he pushed them further, almost hurting me, but I found that very sexy, so much so I begged him for more.

Now lifting me down we took our passion back to the bedroom. Charlie removed my knickers, lovingly nudging my legs slightly apart to allow his tongue to slowly enter my tight, juice filled pussy as I took a sharp intake if breath, closing my eyes to enjoy the most sensual feeling of his tongue lapping around my pussy on a mission to find my clit to tease into submission. His lips now held my clit firmly as I continued to moan loudly, my moaning reaching new heights that echoed around the bedroom as we relaxed on the huge bed that was ours tonight.

I loved seeing Charlie naked, his body was so very toned, lean, and muscular; a delight for my eyes. His aroma added to the pleasure that was all mine, but he wasn't mine, he was married to Helen. My mind now filled with bitter thoughts, draining the smile from my porcelain face, but he was with me and not her tonight, this instantly brought back a warmth to the bedroom.

I took my beautiful new undies into the bathroom, gently slipping them on. The feeling of the soft silk against my skin was so sensual and as I entered the bedroom Charlie's eyes were transfixed. *Lizzy, Lizzy, Lizzy you beautiful whore, my beautiful fucking whore.* His hunger for my curvy body now so obvious as his eyes continued to flirt over my semi-naked skin, his breath warm against the lace that edged of the silky smooth knickers as his tongue weaved its way past the fine, soft, delicate French lace in a bid to seduce my pussy again.

My body quivered, wanting this moment never to end, requesting we paused this moment as I poured us both more fizz, my glass now overflowing with pretty foaming bubbles as they spilled down over my hand and on to my delicate underwear.

Twenty minutes later there was a knock at the door, foreplay was now placed on hold as Charlie went to answer it, wrapped only in a dazzling soft white towel, knowing he was completely naked much to my delight as I saw a glimpse of his thigh that the dazzling white towel had not quite covered, a lean, toned and very athletic thigh.

A picnic hamper and cosy Welsh woollen blanket were delivered, a repeat of our night that was cut so bitterly short. How special was this? I sat on the bed on the blanket in just my seductive underwear and high heels. Charlie sat opposite me, naked apart from the baby soft towel that covered his lower body leaving me yearning for his lean torso.

Charlie opened the basket that contained so much fabulous food, complete with a little wooden box that lay patiently on the top. *Lizzy this is for you.* To my delight the scratched lid read *my forever Lizzy, H L F.* Those initials again, but what did they mean, distracted again I glanced at Charlie before I opened the box that contained a single edible daisy. *Charlie you have thought of everything.* What a treat, smoked salmon sandwiches, lots of individual yummy savoury nibbles, chocolate coated strawberries and cream such beautiful seductive feast.

So now with our picnic over Charlie moved the wicker basket from the bed and pulled back the large heavy curtains to reveal the moonlight that now graced the sky on this very clear, crisp cold night, making a very romantic sky perfect for our dirty love as we led together on the huge bed with the moonlight gracing our room, flooding it with a prefect ambiance for a night of uncontrollable passion.

I was embracing every second of my time thinking if time were to stand still I would have wanted it to be now, this very moment, just Charlie and I in the most magical, majestic place, a place that allowed us both to relax, for now at least.

I straddled over Charlie, removing the towel that had caressed his body, now naked and ready for my undivided attention. His erection was massive, stiff and long, with beads of pearly juice cascading from it, desperate to be relieved from the sexual tension that was clearly engulfing his body. I then placed my mouth around his cock allowing my mouth to be seduced as I lovingly sucked it. *Lizzy, Lizzy you bitch*, he moaned repeatedly. I ran my teeth sharply up and down the massive stem, my tongue in a frenzy rolling over his full throbbing helmet, stopping only for a second so that I could thrust my tongue into his mouth to delightfully dance with his tongue, letting my juice coated tongue slip gently into the back of his throat, seducing every bit of his mouth.

I then silently moved my mouth back to his huge and very juicy cock that was peppering my tongue once again with fresh warm juice. Charlie moaned my name repeatedly. *Lizzy you whore, you fucking whore let me fuck you.*

He then straddled me, gazing at me with every thrust that left me wanting more as we continued to make dirty, raw, and untamed love, a love I knew was perfect for making babies, our baby, but unbeknown to Charlie it was my little secret for now, right or wrong.

We laid together exhausted by love, a love that seemed to be impossible to hide, which now I would embrace, hoping that Charlie would also be allowed to embrace the love we shared, so very content that we fell asleep in each other's arms, sleeping soundly without the constant battle of harrowing voices, vile images, and the distant cries of my baby, freeing me for a while from the torture that was now ruling my life by day and crippling my nightly dreams.

The crisp morning sunlight now crept silently through the window. Charlie kissed me softly with kisses that I adored, his tongue now rolling over my lips onto my tongue and into the back of my throat in celebration of the new day that was about to unfold. We gazed out of the window, it looked so cold but so stunningly beautiful, the rugged Welsh countryside lending itself to the natural winter beauty that never failed to amaze and delight me. Feeling Charlie's naked body wrapped around me both of us wrapped just by a crisp laundered white sheet, while gazing out at the inviting landscape, I felt his seductive kisses roll over my naked shoulder onto my upper arm as he let his teeth nibble my shoulder gently, continuing to the nape of my neck, allowing his tongue to move over my necklace, caressing the delicate chain between his teeth in a bid to be intimate with the beautiful ring which still remained a complete mystery to me, but so obviously not to him.

Suddenly he must have become aware of his own intimacy with the ring and suggested we have breakfast and go for a long walk into the hills. *Charlie that sounds so romantic.* My smile was warm as I indulged once again in his cocky reputation, so a yummy breakfast was served in bed, buck's fizz, bacon and eggs along with a mountain of toast and endless coffee, what a treat.

I needed Charlie to love me on this beautiful new day so I took the lead, inviting him back into bed for some early morning dirty love. Charlie smothered my naked body in sweet kisses, his fingertips once again outlining my curves, over my nipples that were now enormous as they begged his attention. I begged him to seduce me and with that I was seduced, being treated to such beautiful, early morning dirty love.

Now composed and my sexual demands quenched, for now, we headed out through the enormous large oak doors, the intense cold icy blast taking my breath away, brushing against my skin with force, my eyes blurred by the ice cold March wind, but the sun provided a little warmth which was very welcome. Dressed in my boots, scarf, gloves complete with my fluffy hat, I was prepared for the day that lay ahead for us both, to embrace. Both of us were just amazed at this winter wonderland that sprawled out before us, a landscape that didn't seem to end. It was so perfect, so utterly perfect and so very beautiful, taking me back to our first winter together when we would walk through the deep snow that had fallen across the fields outside my house, watching the family of deer frolicking in the woods, a delight for both of us.

Now with the time having swept by we noticed to our amazement that it was beginning to get dark; I was freezing, our clothes now sopping wet from the snow. Holding my frozen hand in his he whispered, *Lizzy lets head back.* As we did, we both reflected on a perfect day, now both of us were looking forward to a long hot bath together and some much needed hot and very strong coffee.

As we walked back towards the hotel the sun was slipping away behind the hills like a huge ball of fire that was now reflecting on the snow, it made the landscape look so very beautiful, setting the vista alight. Flaming orange and fire red snow, creating a magical somewhat mystical wilderness, the vivid sunshine now cast bright shadows over the landscape, everywhere I looked was picture perfect, even on this bitterly cold winter's afternoon. Darkness was now waiting patiently, bringing with it yet another dusting of snow on the silent, but bitter easterly winds that would again freeze the landscape that night.

At last we were back at the hotel but it had been wonderful and had given me time to reflect on the beautiful memories of my mum, being able to spend my time alone with Charlie, time we both so desperately needed.

Coffee was ordered, a large cafetière was delivered to our room complete with homemade biscuits that were very welcome on this extremely cold late afternoon. Charlie then ran us that bath, the bath was large and deep so plenty of room for us both to get cosy. Charlie lit the candles and floated sparkling, glossy snowflakes on the water that glistened in between the thousands of iridescent bubbles that filled the bath.

As we relaxed, sipping our of coffee, laughing about the day, about the out of shape snowman we so lovingly made. This was what I loved the most as we were so natural together, never afraid to show our feelings, knowing what each of us was thinking without question, well almost, as the puzzle of Charlie's reputation, his secret and mysterious life continued to evade me, but it was relentless in its ability to seduce me daily leaving, me in a state of panic by night as his seduction was muted by my overcrowded dreams, allowing the nightmares to still rage on.

With the water now going cold it was nice to slip into the warm towelling robes that felt so soft against my skin, allowing my body to glow. Charlie had brought with him some beautiful oils, again something that he had bought from an expensive perfumery along with my favourite perfume.

The oil felt like silk as Charlie glided it softly onto my skin, the smell was amazing, the delicate fragrance now wafted around the room until it slid under the door slipping silently on to the landing outside our room.

Suddenly I felt Charlie's warm kisses again on my shoulder. *Come on Lizzy, it's time for dinner.* He had awoken me from a perfect sleep. I smiled up at Charlie who looked so very handsome tonight, smiling his cocky smile as he straightened his white smart tailored shirt that hugged him in all the right places. To compliment his look I wore my short black lace dress, high black shoes, black undies, stockings and of course suspenders. *Lizzy you look fucking stunning.* He then once again took in my full beauty, feasting on my body that was now wrapped in layers of sumptuous silk and lace.

As we were shown to our table I felt Charlie's hand gently brush against my thigh, brushing against the lace of my dress that made me shudder in anticipation of yet another night of the most welcome dirty passion.

We were sat together, relaxing in the most opulent dining room that was completely lit only by huge cream candles that sat on tall iron pillars. The heavy drapes were lavish in the richest of reds, autumnal ambers and regal blues, the wall covering elaborate and stylish that created a very relaxing atmosphere. The looks between us were electric as I continually played footsie with Charlie, making him smile as I ran my high heels firmer up and down, his leg in a sensual movement while my gaze was fully fixed on his. *Lizzy you naughty girl.* I blushed, knowing full well I was still the naughty girl he had fallen in love with.

Miles away with my thoughts I wanted this lifestyle, I wanted him, god I wanted him. I could imagine our life, our life together and I was going to have it as I had promised myself in my dreams that were now going to become a reality. I was going to make sure of that, but I knew I had many hurdles to overcome before my childhood dreams would be realised, now suddenly the list was endless.

I loved all his attention to detail, he always thought of everything, he always did even back in the early days. He had that gift of making the simplest of things so special, his ability to cast his reputation over me, enriching my life daily, but not everyone around us approved, especially the other girls who were so obviously jealous that it was me that he wanted to be his princess and now all these years later his bed buddy, his bitch, his tart, his whore, his bit on the side and maybe now the mummy to his baby.

Coffee Lizzy? Yes let's take it in the lounge Charlie. We sat together on the big sumptuous, comfortable brown leather sofa in front of the roaring log fire that was so perfect. We watched the flames flirting around the logs, sparks that crackled and popped, dancing in between the flames that now cast a mellow light, complimenting a perfect love that I never wanted to end. I felt Charlie's hand brush gently against my leg stroking my silky stockings.

His hand moved further, reaching my inner thigh under my dress before teasing the soft lace on my suspenders. Knowing I was getting turned on by my blushes Charlie could not stop smiling, a smile that was once again making me blush uncontrollably.

Now desperately trying to hide my sexual frustration from those around us he pulled me up from the sofa, smothering me in soft kisses before leading me to our bedroom.

Away from the glare of other guests we were free to share the passion that was so obvious to everyone around us, now wrapped in each other's arms lying on the bed, never wanting to be apart as I knew tomorrow would be here before we knew it and the next day seemed very unpredictable as the storm clouds were never far away, ready to invade our happiness once again, having to ride the waves that would undoubtedly try to engulf us in foaming, unwelcome, freezing ice cold water, reminding me that not only me, but now Charlie, would never be free from the storms that threatened everything we both valued.

We gently kissed as the candle light filled the room again with a beautiful, very loving light, allowing us to relax, taking away the painful emotions from our bodies for now only until the haunting images and tormenting voices would fill our lives yet again.

His kisses moved to my tits, my nipples big and juicy, wanting him to suck them, suck them so hard it would hurt, so with that his mouth covered my nipples. He sucked each one in turn, paying attention to them both, while he sucked one he squeezed the other, both gave me the thrilling feeling of being a woman, to feel like a woman should feel when she was in love and being loved by the right man. His tongue was now exploring my belly which was something I loved very much as his tongue revolved inside my belly button, over and over again, leaving wet patches on my skin, silent kisses that stained my skin with tattoos that were so beautiful, wishing I could show them to the world.

Our lips met once again as our tongues entwined with the pleasure of kissing, kisses of beautiful dirty love that we were now locked into once again and as far as I was concerned it was now forever.

Charlie gazed into my dark, emerald-green eyes that now sparkled, stroking my porcelain face with his fingertips. *Princess you were deep in thought earlier what were you thinking?*

I swallowed hard, taken aback by Charlie's request wondering if I should tell him about not using contraception, but now was not the time as it would all become apparent very soon. My mind was made up, or was my dream going to become a nightmare yet again? Suddenly I heard the familiar roar of the storm howling silently which tonight terrified me.

Tell me princess. I smiled. *Charlie, I was just loving the moment I was lost in love, our dirty, but beautiful love Charlie.* I then felt his fingers again seducing the ring on my necklace as he whispered his love for me.

My pussy was now drenched with warm, fresh juice as Charlie's cock was cascading beads of fresh juice like pearls. He pulled away looking at me as he smiled his cocky smile, squeezing both of my nipples, making me squeal with delight.

I was now feeling like a tart, Charlie's tart, as I got on to all fours dressed just in stockings and suspenders, free from my bra and knickers that Charlie had seductively removed from my body. Charlie slapped my thigh gently, repeating his actions again and again as we indulged in a frenzied dirty love session, fuelled for me by a craving for Charlie's incredible love and his seductive reputation.

Suddenly Charlie thrust his enormous cock into my pussy just to tease me, making me beg for more before turning me over again. Charlie's breathing was hard as he moaned, *you bitch, you dirty bitch Lizzy*. His gaze was now fixed on mine.

My mouth hungrily found Charlie's huge erection and once again it filled my mouth so full, it was so fucking huge. *Lizzy, my Lizzy*, he moaned, as his cock was being forced further into the back of my throat, thrusting and peppering my tongue with beads of juice that delighted my senses that now begged for more.

I turned again on to all fours as Charlie began kissing my back, his rolling tongue glided down my spine sending wave after wave of a delightful pleasure. I could feel his cock so hard against my delicate skin, desperately yearning to love my pussy.

I turned to face him. *Fuck me Charlie, fuck me hard*. I screamed out for more, hearing him, his breathing still loud, still so powerful, hard and warm against my neck, embracing once again the ring that still remained a mystery to me but for Charlie it held a secret that he selfishly wanted all for himself. My moaning had now distracted his attention away from the ring, his tongue sweeping over my curves before sliding firmly into my wet, purring pussy that tonight like always demanded more, much more. Charlie's head was now wedged firmly between my thighs.

I continued to enjoy the ultimate dirty love supplied by Charlie with both my hands caressing his head, making sure he knew that I did not want him to stop.

Charlie's cock then found my pussy, slowly and sexily the pressure was much harder now as he started to thrust and moan. *You dirty whore, my tart, my bitch*. Charlie was now fully loving my pussy, I felt the pressure again as thrusting and throbbing inside me was the biggest, hardest cock and fully loaded to the maximum with baby juice that was all for me and I was never going to object.

The moaning from Charlie was deep and heavy from his throat, something so powerful, deep and gritty. I loved hearing him moan my name and with that I felt the warm juice filling my ever demanding pussy to the limits, his moaning repeatedly loud and intense.

His tongue then traced my curves again, revolving around my belly button for maximum effect, sending me wild once again but Charlie had not finished with me as his tongue was on a mission to seduce my clit for the ultimate pleasure. *Cum for me you bitch, you beautiful bitch.* It did not take long before my juices flowed over his tongue smeared his lips.

His fingers were now dancing with my clit, my juices were now clinging to his fingers as I watched him slowly and seductively lick each one in turn, his gaze never leaving my porcelain face. Then once again with his fingers coated in fresh juice they were put into my mouth for me to share this erotic experience we had created together, and his gaze yet again never left mine, wanting to feast his eyes on this most seductive moment that tantalised us both.

Exhausted from love making, we slumped back onto the bed. Charlie looked at me, smiling his cocky and confident smile. *Lizzy, promise me you will always be my beautiful bitch, my whore, my princess.* He knew full well that I would remain his bitch, his whore, completely his forever. I smiled at him, nodding my approval, but was that all I ever would be, knowing that I would possibly be nothing more saddened me.

We woke on Sunday morning very late to the beautiful Welsh sunshine streaming through the window, not a cloud in the ice cold sky. Who could fail not to love the beauty of this amazing landscape that was laid out before us? The snow was still carpeting the lawn, the trees laden heavily, coated from the winter's blizzards that had swept across Wales, bringing with it punishing conditions that tested so many as they went about their daily lives.

Charlie's arms were firmly placed around my waist allowing me to feel his strong body against mine as we both admired once again the beautiful surroundings that had captured our love.

But now sadly it was time to leave, to head back to Cardiff and to the torment that was waiting for us both behind every closed door, something that we would deal with but I knew full well that it would come with massive heartaches, punishing us both for our dirty love affair that was now hiding an ever bigger secret that would bring a devastation all of its own, leaving Cardiff holding its breath in the wake of the disruptive storm that was to be ours.

Leaving the weekend behind us we headed back to normality but what was normality? Would we ever have a normal life together? We always had plenty to talk about, but we seemed to avoid the most important conversation like his wife, my husband and what the future might hold for us both which left me wondering if I was I only ever going to be his bit on the side. I was only in Wales for a short time so the future, my future, was very uncertain, leaving our ongoing love affair balancing on a knife-edge and at that moment my world once again started to crumble as I reached for reassurance from the ring that hung on my necklace as I twiddled impatiently, frustrated by not knowing what the future held for me.

Lunch was fabulous, a cosy affair in a little village pub. We sat in front of a roaring log fire watching the flames once again dance around the logs that sparked and crackled, sending little shards of white flames out onto the stone hearth. The aroma was so tantalising to my senses, bringing back many found Christmas memories. I didn't want to leave, trying hard to make my coffee last a little longer. Cardiff was now insight with our fabulous weekend coming to an end that would leave me alone once again to dwell on the future and Charlie's relentless, never-ending reputation, along with his life with Helen, but we had shared a fantastic weekend, so beautiful, more than I had ever imagined, allowing both our minds to have time to relax from the demanding torture and terrifying torment that we both had suffered just recently.

We arrived at the hotel and sadly it was time say goodbye. I hated goodbyes, but knowing how I felt at this moment Charlie leant over, putting his arm around me reassuringly. *Lizzy I love you.* He gently lifted my tear stained face. *I have a little something for you.* He handed me a box with *I love you* etched in to the lid, along with the mysterious initials that seemed to accompany everything Charlie gave me. I started to cry again. *Princess it's not goodbye.*

But it felt like it this afternoon as I now saw in the distance the swirling, raging black storm clouds, gathering pace knowing that they were heading my way yet again to spoil the sunshine that I had found once again in Cardiff.

As I opened the box I was shocked by the gift he had given me, it was a beautiful pair of pearl and white gold earrings. Charlie was always lavishing very expensive gifts on me, treating me to the finest things like the weekend away, the jewellery, underwear and expensive perfume.

Charlie kissed my hand, taking my thoughts away but in a split second the negative thoughts popped back into my mind as I wondered if he bought Helen presents, if he treated her like a princess, if they had wild, beautiful and untamed sex sessions, all things that spun wildly around in my mind, especially when I sat alone. My mind was muddled by so many puzzles, none of which made any sense. I was unable to put the pieces into any order but all of them were none of my business because as his mistress, his bitch and his tart I had no rights.

I felt flat now as I went to my lonely room, sitting on my huge bed, sobbing tears of loneliness, knowing I didn't have Charlie completely to myself as I was sharing the man I loved, the married man I loved with someone else, his wife, the woman he chose to marry. As I looked around, the room felt cold and very lonely, knowing these four walls would become hard to deal with at times and this cold afternoon was one of them as each wall seemed grey, cold and very unwelcome, allowing yet again lots of negative thoughts to impede on what should have been a time to embrace.

I should have been happy as I had spent the most beautiful weekend with the man who stole my heart, my virginity and in return had given me his love, his dirty love, but now, today, that didn't seem enough anymore, all because I wanted more.

I loved him, I wanted him, but again my mind strayed as he would now be with his wife and not here with me, which made me feel so very bitter. Once again I wrestled uncomfortably with the ring on the necklace, almost willing the chain to break, with my mind working overtime again and with the knowledge that I was facing a disturbed and restless night. I tossed and turned, my mind once again troubled by the turbulent weeks that lay ahead as the storm clouds had now gathered pace, leaving me to wonder what devastation they would bring and how long the storm would last to batter and bruise not just me, but also Charlie.

I was awoken by the alarm ringing loudly in my ear. 6am was here already. I felt mentally and emotionally drained, having been faced by vile images and terrifying voices throughout my dreams. I was still not able to free my mind from the images of Charlie's vile father and from the evil echoes of Dave's voice that continued to fill my sleeping moments, leaving no room in my dreams for the delights of Charlie and that was petrifying, not to be able to revisit our dirty love story while I was sleeping.

With an endless supply of coffee I felt slightly better as I got started on the planner for the week and caught up with my diary. I was starving so I rummaged around and I managed to find some biscuits that I had hidden from the builders and made myself yet another very strong cup of coffee.

As I looked up Charlie was standing in the doorway to the office. My eyes instantly lit up as his beaming smile lifted my spirits. Charlie was looking so sexy today, stood in his hard hat, something that really did turn me on, he gave me a cheeky kiss before we were interrupted by my phone ringing. As the week went on Charlie and I grabbed every chance that we could to be together stealing kisses as well as cuddles where possible, but we had not managed to have a whole night together sadly as he was with her, his wife Helen, which lead me to wonder again what she was really like, the list was endless as I tried to imagine her.

Friday arrived in the blink of an eye and I was due to go home this weekend, dreading it as usual. Charlie and I had not spent much time together this week but I knew with bitterness that I had to accept it. Charlie looked a little sad as he begged me to go back on Saturday morning. *I can't Charlie, Dave might suspect something.* But why did I care? I could not care less about what he thought anymore. *I want you to stay Lizzy.* He held my hands as he continued to plead with me to stay yet another night. I knew full well that I needed his dirty loving to get me through the miserable weekend that I was now dreading, having to go back to Dave's stupid, vile and unwelcome comments, to his inability to understand my feelings or to be able to communicate with me other than the normal few words that he repeated over and over again like a stuck record with the familiar sarcastic comments that were thrown in for good measure which made me think what was the point in going back to a loveless marriage anyway? So delightedly I said I would stay.

I was excited to have yet another night with Charlie and a few wonderful hours of us time together. I called home lying with ease to Dave, saying I had missed the train and would leave it now until Saturday. Dave seemed fine with that as he was going to the pub anyway with his drunken, fowl mouthed companions that all seemed to share the same selfish mentality as him.

I knew I would have to find the strength from somewhere to fight the backlash of his drunken night out, but Charlie's love would be my forever saving grace. The thought of him, us, and the amazing love we shared would get me through.

Saturday morning came all too soon as we enjoyed a very early breakfast together, back in our room I hurried to pack my case as Charlie was driving me to the station, but I had dirty love on my mind again and I was going to seduce him before I left so, as I kissed his neck slowly and seductively allowing me more time to enjoy the delights that were all mine for now, once again I was allowed to treat my senses to the amazing aroma of him while Charlie looked at me with those eyes I adored. *Lizzy you naughty girl, you very naughty girl.* He smiled as I blushed uncontrollably.

In a frenzy my clothes were now discarded onto the bedroom floor, taking full control I commanded him to love me hard and he was never going to object. I smiled cheekily as we continued our early morning dirty loving session before I went back to the life I now hated.

Both of us laid together, satisfied with our early morning delight but Charlie had not finished with me yet as his tongue made its way over my curves, finding and delighting my pussy, enjoying our beautiful juice and like always he was desperate to share it with me so now with both our juices smeared across his lips I was treated to kisses that tasted of our dirty love, giving us both the ultimate sexual sensation as his tongue glided around my mouth and into my throat.

With his cock still solid I helped myself to yet another massive helping of Charlie, knowing he would not object to my increasing appetite. Charlie moaned yet again at the pleasure he was receiving from my mouth, my tongue now coated in more juice that escaped freely from Charlie's cock, both of us loving this unexpected dirty love session.

As Charlie smiled his approval it made me blush and the more I blushed the more his cocky smile increased, stamping his approval, and making my mind up to have Charlie all to myself as I was not prepared to share him with Helen any longer, not now and not ever.

We were then about to say our sad goodbyes. Charlie held my hand, *Lizzy your shaking.* I was, and I wasn't sure why, maybe it was the thought of returning to a life I hated ever more now than I ever had. *I'm fine Charlie.* I shrugged of his concerns, saying goodbye, I hated it as every time was so painful, no easier from the first time.

As I boarded the train reluctantly I watched Charlie standing motionless, looking again like he had the weight of the world bearing down on his broad shoulders. I smiled and waved to him, but today his smiles were muted as I watched his lean silhouette fade to nothing which left me to wonder increasingly if I was asking too much of him, demanding his attention daily, forcing him to make decisions that were out of his control, but he wanted me, he wanted his Lizzy, so why were there so many negative thoughts?

Was I expecting too much? Was I rushing in too quickly, wanting all my dreams to come true, knowing full well I was there was only one man that could grant me those life time dreams? But he was married, his life complicated by secrets and obvious lies.

Suddenly jolted back to the here and now by my phone ringing loudly, much to the annoyance of my fellow passengers that seemed distracted away from their daily rituals, reading their newspapers... it was Charlie, the conversation light and somewhat casual and brief, the conversation felt cold and unloving, maybe it was me, maybe it was all too much for me... maybe it was too much for him, maybe we were rushing our new found love, maybe we needed to step back and take time?

The train pulled into the station reaching the final destination. I took a deep breath for what might lay ahead, knowing I had lied about my whereabouts last night and the massive secrets I was keeping. I had to remain calm, rise above the impending weekend that was before me.

I knew full well that there would be a war of words at some point this weekend, but I was prepared for the backlash, prepared to stand up for myself, or would I be caught off guard?

CHAPTER 19

On arriving home it was apparent things were not good, the sink was piled up with dirty dishes that were coated in the remains of days old food still clinging to every plate and Dave passed out upstairs on the bed from a full drunken binge from the night before, thinking to myself why I had to put up with this shit? But once again I knew I was to blame.

I washed all the dishes that overflowed the sink as Dave did not care even if there was not a clean cup to be had, or clean sheets on the bed, as long as he had the pub and his pathetic mates he was happy. I heard him getting up and I could tell he was in a foul mood, so I braced myself for the backlash of his drunken binge. I could hear him mumbling something as he stumbled down the stairs into the kitchen, semi-naked and stinking of stale beer, days old cigarette odour and unshaven. He was a mess, something I found very unpleasant and pretty much predictable these days, but still something he thought was attractive.

What time did you get back Lizzy? He snarled, his face rigid and tense with anger like a savage animal. I hated even looking at him as he had begun to scare me, his temper now out of control, his vile comments and commands left me terrified.

I got back a while ago Dave and I have cleared up your mess. I snapped as I snarled back at him. I walked past him, letting my anger show, not only in my actions but my facial expression, feeling his hand brush against my arm wanting to pull me back. I could tell I had annoyed him as he snapped. *Well, you need not have done that on my part Lizzy, I'm going out today and I won't be back until later.* That was fine with me, at least I could be on my own without the fear of a war of words between us, for now anyway, I heard him slam the door behind him, almost taking the door from its hinges, wanting me to know he was still annoyed with me, disapproving at my outburst.

I checked in on dad to escape my prison cell, delighted once again to be back at home. I was so desperate to stroll around the garden, absorbing myself in lost memories, finding parts of the garden that brought back such special moments like when I was a little girl helping mum hang out the washing, playing with all the plastic pegs in the tatty homemade peg bag, delighted that I still had all those most precious memories that I could recall, all made possible by this garden. I sat on the old swing that hung under the tree house, letting my mind wander to relax from the misery that surround me at home and from the farce of a marriage that I was still forced to endure all these years on. It still didn't surround me with any emotion, it was never inviting and never would be, but that was my own stupidity.

I then revisited my old bedroom to stand at the window and admire the surroundings without noise, to watch the sun fading into the woods casting its mellow glow as I watched the Owls circling high above the place that they were proud to call home which still fascinated me today, souring high into the sky before swooping into the woods ready for nightfall and the peace that would shroud them.

I walked up the dimly lit street wishing I could turn around and just walk away from the prison cell that awaited me again tonight. The house was dark, cold and empty, but that was no surprise and a welcome relief for me as I sat watching television until late, alone with thoughts that all revolved around Charlie, Wales and my desire to have his baby, but that desire was now laced with so many negative thoughts that spun in my mind, knowing that I was being selfish and having not thought through the never-ending list of problems that would face us.

Dave staggered in very late, very drunk and very bad tempered, slamming the door again behind him, slamming it so hard it would surely have awoken the neighbours. I looked at him in disgust as I glanced at my watch, knowing full well what time it was but just to see his reaction and again he never failed to slur the vile insults that I was becoming used to. I hated this marriage, it was cold, empty there was nothing left here for me but that was something I had known from that early summer's day when I walked reluctantly to take the vows that had silently choked me and had done so ever since.

We got into an argument, a very heated one at that and one that got out of hand very quickly as he began forcing himself on me, dragging me up the stairs by my arm, squeezing it so tight once again, demanding that I did as I was told, sending a sudden wave of terror throughout my fragile body that instantly brought back the vile torment of when I was assaulted by Charlie's father.

Suddenly it was happening again, I was so frightened and terrified, I felt very vulnerable to Dave's demands, screaming at him to stop as Dave fumbled about putting on the condom that I insisted he wore before forcing me to remove my underwear. I just laid there waiting for it all to be over and it didn't take long. Dave screamed at me violently, shedding vile words before he forced himself on me again, he was now snarling at me, showing his teeth in a frightening and menacing way. I was petrified, shaking violently so I allowed him once again to abuse and violate my body while I closed my eyes just to blot it out, but it didn't blot out having to hear his constant unwelcome words while he freely attacked my fragile body that now was so limp from feeling and emotion.

He screamed at me, *Lizzy, you're a bitch, a little bitch.* Then, out of nowhere he slapped my face hard, leaving a burning sting, then his fist hit my cheek with a full aggressive power that stunned my face, making it go numb. I was now in total fear which was terrifying. I jumped out of bed, running downstairs to seek the sanctuary of the lounge, switching every light on as not to be alone.

My face was sore and swollen. How dare he? My body was shaking violently with an uncontrollable fear. I now hated him with a real hate. I could hear him stumbling down the stairs, ready for yet another argument. He was totally unaware of what he had done, repeating his vile words as he verbally abused me again, pulling my hair so hard I thought it would be ripped out of my head, pushing me with force, hard against the front door as my head hit the metal lock. I screamed at him, *you're hurting me Dave, stop!* I screamed *please stop!* My troubled life was now flashing in front of me, suddenly I became aware that I was no longer the storm that invaded my life, it was now Dave that bore that title, it was him that was now bringing the unwanted storms as his voice thundered its way through the house before snarling again, casting his vile war of words as I felt the cold winds of the storm brushing against my bruised and battered porcelain face.

He then raised again his clenched fist in front of my face as I cowered away from him, afraid again that he was about to abuse me once more, to batter my porcelain face that was already heavily bruised. He then suddenly pulled back, *I'm sorry Lizzy, sorry.* He then rushed upstairs, he had then and only then realised just what he had done, hiding behind the door to our bedroom was his hiding place tonight, his bitter spitefulness on show, his guilt brought to the forefront. He had now endorsed in my mind that I was going to leave him, this was my way out of this loveless, cold and now violent marriage, a time when I could at last escape the prison in which I had served my life sentence.

I slept on the sofa in the lounge out of his way all night, wedging a chair under the door handle for added protection as I was terrified that he would abuse me again but I knew I was safe for now as he was so drunk he would have by now passed out on the bed.

My life was in bits, a string of events that had led me to this moment in time, now with a violent husband, my mum so cruelly taken from me, my lover married to another, what the hell was happening to me? My life felt very complicated, clouded by the storms that were continuing to gather pace far away in the distance but still allowing me to hear its violent roar, reminding me that I was once again on a roller-coaster of a journey.

After a very restless night and a violent beating from Dave, I went to the bathroom locking the door behind me, scared to look in the mirror as I knew I was not going to like the reflection that would reflect back. The pain was already crippling my ability to smile. As I looked into the mirror I was shocked at the state of my eye, my porcelain face was now blackened and swollen, complete with Dave's spiteful endorsement of our placid relationship.

Dave you bastard, you drunk bastard. My words coldly echoed around the very cold and sterile bathroom. I hated him, I hated him now with renewed passion that he had turned into a vile, bulling thug, all fuelled by his selfish lifestyle. At that moment the storm swirled around me, taking my body on a violent wave of anger and frustration as my fist violently hit the old cabinet mirror with force, smashing the reflection that was looking back at me, my reflection was now blood stained and tarnished in vile hatred for the man I married. I stood firmly fixed to the floor, rigid as I watched my blood ingrain itself in between the splintered shards of glass before it slithered slowly down the mirror, splattering onto the pristinely white basin below. I watched coldly the torrent of blood that was seeping from yet more open and unattractive wounds.

I was now annoyed with myself that I had reacted out of spite for Dave's appalling behaviour so I applied my makeup thick to try to cover my very blackened eye which was a mixture of dark blue, vivid yellow and black with a tint of burnished red thrown in for good measure. He had really done himself proud, leaving me with yet more scars and heartache to bear and to now have to make excuses for him, excuses that were inexcusable, knowing he would have to see my battered reflection looking back at him through a blood stained tormented vision that today I prayed would haunt him, torment him, and terrify him through the daylight hours and beyond into nightfall.

I thought I would catch the early train back to Cardiff, needing to escape these four walls which today contained so much anger, so much despair and now vile hatred for a man that was proud to call me his wife when we were out together, a husband that thought it was acceptable to abuse me, to humiliate me and batter me for good measure, my so called husband. He was weak, a coward, vile, unloving, uncaring and now violent, all fuelled by his increasing drinking habits and his untamed selfishness.

I buttoned my cosy cream wool coat, wrapped my silky multi-coloured scarf around my neck and took my case without leaving any note, leaving lovingly a blood stained trail in my wake, slamming the door loudly behind me hoping it would wake him from his drunken slumber, hoping he would awake to the realisation that he had now delivered the final and last devastating blow, a reminder that our marriage was now finally over. I knew now I was leaving him for good, my mind made up. I was totally clear on what I wanted from my life and this prison, along with all the things that were contained in it, were never going to be any part of my new life.

I sat on the train trying to block out one vivid emotion from the next, recalling Charlie's vile father and now Dave's vile war of words, completed with his ability to beat me for good measure, words and actions that I now hoped would choke him as tears of hatred blurred my vision, a hatred just kept on building in my body like a raging thunderstorm that was now casting a very dark shadow, so full of bitterness over my life and yet again, almost on cue, I grasped the ring on my necklace but today I felt the ring had lost its ability to reassure me as it too had now started to haunt me, teasing me with the initials that were still a mystery, leaving me again to question what or who they were for, knowing full well they weren't for me.

Suddenly my phone rang, startling me from all the agonising questions that now crowded my mind, it was Charlie. I let it ring, I was too upset to talk to him right now, I needed to free myself from this bitter torment that again raged in head. I knew if I heard his voice it would be impossible to fight back my emotions and distress.

On return to Cardiff I sat in the station coffee shop and ordered a strong hot coffee to help me compose myself for the conversation that I was about to have with Charlie. Then, at that moment Charlie rang again, this time I answered him, desperately fighting back my anguish. I fell silent, lost for any words. *Lizzy, what's wrong? Lizzy, Lizzy where are you?* In a very muffled state I answered him, telling him where I was. He must have known by my anguished voice that I was upset. *Stay there Lizzy.* With that the phone was silent and just as I was finishing my coffee I felt Charlie's strong arms around me.

My head lowered as I just sat staring at the floor, not wanting anyone to see the magnitude of a vile battering that had been made possible by the hands of my so-called husband. I felt sick and ashamed of the thought he would allow himself to even think he had the right to strike me, to invade my body with punches that left me terrified, leaving me petrified to be in the same house as him, let alone the same room.

Princess what is it, let me look at you. Lifting my face gently, my tears clung to my battered face, trying to ease the pain that now crippled my eye and my cheek. *Lizzy what the hell has happened to you? Your hand, you're bleeding.*

I was and I hadn't noticed, my cream pristine wool coat was now splattered in droplets of blood from my fist complete with splinters of glass that stung my skin, all the delicate buttons now ingrained with dried blood. I could see Charlie turning white with rage, he knew instantly what had happened as the rich kaleidoscope of colour now painted my porcelain face in a blend of black, red, blue, and yellow, not even makeup could mask the horrific tattoo that now blemished my face in a story of violence.

Please don't tell me he did this to you princess. I will be fine Charlie. I brushed aside my agony. *Lizzy it's not fine.* He was livid. *Why Lizzy? Why would anyone want to hurt you?* His cocky smile had now turned to rage, a rage that wiped the smile instantly from his face, a look I had never seen before, a look that I hoped I would not see again.

He was drunk that's all, just a drunken argument that got out of hand. *Lizzy for fuck sake that does not make it right please don't make excuses for him.* I could clearly see that Charlie was very upset by this violent attack, the shock and disbelief seemed to have ingrained itself on his face.

Charlie then carefully put my hand in his, *let's get away for a weekend, far away from everyone and everything.* I smiled. *That would be lovely Charlie.* But again in the back of my mind I kept thinking about Charlie's wife and what she thought about him constantly slipping away for weekends and evenings. I felt for her, knowing that she lost her baby recently but I needed him all to myself, so now with my mind made up I was going to have him forever, after all it was my name that was still embroidered on labels that adorned not only his lavish clothes, but also his life.

Now smiling that unforgettable cocky smile he took my hand, kissing each of my fingers in turn. *Let's have a fun weekend Lizzy, say you'll come.* So with my muted smile I nodded my approval, once again thinking about his wife. *Will that be OK for you Charlie? Yes of course it's work Lizzy. But what about Helen? What about her Lizzy?* His voice was raised, I knew then I had touched a nerve. *Helen is not my priority now Lizzy.* I changed the subject. *Charlie, a fun weekend it is.* I smiled a somewhat sideways smile though my pain.

On returning to the hotel Dave had tried to call so many times but I chose to refuse all his calls. I had hoped that he would have got the message, seeing my blood stain reflection in the bathroom mirror, seeing my blood lying cold and congealed in the bathroom basin, but that was obviously not enough so I told the reception desk to not accept his calls as I was not prepared to hear his excuses, his false promises, and his vile comments a moment longer.

Charlie made sure I was comfortable and had everything I needed, kissing my fragile face and lips that were tonight so sore, bearing the brunt of a selfish bully, leaving me alone once again to shed tears of sadness, tears of hate and of love, knowing I would be once again terrorised in my dreams by so many evil demons, all wanting to destroy me and my dreams, past, present and future, now all tormented by the men who had invaded my life, taking with it a part of the real Lizzy for themselves like some sort of sexual, selfish trophy and now the haunting initials that were etched into the ring that continued driving me crazy as to who they were meant for or who they belonged to.

I awoke early feeling refreshed, much to my amazement, having slept well with little intrusion. I thought that maybe I had at last been released from the nightmares of late, free from images and voices that would always terrify me.

I stood at the bathroom mirror blinded by the facial markings that reflected back at me, stunned by the brutal image that appeared before me as I applied my makeup thickly once again, trying to cover the vivid colours that marked my porcelain face, now so clear for everyone to see. My hatred of Dave was still gathering monumental pace as the storm clouds had increased overnight into a mass of the heaviest dark clouds that now contained out of control bitterness ready to shower over Dave when the time was right, but I knew the storm would also be mine unleashing its cruel contents, meaning I would have to seek some shelter if I was to come through it unscathed.

I managed to get to my office without anyone noticing my horrific facial markings, my makeup skills had done the job well, but it could not mask my pain as the pain had silently started to engulf my body.

At last it was 6pm, I felt drained and eager to get back to the hotel but not before Charlie and I had been for a drink and a much needed catch up, snatching a few minutes together. Sadly, before we knew it, it was once again time to say goodnight as he headed home to Helen and I went back to my lonely hotel room with just the four walls for company and the ring, the mysterious ring that was my only comfort that night.

The week went by so slowly but I managed to get a few snatched moments with Charlie, even a few kisses and some much needed cuddles, knowing I would need to wait a few more days until I had him all to myself, until Helen cast him free from her clutches. She was having the lion share of him, my jealousy was becoming hard to hide as I didn't want to be sharing him, to be second best or his bit on the side any more, not wanting to hide our dirty love or having to snatch the odd chance of a kiss or if we were lucky, to share the odd night together, but at the weekend he was going to be mine again.

We both knew what we were doing was so wrong but I could not stop loving him and he felt the same, our love so obviously more stronger and powerful than we ever imagined, that now over ruled our guilt and always would.

CHAPTER 20

Having arrived in London after a long drawn out few days we headed to the hotel which was in a very trendy part of London. It was really posh, we were immediately shown to our room by a porter, immaculately dressed in a very smart grey tweed suit with shoes that shone. They were so highly polished, like he was wearing mirrors on his feet which made me smile.

Delighted to be in London it was great to be with Charlie. It was like a breath of fresh air, a breath of fantastic London air that I absorbed like a sponge, taking in its aroma, its vibrancy, it was alive, my senses now begging for more, inhaling the cocktail of aromas that now seduced my body almost leaving me drunk from the beauty of its powerful cocktail.

We headed to the west end for dinner, a romantic dinner was once again mine tonight, sitting opposite the man that had held and captured my attention for well over twelve long years. We played the flirting game all evening while I continued to blush from the extreme hunger Charlie held in his eyes that still managed to seduce me, leaving me breathless, but eyes that also terrified me as I knew they were hiding such a destructive secret, a secret life that seemed to grow daily, leaving me still to wonder why, but I knew I was never going to be invited into the dark, mysterious life he was leading, as Charlie was hell bent on keeping it to himself.

Back at the hotel we took the lift back to our room, passion was running high as we had missed each other so much that week. It was very apparent from the incredible kisses that were being delivered and received, never wanting the lift to stop at the next floor as we both continued our erotic journey in the lift, pressing the bell to the top floor and back, embracing the seductive kisses that we were now sharing.

We put our kisses on hold for a moment, our room was beautiful with a great view of the most fantastic London skyline, skyscrapers that filled the sky with little lights that were being cast from each one of the windows that almost looked like tiny stars. I gazed out of our window, losing myself in this amazing place and felt Charlie's arms wrap a little tighter around my body, both of us loving the view that spilled out before us.

As our lips met, my body was once again sent into a frenzy of passion as our tongues danced with each other, the dance of love entwined by the sheer passion. Charlie's tongue was now engaged with my throat, sending wild untamed emotions throbbing through my body.

He kissed my hand before looking into my eyes, demanding my attention. His deep brown eyes instantly seduced me, his gaze suddenly moved to the ring, almost flirting with it, seducing it, leaving me somewhat jealous. I gasped loudly, bringing back his attention as he peppered kisses onto my neck, sending yet more wild emotions through my body, emotions that were very welcome that night.

It was my time to take control so I undid his shirt slowly, twisting the buttons undone to reveal his firm chest. He looked so handsome stood just in his jeans and bare feet. His bare torso was stunning, lean, and muscular, I indulged a little longer, feasting my eyes on him, inhaling his very powerful aroma.

I slid my hand slowly down inside his jeans, letting my fingertips meet his hard, stiff cock that was wanting my attention, wanting the attention of my mouth, along with my very demanding pussy.

I smiled contently as he smiled back that adorable cocky smile, repeating only for you as I tried to hide my blushes before peppering his back, his chest, his neck in Lizzy kisses. I then undid his jeans, letting them drop to the floor and unashamedly dropped to my knees to find his erection that was yearning for my undivided attention that yearned to be loved by my most attentive mouth so without any need for encouragement I put my mouth to work, allowing his stiff erection to fill my mouth as Charlie's hands held my head firmly. I sucked it hard allowing him to have the full pleasure of my mouth, slipping nicely into my throat. Suddenly I could taste it fresh on my tongue as my mouth continued to love his huge, stiff, love-filled cock. I felt him tense up, moaning with the rhythm of my mouth that was begging me for more. He then lifted me to my feet, kissing me, allowing his tongue to firmly slide inside my mouth, revolving around my tongue that was coated in fresh, tantalising liquid that had cascaded from his cock, wanting to taste the juice that was now smeared across my lips.

He then gently undid my blouse, allowing my tits to fall naturally into his hands which always made him smile. *Lizzy, Lizzy my Lizzy.* My nipples commanded his attention that I so desperately loved as he sucked them, delivering such a delightful sensation that my whole body reacted to instantly. He undid my jeans, slowly and seductively, pulling me onto the bed for some much needed skin on skin contact that enriched my body that was starving for his undivided attention and irresistible love.

Our lips met again and as they did he straddled over me, caressing my curves, allowing his kisses to follow my curvy body, peppering kisses over my belly. His tongue revolved repeatedly around my belly button.

His tongue made its way to my very wet demanding pussy and Charlie spread my legs a little further as gently and softly his mouth engaged with my clit. My body tensed up with lust that was begging him for more.

My moaning was so loud and uncontrolled as I demanded that Charlie fucked me and fucked me hard. My legs now curled around his strong body as he began to thrust hard, thrusting again and again, moaning repeatedly my name, wanting to fuck me harder, feeling him penetrate a little further. *Charlie I love it, Charlie love me, love me harder, give me what I want.* My intense moaning was so loud now, so demanding. *What Lizzy, I want, I want.* I was now stumbling over my words, *I want your baby!* I screamed.

Charlie was silent as he continued to fuck me hard, his dirty love not fazed by my life-changing command that now echoed around the room, bouncing from wall to wall with nowhere to hide until it slipped silently under the door into the long corridor beyond, flowing out into the streets of London. My secret being swept along on the breeze that now flowed through this vibrant city.

We continued to fuck each other softly as we were both fully in the rhythm of such dirty love that now contained my command and my secret, a secret wish that now London held within its grasp as it silently swept through the streets, waiting patiently for my wish to be granted.

I was loving it as he thrust again and again, his gaze firmly fixed on mine, my blushes apparent with every thrust, knowing I loved it a little rough. Suddenly he withdrew his cock from my pussy, leaving me begging him to fuck me harder. He then looked at me, hesitating for a while. *Lizzy, a baby, our baby, our baby? Yes Charlie.* His powerful smile set me alight, leaving my body tingling while I awaited his response.

Well let's hope it's tonight then Lizzy. I looked at him softly and with a passion that was all for him. *Lizzy, let's make baby love.* I heard London rejoice with his words, knowing Charlie approved of my secret. I was not using any contraception, I knew it was so wrong not to have told him but Charlie had never asked and now I was so desperate to have his baby so it had to be now as I had promised myself at any cost to have him in my life forever.

Charlie looked at me as I looked back at him so naturally, but tonight it was different, as my well-kept secret was now told. Charlie now knew my lifetime wish that had his name on. We both knew it was different tonight and it always would be from now on as we had been given the seal of approval from the city that had now stolen my secret.

We laid together fully aware of our dirty love and what we were committing to. Charlie suddenly sat up, questioning my secret again. *A baby Lizzy, you want my baby? Yes Charlie* I replied. *I do.* I said in a very determined voice, leaving him in no doubt about my secret wish.

I was somewhat elated that I had now told Charlie my most treasured wish, endorsing it with kisses that once again allowed our passion to spill over, making dirty love for the second time that night, hoping to make my dream a reality.

On awakening we shared our amazing love once again. Charlie seemed delightfully determined to grant me my wish, my porcelain face now cupped in Charlie's hands, allowing his eyes to meet mine, his gaze fixed. *Lizzy you're an amazing lady and you will always be my girl.* Suddenly I felt a but coming into the conversation. I held my breath, Charlie smiled, *Lizzy, my Lizzy let's hope you get your wish.*

I was in floods of tears, uncontrollable tears, and as I cried London stood in silence until my tears were dry, tears that seemed to echo through the busy streets below us. Soft echoing whispers that brushed against everything in its path, leaving a trail of delight, sweeping smiles that coated everyone's face.

With the morning sunshine streaming through the window I was excited to be here in London, somewhere I had not been since I was a child. It was now all fresh and new with a vibrancy that I loved, I wanted to explore a new found freedom, alone with Charlie in this huge city that had clearly captured my heart, embracing me in its zest that thrilled my senses, taking me on yet another journey in my life, inhaling air that was alive and that thrilled my body as it now knew my secret.

The warmth was so apparent as we stepped out of the hotel on that beautiful sunny April day, peppering warm kisses on to both our faces that seemed so refreshing after the bitterly cold winter that we had just endured.

As we reached the park it was stunning, all the trees were now bursting with heavy bud and glorious blooms, the glorious songs from the birds singing from high above us, flower beds that looked so beautiful, forming an intricate coloured woven carpet of sunshine; yellow, pastel blue, decadent purple, gleaming whites, and delicate pink.

The sun was now peppering the park in pockets of warmth, the smell of newly cut grass filled the air. It was such an evocative smell, one that took me back to my childhood when dad used to cut the grass in our garden at home and once again that aroma allowed me to be transported back in time to the garden I loved and adored, a place that held spellbinding memories for me as my birthday parties were held every year in the garden, allowing my friends the freedom to embrace what the garden held for me.

We walked holding hands and before long the conversation led us to the subject of babies, a conversation that we had never spoke about until now. This was a brand new conversation for us both, although it had been constantly in my thoughts.

Charlie squeezed my hand. *Lizzy, what you said last night.* London suddenly froze, holding its breath once again as I waited for Charlie's words to fill the air. *Our baby is it what you want? Yes, more than anything Charlie, I would love your baby.* Charlie then smiled his cocky smile, allowing London to breathe a sigh of relief and for me to now not have to choke back any bitter tears of rejection, squeezing his hand and taking in yet another deep breath. *I know it's not right Charlie.* I yet again twiddled nervously with the ring on the necklace. *Lizzy let's not talk about that now.* Yet again I felt he was sweeping the most important conversations under the carpet rather than face what was going to become a reality.

Charlie never talked about his home life or his private life that obviously held so many secrets, something he obviously didn't think seemed important as it was only us that mattered, but his casual words and lack of commitment to Helen terrified me, knowing he was married, knowing the reputation that still surrounded him, shrouding his life in constant suspicion.

I sat again seeking comfort from the ring as I twiddled relentlessly, almost breaking the chain. I felt Charlie's fingers entwining with mine, taking my fingers away from the chain, to hold both my hands for reassurance. *Lizzy, I love you.* With those words it felt like there was yet again a huge, but coming something that I was not going to like as London again froze in silence awaiting Charlie's muted answers.

Sorry Charlie, maybe I should not have said anything, but the moment felt right, the love felt right. Princess it's fine, it's fine, I have thought about it too and I love the idea. My face beamed at his reply, as did Charlie's, London was now smiling for us both but I don't think I had really thought it through completely as now lots of negative thoughts were popping into my mind as to the effect that us having a baby would put on others and us. Once again I had gone full steam ahead, never thinking about the consequences and as I looked up to the sky it reminded me that the storms were imminent and that they would be relentless, bringing dark clouds that would cast so many unforgiving shadows from the past as well as the present to complicate further our already teetering dirty love affair.

Now with strong, hot coffee we sat and talked while overlooking the lake, our conversation seemed slightly casual today, but my mind was made up, I wanted Charlie's baby desperately but I would put no demands on him as he was married to Helen, something I still felt somewhat guilty about, that I was sleeping with her husband, being his bit on the side, his tart, his whore, and his dirty secret, but he was promised to me the day our eyes met for the very first time.

Suddenly I had started to wish that I had not said anything as it seemed to have made things more complicated in some ways. The more we talked about it the more I knew I should not have told him, I should have kept my secret to myself not letting him or London know what was mine and what should have remained my secret.

I leant forward to kiss Charlie, whispering thousands of I love you's as he smiled that wicked, cocky and at times arrogant smile, a smile that reassured me that he felt the same, wanting us to share the precious gift of a baby, a new life that we would make together.

We laid on the grass for a while in the sunshine that was warm, peppering soft spring kisses on our faces. This was a perfect way to spend our time together, Charlie now laid on his side looking at me as he picked a delicate, perfectly formed tiny white daisy and said, *Remember these Lizzy?* I smiled. *How could I ever forget Charlie?* Blushing again, so much so my face was burning, not from the sun but from the thoughts of those very special and seductive daisy chains.

The sun was now disappearing slowly behind the London skyline as it began to set. Suddenly London once again came to life, bringing with it a vibrancy that I loved, the unique aromas, the constant noise, the hustle and bustle that seemed to entice me in to its very different life from the life I had back in the Wiltshire countryside which seemed a million miles away from the here and now.

Back in our room Charlie ran us a bath full of soft foaming bubbles that cascaded on to the bathroom floor in small piles of a pretty foaming mess, bubbles that were so perfect and round, bursting when they brushed against each other, unleashing the pretty, delicate fragrance they held.

Room service had now arrived, champagne on ice and in a very fancy silver bucket to celebrate my secret as we sat in the biggest bath ever sipping champagne, loving our time alone together, embracing every second of our time in London. Charlie's gaze was firmly fixed on mine once again. *Princess I love seeing your tits covered in bubbles, it's so sexy, so very sexy it makes me smile every time.* He was right, it did always make him smile.

Our eyes were now flirting and dancing a sensual dance with each other, it was obvious that we both had love on our minds, baby love, so with that in mind we left the bathroom for something more comfortable.

Charlie then sat in the chair that had no arms, it was perfect for straddling him, perfect for some serious dirty love that we now needed and once again I watched him feast on my curvy body, once again seeing the hunger growing in his eyes.

I sat on his legs, ready to straddle his love filled cock, so as I held the back of the chair with a firm grip I let my pussy relax to ride the enormous cock I loved. We found the perfect rhythm as he slowly thrust it gently into my increasingly demanding juice drenched pussy.

I moved slowly, almost letting his cock escape my pussy. *Princess you bitch.* With that he thrust it all the way, hard and with a powerful force, making me screech with passion and begging him for more as we both continued to moan loudly, embracing the moment.

I was left breathless as always from being loved by Charlie as he held me tight with an intense dirty love that was so special. Charlie's fingers were now clenching the bottom of my spine, both of us not wanting to move from this amazing position. Charlie whispered. *Princess, let's continue this later.* He smiled his trademark smile that always delighted me, that tantalised my emotions for what was to come.

As Charlie made his way to the bathroom I could see his naked torso reflecting in the mirror, a reflection that I just adored. He was so handsome with his distinctive look, his lean body so sexy, something that was mine and always had been.

Tonight as we stepped out from the hotel hand in hand like any normal couple it felt so right, now not having to hide our dirty love that allowed us to enjoy our evening, allowing us to be us, to ride the journey without people ready to point fingers and to judge what they saw with blinkered eyes.

We kissed goodnight lying in each other's arms as we were so tired from the day's events and happily exhausted from making beautiful baby love. I hoped my mind was again free from trauma, free from terrifying voice's and vile images.

Sunday morning came and a late lazy breakfast was served before we headed to the very posh Knightsbridge for some window shopping which I loved, now hoping that one day I would return to London again as it had stolen a piece of my heart which I was happy for it to have, as I knew if I left a little love in London I would have to return to collect it one day in the future.

4.30pm was here already and we were back on the train heading back to normality, but nothing was normal as I was back having to share Charlie with Helen. I kept thinking about her and how guilty I should be feeling, but I didn't feel guilty, not in the slightest as I would never be able stop loving her husband, not now, not in the future, because the future was ours, not theirs.

Back in Cardiff as if it was only yesterday Charlie and I now had to say yet another goodbye and as normal he held both my hands outstretched, smiling his trademark smile, looking at me with passion and still with hunger in his eyes. *Lizzy, my stunning Lizzy, I hope your dreams come true Princess.* He beamed that all familiar cocky smile, his smile once again held my gaze, lingering to say the last goodbye, begging for just another kiss and another, to be replaced by another. Charlie then headed home to her, his wife, to resume their lives as husband and wife, leaving me once again alone in my room, alone with thoughts that were now delivering so many negative thoughts and tonight was no different as wave after wave of negativity embraced me of what the outcome of my secret might hold.

CHAPTER 21

Monday morning was here already, the alarm rang loudly in my ear distracting me from my dreams that had thankfully been free from vile images and tormenting voices, it was now the start of a new week after we had such a wonderful weekend. Work would seem so dull in comparison, knowing the normal day to day routine would be waiting for me, paperwork and yet more paperwork piling up into some sort of tower, ready to topple over as it groaned under the strain.

I opened my top drawer to get my phone book and to my delight in my drawer was a box, a little wooden box and scratched in the lid the words *read for our baby* followed by the now the haunting and habit forming initials *H L F*. As I opened it my heart was racing, our baby, tears filled my eyes, tears of joy that now blurred my vision, knowing we would hopefully have the baby that we both wanted so much, fulfilling my dreams, a beautiful silver daisy broach laid in the beautiful box, It was so lovely, he must of bought it in London when he slipped away for a few minutes. It was so pretty and so very delicate, such a special loving thought for our baby that would be conceived through love, everlasting and eternal love that had consumed us for so many long years.

It seemed so cold in my office today, even though it was April, so I made coffee in a bid to keep me awake and try to get warm. Charlie popped in to my office, instantly bringing some much needed warmth. As I threw my arms around him he smiled instantly on spotting the box which lay open on my desk for me to admire. *You found it Lizzy. It's perfect Charlie.* I then kissed him to thank him for the unexpected gift.

You heading home at the weekend princess? Yes I will have to see dad and make sure he is OK. I was hating the thought of seeing Dave, knowing I had to face him at some stage but I would not put up with his abuse and his temper anymore, so armed with renewed strength and power I was ready to face Dave, ready for his sarcasm, his bullying, and his violence, ready for the violent storm that was now Dave.

The week dragged, I saw Charlie now and again snatching kisses with the odd much needed embrace thrown in, but it was never ever enough to suppress my ongoing cravings, knowing time was precious, as were moments we spent together. It always brought a smile to my face however, my smiles could not hide the lingering thoughts I had about Charlie's wife and his home life as it did not add up, something was not right, something that continually tormented my mind. Nothing about Charlie's private life seemed to make any sense other than when he was with me, but even then his eyes hid a magnitude of secrets that I would never know and thinking to myself maybe I didn't want to.

Friday came and my bags were packed ready for the journey, Charlie was taking me home but I could not say it was home any more as it was not, it never had been and never would. Homeward bound and once again the conversation turned to the future, knowing it was not so easy to predict what it held for us both, but we could be sure our love would continue near or far, forever, wherever we were in the world.

As we said our goodbyes I twiddled again nervously with the ring on the necklace in anticipation of what lay ahead of me behind the cold unwelcoming front door, so with lots of kisses and special I love you's Charlie held my hand, not wanting to leave me, his smile so powerful. *Meet me tomorrow Lizzy.* I jumped at the chance. *See you tomorrow you know where.*

He then kissed me and he was gone, speeding away through the country lanes leaving me alone again, but I was left smiling in anticipation of visiting the old shed again and how romantic it was going to be, so now with a spring in my step I walked up the dank and uninspiring street nervously and now very concerned as to what I might face. I prepared myself once again for the backlash and possibly a drunken beating, taking a deep breath in as I forced the key into the lock, wanting to turn around and run for miles, but to my surprise it was clean, tidy and Dave was cooking dinner but I knew full well this was only an act of total guilt that had overcome him, it was so obvious. His actions had been made in a desperate attempt to try to cover what was now a habit of violence and his intolerable behaviour, but it did nothing for him except enhance his guilt.

But his guilt changed nothing about the way I felt, as our marriage was over and over for good, that was for sure. Nothing could or would ever change my mind but I was tired and had other things on my mind, much more important things that did not include him, the effort he had made was far too little, far too late as it was only a drop in the ocean as far as I was concerned and would never make up for the violent beating he gave me, leaving me now scarred for life, tormented by his abusive behaviour, along with his foul and spiteful comments. It was now only a matter of time until I ended our sham of a marriage so that I could be free from his name that had clouded my young life, making it a total misery, dragging me along for the last seven uneventful, boring, and underwhelming years, talking me down, chaining me to his demands and coating me in vile unfounded words daily.

We sat watching television on opposite sides of the living room, not saying anything to each other, there was nothing left to say in this marriage, not for me anyway. Silence descended over every room in this prison, casting a cold, uninviting light that Dave was happy to call his home and tonight was no different from any other night we had spent together as he headed to the pub to seek the company of his vile comrades and the companionship of the bottom of a glass.

I went to bed about midnight and Dave was still out. Two hours later I was awoken as I heard him stumbling through the front door, slamming every door in his way. I cringed at the thought of him being at home so I pretended to be sound asleep as I did not want a repeat of the last time I was here, my body once again shaking with anxiety of being beaten and abused for the second time in as many weeks, my fingers rigidly holding onto the ring that still hung patiently from my necklace.

The night passed without incident much to my surprise, but my dreams were visited once more by the images and voices that I hated but that I had come to expect, along with my baby's muted cries far away in the distance.

We were both awake early and I was off to see dad for the day as Dave was going out with his vile friends which was perfectly fine with me, we were ships that passed in the night now. We had to face it, our marriage was just a waste of time, something I had known from the day he forced a cheap engagement ring on my finger which he seemed to think gave him the right to bully, control and abuse me.

I wanted to see dad to make sure he was coping with life without mum, knowing he would put a brave face on for me to try to hide his ongoing heartache. I braced myself, taking in a huge, deep breath as I unlocked the front door. Suddenly mum's perfume invaded my nostrils, again instantly making me glance up the staircase onto the landing as I felt mum's presence disappearing into my bedroom, knowing she was looking out of my bedroom window across the garden she loved so much.

As I glanced around the house nothing had changed. Mum's clothes still hung in her wardrobe, her makeup bag still where she had left it, treasured keepsakes adored her dressing table, photographs that held memories that we all cherished, it was obvious that dad was still finding life without mum very hard to deal with.

Once again I spent time alone in the garden recalling all the times I had spent here in this perfect garden when mum would read to me in the shade of the apple trees. Such treasured times were brought back to life in multicolour, still vivid in my memory, never allowing me to forget my wonderful childhood that was filled with so much love.

After lunch I headed to the little shed, knowing how special and how lucky I was as I pushed the door open to see Charlie sat in the chair. Suddenly I was consumed with tears while trying to capture the aroma that was contained within this little shed. *Why the tears Lizzy? It's perfect Charlie.* Now with memories still fresh in my mind, just the way it should be as I never wanted to forget any of them. Like the little lamp we once used still sat on the grubby window sill waiting to light this little shed again if needed, the grubby window and the vast amount of wavering cobwebs that now seemed to be clinging to everything.

Now in a frenzy of afternoon lust we instantly started peppering each other's bodies in sensual, dirty love fuelled kisses. I was feeling very frustrated through lack of Charlie's dirty love this week, both of us tense with passion, ready to be unleashed.

My kisses were tender and soft on his balls that were fully loaded and ready for some very dirty love, Charlie was loving it so much his moaning sent a deep cold shrill down my spine.

His body was now fully tense as I moaned with sheer delight, repeating his name, begging him to fuck me, to fuck me hard, but Charlie had other things on his mind. Instantly his fingers danced delicately with my pussy, coating each one of his fingers in my juice, his gaze fixed on mine as he slowly licked each one free from the juice that clung to them, following my gaze, allowing us both to indulge in such a seductive ritual.

I was now completely content with Charlie's cock delivering all its dirty love as Charlie applied the pressure that I loved and craved, his cock was now filling every bit of my naked, demanding pussy, his hands resting on my hips letting his cock take full control as we moaned in unison to the rhythm that was ours. Charlie then grabbed my fingers, sliding them gently into my pussy, moaning passionately. *Feel our juice on your fingers Lizzy.* Our juice was now all over his fingers and mine as Charlie licked my fingers free from juice as I licked his, fuelling yet more dirty love that flowed through us on this sex fuelled afternoon love session.

Charlie looked at me, smiling that cocky smile that captured my gaze. *I love making babies with you Lizzy.* I smiled at him as I never dreamed we would ever be having this sort of conversation here in this very place that had stolen my heart all those years ago.

There was something about the little shed that was very special to both of us, it held so much love in its thin walls that now held the full intense story of our love.

Knowing what a long loving and at times painful relationship we shared, all the tears that had fallen here and all the laughter that was contained within these walls made this little place so special.

We must have fallen asleep as it was getting dark when we awoke and I needed to get home to be undetected by Dave wanting to know my whereabouts today. Charlie held my hand as I got up to leave, wanting me to stay a while longer. I could not resist, how could I? Just to be here in this little shed for a while longer to absorb more of its charm that now demanded my attention.

An hour later I dressed my naked body, but not before I had indulged myself a little longer in Charlie's dirty love before I headed for home or to the prison I lived in. I was happy that I had managed to spend a lovely afternoon with Charlie, unbeknown to Dave and to Helen, deceiving the other two people who unbeknown to them had become part of this tangled, destructive and somewhat poisoned love story, Dave more so as he had been involved for many years while I continued to indulge in my love for a bad-boy wanting nothing more than his love.

I got home to an empty house, relieved that Dave was not back yet. I sat watching television, just relaxing, letting my mind wander every now and then to Charlie, Helen, and I, the love triangle that had a habit of just kept creeping into my mind, not allowing me to fulfil my dreams.

I must have fallen asleep as I was awoken by Dave coming home. He was never the quietest of people, slamming doors, shouting and balling his way into the lounge like an out of control whirlwind, stumbling around while juggling his vile insults.

I glanced at my watch, it was 10pm, he smelt of stale beer and cigarette smoke. It was so obvious that he had been drinking all day, his mood suddenly somewhat lighter, knowing not only he smelt of his disgusting habitual odour, but now it was accompanied by the chilling and sickening smell of guilt. *I'm meeting the lads down the pub in a minute, you coming Lizzy?* I was taken aback that he was inviting me to join him, yet another attempt to make up for his guilt, a guilt that was completely wasted on me.

No it's fine I'm tired you go though; you have obviously made plans Dave. He did not put up a fight or comment, he just went, but at least it meant that there would be no rows or war of words tonight hopefully. I took a bath and watched a little more television before I went up to bed about midnight, not knowing what time Dave would get in as he would probably be very drunk and full of himself, spewing the most vile, evil and disgusting comments that he seemed to do regularly now.

At 1am the door slammed, shuddering violently behind him. He was home and very drunk and suddenly I was terrified, rigid with fear as to what I would be faced with tonight and again I was living in fear of a violent beating. My body froze, bracing itself for the battle I might face tonight. *Lizzy, Lizzy.* He was shouting my name at the top of his voice from the hallway. I got out of bed and went to the landing. *What is it Dave?* I shouted at him, my voice howling down the stairs. *Come down here Lizzy. No Dave I'm tired for god sake. Lizzy,* he shouted. *What?* I screamed back again, enraged that he was drunk again, I was so annoyed with him thinking he still had the rights to treat me the way he always had as the war of words left my mouth. Suddenly I felt a cloud of anger wash over me, an anger that frightened me as a torrent of abuse left my mouth, something I found very hard to deal with and now I could see this turning into a heated and ugly row, both of us angry for different reasons. Mine was justified, but Dave's was not.

Dave staggered up the stairs, tripping as he went while I watched him take every step, hoping desperately he would fall. I was almost willing him to fall, what a complete idiot he was. *Lizzy you bitch,* he snarled. He got to the landing wanting to kiss me, I screamed at him. *What did you call me Dave? I called you a bitch, you always have been Lizzy.* I just glared at him as words now failed me, knowing my words would be wasted on him.

Returning to the bedroom I said and did nothing, tensing myself ready for yet another cruel unfounded beating, fuelled once again tonight by his drinking. Dave got into bed, the strong smell of beer was very apparent, his hands then started to creep over my skin and once again it brought back the vile memories of Charlie's father. Dave started to make demands on me. *Come on Lizzy, I want you Lizzy. No!* I snapped, *I'm tired Dave and your very drunk.* Suddenly the insults increased, repeating over and over again the most vile comments as they just kept erupting from his evil mouth like an open sewer.

I limited what I said as I was a little scared now and I did not want a repeat of the last beating he gave me. His face was red with temper, straining with rage. *Lizzy.* He snarled at me again as he struggled to put on the condom that I demanded he used. I just laid there to allow him to abuse my body again and not for the first time as I closed my eyes in a desperate attempt to blot out his vile abuse and the ragging storm that I was allowing to happen, but I was allowing it for one reason only, to avoid the beating that was going to be mine if I objected to him abusing my fragile body.

With my heart pounding I waited for the appalling ordeal to be finally over, my mind elsewhere, certainly not here and certainly not with Dave as tears again were staining my porcelain face, tears of stupidity, tears of frustration that I had let him win, letting him take my body once again for his evil pleasure, all the time Dave making sure I knew what would happen if I didn't let him.

He was not loving in any way; he never had been. I was totally repulsed by him, it made me feel sick, the thought of him abusing me and even worse that I had allowed it, but sadly on this occasion I had no choice as I feared a cruel unfounded beating, knowing my fragile body could not take anymore.

Now with the vile ordeal over, my body was free from his as I waited in silence for him to pass out as he was so drunk. Sadly, that was his life now, revolving around drunken binges. How sad his life had become and would get worse as time went on without doubt.

I crept out of the bedroom to seek solitude in the spare bedroom where I felt safe as I could lock the door behind me, creating a much needed barrier between us as now I could not bear to be in the same room as him. The thought of him touching my body left me very cold, complete with a numbness that crept through my body like a dark shadow, making my heart jump sideways, clawing sharply at the heavy scars that now covered my skin, scars that I wanted to rip open to allow them to bleed, freeing the blood from my body that had been tarnished by evil in a bid to let the old blood drain away to be replaced by new, fresh life-changing blood.

I awoke early. The house was very quiet and peaceful, sadly I knew it would be short lived and it was as suddenly I heard Dave stumbling around, knowing he would still be very hungover from his drunken binge of last night. We ate lunch in total silence, there were no apologies, not even a sad sorry from him, there was nothing left in this marriage, nothing at all, it was empty from any emotion and any warmth. My mind was made up, it was over for good, I would be divorcing him. I said nothing to Dave but I think he felt the same. At last it was 3.30 and time for me to escape, so while Dave relaxed in the lounge in his own little world I walked out of the front door saying nothing, just slamming the front door firmly behind me, leaving Dave to wallow in his own self-importance, knowing he would already be planning his night out drinking tonight, to revile in his own self-importance, to boast and brag in front of his selfish friends.

Arriving back at the hotel, Charlie and I headed up to my room, eager to spend a little bit longer together. Charlie made coffee as we sat and talked for a while. *I must go soon Lizzy; you do understand princess don't you?* I nodded, but it did not make it any easier to accept that he was going back to Helen, leaving me alone again to dwell on my future plans, whatever they were going to be as the future was so very unpredictable, but one thing was for sure, my marriage was finally over and I was ecstatic that I knew I would never have to go through the vile, unloving, uncaring chore of sex with Dave.

Monday morning was here again and I was on site at 7.30am knowing I had a few busy weeks ahead with the final fitting and build. Glancing at my desk the paper tower was getting bigger, turning into a mountain daily and today I had a site meeting booked for 10am. I was not hosting the meeting this time and I was relieved that it was the site managers turn as I had not prepared any notes, but I had ordered bacon rolls and coffee to be delivered at 10.30am for all the trades men, contractors, and builders.

All the contractors arrived for the brief at 10am, I was late as usual so I crept in at the back unnoticed. I could see Charlie clearly in the midst of the crowd that today seemed to have grown tenfold. The meeting finally started and it was all praise for the build, and everyone connected with it and now the end was in sight as I breathed a nervous sigh of relief.

Bacon rolls and coffee arrived on time so with that we broke for fifteen minutes. At last I could talk to Charlie who once again looked very preoccupied today which now convinced me that there was a part of his life that I would never be part of. I knew there was something wrong and once again I felt it was me that would get hurt in some way, crushing once again any dreams I now had.

What was it that he was hiding? Was it Helen? Was it me? Was I making his life complicated? I didn't know, maybe this was not the right time for us to be together, maybe I should end it now and for good. My words echoed loudly in my head as they spun around me. At that moment I felt Charlie's hand brushing against mine, gently stroking my fingers with a nervous energy. *Do you fancy a drink later Lizzy? Yes Charlie of course.* I blew him a warm kiss just to endorse my love for him.

I went back to the office to struggle with the endless pile of paperwork that was sprawled across my desk like a range of mountains but I could not stop thinking about Charlie, he really was not his normal self.

My day was now over and I knew deep down I would need a drink to brace myself for the conversation that Charlie and I were about to have, good or bad. I had to prepare myself, my nerves were on edge once again as I repeatedly embraced the ring on my necklace. Charlie was waiting for me, leaning casually against the office wall, staring up at the night sky.

The air was heavy with pent up frustration, neither of us prepared to say the first words or to hold hands. The cold stark reality of our secret affair was starting to raise its ugly head. On arrival at the pub Charlie ordered the drinks and was now sitting next to me on the comfy sofa. He looked so unhappy, his face eaten up with pain.

You wanted to talk Charlie? Yes Lizzy. His hesitation was now worrying me, seeing the pain that swept across his face, I knew it was going to be devastating as he fought to hold my hand while I twiddled once again nervously with the ring on my necklace. *You want our baby don't you princess?* I glared at him, stunned by his question. *Yes of course, yes I do, don't you? Yes I want you to have my baby Lizzy.* But there was always a but. *But it's Helen.*

Helen again. *But what Charlie?* I snapped in a very sharp voice, his expression now changed, spitting out words that tonight confused me and that stunned me into complete silence. Charlie hesitated. *What is it Charlie?* My tone was one of annoyance. *Helen's pregnant.* Stunned and saddened once again I could not speak as I was suddenly choked by the words I had just heard. I felt sick, hurt and disappointed yet again as my dreams were now crashing down around me, the storm as promised was now overhead and bringing with it a tidal wave of destruction.

Charlie was now looking at me intensely for some sort of words or reaction, tears once again welled up in my eyes that had instantly gone from the brightest emerald green to the dullest of grey in a split second, my smile now disappointing.

I was so damn jealous, my whole body totally eaten up with jealousy. I wanted his baby, his and mine and at that moment I wanted to walk away, walk away from this battle, this ugly love tug-of-war battle that pulled us both in different directions. My head told me to walk away and to walk away now, but my heart nailed me to the floor as I was unable to break free from our roller-coaster love affair, unable to free myself from being his hostage.

I stood up to leave, feeling Charlie's hand brush against mine, sweeping it away in total disbelief, turning the volume down in my head as I did not want to hear the continuing saga anymore, thinking now I should be free from everything that had been my down fall in my life, to walk away from all the torment that I had created, from the storms that were all made by me from my ongoing desire to love a bad-boy. *I'm fine Charlie,* I snapped, my voice bitter and laced with anger. I suddenly cast my gaze sideways to see others glaring at my outburst, pointing fingers, and witnessing my distress.

Clasping my hand tightly he begged me not to go. *Please don't go, listen to me please, Lizzy this does not change anything for us.* I glared at him. *Well it certainly changes things for me Charlie.* I snapped in a loud and very unwelcome voice as Charlie pulled me gently back onto the sofa, allowing me again to see out of the corner of my blurry eyes couples huddled together, whispering and finger pointing, still witnessing my obvious distress.

Charlie held my porcelain face with both his hands, kissing away the tears of what had become excruciating as always. *Lizzy, I only found out last night, Helen's only a few weeks pregnant, she's in the very early stages, but I had no idea Lizzy. Charlie please don't worry; I'm pleased for you both.*

The tone in my voice was still tinged with a very guilty hate, a hate that was so hard for me to hide right now, my voice was still raised.

My unhappiness was so clear to see. *Lizzy can I come back to the hotel with you, we can talk more.* Exhaling loudly, *I don't know Charlie, I don't know what more we can say, it can't change anything, not now.* Once again I felt my life spiralling out of my control on that night.

I was pissed off and he knew it, but I loved him, I wanted him, I wanted his baby. *Lizzy please, please let me come back with you, I beg you Lizzy.* I scowled at him as voices in my head told me to run away, to free myself from the bitterness that was now ruling my life daily, to break free from not only Dave, but now Charlie too, a complete break from them both, knowing I had others waiting to take their place if needed, daily offers of dinner dates, evenings out, weekends away and every other sort of invitation you could think of, these were never in short supply, maybe that was what I needed right now.

But he seemed so unhappy and now I felt I was spoiling the precious most beautiful news for him, and I had no right, no right at all as I was only his bit on the side, nothing more, and now that was all I was ever going to be, his trophy, his school boy crush, his tart, his whore, and his mistress.

I questioned him, needing to know how he felt. *Charlie are you happy about the baby?* He hesitated. *Yes I am, but it's been a shock, as you know Helen and I don't sleep together anymore Lizzy, we don't have what you and I share.* I snapped again instantly as I glared at him with my nostrils flaring and my voice raised to the maximum. *Well obviously you do have sex Charlie or Helen would not be pregnant.* The cosy pub was now full of my bitterness as I watched in horror as the others around us did nothing apart from finger point and whisper. I sounded like a real bitch, my unhappiness now very apparent and very raw to everyone else in the pub and Charlie knew it too, I was hurt once again by his untimely news.

My mind was now completely confused by the conversation that had once again shattered my newly made dreams as well as destroying my childhood fantasies, once again I twiddled irrationally with the ring that hung from the necklace, wanting tonight to snap the chain out of anger, to throw the ring back at him and to demand the answers that surrounded it. I glanced at him, suddenly I was stunned at how cruel I was being to him, I squeezed his hand in a bid to gain his gaze. *Charlie, come back to the hotel with me and you can make the coffee.* He smiled that cocky smile that seemed to make everything right, but we both knew it wasn't, it was a total mess for me, and I guessed it was for him also, knowing his loyalty was now going to be compromised, or was I going to be side-tracked for Helen.

We left for the hotel holding hands except the conversation was now cold and frosty, sparse from the fun and laughter that normally surrounded us. Tonight I felt the chill of the bitter wind blowing in on the storm that had been predicted so I braced myself again for the coming storm that was sure to leave my love for Charlie hanging in the balance.

At the hotel we talked until late, things seemed a little more clear for us both, for now anyway, but in the back of my mind I knew it would end in bitter tears either for me or for Helen, or for that matter both of us.

Can I stay Princess? I gasped at his request, how dare he be so fucking casual, thinking that staying tonight would make things right. *No Charlie,* I snapped in a raised voice. *Helen needs you and I'm tired.* I felt emotionally drained with so much turmoil swimming around in my head. I felt like I was drowning in a sea of turbulent love as now the waves continued to crash into each other, blinding my thoughts, not allowing me to think clearly, leaving my mind clouded by so many dark and unforgiving waves.

I felt I needed space for the first time in our long relationship. I felt I needed to breath, to be able to breath my own air, not the stale second hand air that tonight surrounded me. I wanted to be completely alone to come to terms with his news so we said a sad goodnight and as normal we blow kisses until out of sight, even if they were muted by my inability to be happy for them both and to return the smiles that Charlie wanted to receive.

I slammed the door behind me letting him know just how I felt and as I did, my limp body slid down the door, ending up in a crumpled heap on the floor sobbing so hard I felt sure I could be heard in reception. Having been in the crumpled state for what seemed like hours, ignoring my phone that was ringing constantly knowing it was Charlie, but tonight I had lost interest and that terrified me, it was now well after midnight. I struggled to get myself up from the floor and into bed, my emotions were not allowing me to think rationally as I tossed and turned all night, unable to get things straight in my head as wave after wave kept on crashing and clouding my thoughts, each one now tormented by another, finding Charlie's news very hard to digest. Tonight had made me realise I was always going to be the bit on the side, the bitch, the whore, the tart, nothing more. But it had not stopped us from falling in love once again and I had fallen even more deeply with the boy who had stolen my heart along with my virginity.

As I laid still and silent my body now frozen by Charlie's words, I relived them all over and over again until they became muddled and confused, but tonight I came to the conclusion that I had now received the final impact on my fragile emotions, taking me to an all-time low, recalling all the bitter blows my body had endured to have Charlie's love.

Our baby loss, my vile assault, my unwanted marriage, mum's death, Dave's violence and now this, my body could not take any more as I was hitting rock bottom and I was sinking fast. Once again my life seemed to be darkened by more emotions that hit my fragile body repeatedly, knowing that this was the start of the storm that had waited to unleash its devastation, dark rolling clouds that would clash violently with my emotions.

The next morning I woke early in the city. Awakening with sleepy eyes, consumed by my agony and heartbreak. I phoned the office to tell them that I was sick and that I would not be in for a few days, not wanting to come to terms with the future that would lie ahead for Charlie and Helen being it was my dream to have their future, but now Charlie had stolen that and given it to Helen, when it had always been promised to me.

I stayed in my room all day, I did not even get up. I just laid still, silent, and motionless, just going over and over in my head repeating Charlie's words. I had to think hard and long about what I wanted for me and my future, needing desperately to have my time alone without intrusion.

I was feeling hurt that Charlie and Helen were still sharing a bed and being intimate, but I had no right to object, I thought his love was only mine and suddenly I realised that I had been used yet again. My body was allowed to be yet another man's trophy, thinking that was all I would always be, just a selfish trophy won by the highest bidder.

My mind was now in overdrive as there were three of us in this relationship, a relationship that had only been made for two. Charlie now seemed to be content in having his cake and eating it and I allowed it out of unconditional love. I was allowing that to happen, stupid Lizzy once again, I was letting it happen to me again. Where was my self-respect?

Charlie had rang the hotel so many times and each time I refused his calls as I wanted to wallow in my own pity and it felt okay to do so today as I had good reason and it seemed justified, wanting to rebel against everything. I drank strong coffee all day knowing I had not eaten for the last few days either. I felt weak, sick, hurt and very alone, wishing desperately that I could take a walk in the garden and to stand at my old bedroom window to recapture happy times, freeing myself from this torment that filled my head to breaking point, leaving me miserable.

Knowing full well today I could not stick a plaster over it and make it better this was something that would take time to heal, the scars that had already marked my body were leaving permanent reminders of my wounded and battered life, the wounds increased, all of them had Charlie's name ingrained in them.

I knew right from the start, back on that very cold January evening when I heard Charlie's voice again for the first time in a very long time that we could never be together properly as a couple, maybe then I should have shut him out of my life completely, knowing full well that my life would be less complicated and less tormented mentally. It was something that now ruled my life on a daily basis, having to face the fact that I was never going to be allowed to lead the life I craved, the life I had dreamt of with Charlie, my life denied of my dreams or that's how it felt that day.

Charlie and Helen's baby changed nothing for me, it was nothing to do with me so I had to blot it out of my mind, not giving it any more thought or any more of my constant heartache. Charlie called again after work and I took the call reluctantly as I did not want to get bogged down with tearful emotions that just took us round in a never ending circle, full of pain and devastation. *Lizzy I'm worried about you. I'm fine Charlie* I snapped. A long silence followed at both ends of the phone as I didn't know what to say, my mind was in a constant spin. *Lizzy I'm coming over now.* With that the phone went dead.

Twenty minutes later and I was in Charlie's arms, both of us sobbing, both of us so sorry. The pain of our relationship was tonight at an all-time high but it felt so good to be in his arms again but my vision was blinded once more by foggy tears, my mind clouded by the violent storm.

Let me look at you Lizzy. My tears were still flowing as the hurt continued at pace. Charlie held my tear stained porcelain face gently in his hands. *Lizzy your too beautiful to cry, your my beautiful girl, I know I have hurt you so much, I'm so sorry, how can I ever make this right?* He looked at me again with those deep brown eyes that were now tear stained, holding on desperately to my gaze. *Lizzy do you want me to leave Helen? Would that make things better for you*? I was frustrated at what I was hearing. *No Charlie*, I snapped. *It would not be right and not fair on Helen; I would never ask you to do that.*

I quickly changed the subject, wanting to forget the unhappiness that clouded my life tonight, so with the tears gone for now the laughter had returned, complete with the smiles that said it all. Charlie looked for now like he had a weight lifted from his shoulders.

The mood was a little lighter but our conversation left me cold with words that didn't inspire me, but as we said goodnight his embrace was firm and meaningful, leaving me fully aware he did not want to let me go as he lingered at the door for yet more kisses. His eyes were begging for my forgiveness, hungry for my love, desperately wanting reassurance that I was OK.

Once Charlie had left it gave me time to think, to think about my future and what I wanted from it. I was not going to let the sadness from my past along with the fear of my future destroy what was going to be my happiness. I clung tightly to the ring that still kept its own secret life, knowing one day I would have it all and maybe the secret of the ring would be mine.

Awoken by the most vivid nightmare I headed to the office early as I needed to catch up, having missed yesterday's work, so with the coffee flowing I tried to sort the mountains of paperwork that was now falling off my desk and with my phone in constant meltdown and my head spinning out of control I sat down for a while to get my breath back.

Sadly, I could not hide from the mass of contractors that continued to flow through the office asking questions, constant questions, all I wanted to do was scream at the top of my voice to let everyone know of my continual excruciating heartache, a heartache that was all made possible by my dirty love for a married man, a man I had loved all my life, a man who had broken my heart on more than one occasion.

More coffee, more questions, I thought my head would explode at any minute. I needed to get some fresh air as I felt stifled and suffocated by the second-hand air that circulated within my office so I headed off over to the build. I felt very light headed and sick, but put it down to not eating so I promised myself I would send out for something as soon as I had seen Charlie. Then, suddenly and without any warning, I felt very faint and with that I could not remember anything. I woke up with contractors all around me, fussing and flapping around, all looking very worried, all wanting to help, but fussing over nothing, let's get you to hospital Lizzy.

Charlie helped me up, then drove me to the hospital. I kept telling him I was fine, he kept telling me I was not, maybe stress was the reason I felt so fragile, agitated and not me. Charlie came into the waiting room with me holding my hand throughout our long wait. I stood up to leave, repeating I was fine and ready to go. *No Lizzy*, Charlie insisted, easing me back on to the uncomfortable plastic rigid seat where I fidgeted trying to get comfortable. I sat nervously pulled at my hair, twiddling it around my finger as I watched the comings and goings, nurses scurrying around taking care of the many people that were in need of help, leaving me to question why I was here to waste their time. I hated watching people in distress, smelling the fear, and hearing their painful cries.

Suddenly I heard my name being called so I left Charlie nervously waiting alone in the waiting room while the doctor examined me, took some blood, checked my blood pressure, poked and prodded asking me about my health, my family health history and family history. His expression was cold while he stared at my notes, silent apart from the odd cough and occasional sharp intake of breath which worried me. I hated all this, it was just such a waste of time when all I needed was something to eat and something to drink, knowing more hot strong coffee and biscuits would sort me out.

Wait hear please Lizzy, I need to wait for your results, but it will be a while. I just twiddled again with the ring on my necklace while staring around at the four very clinical walls that surrounded me, walls as pale as my porcelain skin that now lacked any colour as all my emotions were now drained from me, suddenly taken away from the four sterile walls, by the nurses who had brought me some toast and coffee insisting I eat. I was worried that Charlie was still waiting for me, he should go as he had been here for hours now, and it was getting late.

The doctor came in with a nurse and sat by the bed. *I have had your results back Lizzy.* After asking yet more personal questions, he took a deep breath in and smiled, *Lizzy I'm pleased to tell you you're pregnant, you're expecting a baby, congratulations.* I gasped, stunned by the news I had just been given. I could not take it in, I was pregnant, I was pregnant with Charlie's baby.

The doctor looked at me, *I want to keep you in tonight Lizzy I want to do more tests. More tests?* I questioned, panicking that something was wrong. *It's just routine and nothing to worry about Lizzy.* I felt my smiles radiate through the hospital, my heart jumping with uncontrollable joy, my face hurting from my extended smiles.

CHAPTER 22

Knowing Charlie was still outside in the waiting room I asked the nurse if she could tell him to go. She smiled, *Don't you want to tell him your fantastic news, to share it with him? No, he can't know.* I snapped at her, she looked at me slightly baffled by my hesitation not to tell Charlie. Minutes later the nurse informed that Charlie had gone. She smiled. *Oh, he said he will see you tomorrow and to ring him if you need anything.* But tonight I needed nothing, not even from Charlie as I had been given the gift I craved, needing time alone to digest this most wonderful news, the most incredible news in my own time, to embrace the news I had yearned to hear for so very long.

I must have conceived instantly, my desperate craving now a reality, pregnant. I was pregnant, I kept repeating the doctors words to myself just to make sure it was digested. I was pregnant, my hands now resting on my tummy which was still so incredibly flat. I was pregnant with Charlie's baby, our beautiful baby, my dream had come true and at last I would have something that was mine and Charlie's apart from our wonderful lifetime of dirty love.

My thoughts stopped instantly as I was in total shock, stunned as to what Charlie would say and to what his reaction would be. My mind once again over-crowed by so many thoughts. Two men, one wife, two babies and me, the bit on the side, the tart, the whore, Charlie's bitch, what a mess!

My thoughts kept me awake all night, going over and over everything, retracing again to the doctors words just to make sure that I had correctly heard the incredible news that I had longed to hear. Charlie, Dave, Helen, divorce, and a beautiful baby. I had to get my long and very overdue divorce from Dave as I feared for us both at his violent hands, I could not and would not put my precious baby in danger.

With the tests all done clear in the knowledge that Charlie would become a dad to two babies within the space of a few weeks or so, I realised that he had been a very busy boy, sharing his love between Helen and myself. Once again my sarcastic thoughts were laced with bitterness, knowing that he and Helen had been intimate and making babies on the nights that we were not together, knowing he had spread his love between us both leading me to wonder if there were others receiving his love, spreading it ever thinner, not something I wished to dwell on as it was too hard to contemplate with the added realisation that he had made both Helen and I pregnant around the same time, knowing that Helen had fallen pregnant so soon after her miscarriage. I then realised that it had to have been when I was back in Wiltshire, just after my mum had died, while I was grieving Charlie and Helen were making love, sharing a love that I had thought was only for me. But then I had no right to expect anything else, so shaking my head free from negative thoughts I diverted my thoughts to my thrilling news, knowing Helen would have experienced the same emotional happiness that I was feeling right now, but without the heartache that I was feeling, or did she have suspicions about her husband? So many negative thoughts were pulling me into so many different directions.

I was discharged from the hospital and given my dates to see midwives. I could not believe it, my dream to have Charlie's baby had come true so very soon, but I had something else that couldn't wait, so back at the hotel I called the family solicitor with urgency and started divorce proceedings. I could never go home now, my mind was made up, time to leave my farcical marriage behind me and not before time.

Charlie rang constantly to make sure I had everything I needed. I so wanted to share the amazingly beautiful news with him, it was so hard knowing full well it would be become so much harder as time went on to keep it my secret. Charlie questioned me repeatedly about my hospital stay and the doctor's advice so I took a deep breath, nervously twiddling again with the ring on my necklace as I fought back the tears of joy I wanted desperately to share with him. *I have got to rest again today, I have been over doing it and I have not been eating properly, generally not taking care of myself. Lizzy you need looking after, can I come over tonight?* I hesitated, worried I might let slip my secret, but I needed to see him. *I would love that, yes of course Charlie. Can I stay the night princess?* I wanted him, so how could I refuse his request? *Yes Charles. Lizzy see you at seven, I will bring food and Lizzy you will eat it.* I giggled at his loving comment, the laughter was back to bring some much needed smiles.

I had decided to tell him about the divorce but not about our baby, that was going to be my secret for a while longer, knowing I still had my ever increasing suspicions about Charlie's secret life, the life that I was never going to be part of, that was still shrouded in so much mystery.

Evening had arrived and Charlie was stood at the door, throwing his arms around me, showering me in beautiful kisses. His beaming cocky smiles were so encouraging as I squeezed his hand for reassurance. *What a week, we have had your super news, me flaking out, heavens what next.* Keeping it all light as not to get bogged down with the love triangle we were in and the constant heartache it brought every time it raised its ugly head which in return sent my life into meltdown.

I have news for you Charlie, I smiled. *What Lizzy?* His eyes lit up as he anticipated my reply, his cocky smile radiating around the room. *I have been thinking about this for some time and I put the wheels in motion today, I'm divorcing Dave.* His expression suddenly changed, but through a muted smile he agreed that it was great news, knowing full well that I was not prepared to put up with his inexcusable behaviour, living with the fear of regular unfounded beatings that were fuelled by his dependency on drinking to excess. Charlie looked pleased, but slightly disappointed as I could see in his expression he was hoping to hear the news that I was keeping from him, but it was my secret for now and that would allow him time to enjoy his own happy news.

You seem to have it all planned out Lizzy. I nodded in agreement and with that he pulled me in his arms which tonight felt right once again in what had been a very stormy few days, but I continued to ride the waves that pounded my fragile body, leaving me weak, unable to fight against it, so I swam in the foaming, cold unwelcome waters, fighting for every breath I took on the journey to have what I wanted, to have it all, but the storm was not over yet as the clouds were once again waiting to shower us both in heartache. Charlie then led me to our bed where we laid naked side by side. It was amazing just to be held, knowing I was in love and being loved by the right man and now not having to live in fear from the false, farcical marriage that had been mine for so many long and unloving years.

As lingering kisses led to passionate ones, Charlie's kisses rolled over my curves, his tongue rigidly tense as it found my clit, sending me wild with dirty passion as I begged Charlie to fuck me hard and rough and I was not disappointed, his dirty loving was intense, feeding my desires once again, but in the back of my mind my thoughts were that at least he was with me and not Helen as she would not be receiving his huge dirty love tonight, for now it was mine. Bitterness once again was creeping through my body, playing its part in my agony to have Charlie all to myself.

On awakening early, Charlie made coffee before popping out to collect breakfast and insisting that I ate it. I hated myself for keeping this special secret from him as I knew he would have been delighted by the amazing news I was keeping to myself, but I had my reasons, many more now that I knew Helen was also pregnant.

Friday night came and another week was over, bringing me yet another week closer to the end of my time here in Cardiff which filled my body with such deep overpowering sadness, but for now I intended to embrace every moment, good or bad. Charlie met me after work, we went for a bite to eat and a drink, my feelings were always the same, nothing had or would change my love for him not even now when I knew full well that he and Helen still remained locked firmly into their marriage, but I loved him so bloody much it hurt. It hurt because he would never be mine, not properly, as long as he was with her. I was jolted from my thoughts by Charlie, *Lizzy are you OK? You were miles away. Yes I'm fine Charlie, it's just one of those moments.* I kissed his hand while squeezing it for reassurance, changing the subject quickly as I always did when the going got tough.

I am going to miss you this weekend Lizzy. I glanced at him trying to avoid any eye contact, terrified that tonight after my constant questioning I might see the forthcoming storm that I knew was gathering in his eyes, so I waited to hear his plans with my head slightly lowered. He hesitated and once again the alarm bells rang loudly, so I asked the about his plans but still Charlie skirted around my question, arousing my suspicions further, so I asked again, raising not only my voice but my eyebrows. My annoyance was fully on show, suddenly there was an admission. *I'm seeing some old friends, a boys weekend that's all.* Now with the door slammed firmly closed on my questions he changed the subject, not wanting me to question him anymore in a bid to shield his private and mysterious life.

My silence now filled the room, leaving a chill in the air, a chill that seemed to have sent everyone shivering as Charlie fumbled to find my hand, squeezing it, trying to reassure me with his trademark cocky smile, but tonight it was as if he was a moth caught in a flickering flame, with his reputation fully on display and with nowhere to hide. *I need you princess;*

you're my girl and I can't live without you. But what about Helen? He then kissed his fingers, placing them gently on my lips. *That's my problem Lizzy, I don't want you to worry your beautiful head.*

As we said goodnight I was left alone again as he went home to Helen and to his very secret mysterious life that involved vast amounts of money, endless and some very secret phone calls and of course his hesitation to enlighten me about the people and places that revolved around his life and his spiralling reputation. Going over and over so many scenarios in my head I must have fallen asleep so soundly, my mind having allowed me for a while to rest from the constant daily torture that seemed to be my life now, Dave, Charlie, Helen, our baby, their baby, dad and of course the build.

Saturday was here and instantly as I awoke my thoughts were with Charlie and his so called boys weekend, wondering if he had given me any thought, but I needed to be pampered and I was looking forward to it and on returning to the hotel after my three hours of total relaxation I felt the need for food as I was starving, having started the craving for crisps, wondering if it was normal so early in my pregnancy, but this evening I didn't care so armed with my stock of crisps in all flavours I was looking forward to having a peaceful evening.

I picked up my key from reception, the porter said, *Lizzy a delivery came for you today, it was a beautiful bunch of white daisy's.* The porter then handed me a large vase for them, his smile warm, offering to carry them for me to my room which I accepted without hesitation.

I went up to my room, the flowers were so beautiful, the perfume tantalising to my senses, filling the room with glorious love, complete with a card which read…

My one and only Lizzy, H L F. Those haunting and taunting initials, I wondered if he was thinking about me that night, as much as I was thinking about him.

I spent the evening relaxing, looking at my flowers while I munched my way through a mountain of chicken, plain even cheese and onion crisps to quench my new found craving.

I laid in bed thinking deeply about Charlie and where he was tonight and with who, also about our baby, us and the future, my future, not knowing where it would take me, but I knew my love for Charlie would be my continuing strength throughout my life. My thoughts then led me to Dave as he would receive the letter from my solicitors next week outlining my wishes to end our farcical marriage and then I would be free from him for good, free from the miserable life I had allowed myself to endure for so many years. I relived the weeks of torture that I began to think was all normal, but knowing full well it had been forced upon me, forcing his control over my life.

Having fought the unwelcome visitors that had interrupted my nightly dreams I felt slightly jaded, having awoken with a startle laying in a pool of cold fluid as the haunting images had allowed me nowhere to hide. Vile images, haunting voices and tonight there was a new visitor, a female that I didn't recognise. I wondered why she had entered my world tonight, her vision hazy and her voice muted, but I knew that she along with the already familiar visions would return during the hours of darkness to haunt me again.

At last Charlie was waiting for me outside, revving the engine of his pristine, sleek car, something he knew made me mad as he smiled that cocky smile that I loved. *Lizzy, I have missed you.* We kissed our hello's repeatedly as he held my porcelain face, cupped in his hands for total reassurance, now sitting cosily together in a secluded little country inn. Charlie's fingers traced the outline of my immaculate painted face, my blushes were now apparent to everyone around us in the pretty restaurant, but still he skirted around what he had done this weekend with the boys, freezing me out every time I approached the subject, so I knew to leave my questions unanswered for now, simmering on low.

On arriving back at the hotel, once again Charlie's kisses were like exploding fireworks on my pretty painted lips that left my body wanting more of what Charlie's dirty love gave me. He undressed me passionately whispering is undying love for me. I felt the same way about him and he knew that, I didn't need to tell him.

I kissed his neck slowly, sexily, and very seductively. He moaned, *princess you bitch.* His body was tense with passion and emotion as I continued to pepper kisses over his chest, my fingertips feeling his heart beating as I dug my nails gently into his skin, now and again making him tense up with pleasure, running my fingers over his six pack, on to his washboard stomach, avoiding his erect, full cock that was now demanding my attention as he moaned again.

You whore, suck me Lizzy, fucking suck me. I chose to avoid his demands for now. *Princess my bitch, my beautiful dirty bitch.* His moaning was now so loud, so encouraging. I resisted the temptation a while longer before I gave in to his constant dirty moaning as I placed my mouth tightly over his huge erection and as I did, his body was rigid with tension.

I sucked him slowly for maximum effect, letting my tongue glide over the tip of his full helmet. *Princess I love it*, he moaned. I pulled his cock free from my mouth, leaving beads of pearly juice fresh on my lips. I then kissed him hard to allow him the taste of his juice that was now smeared across my lips from his juicy cock while Charlie allowed his tongue to revolve wildly around my mouth for the ultimate dirty love.

Suddenly his head was firmly locked between my thighs as he licked my pussy hard, his tongue gliding over my newly waxed lips. I could hear him moaning again, his moaning raised to maximum. *Princess you taste so fucking good*. His tongue was now on a mission to make me explode with the juice that he longed to taste.

Having suddenly changed positions, his huge cock was once again in my mouth, filling it so full to the point I could hardly breathe, but it was so good, so bloody good. Charlie then put a little more pressure on my mouth, requesting that I make him explode to have his juice. *Swallow it you beautiful bitch*. Charlie's juice was now thick in my throat, filling my mouth so full of dirty love that now coated my tongue, and my lips. Charlie kissed me hard, running the firm tip of his tongue over my lips that were now smeared with warm, newly delivered juice, his tongue once again revolved around my mouth.

Charlie seemed content again with having his cake and eating it while Helen was at home being the loyal wife and me, here in a hotel room being his bit on the side, his whore, his tart and his bitch, while having the secret life that his ongoing reputation fuelled, so he already had it all while I waited patiently for that privilege. We said our goodnights complete with lots of kisses as I begged for another, never wanting the last kiss to end, so now as I lay still beside him I switched the lights off, hoping that the day would never end, so that I could escape the torment I knew would be mine again tomorrow.

It was now Monday morning, and the alarm was ringing so loudly. Blurry eyed I turned it off, realising that another day awaited me, another day that was sure to bring more heartache, so I rolled over wanting to enjoy Charlie's body awhile longer but as I sat up in bed I suddenly felt very sick. I rushed to the bathroom to hide my secret from Charlie. Morning sickness had struck, not the nicest of ways to start the day so I cleaned myself up, brushing my teeth over and over again to remove the horrid taste from my mouth, returning to the bedroom to find that Charlie was stirring. I loved to watch him sleep, nudging him gently. *Morning sleepy head.* I kissed him, he then pulled me back on to the bed, wrapping me in the crisp white laundered sheets wanting to make dirty love. I smiled blushing at his comment, as I straddled him to selfishly indulge myself once again.

I knew we would be late for work but I didn't care as Charlie was much more fun, Charlie's hands were now firm on my hips as I started riding him. *Princess, you horny bitch I love it.* I kept riding him, increasing the pace at his repeated requests for more, *Lizzy you sexy lady, let me fuck you hard.* Charlie commanded, knowing I was never going to deny him his delightful commands, not now, not ever.

Our unexpected early morning loving was going to make us very late for work, we laid looking at each other, smiling at the love we had for each other. *You're a naughty girl Lizzy.* I blushed again, *Charlie we are going to be so late.* He laughed. *Well Lizzy, you can explain why.* I smiled as Charlie grinned just like a naughty schoolboy.

We headed to the build, now over two hours late, arriving on site both Charlie and I received some very funny sideways looks, even a few whistles and cheers thrown in for good measures from the builders as they all must have known why we were both so late. I blushed as I hurried to get to my office to hide away from the constant whistles and suggestive comments that continued to echo around the site. Charlie's smile was the give-away, letting everyone know what we had been doing, now most of them knew we were lovers and that I was Charlie's bit on the side, but unbeknown to them I had been his tart, his bitch, and his whore since I first came to work here in Wales.

It was now May and my final date was to be the end of June. How time had flown since my arrival here in Wales, back in very early January, and how my life was again about to change, knowing I had many challenges ahead, many heartaches and endless decisions, but delighted that I would be possibly starting to show my beautiful baby bump to the world, allowing everyone to witness my secret, a secret that I was still keeping from the most important person, the person who was responsible for making it all possible.

With the weekend now fast approaching once again I was heading back to Wiltshire to box up my life, to move out of the house that had imprisoned me for so long, my sentence now over and the penalty paid in full.

I didn't have much, but what I did have were cherished things that I had to have. Dave would have received the letter from my solicitor by now so I waited with bated breath for the backlash, but as I had not heard from him I guessed he had accepted it willingly, as we both knew the end of our marriage was in sight and not before time, both of us needing to escape the torment within our farce of a marriage.

I saw Charlie a couple of evenings during the week, but not to stay over and especially on those nights my night time visitors remained, haunting and unwelcome and again the female vision made an appearance, but who was the ghostly vision who wore a full length white gown of silk and ornate lace, almost like a wedding dress, but I couldn't see her face as I wrestled in my dreams to find her identity. She breezed in and out loudly with menace, wanting to make her presence felt but who was she? And why was she here again tonight leaving me in a pool of unwanted cold fluid that had escaped my body?

It was Friday already, it felt like I had hardly seen Charlie all week, Helen was certainly having more than her fair share but Charlie and I had made plans to have lunch together, we were going to the lovely cafe just around the corner where I sat drinking coffee on my first day here in Cardiff, unaware then of what a monumental journey that was ahead for me on that freezing cold January afternoon. Charlie was already there waiting for me at our little table by the window and as I walked through the door his eyes lit up just like his beaming smile. He stood up, taking my hand in his. *You beautiful, stunning creature, the Welsh air really is good for you.* I smiled at him, if only he knew the real reason.

We ordered lunch and as we talked my eyes were fixed on him, fixed on his every word, listening to him speak, watching his rugged jaw uttering my name. He was so incredibly handsome and so very sexy, he was never short of female attention as so many still lined up to seek his attention, searching for that cocky smile, knowing his reputation that still managed to seduce not only me.

I will miss you this weekend Lizzy. Casually returning my response, *I will miss you to Charlie, have you got much planned this weekend?* I needed reassurance about my suspicions, needing desperately for him to tell me his well-kept ongoing secret, hesitating again to find an excuse. I nervously wound the ring around my necklace until I could not wind it any further while I waited for his reply. *I'm taking a trip up to the cabin.* I looked at him questioningly as my mind once again was thinking about what he was hiding from me, wondering whether I should question him again, to ask him outright, but again I declined, holding on to my escalating suspicions as tight as I held the ring on my necklace.

I had begun to wonder if he was having a little intimate weekend away with Helen, if he was meeting up with mates or something else, something much bigger as now my suspicions were once again out of control and fuelled by negative thoughts.

Suddenly Charlie brought me back from my deep thoughts as time together now was limited, due to the time I had left in Wales. I think it made it harder to cope with knowing that we were approaching yet another terrifying earth-shattering goodbye and I wasn't sure if I would be able to cope this time as I had already had a dress rehearsal all those years ago. It was heart wrenching then and this time would be no different, but now it would for sure be harder to deal with by the secret I was keeping from him, also my resentment of Helen was still festering in my mind. I often wondered what she was like, was she as madly in love with him as I was? Was she slim, beautiful and sexy? Did she look like me? Did she remind him of me? So many things that had crossed my mind over the last few months. Charlie hardly ever said anything about her so I had no idea if she was a long term threat to my happiness or if I was a threat to her. I had to find out somehow, there had to be a way for me to get the answers I so needed.

With another week over, Charlie and I stood again on the station platform holding hands, saying our loving goodbyes as our unending passion spilt over into a terrifying sadness knowing our time together was about to come to an end. *I love you Lizzy, I never want you to forget it.* He squeezed my face between his hands for reassurance, making my heavily painted lips pucker up, but once again his words worried me, was he trying to tell me something in around about way? But what? Again I reached for the ring that somehow gave me the strength I needed today.

CHAPTER 23

A s I sat alone on the train staring out of the carriage window into nothing, I started to reflect on my loveless, farcical marriage that held nothing but bitter and empty emotions, bitter hatred and empty promises that tomorrow would be a better day, but tomorrow was no different to the last, so without any hesitation I removed my cheap engagement ring and my even cheaper wedding ring. My farcical marriage was over for good, so with that I opened with force the little grubby window of the train, tossing them both away into the early evening air like discarded rubbish, yesterday's trash gone for good at last. I was free of the band they called marriage, free from the tight numbing grip that Dave's cheap rings had on me that had stifled, suffocated, choked and ruined the last seven years, a marriage that had been built on a farce.

A marriage that took me from being the fun loving Lizzy to the down trodden, bullied, battered wife that Dave had moulded me to be, right from that first night when I stupidly allowed him into my fragile world. I walked nervously into the house which again tonight was dark, cold, and silent from unwelcome comments, that was a very welcome surprise. Dave had left me a simple but brief note on the kitchen table saying, *take your stuff and go*, leaving me relieved that there would be no war of words this weekend, that meant for once I could sleep in this house without fear, smiling to myself that at last I had made the right decision to leave this cold, unwelcome prison, to start living my life, the life that I craved as a child.

I ran upstairs to find my secret box, hidden away from Dave's prying eyes, neatly tucked away under the floor boards in the airing cupboard with bedding piled on top for the extra security that these special gifts and love letters deserved.

On opening the old dusty box with its crumpled corners I found my daisy rings, one for love, the other for eternity. Hurriedly I placed them both on my wedding finger and they looked perfect together. At last

I could wear them and be proud to show them off as both rings were a celebration of my eternal everlasting dirty love with Charlie.

Now I needed to see my dad to explain the imminent arrival of his new and hopefully welcome house guest. On arriving at the house my mood changed instantly, the house was still bearing the grief of mum as the cold exterior greeted me, the front door unwelcoming, lifeless, and still. Even the front garden looked dull with blooms that should have been radiant in colour, but today they looked tired, bereft from sunlight and still shrouded in grief.

Dad however seemed on good form, delighted to see me, welcoming me back with open arms. He didn't seem shocked at my request to move in and as I explained further what had happened, dad's reaction to my story was of torture, hearing my terrifying story of how I had been abused at the hands of Dave, he seemed unable to comprehend my life with a man who was always putting on a front for those around him and was delighted that at last I could start again. He didn't ask the finer details, he didn't need to as it was so obvious to him that Dave had not treated me with any respect, but I also was guilty of that, betraying him behind his back, but I was shocked and surprised that Dave had not mentioned it to him, calling my name into shame, spewing vile lies about me, but he hadn't, and I was relieved about that.

Now with only the darkness for company I was eager to start packing my life into boxes. I found my tatty passport that had laid dusty and unused for so long, something Charlie insisted I found so I put it safe inside one of the many boxes that were now to be my life.

Tonight it felt like a heavy weight had been lifted from my fragile shoulders, a heavy weight that had been my burden for so long, but now I celebrated, knowing I only had to endure this house one more night, the house that was never a home, only a prison cell that had dragged me down, spiking my life in nothing but anguish, pain and unlimited and humiliating suffering at the hands of my so called, only as he always reminded me, husband. I was delighted to now be alone on my final night here, free from Dave and the constant worry of his violence, it gave me time to reflect on how it went so very wrong and looking back it, it all started the night I stupidly allowed him to force a ring on my finger, to allow myself to become his ultimate trophy.

I glanced back down the stairs, my things now all boxed up, my short life now encased in cardboard. I grabbed some much needed sleep as I felt shattered but very happy that something positive was happening at last, something that I had commanded to happen, taking my life into yet another chapter, but tonight like most nights I knew I would be denied the peaceful sleep I needed.

With a fresh new day here at last I looked again at my life that was now boxes all piled up in the very small hallway, but they were mine to start again with the van loaded and waiting outside at last it was time to go. I smiled to myself as I bitterly slammed the front door behind me before locking it for the very last time, feeling nothing but relief as I put my keys through the letter box without a note, without anything, there was nothing more to say. I was now free at last from the storm that was Dave but I knew there were many more, far away in the distance that would surely blight my life, bringing so much more agony along the way.

Dad was waiting for me patiently, he had given me my own space downstairs, complete with my own bathroom. My bedroom was ready, complete with a double bed and a big wardrobe, so plenty of room for my clothes, this was now going to be my home once again, to visit lost memories, recapture hidden memories that laid behind every closed door in this vast house, to allow myself to find me again, knowing full well my life would once again be enriched by this house that I was always proud to call my home.

I was feeling emotional being back at home, the home in which I grew up. I took a much needed visit to my old bedroom to stand at the window, to allow myself to be transported just for a split second, to take the many journeys that were now ready to be recalled, but today I wanted more, much more, so I lay on my old single bed and instantly I remembered the afternoon that Charlie seduced me right here on this very bed, his aroma now fresh in the room, his words still so vivid as they echoed from every wall with his cocky attitude fresh in my mind.

I walked for a while alone in the back garden, the perfume from the flowers was incredible, so powerful, invading my senses with memories of mum, my childhood, and the love I had received from Charlie right here in this garden and once again the garden let me freely recall those sunning times that brought constant smiles to my face. As I looked across the fields into the woods I was yet again lost in wave after wave of a stunning multi-coloured journey. I could hear the breeze clearly rushing through the trees that always drew me in suddenly, a shiver ran down my spine as I could feel mum, she was here with me, my senses enlivened as I recalled her perfume.

Dad and I sat in the garden and talked at ease, he wanted to know about work, the build and Wales. This was the perfect place to sit and tell him my incredible news while we sat and enjoyed this beautiful garden together, sharing memories that we both loved, so with a large intake of fresh evening air I told him I had some special news for him. His eyes lit up, at last I could give him some good news for a change as we seemed to have been in the grip of sadness for far too long.

I crossed my fingers and everything else, hoping that he would be happy by my unexpected news. While smiling my uncontrollable smile and twiddling once again with the ring on my necklace, I blurted out my unrehearsed speech. *You're going to be a grandad. What Lizzy?* He looked at me with tears in his eyes. *A grandad? Me, a grandad? Again, Lizzy I am so pleased for you, but Lizzy.* He looked and sounded slightly confused and I knew exactly why, so with my hand on his I put him in the picture. *It's fine dad I have met someone at work.* I stumbled to get my words out, knowing dad would not approve and certainly not once he knew who my mystery man was. *But what Lizzy?* I gasped, *he's married.* Dad looked disapprovingly at me, *Lizzy, Lizzy. I know dad, I know, it's fine, he will never know, it's my baby.* He gasped. *You're not going telling him Lizzy? No dad, it's too complicated, so I am going to be a single mum.* Dad seemed very disappointed and a little cross, but he admitted it was wonderful news. *Mum would have been pleased wouldn't she? Lizzy she would be so proud of you.* I knew he was upset that I was not going to tell Charlie and I knew deep down I was being selfish to him and to our unborn baby and like a lightning bolt I now also realised I was also being selfish to myself, but at this moment it was right for me.

You're the first to know dad. Lizzy don't you think you should tell him. No dad, he will never find out he can't. Why Lizzy? He just can't dad. With that we said no more, but I knew my news would surprise and delight many, but for some they would look at my news with shame and disappointment. We sat in silence enjoying the warmth of the evening air, listening to the calls from the wildlife that surrounded us, watching the owls swooping home, something that still delighted me, hearing their shrills and whistles once again.

So now as a chill descended across the garden I headed for the sanctuary that would be mine and it felt great, a new start, no Dave, no farce of a marriage, only me, my baby and of course my forever Charlie.

With an early night needed I headed to bed, not knowing if I would tonight be haunted by images and voices that had now become such frequent and unwanted visitors. As I drifted off into my dreams the battle began, jostling images that tonight seemed more aggressive than ever as each one fought against the next… Paul, Dave, Roger, and of course Charlie's vile father ruled my sleep, but a vision stood back from the rest, the female vision that until now remained muted but tonight I heard her loud and clear as she growled at me, her face tangled and distorted by evil emotions, her howling and aggressive admission that she was the impending storm, this made me jump from my sleep, leaving behind me a fluid soaked bed, her face was now real, her harrowing words haunting, but who was she? Why was she so intent on interrupting my sleep?

Sunday came and I awoke to a familiar sound as the church bells rang out in a celebration of my homecoming. Bells that today were very welcome, knowing that I would enjoy the heavy, earthy sounds that came from the bell tower, something I had so obviously missed more than I thought.

I was heading back to Cardiff today, but not before I had stood at my old bedroom window looking out over the many memories that were laid out before me, every one of which was a delight that seemed now more vivid in colour, more vibrant and more powerful, something that had so obviously been muted over the last seven years.

Suddenly a cold unwelcome shiver hit my spine as I glanced into the mirror. Today it wasn't my reflection looking back, it was a haunting image that I had seen before during the hours of darkness, the female vision that today terrified me. I closed my eyes, not wanting to see the anonymous vision again so I turned my back on the vision that was staring back at me. A beautiful, slim, elegant woman with long flowing blond hair, but she was angry scowling at me, suddenly a cold breeze filled my old bedroom as her muted voice was now terrifying, reminding me that a massive storm was building and heading my way, so not wanting to see any more I made my exit from my old room, slamming the door behind me, but I still I had no idea who she was and why she wanted to disrupt and challenge my somewhat fragile life now.

Putting the last few minutes behind me it was time to go, so I excitedly rang Charlie, I was delighted to hear his voice and eager to know about his weekend, but as expected he was hesitant at my eagerness, almost lost for words. *Yes it was fine, it was nice to have some peace and quiet.* Again it aroused my suspicions about him not being happy at home or was that just another smokescreen to hide his ongoing reputation or something much bigger? Hiding something I was never going to be allowed to be part of.

I was feeling in need of some serious, horny and very dirty love and I intended to seduce him tonight. Back at the hotel there was suddenly a knock at the door, my room service was delivered, my smile was beaming. Charlie was here at last holding my hand, gazing at it, smiling his cocky smile. *Lizzy, you still have the rings I gave you*, chuckling to himself. I kissed him repeatedly, letting him know that the rings would grace my finger forever, to celebrate our eternal love. Charlie took my hand to kiss the rings, endorsing his love. He was pleased, I could tell from his face as he was smiling that amazing smile that took my breath away every time. My eyes locked onto his rough, rugged look, his chiselled jaw and of course his eyes that seduced my every move.

He then kissed my lips hard, smudging my pristinely applied cherry red lipstick before kissing my neck passionately, leaving a trail of lipstick coated tattoos on my delicate skin while whispering his love for me, repeating his words over and over again, his breath warm and tender against my skin as I felt his tongue once again engage with the ring on my necklace, seductively gliding his tongue over the raised pattern.

Taking him away from the sudden seduction of the ring I kissed him in my usual way, allowing my tongue to meet his, sparking sensual emotions for us both as I once again slid my tongue hard into his throat, commanding my dirty intentions for this evening.

Freeing me from my kisses for now, his gaze fixed on mine. *Let's have a weekend away at the end of the build, it would be a fantastic way to celebrate Lizzy*. I smiled, *but what about?* I think he knew that I was going to mention Helen so he kissed me again, our kisses so tender, so powerful, avoiding for now having to answer my delving questions, but I repeated, *what about Helen?* I muttered. *What about her Princess?* His answer was very casual. *Where will you say you're going? Leave that to me Lizzy*, he said firmly. With that I said no more as I felt I had touched a nerve and a sensitive one at that, but it left me to wonder, did he care about her at all? At that moment I felt sorry for her, as if he had abandoned her for me.

I was suddenly brought back from my thoughts as I felt Charlie's fingers creeping inside my blouse. He undid the pretty, pearly buttons on my silky blouse before letting it fall to the floor, his eyes firmly fixed on my full, rounded tits. I stood in just my jeans and bare feet, allowing Charlie's eyes to feast on their full beauty as my nipples sprang to life, commanding yet more attention.

Our kisses had now become uncontrollable, then, without warning he dropped to his knees, unzipping my jeans with passion, allowing his fingers to slide along the lace edge of my black knickers. His rigid fingers were dancing delightfully with my increasingly demanding naked pussy. He nudged my legs apart firmly and I then felt his tongue replace his fingers, his tongue being greeted by my wet, very excited pussy. I was now moaning with pleasure, my moaning now so loud. *Charlie I love it*, I screamed.

My jeans were now abandoned in a passionate flourish as Charlie firmly removed them. I stood totally naked in front of him. *My god Lizzy, my amazing whore, my dirty little love secret.* On hearing his words I made my demands again for Charlie to lick me hard as I moaned over and over again, not wanting him to stop, wanting to feel like his tart for a while longer.

We moved to the bed and as we did he kissed my tits, peppering them in glorious dirty love. Then my tummy got the kisses that only Charlie could deliver, feeling his tongue revolving inside my belly button, something that sent me wild with pent up passion that needed to be unleashed. *Charlie don't stop, I love it*, I repeated my dirty delightful commands as he continued covering me completely with his sweet kisses that were so juicy while lovingly drawing his fingers down over my curves, tracing his way over my nipples which were now standing to attention, demanding to be sucked. My tummy got the Charlie love and kisses almost like he knew I was pregnant just like all those years ago in the barn when just like tonight he hesitated to move his kisses from my belly.

His cock then slipped perfectly into my ever demanding pussy as he held my hips and rode me hard, thrust after thrust, I demanded more. *Princess, princess, my princess,* he moaned delightfully to the rhythm of our dirty love as his juice filled my pussy full of fresh, warm, dirty love. Charlie then continued his quest by riding me long after he had climaxed, his cock still solid and full of dirty love.

With his cock relaxed from the almighty grip of my demanding pussy it was suddenly replaced by his tongue that rushed to taste the baby juice that we had so lovingly made together. His lips then met mine as his tongue danced silently on my lips, tantalising me, allowing me the beautiful taste of baby love we had just made.

We loved together, laughed together, we were brilliant together. Nothing should be standing in our way, but it was, and it was what I questioned in my mind so often and increasingly more almost every day. Only two things in my mind kept him here, either Helen or the secret, mysterious life fuelled by his reputation, but which one or both needed to free him from their so powerful clutches? My mind once again began drifting far away from the love that was being echoed around the room.

I had to find out what and soon. I noticed Charlie's wallet lying open on the bedside cabinet along with his phone, maybe they held all the answers I needed? I was furious with myself for even thinking of snooping into Charlie's private life, but maybe that was my only way as once again I became frustrated with myself, clutching relentlessly with the ring on my necklace before being brought back to the here and now. *Coffee Lizzy?*

While sharing our bath and drinking our coffee together things felt right, so totally right. Charlie seemed relaxed tonight and in good spirits. *Can I stay tonight Lizzy?* I looked at him smiling delightfully, *yes of course, I can't get enough of you Charlie, I'm addicted to you.* Knowing my words just played into his hands once again I was allowing him to have it all.

Charlie seemed to now be on a mission to make me pregnant, allowing me fully to receive every bit of his dirty love, but little did he know he already had and I felt guilty that I could not share the most wonderful news with him at the moment, but I still needed more time as the mystery of what he was hiding was hard to deal with, allowing my suspicions to grow daily, but still I gazed at his wallet and phone wondering if I should be so stupid as to indulge my growing suspicions by opening the wallet.

After a calm night with little intrusion Charlie woke me with coffee and with kisses that thrilled my senses. How I wished it could be like this every day, looking at Charlie I knew he was thinking the same as his eyes were watching me intensely, hungry for my gaze, unable to let me free from his intense stare. *I love you Lizzy*, his smile this morning was cocky and alive the smile I loved.

Wait for me princess. He brushed his hand against mine, once again repeating the same chilling words that washed over me as I looked at him, his face today again consumed by pain, but what was hidden behind that pained expression? I held his hand as I repeated my love for him, once again his words now haunted me on a daily basis. Something was not right, but unless he told me then I would never know as he seemed to repeat the same spine chilling words regularly now.

I was not seeing Charlie tonight as I had a pile of paperwork to do and he was busy at home, or so he said, but again today my doubts and lingering suspicions were awoken by the lack of commitment to let me be any part of his secret mysterious life he was so obviously leading.

It was Friday before I knew it, Charlie and I had a few evenings where we went for a drink after work, but nothing more than that. My body was once again craving his love and attention, knowing I was going back home today. Charlie offered to drive me home and would not take no for answer which delighted me.

Back in Wiltshire and back to the home I adored, Charlie and I kissed our goodnight, he leant over and squeezed my hand. *Don't forget your passport.* I looked at him questioningly. *The weekend away we talked about Lizzy. Charlie where?* I squealed excitedly.

It's a secret Lizzy. He then kissed me again and with that he was gone as I heard his car roar away into the darkness through the pretty Wiltshire country lanes, but what were his plans this weekend? He wasn't with Helen or with me come to that and we hadn't made any plans, only to catch up on Sunday evening so again my head was sent spinning as to what he was doing and with who. But I had to stop worrying about it as it was none of my business although it didn't stop me from worrying, leaving me terrified knowing that he was leading a dark, very secret double life fuelled by the reputation that still surrounded him.

On awakening early aroused from my sleep by the church bells, I rejoiced at the wonderful sound that now echoed throughout the house, the heavy intoxicating thud of the bells, smiling to myself that it was the simple things in life that I loved the most.

I left my fluid soaked bed linen behind me after yet another turbulent night of unwelcome visitors that had once again managed to intrude on my dreams, leaving me terrified to look in the mirror as the unknown female visitor had made it clear that she was always going to be watching me near or far.

I got ready and headed for town wandering around the shops trying to make some sort of sense of the future and the impending goodbye that was now in sight, ready to crush my world once more. My head was spinning again, I just wanted to head back to the childhood sanctuary I adored.

Dad and I sat in the garden talking well into the evening as the warmth of early summer was with us. I enjoyed being with dad, he was great company and as we talked about mum her presence was once again apparent and gracing our lives.

I was thinking of my future and my baby that I would hold in my arms, knowing Helen would also be feeling the same as I did, but at least she had someone to share the happiness with, unlike me, but I could not bring myself to share it with Charlie, not just yet anyway and if I did then it would be in my time, when I could be totally sure of his commitment to me, but for now that was on hold as I continued to worry about the secret life that he was so obviously leading, the never-ending phone calls, the mysterious weekends, the vast amounts of money and his endless lies to Helen without any guilt which left me to wonder if he told the same lies to me.

Sunday afternoon was here, it was sunny and bright as I walked around the garden to relive yet more memories of my life here in this garden, looking beyond into the fields and woods that suddenly triggered tears that were so powerful and painful, blinding me from the stunning views into the woods that were laid out in front of me as this terrifying emotion swept over my body like a dark, heavy cloud that was now embracing me, clouds now littered the sky that today was full of fear of me being alone without Charlie. Tears were now streaming down my face; this was the reality. I would be alone and a single mum while he and Helen continued playing happy families back in Wales.

Back at the hotel and Charlie was waiting for me, ready to smoother me with loving kisses, knowing it wouldn't be long before he had to slip away, but I needed his company a little longer, suggesting that he came up to my room for coffee. Charlie jumped at the chance as we headed to my room in a desperate attempt to keep him here with me and not to return to Helen.

I was restless today, my mind spinning as I kept repeating how much I loved him. I continued to twiddle with the mysterious ring that I had worn around my neck for the last twelve or so years. *What's wrong Lizzy; you seem on edge? I'm fine Charlie, just. Just what Lizzy?* I hesitated to find my answer, thinking on my feet I blamed it on being tired today.

Reassuringly Charlie held my porcelain face in both his hands, kissing away the tears that were now once again refuelled by emotion, staining my skin in heartache and as I looked at Charlie he looked like he had the weight of the world on his shoulders and once again my suspicions were brought to the forefront as he was holding my hands again with his voice lowered, his smile not so visible tonight. *Lizzy, I will not be on site in the morning.* I looked at him questioningly, still he seemed reluctant to explain why. *Sorry Lizzy.*

Helen, Helen again I gasped, turning my gaze away from his as he squeezed my hand tightly, knowing just mentioning her name annoyed me, sending me into a state of panic. I instantly pulled my hand away sharply. *Lizzy, please look at me, Helen needs to have an early scan and check-up. I have to go with her Lizzy. I'm fine Charlie, please don't fuss.* My voice was harsh and with an abrupt tone. *I have to accept it Charlie.* And I did, but with such jealousy, it was hard, harder than I ever imagined trying not to show my jealousy and my increasing bitterness that now seemed to grow by the day.

Monday morning was here in the blink of an eye and the paperwork was piling high. At least it would give me plenty to do, keeping my mind free from the torment of the love triangle that was Charlie, Helen, and me. We now had a date for completion, July 1st and my work here would be finished which I was now dreading, having to leave Cardiff, Charlie, and the love that I had found here, leaving him and Helen to resume their marriage with no distraction from me, but I knew that many others would once again distract Charlie by their beauty.

Suddenly I glanced up at the clock. It was 3pm, Charlie was back on site, he came in to the office. *Lizzy you OK? I'm fine Charlie,* I said coldly with a bitterness in my voice that today echoed my envy of Helen. I carried on with my paperwork, not giving him any eye contact today. Charlie leant over my desk that now was groaning under the weight of paperwork that remained piled high. He kissed my hand. *Thank you Lizzy for understanding.* I pulled my hand away sharply, not wanting to embrace any intimacy from him.

I was bitter, envious and above all very jealous at what he and Helen were sharing at this moment. I put on a brave face for him, but deep down it hurt so much I don't think he quite understood how I felt, he probably never would, but that was my fault for not telling him about our baby.

Fancy a drink after work Lizzy? I snapped back, *yes Charlie, that's if you don't have to rush home to Helen.* He looked at me almost cross at my unwelcome tone that instantly wiped his adorable smile free from his face with my spiteful and bitter outburst. Charlie then walked away, slamming the office door behind him not saying a word, leaving my office cold and sterile.

This was all becoming very hard for me as it had started to reflect not only in my voice, but now in my actions, as I was getting increasingly annoyed. I constantly felt that I was second best, being just his bit on the side, his whore, his tart, something that could be taken away in an instant when Charlie got bored of me being his secret, as he was in total control of this relationship, but he would say otherwise.

We met at the pub for a drink after work. I enjoyed the walk from the office as it always gave me time to clear my head that now seemed in a constant whirl what with the love triangle that I was in along with my divorce, babies, and our final goodbye. We sat and talked mainly about work, avoiding the most important things, the things that needed to be addressed.

With the small talk over and a snatched hour or so, we walked back to the hotel. We kissed goodnight and of course lots of I love you's followed from Charlie as he waited for my words of love to be retuned, but tonight I found it hard to say them as I was completely devastated and consumed with sadness that seemed to mute my words of love, but Charlie knew I loved him without doubt, but my resentment for Helen seemed to now rule my world on a daily basis.

Tuesday evening came and Charlie picked me up from the hotel ready to enjoy our evening together and it seemed as if we were the only ones around in this very cute remote pub as we were cocooned in a perfect blanket. If only it was that easy in reality, but it would never be easy as I seemed to have made sure of that with my stupid actions over my teenage and young adult life, allowing myself to let things happen to me, never standing up for what I really wanted. If I had done then things would have been so different today as I would be living my dream without doubt, the dream I had as a young girl to have it all, to have it all with Charlie, the person that had stolen my heart, my virginity and my soul, embracing me in chains that still to this day shackled me to him, heavy metal chains that some days left me weak, lifeless and unable to see things clearly, blinding me with unconditional love.

Returning to the hotel we sat in his car, our kisses warm and flowing as he whispered I love you so much. *Lizzy.* Suddenly I burst into floods of tears as everything was becoming so emotional now, the slightest thing and I was in tears. Charlie pulled me into his arms just to hold me close, not questioning my tears as no explanation was needed, he knew full well why I was so emotional, but sadly he didn't know the full extent of my tears.

As Charlie held my tear soaked face with both his hands kissing every tear gently away, smiling his so familiar cocky smile, my blushes tonight brought a smile back to my face, for now anyway, as I knew it would only be short lived until the next tidal wave of emotion would engulf me, leaving my fragile body wrecked and once again in agony. Charlie then gave me an envelope covered in millions of kisses and big red hearts that made me giggle. *Open it later Lizzy.* His kisses were as passionate as ever, his arms so strong as he embraced my quivering body until it was time to say goodnight.

I went to my room excited. I opened the envelope with my hands, shaking in anticipation, the pretty card inside read...

Make sure you have your passport ready on the 2nd July as I am whisking you away for a lovely romantic break, just you and me. Oh and Lizzy, never forget I love you, H L F. Again, the taunting initials that sent a cold shiver down my spine, my gaze once again drawn to the letter. He had even drawn a little daisy in true Charlie style with a blunt pencil which made me smile.

Friday was here in the blink of an eye it seemed like every day now blended into another as they were flying by now, possibly because the end of the build was so close and the dreaded day that was fast approaching when I would have to lock my office door for the final time, leaving behind me a trail of love, lies, deception and growing hate.

Charlie popped in to my office at 6pm to say goodnight and again he looked troubled, like he had the weight of the world on his shoulders, maybe he was feeling the powerful pain of our impending goodbyes, maybe it wasn't just me that felt the agonising pain and destruction it would bring.

Charlie was going out tonight and we had made no plans to see each other over the weekend. I didn't know where he was going or what his plans were for the weekend as I never asked and he never told me, so I was alone again with my thoughts that as always lead me to wonder again about his mysterious, private life which I was now finding intriguing and just like before his reputation continued to seduce me, but now I was left wondering if I could trust him.

With a new day unfolding I took the early train to Devon to see a very old friend. She was a couple of years older than me, the sensible one, the practical one, and a very gifted one who definitely had her head screwed on.

We found a lovely cafe to have our much needed coffee and long overdue catch up, thinking I would tell her my exciting news, but I hesitated, putting it off until later in the day, maybe over lunch, still worried about hearing and seeing her reaction.

My mind continued to wander, wondering about Charlie and yet again his mysterious weekend, questioning myself over and over again. Was he having a romantic weekend with Helen? Or did he have another mistress ready to be my replacement once I had left Cardiff? I knew he was never short of female attention which was something he clearly enjoyed.

I was brought back to reality while nervously spinning the ring on my necklace by my friend asking me what coffee I wanted, week, strong, sugar, with or without. *Lizzy* she snapped. *Yes, coffee, sugar, and cream lots of cream. Lizzy you were miles away.*

With the shopping now done it was time for lunch, so as we sat outside in the beautiful warm sunshine at yet another pretty cafe my hands were shaking and somewhat cold with nerves, and once again my fingers reached for the ring on my necklace, but knowing it would be nice to share good news for a change instead of bad news, so this was it. I sat bolt upright, taking in a rather large deep breath ready for her reaction before I blurted out *I have news for you.* She looked at me over her huge coffee cup, sitting up straight to receive my news, wriggling in her seat to get comfortable and placing her cup back into the saucer. *What? What Lizzy?* Again I hesitated, fidgeting once more, ready for the backlash of my antics. I whispered, *I'm pregnant. Lizzy, your pregnant?* She coughed and spluttered, *pregnant, a baby Lizzy? Yes.* Her voice was raised with excitement, attracting others to suddenly witness my news here in the pretty coffee shop courtyard setting.

When? Who's?, What? She gasped to find her words. I giggled at her. *It's due at the end of the year and it's Charlie's. But he's married and he and his wife are also having a baby.* As I recalled my words it now seemed utter madness when I said it out loud again, another reason why I had not told Charlie and today, as I heard my words in my mind it sounded so very casual.

Well congratulations I'm thrilled for you Lizzy, you don't do things by half. Her expression clearly told me what she was thinking, *Charlie?* She questioned. *Yes,* I replied. *I know that name from years ago, not that*

Charlie? Yes, that Charlie, I smiled. *Lizzy, you two were so in love, I can remember that.* I nodded, blushing at the same time. *Lizzy have you been seeing him while you have been married?* I nodded, somewhat ashamed, blushing again that now she knew my sordid dirty secret, but to my surprise she made no more comment other than raising her eyebrow before finishing her coffee.

With my incredible secret told and a sense of relief, we could now go shopping for baby things. I was completely shocked at how much such a little person would need but I bought a few beautiful things, so small and cute, reminding me how very special my love for Charlie and our baby really was.

I had enjoyed my lovely day in Devon, but I longed to have a long hot bubble bath and my comfortable bed as my feet had taken the strain today, so we said our goodbyes and I was off back to Cardiff, happy that I had shared my sensational news with someone other than my dad, even if it had shocked her into silence at one point.

I slept so well, free from intrusion, free from vile faces, haunting images that most nights left me in a cold pool of fluid, terrified at what the next storm would bring. It was late when I awoke, not that it mattered as it was Sunday and I had no plans for the day. It was mine to do as I pleased, but yet again I was alone with my ever increasing negative thoughts while drinking even more hot and very strong coffee, getting completely lost in myself with thoughts of Charlie and Helen, as the love triangle once again reared its somewhat traumatic and now very ugly head, knowing the mess we were now facing was made by me all those years ago, by falling in love with a boy who had stolen literally everything from me, leaving me naked, vulnerable and weak with nowhere to hide.

Suddenly I was brought back to reality as my phone was ringing very loudly, it was Charlie. I was thrilled to just hear his voice, *Lizzy do you fancy a picnic this afternoon? Yes.* I squealed with delight, what a surprise and as promised Charlie was outside waiting for me complete with a luxurious picnic hamper.

We drove off in to the Welsh countryside finding a cliff top vista to enjoy our picnic that over looked the sea, along with a breath-taking view that delighted us both, the salty sea air was now filling my nostrils, the sun delightfully kissing my porcelain skin as we sat on the old crumpled tartan blanket with the sun shining and not a cloud in the sky, a perfect

Welsh summer afternoon. We laid back, both of us looking up to the sky in complete silence. It was just so beautiful, just perfect as there was no need for words. We listened to the waves crashing onto the shore below us with the gulls swooping and squawking overhead.

Just then Charlie straddled over my legs. *You look so sexy today princess, you look amazing, just fucking amazing Lizzy, Wales is certainly agreeing with you.* I smiled and blushed by his comments, my cheeks were rosy-red from his endless and lavish comments.

He gazed at me lovingly as his fingers were now twiddling with my hair, something he often did and something he has done right from the start when our love was so virginal. *I'm going to miss you so much Lizzy.* I found his words painful as his lip dropped slightly. I put my fingers over his mouth, whispering *not now.* He then leant forward and whispered, *I love you so much Lizzy, so very much, I can't bear the thought that I will have to say goodbye to you once again.* It was obvious that today both of us were being tormented by the final goodbyes.

Still sitting on my legs he held both of my hands, *it's been great having you here in Cardiff, I have loved falling in love with you once again Lizzy.* His eyes were then drawn to the ring on my necklace, dazzled by the sun rays, making the ring sparkle, suddenly his fingertips caressed the ring so I closed my eyes wanting to enjoy the seduction the ring so obviously held for him.

His hand then slid inside my pristinely ironed t-shirt heading straight to my huge tits. I was today free from underwear as he ran his fingertips roughly over my nipples, making them stand to attention, big firm and very round.

He then pulled his hand out from inside my t-shirt, pulling it down tight over my enormous tits, attempting to suck my nipples through the delicate cotton fabric, leaving behind two very wet patches which he thought was very funny, he was unable to contain his laughter which was very contagious as we both shook with laughter.

We sat with our arms draped around each other, looking out at the beautiful sparkling sea with huge rocky crags that hung from the large expanse of the cliffs all around us. The sky was a perfect blue with no clouds to mar its beauty, it was hard to tell where the sea ended and from where the sky began, both so perfect in colour, combined with the earthy tones from the cliffs it made a spectacular landscape, perfect for an escape from the normal day to day torment that was my life at the moment.

We ate our picnic enjoying each other's company and to our surprise we seemed to be alone now. Charlie suggested a little Sunday afternoon loving. I smiled at him, my blushes burning my skin. Taking my hand we moved somewhere very secluded where we would not be interrupted as we made ourselves comfortable.

He straddled my legs while his hands glided inside my t-shirt once again. *Princess, your tits are amazing.* I blushed as my nipples sprang to attention, just begging to be sucked. Charlie then removed this shirt. He had the most perfect chest, strong, solid, the perfect body. I ran my nails down his back which made him tense up his whole body, rippling firm and taught.

He unzipped my jeans to reveal that I was free from knickers as I wriggled, freeing my jeans a little to expose my bare thighs. *Lizzy you naughty girl.* I blushed again, knowing I was being the little tart he wanted me to be, but I wanted to be his wife, not his mistress, not his whore or even his bit on the side. I let his fingers slide into my pussy with a firmness that I loved. I was loving the intimacy between us and I relaxed to let him take full control, his kisses were now hard on my lips as his fingers worked further into my wet demanding pussy. Charlie was moaning delightfully as he enjoyed my pussy, whispering, *you're a sexy lady Lizzy.*

Suddenly I was treated to something we both loved, his fingers were now covered in fresh baby juice as he gave me his middle finger to lick and suck, his gaze was fixed firmly on mine. He then did it again, now all his fingers were coated in my juice. He licked each one of them in turn to taste the juice from my constantly demanding pussy. I watched him intensely as he enjoyed this most erotic act that left us both wanting more.

He then pulled my jeans free from my body that was now semi naked so that he could fill my pussy with his enormously big, long love filled cock that was throbbing, begging for my attention.

Smiling his perfect cocky smile he whispered, *fancy making babies Lizzy?* I blushed. *Lizzy, I want to make you pregnant, I want you to have my baby, our baby.* He smiled again, his intensely cocky smile.

He rode me hard, holding my hips firmly as he continued repeatedly, moaning *Lizzy I love you, I love you so much.* Allowing my body to embrace Charlie's wonderful dirty love, Charlie's words now commanded my attention, *Lizzy, Lizzy Lizzy, I could love you forever.* There was a silent pause before I gave my answer, *then why don't you Charlie?* He smiled at me lovingly, *is that want that Princess? Yes, I always have and always will.* My answer seemed slightly casual this afternoon as if I had given up on anything more than being his bit on the side and that was terrifying for me, just letting our love slip away, it almost felt like I was too tired to fight the battle anymore.

With that he screwed me even harder, my juice was now clinging to his cock as I felt his juice fill my pussy, knowing Charlie's cock always remained solid for a long time after climaxing, enabling him to move the juice around my pussy for maximum effect.

His erection was still so solid, it seemed a shame to waste it so with that he filled my pussy once again, screwing me hard, so hard, making me scream for more. *Princess you bitch, my whore, Lizzy, Lizzy, my god I love you, I can't let you go, I just can't.* Charlie seemed very emotional today, his comments were at times very powerful, and I wondered if the impact of my leaving had just hit him or was he telling me to stay, leaving me totally confused.

Composed and fully clothed we laid on the grass once again looking up to the beautiful sky above us, staring at the vast and unending cloudless beauty that just needed to be admired in silence, *Lizzy what are you thinking?* I chuckled at his question, *I'm thinking that I love you Charlie.* Suddenly he touched my hand, gripping it firmly in his, *I love you to Lizzy.* We both seemed to be getting very emotional again with emotions that seemed to be engulfing both of us and Charlie must of sensed it, suggesting that we went for a walk along the beach, so with our arms wrapped around each other we walked through the waves that washed gently against the shore and now with the beautiful sun setting across Wales it was casting a beautiful shimmer across the water, allowing us to share yet more beautiful moments together to recall in the future.

Charlie's eyes fixed on my porcelain face, his voice quivering with emotion. *Lizzy, I can't let you go.* His face was crippled with pain, knowing our final goodbye was almost here, I squeezed his hand for some kind reassurance. *I know, I know Lizzy, but I can't bear the thought of you leaving.*

I then kissed him hard, *I love you Charlie.* He then smiled that intoxicating smile that I knew and loved so much, we both knew that we would at some stage be lovers again, to be in each other's arms and making beautiful dirty love. It was inevitable as far as I was concerned, but when? Who could say? Our future was so very unpredictable, balancing on a knife edge, just as it had done for all the years that we had been in love.

We walked back to the car still wrapped in each other's arms, addicted to each other's love, never wanting to be parted from a love that still amazed us all these years on from the very early days of our unconventional virginal love.

Monday came as did the rest of the week and uneventful it was with the pressure firmly on me for the final stage of the build, my mind kept occupied by the ongoing pile of paperwork which for once was a welcome distraction from the impending goodbye.

I saw Charlie a couple of evenings through the week, but not to sleep with. I was getting a little frustrated sexually and emotionally and very jealous that Helen was having Charlie all to herself, so at times it left me feeling like second best, leaving me feeling very alone and once again fragile, dealing with the regular night-time visitors that now seemed more vocal and again the female visitor. It remained a mystery why she wanted to invade and disturb my sleep, scowling bitterly at me.

It was Friday and I had Charlie's dirty love on my mind, so while he was working I slipped him a note. He smiled, amused by my actions as he read my note which read *Meet me at the hotel at 2pm*, and once again his cocky smile delivered my answer.

Right on time at 2pm there was a knock at the door, my breath once again taken away by his presence as he beamed me a radiant and very cocky smile, a smiled that this afternoon made me blush uncontrollably. He picked me up in a sweeping movement in his strong arms and laid me gently on the bed as he straddled over me fully clothed, complete with his hard hat. *Right Lizzy I'm here now.* He peppered my porcelain face in kisses, smudging my perfectly painted lips.

Tell me what you want Lizzy. I blushed. *Charlie you know what I want.* I blushed again. *Princess, you beautiful whore, my whore.* He slipped out of his shirt before removing his trousers, he was of course free from any underwear as was I, something we both loved.

He straddled me again, his cock was stunningly rigid as normal and again his cocky smile commanded my attention, my eyes following his every word being seduced completely by his presence. His gaze was now firmly fixed on mine as my head laid on the freshly laundered pillow cases. Charlie moved up my body, his huge cock was now level with my mouth as his hands firmly clenched the headboard, his arms outstretched watching my expression. *Princess, eat me, eat me hard.* So without hesitation I took his throbbing cock in my hands, slowly drawing the skin back to admire the huge purple helmet. I felt Charlie tense up, his body was rigid with dirty love. *Lizzy, Lizzy you dirty little whore.* I continued to rub him hard, my nails slid easily down the solid stem of his cock as I repeated my love for him. I could feel Charlie's eyes watching me as I moved my fingers seductively round his huge, pulsating cock, watching his face tense with lust.

Without any encouragement my lips were placed firmly over his bulbous helmet that had already started to dribble the juice I loved. His moaning increased, repeating my name. *Lizzy you horny bitch, you whore, my dirty whore, I love you sucking me, princess.* Charlie moaned deeply, *you beautiful girl is your mouth ready for all my juice, for my baby juice.* I said nothing, I didn't stop, I couldn't stop, I just kept sucking him the way he loved it. *Bloody hell Lizzy*, he moaned. I then felt his body tense again as the warm juice hit the back of my throat, filling my mouth so full. My lips were now smeared in fresh, warm juice ready for some dirty kisses.

He then looked at me, placing his mouth against mine. His kisses were delightful, his tongue was moving the juice from one side of my mouth to the other, allowing us both to be treated to the ultimate seduction.

I wriggled to get out of my jeans, I too was commando, this also allowed Charlie's fingers to slide nicely into my pussy that was now drenched with juice, needing to be satisfied. I straddled his right leg, letting my naked pussy glide gently backwards and forwards to satisfy my ever demanding sex addiction. Charlie once again moaning, *ride it princess, ride it you bitch.* As he continued to watch me, *ride it, ride it hard princess, you fucking whore Lizzy, ride it hard.* My pussy then burst with juice, so much juice flowing from my naked and very demanding pussy, leaving me satisfied for now, but just for now.

Suddenly his phone rang, he ignored it it rang again. I should have questioned it, but I didn't, yet again I let it pass. I looked at him, his normal cocky self suddenly had just vanished, his skin was pale, *what is it Charlie?* I questioned, *nothing Lizzy it's just Helen.* He spoke with a slightly cool edge to his voice, *do you need to go?* He hesitated, *no Lizzy I don't. Well then, love me again Charlie.* I smothered him in Lizzy kisses, *Lizzy* he smiled, he did not need encouraging as before I knew it we were making baby love again that left us both breathless and content from an afternoon of extreme dirty love, passionate dirty loving made possible by Charlie and how we both loved it.

CHAPTER 24

I was now once again back at home and dad was fine, he looked in good health and pleased that I was at home for a weekend of rest, to have time to myself to refuel my body from all the pain and turmoil that my body was experiencing at the moment, fuelled by the constant love tug of war, the love triangle that was Charlie, Helen, and me.

I now had a date for my scan which was only a few weeks away, Charlie was still so unaware of the baby that I was carrying. I felt very guilty, but that was my choice for now, or until my mind was more clear on the secret, mysterious life that he was leading and the impact that it might have on us all, also the relationship he still so obviously had with Helen.

With a night of turbulent sleep ahead I tried everything I could to blot out the endless supply of vile images and intruding voices that would for sure blemish my dreams that night and right on queue they trampled over everyone, crushing my dreams, but one image remained still and motionless, silent from any words, her face frozen from emotion which terrified me, not knowing who she was and why she wanted to enter my world.

I woke feeling refreshed and much to my surprise I was up early sitting in the garden sorting out my post, filling my diary ready for the coming weeks and months ahead, listening to the silence that filled the garden as the sun had just made its appearance, filtering through the trees that flanked the fields beyond.

Sunday had arrived all too soon, but before I took the train back to Cardiff I wanted to engulf myself in yet more memories so as I stood at my old bedroom window allowing the woods to draw me in, to let me look back at the past that I had left there and again today, like most days when I was here, it never failed to embrace me, the vivid kaleidoscope of a gift that just kept on giving for me, to unwrap again and again without question.

With my memories now recaptured I was heading back to Cardiff. I had not heard from Charlie over the weekend which once again played on my suspicions, arousing my ever increasing torment that he was hiding a double life, fuelled by his reputation that he had carried with him all his life, something that he was never going to give up, no matter what and that terrified me. With a lonely night ahead and still unaware of where and with who Charlie had shared his time with this weekend, I knew I was heading for a disturbed and turbulent night that would be sure to test my resolve to the limits.

Monday morning and Charlie was waiting for me in my office, sat in my chair with his muddy boots draped over my desk, something that I strongly disapproved of. I could not help myself but smile at him as he retuned me his trademark, cocky smile. We shared a quick and much needed kiss and cuddle knowing we both wanted more, but I had work to do, as did Charlie, but not before I had questioned him about his weekend, however, he skirted around my questions, avoiding any eye contact with me as my gaze was fully focused on him and his long awaited response. In true Charlie style, I was none the wiser. Now alone, my office seemed cold and lifeless, knowing I was finished here on Friday and that was to be my last day. It was hard to believe the fantastic journey that I had been on in the short space of time that I had been here in Cardiff, having found Charlie's dirty love once again, being his secret tart, his bit on the side and now being pregnant with his baby, but that all came with a hefty price tag of broken promises, broken hearts, hatred, lies, guilt, and deception.

My mind was once again still playing games with me, it had been for some time now. What was the real reason that kept him here? My mind was baffled and tormented, something else apart from Helen and their baby was keeping him here, nailing him to his lifestyle that revolved around Wales, but what? What was I missing, and would I ever be more than just Charlie's tart?

As Friday approached I was saddened and distraught with the thoughts of having to say a sad goodbye to everyone that I had come to know, knowing I would be in bits, it would be a very tough day with many tears that I would undoubtably shed, for Charlie and for the many friends I had made here in Cardiff, along with the beautiful Welsh landscape that had seduced me over the last few months. I had captured its beauty within the three seasons of being there, winter, spring, and summer, all a little similar to what I would have experienced back in the beautiful Wiltshire countryside.

My next site details had arrived and were laid spread out on my desk ready for my attention, now unleashed from the huge brown envelope that had keep its secret until now. I was off to London, what a great opportunity for me to really get to know the London I already loved, and there I would be free to show off my most adorable baby bump without worry, finger pointing, disapproving looks and whispering.

I was looking forward to being in London, but with a strange apprehension I almost wanted to be there now to be away from the ever increasing bitterness that I had for Helen and her life with Charlie, fearing the terrifying sadness that Friday was sure to bring, so for now until the posting was confirmed I was going to hold off telling Charlie.

In the blink of an eye the dreaded day was now here. I sat in my office alone, staring at the four walls that I had grown to love during my wonderful time in Cardiff. The reality was now hitting hard as I was going to walk out of the door later today for the last time which I was dreading. Suddenly I had the urge to be totally alone so I locked the door, with only my emotions for company as my body slid down the door heavy with emotion, my face now smothered in cold and unwelcome tears, my body crippled by pain as I gathered myself up from the cold harsh floor.

My thoughts were now taking me once again on the journey that I had taken while here in Cardiff, falling in love with Charlie once more, allowing me the freedom to be me, finding the powerful strength to end my farce of a marriage and now to have become pregnant with a baby I craved. I sobbed uncontrollably tears for Charlie, us, our baby, and Wales. Nothing could have prepared me for this day as it was worse than I could have imagined. I grasped the ring on my necklace for some reassurance and comfort.

So many emotions were whirling around in my head; sadness, happiness, love, and hatred. You name it, I was feeling it, tears again that just cascaded down my porcelain face, my eyes blurred with bitter tears that stung my eyes.

Suddenly I heard the door being tried, it was Charlie. I unlocked the door and fell into his arms, sobbing again. *I don't want to leave you Charlie. Lizzy, my darling Lizzy, I can't let you go now, not ever.* Those words were a joy to hear, but I knew that it was a promise that would be hard for him to keep.

I suppose I was feeling all the emotions of being pregnant, along with the feelings of being alone again without Charlie and in a big city

I hardly knew, but now loved without any question, knowing its vibrancy already flowed through my veins, its seductive aroma ready to seduce me again.

My tears had now gone and my smile retuned as Charlie's arms allowed me to be me. *Lizzy, we are all going out tonight to celebrate the end of the build, a surprise party. We all want you to come.* I gulped, trying to hold back again the words that were now choking me. *I would love that Charlie.* I noticed him looking at the rather large brown envelope that now sat on my desk, questioning if it contained my new posting. *Yes Charlie, it's been confirmed today.* I took a huge intake of breath, *I'm off to London.* Charlie looked ashen and somewhat shaken by my new location details. We both knew it was going to happen, but I suppose it was now so real, laid out in black and white before us. The thought of us at opposite sides of the country was now hard to deal with, we both looked at each other unsure of what to say or do to ease the apparent pain.

Suddenly and to my complete surprise Charlie took my keys from my hand and locked my office door, pinning a hand written sign on the other side of the door saying *do not disturb out to lunch. Lizzy, I am going to show you just how much I will miss you.* He then took me in his arms, looking at me with tears in his eyes. *I want to love you Lizzy, right here, right now.* I blushed with a passion, I could feel the hunger as he then lifted me on to my desk, sweeping aside the neat pile of paperwork, letting it float to the floor like confetti in a breeze. My blouse was instantly discarded, almost ripped away from my body in a frenzy along with my bra which now laid on my office floor in a crumpled heap.

My short skirt was now revealing my most beautiful underwear that Charlie had bought me as I sat on my desk, my body now a feast for his hungry eyes. Charlie stood in front of me with dirty love on his mind, he leaned me back over my desk removing my knickers seductively so that he could love my pussy with his huge demanding love filled cock that I had come to love.

We were loving this unexpected afternoon delight, this was very horny and so very welcome on this sad afternoon. Charlie was now gazing at me, his eyes begging for more. *You love this don't you Lizzy?* I nodded my full approval as he delivered thrust after thrust of pure dirty love, again and again, long loving thrusts that we both loved, leaving us both breathless. Charlie's eyes once again hungrily explored my body.

With passion raging its way through my office Charlie's head was now locked between my rigid and toned thighs as his tongue revolved inside my juice filled demanding pussy for the ultimate dirty love, his lips now smeared and drenched with my juice as I let the tip of my tongue run along Charlie's lips, licking them free from the tantalising taste of baby juice that coated them.

I was receiving Charlie's dirty love for the second and final time in my office as Charlie moaned. *Lizzy you are amazingly fucking sexy, I can't get enough of you.* I smiled content at our never ending love, both of us amazed that we were still dirty lovers all these years on, but knowing full well there was never going to be a happy ending to our love affair, however many promises we made to each other.

His gaze was now firmly fixed on mine. *Lizzy I'm going miss you so much I can't bear the thought of you away in London.* Again, all he had to say was I'm coming with you as then we would never have to be apart, never have to say anymore sad goodbyes. We could start a new life in London together, but sadly those words never followed and I could not understand why, as yet again I reached for the mystery ring on my necklace, twiddling it uncomfortably, searching for any comfort it could give me today.

With our lunch time loving now sadly over I started to pack up the office that I had loved so much during my time in Cardiff. 6pm and my last day was now over, it was hard to believe as my job here in Cardiff was done and completed. Sadly I would miss Cardiff so much as it had once again allowed me to fall in love with Charlie. As I was locking the office door for the last time I held the key for as long as I could, to embrace the love this office had given me, to recall hearing the chaotic laughter, continual talking, bloke jokes, whistling and all the love along with the continual ringing of the phone that had filled this little office since that very first bitterly cold January afternoon.

Back at the hotel my face was stained once again by tears. I was excited about tonight, I wanted to look my very best this evening to make Charlie proud to be seen with me as it didn't matter tonight that we were seen together as everyone at the build knew our dirty secret. Dressed in my black, curve hugging, very mini dress complete with high heels I headed out to meet Charlie for our final goodbye.

I saw Charlie waiting for me, he was looking so handsome. He handed me a glass of ice cold bubbly, the champagne was so cold on my lips, knowing a fabulous night would lay ahead to celebrate not only the build, but our dirty continuing love and hopefully our everlasting love affair. *Lizzy you look stunning, so very fucking stunning*. He smiled that cocky, trademark smile and tonight once again he looked like that cat who had got the cream while gliding his eyes over my body in a seductive sweeping movement while undressing me with his eyes.

With speeches and formalities over we danced the night away. Charlie and I even managed a few slow dances, allowing the passion to build between us, to have that intimate closeness on our final night, knowing we had not danced together in public since before my farcical wedding when we shared lots of sexy whispering on the dance floor and tonight was no different as again I felt everyone's eyes on us, now they were in no doubt that I was Charlie's little dirty secret, well not so secret now.

It was very late when the party finished and as we all began to make our way home Charlie's phone was ringing repeatedly, every time he chose to ignore it and every time I looked at him waiting for him to say something, but he remained tight lipped while he held my hand tightly and whispered *I want to sleep with you tonight*. I looked at him with all the love I had, not needing to reply, so in return I smiled and nodded my approval.

Returning to the hotel we went straight up to my room, our kisses were warm, very tender, and extremely intense. Charlie kissed my neck, whispering *let's make baby love princess, lots of baby love*. My smile was uncontrollable now, as was his.

Our lips were peppering kisses on every part of each other's bodies, each enjoying the sensations that we were creating as the passionate tension filled the room with the pungent aromas that were Charlie and me.

My demanding pussy was wet with total lust for him as he stripped me bare of all my clothes for the second time today, but now they were covering my bedroom floor and just like earlier in my office the frenzy of dirty uncontrollable love resumed.

Just fuck me Charlie, I demanded. He then lifted me up and put me on the bed. I was now on all fours allowing me to feel every bit of his delicious cock. I could feel his balls teasing my pussy as he continued thrusting hard. I loved it, but tonight I wanted rough love as I commanded Charlie to fuck me harder.

You want it rough Lizzy. I moaned encouraging him as he was now thrusting and forcing his huge, solid cock, making me scream out wanting more, demanding him again to fuck me harder, *Lizzy you amazing whore, I want to make you pregnant, I have to make you pregnant.* His words were so powerful and strong, sending my emotions into free-fall.

When the night's loving was over Charlie looked at me lovingly, smiling the smile that I loved so much, but tonight he seemed slightly sad as his trademark smile was now tarnished and replaced by torment, a torment that once again terrified me, my baffled expression begged his torment.

I can't let you go Lizzy, I want to be the one who loves you every night, to hold you when you cry, to kiss away your tears and to warm your hands in mine. Both of us were saddened by such emotional torture that was now wrecking our hearts, eating them up and spitting them out, all of them tarnished with poison.

Having fallen asleep soundly I woke with a startle, the female visitor had awoken me from my dreams, her presence now harrowing as she still remained silent from words. Steely faced her expression terrified me, leaving me soaked in yet another pool of liquid. Now awake I knew I would have to wait to see the vision again, but her vision would now rule my daylight hours too.

Saturday morning was here, and my heart was still in tatters as we just laid in bed drinking coffee. Both of us seemed shattered by emotions that were rocketing throughout our bodies, leaving them in fear of what would lay ahead for us both, knowing the road ahead would be a long one without any possible end.

We made dirty love again, we both loved the morning loving that was fresh and new, just like the new day, but today it was tainted with sadness as Charlie had to leave me, his lifetime princess, to go home to Helen, back to his life with her, leaving me alone to relive my past hopes and dreams.

With his phone now in complete meltdown, I was guessing the calls were from Helen. I listened to the muffled and somewhat heated conversation that seemed to make Charlie a little on edge. *Lizzy I have to go, I'm sorry. It's fine*, I snapped. He grabbed my hand. *Lizzy please don't, I hate seeing you so upset. It's fine, I'm fine Charlie I'll cope.* My bitter resentment for Helen was once again rearing its ugly head and this was just the dress rehearsal for when the day for the final goodbye would come.

Forcing a half-hearted smile I kissed him goodbye. My kisses were cold, bitter and empty as he once again squeezed my hand for reassurance before I brushed it aside. *Lizzy please.* His expression was now somewhat confused. *I'm fine Charlie. Lizzy never forget I love you*, repeating again his words as I slammed the door firmly behind him letting him know my frustration while keeping a tight lid on what was only a matter of time until I unleashed my bubbling frustration, knowing I was moving forward with my life while he remained stagnant with his here in Wales with Helen, again today I felt no commitment from him, only empty promises.

I spent Saturday afternoon alone with my ever-increasing negative thoughts, going around in circles and always ending up no clearer than when I started, leaving my head clouded by a grey mist, but through the mist I saw the vision that had been haunting my dreams recently, the tall, slim vision that again today remained silent, her face tormented and riddled with hatred, her vile stare firmly in my gaze. I blinked repeatedly, trying to remove the vision, and for now it seemed to have worked as she faded back into the grey mist.

Back to my thoughts I wondered why Helen put up with Charlie slipping away so often and why did he not just commit to leaving with me, to love me, his life-time princess, or staying with her, his wife. His words always convinced me that he loved me, but his words were never enough, they never would be as now I needed more, much more than words, it now had to be a commitment.

Sunday night came and I packed my case, I was so excited to be spending a few days together with Charlie before I left Cardiff for good. I knew it was going to be very hard and tinged with sadness, the emotion hard to contemplate as we approached our final goodbye, so tonight I knew I would yet again face the nightly terrors that formed an ugly queue, ready to wage war and disrupt my dreams.

Charlie arrived early as promised and was patiently waiting for me as I rushed out to meet him, eager to feel his kisses warm on my lips, to have my body filled with all the love I knew we had before we headed off, just as the sun was starting to rise over Wales.

I still had no idea where we were going, other than I would need my passport, so it was a trip either by plane or sea, he was to be mine for the next few days.

We drove for a while before arriving at the airport. Once inside we headed for check-in desk three. I kissed him with excitement as I now knew we were going to Paris. I gasped, *Charlie, the city of love? Yes Lizzy, only the best for my girl*. He squeezed my hand with excitement, we arrived a short time later at the most pristine hotel I had ever seen, it stood proud in a pretty Paris street away from the main hustle and bustle, but very typically Parisian.

We checked in as Mr and Mrs Stevens, bringing a lump to my throat just hearing Charlie say Mr and Mrs Stevens in some sort of broken French which he found very funny. He tried hard to keep a straight face while he continued to flirt with the pretty French, immaculately dressed receptionist, so to distract him I kissed him, making sure he knew I was watching him, but I knew he did it just to tease me, knowing that it would make me mad, which it did.

We were shown to our room, resplendently French in style. A big open airy bedroom, decorated in neutral colours, whites and creams, a large French wooden bed commanded centre stage in the room, complete with beautiful crisp white linen. French style furniture completed the look as wooden shutters adorned the windows, making for a very beautiful French hotel.

I had never been to Paris before, Charlie had, but not with Helen or that's what he had told me. Yet again the negative thoughts now invaded my mind, but I was pleased he had done this for me, to share our love here in Paris, the city of love for lovers which I found so very romantic.

Excitedly he then whisked me off to the very impressive Eiffel Tower. It was huge and commanding, the Paris landscape was in all its glory standing proud to be French. Charlie insisted we went right to the top and what a view it was, an amazing view overlooking Paris in all its glory, passion now hung heavily in the air, blanketing not only us in a cocoon of love, but for all the other couples that were just like us, wanting to share their love. Charlie held my hand, the hand which was adorned by the daisy ring. *Lizzy I love you; I love you so damn much.* His hand was so firm, letting me know I was his girl. *I never want to be without you Lizzy.* I froze to the spot on hearing such heart trembling words that brought a lump to my throat and with a trembling voice I said, *we will always have each other Charlie.* My heart remained heavy as I knew it was going to be almost impossible to continue our love as life would always find a way to cheat us out of our dirty love that should be allowed to flourish freely, but now, just like always, there were so many obstacles standing in our way ready to trip us up and to watch us fall.

I felt the tears once again blurring my vision, tears that stung my eyelids as Charlie held me close, allowing me to hide my terrifying sadness from him for now and to hide my emotions from everyone that was witnessing our tormented love. *Princess please don't cry.* I knew it would all be very emotional as this was our beautiful, but staggeringly sad final goodbye. Charlie's arms firmly cradled me as we just gazed out over Paris and all its beauty. You could not help but fall in love with it as everyone said, Paris was a very romantic city, and they were not wrong.

Lightening the mood, Charlie suggested we went for coffee and some much needed distraction from our heartache and the painful goodbye that we were yet to experience, so we settled ourselves outside at a pavement cafe in the centre of Paris just people watching, watching everyone going about their business, watching couples in love, families having precious time together, ladies wearing the most beautiful expensive clothes, looking so very glamorous and elegant, breathing in the unique air that was heavily laced with expensive and provocative aromas that spilled out from the endless perfumeries that lined every street. I continued to inhale the luxury, allowing the delicious aromas to fill my nostrils.

We sat with our coffee holding hands and it wasn't long before the conversation led Charlie to once again repeat his constant need to make me pregnant, but I could tell from his expression that he felt he had lost his quest to allow me my dream and once again I hated myself for keeping my secret from him. As I fought with my guilt I suggested we went for a beautiful walk along the river, as ever hand in hand and it felt good as we seemed relaxed, away from the daily torment that had been our lives for the last few months. We were now able to walk wrapped in each other's arms, to kiss without question, breathing in the freedom that we both yearned. Charlie kept mentioning our baby, I was lost for words as to know what to say, I just looked at him smiling, joking that he would have to try harder, making him smile the trademark smile that I adored.

As we walked together hand in hand, the sunshine was perfect, allowing us to relax away from the secret dirty love affair we shared, hiding it away from Helen back in Cardiff, but I did on occasions feel sorry for her and today was one of those days when my guilt just ate me up, adding to my already escalating emotional state.

With the daylight behind us, Charlie took me to a superb French restaurant, wining and dining me. It was the most amazing place, but seriously expensive as we drank the best champagne and ate the most fantastic food.

Arriving back at the hotel relaxed, we headed straight to our luxurious room, passions were at an all-time high. Charlie laid me on the big French style bed, looking at me with those eyes that asked for my dirty love, but tonight held a sadness. *Lizzy, Lizzy, Lizzy I will miss you.* His fingertips outlined my tear stained porcelain face.

I will miss you too Charlie. Once again my eyes were filling with tears as my heart started crumbling in to a million pieces, every one of them had Charlie's name tattooed across them. It hurt so very much, it was hard to explain the pain I was feeling for Charlie as I continued to keep the one amazingly perfect secret from him that he craved to hear, but I questioned myself repeatedly whether I should tell him now or keep it my secret a little longer. If I was going to tell him then here in Paris would undoubtedly be a good time, a special time, but I held back once again to not allow Charlie to know my precious and closely guarded secret just yet.

Charlie undressed me slowly, bit by bit, allowing my clothes to fall into neatly formed piles on to the floor before starting his quest to seduce my body, kissing my tits, paying extra attention to my nipples which seemed more sensitive now, before he moved his attention to my belly, peppering it with loving kisses. My belly was starting to fill out, but Charlie had said nothing as he just delivered beautiful comments of how lovely it was going to look when I was carrying his baby.

His tongue was now revolving around my belly button, then with sweeping movements his tongue glided with ease to my demanding, naked pussy. My legs were open, ready for his kisses as Charlie's head was now buried firmly between my thighs, delivering such sensitive kisses that I adored as I continued to beg him never to stop.

Charlie's fingers replaced his tongue as they danced with my naked pussy that was craving and demanding his dirty love. Suddenly he let his teeth run wild in a bid to tease my clit, making me tense up. His tongue once again flirting with my pussy on a mission for my warm, newly escaped juice that now coated his tongue and smeared his lips.

His cock was now standing to my attention, rock solid, with his balls hanging low and heavy with dirty love and it was all for me.

I straddled him, kissing him, running my fingers firmly down over his lean body, tracing the untamed outline of his torso, making his body tense up before my fingertips met the firm helmet of his cock which begged my fingers to run around its huge purple juicy head. I slowly drew my fingers down over the skin, working gently and slowly. His moaning was now so loud, my actions were having the desired effect as his whole body was tense with pent up passion that was about to be unleashed. Charlie increased his moaning to encourage me to love him more. *You bitch Lizzy, my beautiful bitch, you adorable whore.*

My lips then locked around his huge, love filled cock that was full of dirty love that was now escaping, leaving warm dirty love smeared across my lips as Charlie held my head gently while I sucked his cock, not wanting to free my mouth from the pleasure he was receiving, his moaning became very gritty and harsh.

My pussy was now demanding more, demanding Charlie's cock to fuck me hard as I started to ride him, his hands now firmly on my hips controlling the rhythm of my hard and dirty loving. I built up the rhythm, his gritty moaning became more powerful. *Lizzy let your juice slip down over my cock.* He repeated again his never-ending need to make me pregnant.

Guilt once again quivered through my body. I hated myself for not telling him, but my reasons where mine and mine only, feeling it would make things more complicated, not that it could be any more complicated than it was now.

We awoke on Tuesday morning to the sun streaming through the bedroom shutters, bathing the room in warm French sunlight so bright, it lit the room with stunning patterns that were made possible by the old shutters that adorned the windows.

Charlie was up and making coffee for us, so I slid out of bed wrapped only in a crisp white sheet, wrapping myself around him, hugging him so tight, giving him the Lizzy kisses and in return I was treated to kisses that were so soft on my neck, allowing my senses to be filled by Charlie's powerful aroma.

We drank our coffee ready for another lovely day. We headed out in to the Paris streets, the sun was warm and delightful on our skin, perfect for a boat trip down the river which was beautiful and so very romantic, you could feel the love that once again hung heavily, filling the air, a pungent aroma that was ours, something so unique you couldn't pinpoint to what made it so special.

Lunch was over and romance was filling our hearts to the limits, Charlie's arms were firmly around my tiny waist. He whispered, *Lizzy lets*

289

go shopping, I have to collect something for you. I gasped as we entered a very posh jewellers where a gentleman dressed in a very expensive tailored grey suit brought out a small velvet box and gave it to Charlie. Charlie then looked at me with that *I love you* expression, handing me the box. Trembling, I opened the box while Charlie smiled, *I love you Lizzy.* My tears were now uncontrollable.

I felt so loved that Charlie had gone to all that trouble to have made for me a pair of very expensive platinum earrings in the shape of delicate daisy's, complete with a note attached to the box which read, *My Lizzy, My lover, and My forever girl, we will never be apart, as life won't let us. H L F* completed the note. I squeezed his hand as I fought back tears of every emotion, from happiness to complete devastation.

After composing myself and with our love fully apparent now to everyone in the jewellers, Charlie's lavish gesture once again refuelled my suspicions of his mysterious, dark private life that so obviously revolved around huge sums of money.

We then took a stroll through the avenues of shops that graced these beautiful streets, the most stunning, glamorous boutiques that stood proud in this beautiful city with clothes and lingerie that were displayed in windows like works of art that were so elegant and sophisticated, but they too came with a very hefty price tag, just like our dirty love.

Back at the hotel we dressed for dinner. I wore a short black lace dress, complete with six inch heels and of course my earrings that I wore with pride. I wore my rings along with everything Charlie had bought for me, bringing endless and eternal love to my life.

Being in Paris made me realise how lucky we were to have each other, to have been given a second chance of a perfect love. Well, almost, as my life was never going to be perfect as I had now begun to realise, I would never have it all. It was all a dream; it was always going to be my dream that now would never be realised.

I was proud to be with Charlie, to be his girl, his lover, whatever I wanted to call it, but it was so wrong, so very wrong. We both knew it was forbidden love as I was left feeling very guilty at times, but my need for Charlie's love was more overpowering than the guilt I felt for Helen as his love and our love overruled anything that I could possibly feel guilty about, except our baby, that was at this moment my biggest burden of guilt, not to be able to share it with Charlie.

We enjoyed a very special evening, our last evening together that left my heart broken into the smallest shards that managed to puncture every bit of my already fragile heart, leaving my tattooed skin bleeding. Back at the hotel we made dirty love as passions again were on an all-time high, our final dirty loving, but tonight it felt rushed and unloving, as both of us were completely eaten up with enormous sadness, our hearts, and souls now in utter turmoil as we were saying goodbye to a lifetime of dirty love. What the hell were we thinking? Wrapped in each other's arms we must have fallen asleep, so desperately unhappy, trying to blot out the fragile state of our hearts that were now laced with terrifying sadness.

We awoke the next morning, just as the sun began to break through the shutters that adorned the windows, just like yesterday, but today was the start of a new day, the last day that Charlie and I would spend together. Just thinking about it sent my body into a terrifying mass of sadness, a sadness that I knew I could not hide, tears now sprang into my eyes as I fought to choke back the pain that seemed to stick rigidly in my throat, stifling me of air.

Alas it was time to get to the airport for the short journey back to Cardiff, a journey that I never wanted to take as it was yet another step closer to our final goodbye. Charlie held my hand that was now shaking violently, at a loss for words, fighting back my emotions, fighting back the tears I so wanted to shed, but not here in this beautiful city.

Once back in Cardiff, Charlie's phone was once again ringing frantically, to the point of being in meltdown. I could see the ongoing harassment it brought to him, but he didn't bother to answer the calls and again never mentioned it, but it raised my concerns, before I could say a word he switched the phone off, not wanting it to interrupt us again.

Charlie dropped me back to the hotel, it was going to be my very last lonely night there, just how it started only a few short months ago. The feeling of loneliness was so overwhelmingly sad, knowing Charlie was feeling it to, I could see in his beautiful brown eyes that he was hurting, both of us not knowing what to say or do for the best. Maybe it was better that I was now going to be on my own for my last night in Cardiff, alone like my first night, to give us both some space to deal with this agonising time we both had to face tomorrow.

I sat alone with my coffee, my mind racing between Cardiff, London, Charlie, Helen, myself, our baby, and his very secret, mysterious life that

I was not part of. I continued to ask myself questions that I could not answer. Should I tell Charlie about our baby or not? Do I stay in Cardiff, or do I go? Once again my reaction was to seek the comfort of the ring that hung on my necklace as I impatiently twiddled it, moving it around and around until it cut sharply into the skin on my neck.

My hands were resting on my tummy, our baby, that was such a huge thing in my life right now, knowing I was going to be a single mum having to go through labour on my own. I had to be very brave now for myself and for our unborn baby, this was going to be life changing as well as life challenging.

I started to shed the tears that had been on hold until now, tears that wee cold and wet on my face, tears that could not be kissed away tonight, shedding the many tears I had for us, for Charlie, for our dirty love which always seemed to end in tears like now and just like all those years ago.

I was going to miss Charlie, Cardiff and everything that went with it, the many friends I had made, the love I had found and rekindled once again, the list was endless. Cardiff had given me back my life, but had also managed to complicate it, leaving me the victim yet again of Charlie's dirty love and being his forever hostage, but I never wanted to be free from those chains that locked me into his love, a love I had felt since that day when fate played its hand, embracing our love with a tightening grip, as the chains were pulled tighter, as my emotions frayed, unravelling with every second that ticked by, ticking down to our final goodbye, a goodbye that I never wanted to say, how could I? My scars had now become my every day attire.

After a night of interruption, haunting images and harrowing voices, my body laid rigid in a pool of cold unwelcome fluid. I wondered how Charlie was feeling, if he too was reflecting on how this whirlwind adventure had changed our lives so dramatically. I took the journey again recalling the first time I saw his name in the local paper and how I felt that night, how terrifying that phone call was, but how delighted I was to hear his voice that sent wave after wave of beautiful emotions rocketing through my body.

We were now saying the most saddest goodbye and that was petrifying as I knew I could not live without Charlie in my life. He enriched it every day with his trademark cocky smile, to love me just like he promised twelve years ago, and to treat me like the princess he still to this day called me.

Charlie was waiting patiently for me outside and as soon as I saw him I started to cry, my bitter tears were at an all-time high. *Lizzy please don't cry.* But it was inevitable and impossible not to shed the tears that blinded my vision like a thick fog, debilitating my every movement, my every thought, it was all so damn sad. It should not be like this, Charlie held my shaking hand, begging me not to leave. *Don't go Lizzy, stay please.* I was startled by his words, at last he was asking me to stay, but it was all too late and he knew that. I questioned in my head why his words had come so late, *I can't Charlie, I have to go it's too complicated for me to stay.* He looked at me with a questioning expression, one that I did not want to answer or dwell on, so I declined again, keeping my secret to myself that meant I could never stay now.

I don't want you to go Lizzy, Charles hand squeezed my hand tightly. *Charlie, dad needs me, and my contract has been signed for London and the list goes on.* My hands were shaking, my voice quivering. *You have Helen and a baby on the way, they are two of the reasons I can't stay Charlie.* My words must have seemed cold today, without warmth almost pushing him away, only two Lizzy, you mean there are more reasons, I couldn't look at him, staring into the palms of my hands, as I caught the harrowing tears that was my life once again, Charlie, I'm sorry I just can't stay.

Tears now engulfed his face; his face being so pained by the hurt our love was causing us to endure today. We sobbed inconsolably as we sat together in his car, embraced in emotional sadness, neither of us wanting to be the first one to pull away as that would allow us to have to say the final goodbye, to have to utter the words that would jolt us both sideways.

Arriving at the station my body felt like it had melted into a watery puddle in which my reflection was distorted by pain and anguish. I cried more uncontrollable tears that splashed onto my bare skin, stinging the already open wounds that tattooed my body.

As we held hands our kisses were uneasy and flat. I could not bear it, the hurt in my heart was terrifying as I whispered *I love you Charlie, I love you so very much, so very much. Princess, my beautiful princess, my beautiful Lizzy.* He caressed my face, *stay Lizzy please.* Charlie was now sat with his head heavily cradled in his hands which I had seen him do before when things were so obviously heavy on his mind, he was being emotionally crippled by this very unwelcome goodbye.

I was now walking away from the man I loved, the man that I had craved all my life, what in the hell was I doing? Was I about to make the worst ever mistake of my life by leaving Charlie? Of course I was, but I had no choice because if I stayed in Cardiff it would put more pressure on us both, something that might ruin what we had and what we had shared, our dirty love, a beautiful dirty love, this was so hard and so utterly unfair as it always had been and probably always would be. We seemed to always be saying goodbye as our lives seemed to revolve so easily around sadness and constant goodbyes.

CHAPTER 25

As the train drew in it was time to go. Charlie held me for as long as he possibly could, our tears were now obvious for everyone to see. It was heart shattering as we said our goodbyes, our long I love you's, our beautiful I love you's, the cold reality was here all too soon and once again we seemed so unprepared for this huge emotional roller-coaster that never seemed to be able to stop, to allow us to get off even for a split second, to recover from the constant pain of life we seemed to be enduring.

Charlie blew me kisses until out of sight, I caught every one of them and returned them a million times. I turned away, blinking away my tears and Charlie was gone. My first love, my lover, my forever Charlie, I could not believe I had let him go so easily, but I felt let down by him that he hadn't made more demands on me to stay earlier, to ride out the continuing storm together, but I had let him down in return by not telling him the secret he longed to hear, the secret we had lovingly made together.

I cried all the way home, crippled emotionally and physically by the impact of our goodbye. This was going to be so hard, almost like grieving, reliving the past. The sadness was so hard to deal with, but it would never be any different as I once again made the decision to allow the heartache to continue, by keeping my secret from him.

Dad met me from the train as I struggled with two unruly suitcases. I was so glad to see him, knowing he knew exactly what was on my mind as my tear stained face told the desperately sad story witnessed today by my fellow passengers. *Come on Lizzy let's get you home and make you some coffee.* Home, I was home again. This was now my life… beautiful memories met me at every turn, memories that would embrace me.

It was about 4pm and dad was sat in the garden when the doorbell rang, it was too late for the post, and we were not expecting anyone. As I opened the creaky front door a lady stood with a beautiful mass of large white daisy's wrapped in pale pink cellophane and soft tissue, I hurried inside to read the card, it read:

I will never stop loving or missing you. X. You're my world, you always have been and you always will be. Lizzy, a life without you will be impossible. H L F. Until we make Daisy chains again.

What the hell did those haunting initials mean? Was I supposed to understand them? Was it a code that linked us together? Something from our past maybe, the mystery continued.

In bits once again I started to cry. Dad came in and saw the flowers, he must have put two and two together, smiling, *they are lovely Lizzy, someone cares about you very much.* I nodded through my tears, *yes he does dad.*

As I put the flowers into water I was thinking constantly about the man I loved and that I had left alone in Cardiff to resume the life that he had with Helen, to continue leading the dark, mysterious life he was so obviously leading that was ruled and fuelled by his ongoing reputation.

I had to somehow forget him again, knowing I was being completely stupid as I never would. How could I? My mind again in a constant sea of turmoil, I must have fell asleep on my bed which felt very lonely and cold, I woke up late, the house was in darkness, dad must have already gone to bed not wanting to disturb me.

I was now feeling totally alone, agonising if I should have stayed in Cardiff, to have stayed and been Charlie's bit on the side, his whore, and his bitch, to have told Charlie about our baby. Maybe I should have made demands on him to leave Helen, to put more pressure on him now with so much going through my head, I never thought it would be so hard to have it all, but one thing was for sure, I loved Charlie and his baby that I was now expecting.

I awoke the next morning, having been visited relentlessly during the hours of darkness by haunting images of the many frequent visitors, along with voices that echoed through me, sending my body into a trembling mess. my head was now splitting, I felt so drained emotionally. All I wanted to do was sleep, shutting out such tormenting sorrow.

A day in the garden to relax was in order. I relaxed overlooking the best view, the view I loved in the warm sunshine surrounded by sweet smelling blooms in what was a perfect garden allowing my body to recover from the devastating terror.

This was just what I needed having burnt the candles at both ends recently, a few days rest was a good idea, if only I could let my mind relax and not overdo the mass of negative thoughts and what ifs, there were so many that I could not find an answer for.

I had a pile of letters to sort so I sat in the garden going through them. Most were junk, but this garden always proved to be a distraction as I gazed around at the glorious blooms, inhaling the beautiful perfume that sparked such provocative emotions. Glancing back at the pile of post there was a letter from the solicitor. Dave was selling the house and I was entitled to half. Everything in the house was Dave's to start again with, along with all the permanent reminders of the loveless life we spent together, having to endure the miserable marriage we shared. Every stick of furniture containing bitter reminders of the seven year marital farce would be his, along with all the misery ingrained in it, like the bathroom mirror that had witnessed the vile person Dave really was, just like his tortuous behaviour that was now ingrained on my skin, knowing he had wanted to keep me his prisoner, instructing me on so many occasions to jump to his commands, to be the down trodden wife... but now that would be someone else's life with Dave.

I had not heard from Dave since I walked out on him and that was fine by me as I never wanted to see or hear from him ever again, to never have to relive the farce which let myself become a victim of his abuse, violence and bitter hatred, taking everything from me for his selfish trophy.

I was now thinking about my scan, my thoughts lead me to Charlie, wishing desperately that he could be part of it. I was faced with a heart-breaking dilemma, to tell him or not, knowing the next few days would remain tormented for me as I constantly had Charlie on my mind. My dilemma was building and not being made any easier, so I took another visit to my old bedroom to stand at the window that allowed me to rethink the dilemma I was facing, hoping I might find the answer. I let myself escape to a place where everything was calm, beautiful and free from ugly torment, but the answers were not here for me to collect today, they never would be as I had to make the decision that weighed heavy on my mind, while I clutched desperately to the necklace that held the ring which I had grown to love, that still seduced me every day by its secret.

My thoughts were of our baby and Charlie, if I told him would he want to know? His quest to make me pregnant was now a reality, would he hate me for not telling him sooner, for not being part of the amazing journey we should have taken together? So many what ifs, my head was spinning around, questions clashed together like booming thunder and vicious lightning. There would be no rainbow today to cast its brightly coloured structure.

I received flowers every day for a week, daisies of course, and always wrapped in pink tissue and glossy pink scrunchy cellophane and always accompanied by the initials that now taunted me... *H L F...*

Charlie also rang every day without fail and every call was laced with bitter emotions, neither of us knowing what to say to make things better and every time I shed so many heart breaking tears, but that showed me just how much love we would always have, we really did have something unique and amazingly powerful.

The following days melted into one, my scan was now just days away. If I was going to make my final discussion it had to be now, so I slept on it one more night as I wanted and needed everything clear in my mind. My dreams were now taking me on a very colourful journey around the garden that I loved, desperately trying to awaken more thought provoking emotions in the hope it would trigger a reaction, a reaction that would finally make up my mind for me.

As I awoke refreshed after a rare night's sleep without unwanted visitors I laid in bed thinking I had to be fair on our baby, so with that my mind was made up. I picked up the phone and dialled the number that was so very familiar and that I had rang millions of times before, but this was the most terrifying call that I would ever make, but it was now or never, so I took a deep breath to prepare myself for being rebuffed. My heart beating so fast and hard, my hands were trembling at the thought of hearing the voice I loved. The phone rang, it seemed he would never pick up when suddenly my breath was taken away by the voice on the other end of the phone which remained so powerful and seductive.

On hearing his voice I was suddenly lost for words. *Lizzy what's wrong?* I started to get emotional. *Lizzy don't cry, please don't cry.* My voice was now quivering, tears again blurred my eyes like a thick fog as I muttered my words. *I need to see you Charlie.* He was obviously worried, asking me repeatedly if I was OK. I reassured him I was fine, but that I missed him so much.

The air was now heavy with anticipation as I held my breath, waiting for Charlie's words. *That would be great, I will book us somewhere nice Lizzy.* Delighted once again that I was going to be back in his arms with the man I still loved so deeply. *Lizzy, are you sure you're OK?* I gulped back the massive lump in my throat that was now choking me. *Lizzy talk to me. I'm fine Charlie.*

We chatted for a while as I tried to keep the conversation light and airy, my heart was still beating so hard as my feelings once again were aroused by him, by his deep stunning voice that never failed to seduce me. We said our goodbyes and as normal, more beautiful I love you's and I miss you's followed. Charlie had not even mentioned that he thought that I might be pregnant and having his baby, I couldn't believe it had not even crossed his mind, but maybe he had given up any hope, unable to keep his promise to make my dream come true.

At last I was on my way back to Cardiff for the weekend, leaving me with butterflies that danced delicately at the thought of seeing Charlie again, knowing it would be so emotional for us both, as the news I was going to deliver would completely change our lives forever in more ways than one, our future was now in waiting, hanging in the balance and if the past had been any sort of rehearsal then we were in for a very stormy and turbulent journey, but hopefully we could weather the storm that was brewing, bring more torment, sadness and of course heartache that was never far away, as it continually ruled my life, as it had done since the vision in my bedroom mirror was one of a swan and since I let myself fall in love with the boy with the bad reputation that had stolen my heart, taking me his hostage, never allowing me to be free from his love, but that I allowed out of love, the love I only had for one man and that would always be him to the day I took my last breath it would always be Charlie.

Train pulled into the station. This was it, I took a few long deep breaths trying to keep calm, my hands shaking and cold with fear and once again I clasped my fingers tightly around the ring on my necklace as I fiddled nervously with it, suddenly through the train window I spotted Charlie who was there waiting for me as always, leaning against the wall which always made me smile with his calm and cocky attitude fully on display.

I ran to him throwing my loving arms around him. We held each other so tight, receiving the kisses that once again took my breath away, every kiss replaced with another more powerful than the one before. *Lizzy*, he whispered, I have missed you so much. You look so stunningly beautiful. He held my arms outstretched, wanting to feast again on what was always going to be his, again this weekend without doubt.

He looked at me with that same intoxicating smile and with his adorable deep brown eyes that drew me into his love, a love that took me on a journey that had led me here to be reunited to the only man I had ever loved, or was prepared to love, despite his secret and mysterious life, a life I would never be allowed to enter, but still it seduced me and in a strange way I found it very romantic.

On arrival at the hotel I was stunned as Charlie had booked the beautiful lavish city hotel in which we had the end of build party. Amazingly we were able to check in, the receptionist smiled a warm welcoming smile as she asked him in. *What name was the booking made*? Charlie replied, *Mr and Mrs Charlie Stevens*. That made my heart sing. Charlie took my bag as we were shown to our room. It was amazing, a jacuzzi bath and very large bed complete with lovely crisp white laundered sheets, everything that I adored.

Is this OK for you Lizzy? Again only wanting the best for me. *Yes it's fantastic Charlie.* Our kisses were once again so passionate and full of love, nothing had changed our love which was still paramount, so obviously true. Charlie suggested we went out for coffee to the little cafe that we had grown to love. *Lizzy, is everything OK?* His face was pained and so sad, maybe he thought it was bad news. I gulped, the moment of truth was about to be told, but how would I tell him? I had to find the strength from somewhere and I would, after all I had come here to tell him the most beautiful and amazing news.

As we sat holding hands across the table in the cafe I loved so much, the familiar pleasurable aromas now filled my nostrils. The pretty waitress, the lovely Welsh girl had unknowingly led me back into Charlie's arms. I was lost in the moment as Charlie looked at me, smiled his trademark smile. *Lizzy I have missed you so much.* He squeezed my fingers. *I have not stopped thinking about you, not for a minute.* Just then our lips met, lingering, not wanting to miss this amazing and most powerful feeling that was surging through my body.

As he looked at me waiting for me to say something, my thoughts mingled into one as I hesitated yet again. Would he be happy about my news that I was about to deliver to him? Tears were now clouding my vision, my lips quivering in anticipation of his reaction.

You're worrying me now Lizzy. My hands were shaking, cold and sweaty, my mouth so dry, so much so my tongue kept sticking to the roof of my mouth, so I took yet another rather large sip of coffee, before I took a deep breath squeezed his hand lovingly, his eyes fixed firmly on me watching my mouth waiting for my words that were about to deliver my huge overwhelming secret. *I'm pregnant Charlie, I'm pregnant with our baby.* His brown eyes burst with tears, *Lizzy our baby, our baby Lizzy wow.* I could see and feel his hands shaking as he was now holding his head with both his hands. *Wow Lizzy.* He seemed totally taken aback by my news that had stunned him into silence.

He stood up and kissed me, his voice now raised, *Lizzy I love you, I love you so much.* We were now both shaking as he kept repeating *our baby, our baby. Lizzy our baby. Yes Charlie.* He was consumed by absolute love that sent wave after wave of love through the little cafe, bouncing love from every wall. It seemed as if we were now cocooned once again in a bubble of love, while others looked on in amazement at our news.

I'm just so shocked Lizzy totally shocked, my baby. He then placed his hands on my belly, *my baby, our baby Lizzy thank you, thank you so much.* Watching his expression I could see he was in love with our baby already and totally happy with the news that he had just received. *How long have you known?* I hesitated again. *For a while Charlie. Lizzy why didn't you say. So many reasons really, you had just found out Helen was pregnant and I thought it would complicate things even more, I needed time to digest the most perfect news.*

Leaving the little cafe behind us, still reeling from our news we walked back to the hotel, cocooned in each other's arms. Charlie was still stunned by the news I had just given him. Tears appeared in his eyes once again, his voice trembling with excitement, now looking back I should have told him a long time ago as we could have enjoyed the early part of the journey together. I had been a fool, a total fool and as I looked at him I fell in love again, smiling his cocky smile. Screwing is nose up he cheekily asked, *when did I get you pregnant Lizzy?* Smiling back, I revealed to him that it was the time when we headed to the beautiful castle for a dirty weekend of love, confessing that when we headed to London for a weekend of passion that I was already pregnant. *We even talked about making babies.* He smiled. *Lizzy I remember it well*, chuckling to himself.

Over dinner our baby was the topic of conversation, it was all we could talk about which made a very refreshing change from being bogged down by work or Helen, subjects that still remained in the background and would crop up sooner or later, knowing he had made us both pregnant within a few weeks of one another. Our conversations would then once again be tainted with sadness, bitterness, and guilt and not so delightful as they were right now.

Back at the hotel we were lovers once again as Charlie unzipped my dress, letting it fall to the floor. I stood in my undies and high heel shoes delighted to be showing off my not so little bump to Charlie. He kissed my neck, slowly seducing the immaculate ring that hung around it lovingly, before he dropped to his knees kissing my belly, revolving his tongue inside my belly button, peppering my belly with soft wet kisses.

Charlie then laid me on the bed, freeing me from my underwear to reveal the full beauty of my newly naked pussy. Charlie's lips felt the smoothness, his tongue was tense and rigid, sending wave after wave of the tantalising sensation that I had missed so much, his dirty love, his dirty passion, and his very dirty sex, all still so addictive.

He then straddled my legs; his breath was warm against my nipples that now begged to be sucked as they instantly stood to the attention of Charlie's lips.

He leant forward to kiss me, allowing our tongues to engage with one another, again on a journey of perfect dirty love, dancing delightfully together as Charlie let his tongue glide over my lips and on to my tongue. Charlie's whispering and moaning sent wild ice cold shivers down my spine. *Princess I'm going to fuck you forever.* I was not objecting, and I never would, something that would never change. Charlie's cock gently slid into my extremely demanding wet pussy on a mission to make up for lost time, his thrusting hard, long, and powerful as I demanded him to fuck me harder.

My legs were now relaxed over his strong arms as he rode me softly and gently, delivering amazingly dirty love, very tender and caring. At that moment it felt like we had everything, but I somehow knew it was never going to be perfect.

I was moaning hard and very loud now, allowing all my pent up sexual desires to be unleashed. I could feel the pressure from Charlie's rigid, rock solid cock that allowed my juice to cling to it. Suddenly I felt him tense up, allowing his juice to fill my pussy, making sure I had received it all as he delightfully continued to thrust until I had. His kisses were now drenching my body on a mission to free me from the juice that filled my pussy for the ultimate dirty sex, so with his head now firmly between my thighs, his lips locked onto my clit, sending me wild with dirty desires as our juice was now smeared around his mouth and over his lips. He loved to share this with me on every occasion and tonight was no different. I had received the most incredible, beautiful dirty love, leaving me once again totally addicted to our love.

I awoke early to watch Charlie sleeping, something I had not done for what seemed like such a long time. He was a very handsome looking man and still to this day he was never short of female attention, as I knew full well when we were out together girls would always give him a sideways smile, or turn their head to look again in a bid to attract his attention, but it was me, his girl, his Lizzy that he wanted to love so much.

I kissed his lips gently to wake him, he stirred, whispering my name. *Lizzy my beautiful Lizzy.* He swept me back against his naked body while I took a sharp intake of breath, catching the power of his aroma that now lingered on the crisp sheets that had been pushed to one side so that we could admire again each other's bodies.

As we looked at each other I was consumed once again by our overwhelming love that seemed to take me once again on a journey that filled me with such evocative memories, spanning over the many years that we had been lovers. Suddenly I was brought back to reality, away from my journey for now, by an overexcited Charlie. *Lizzy I fancy going shopping; I want to buy something for our baby.* I laughed and smiled at him; he was so excited, just like a big kid.

We headed out for lunch, sitting in the pub garden, flanked by the castle walls. Its imposing structure was magnificent, a gracing backdrop for a perfect Sunday afternoon as the sun managed to pepper kisses on our faces. Once again we talked excitedly about our baby, I touched on the subject of Helen and their baby, he looked at me and his face was saddened once again. *I will be there for them Lizzy.* It now felt that I had split him in two different directions, and I hated myself for that. I grabbed the ring on my necklace for comfort, trying somehow to help justify my increasing guilt.

I touched his hand lovingly, sweeping my fingers over his. *I don't expect any commitment from you Charlie, all I want is you to be a part of our baby's life, even if you chose not to be in mine.* He looked at me, puzzled by my words. *Lizzy I told you, I can't let you go, I can't and won't let that happen ever again.*

I let you go once to another man Lizzy, something I have regretted every day of my life. These were tear provoking words that I really hoped he meant so with the sentimental chat over for now we headed for a large department store in the centre of Cardiff as Charlie had said he wanted to buy our baby's first teddy bear, so now we were on a mission to find the cutest teddy in the world. *That's the one,* Charlie said. It was white and fluffy with a huge red bow.

There was now only one place that would make today perfect, as coffee was needed it had to be our favourite cafe where we sat at the table by the window, that seemed to be the right place today, and once again it managed to cocoon me in a blanket of utter love, all before I had to get the train at the end of a perfect weekend, once again made possible by Charlie and his endless ability to make me feel special.

We said our goodbyes, loads of beautiful kisses for me and our baby. People must have thought we were mad as Charlie kissed my tummy on the station platform, making us both smile. I giggled as he held my hands outstretched in front of me wanting to admire again and again my baby bump.

He then held me close as he kissed me, whispering *I love you more than any words Lizzy.* We were now not wanting to be parted from each other. Charlie held my hand for as long as was possible before I had to board the train for the long and lonely journey back home to Wiltshire, the air was stagnant with dark clouded skies, making it impossible for either of us to smile. I reluctantly boarded the train, my legs were heavy and unsteady, with no support for my already fragile body, but I knew I had renewed strength, I just needed to find it. I looked at Charlie, his body too seemed to be limp of any life, wondering if now I had caused yet another problem to complicate his already chequered life, knowing he too would now have to dodge the raging storm that we had created together.

CHAPTER 26

We blew thousands of kisses to each other until each of us was out of sight. The journey home gave me time to reflect on the news I had just shared with Charlie, letting myself drift off wondering if he made Helen feel equally as special. Once again my thoughts led me to a dark, mysterious place that I hated, back to the bitterness that still surrounded our lifetime of dirty love that now made me doubt whether I should have allowed him the beauty of my secret.

Arriving home late I placed the fluffy teddy in pride of place in the nursery. It looked so very cute, instantly bringing a smile to my face, putting aside for now my negative doubts, but I knew full well they would return bigger and without doubt send me into a blind panic.

Every day that Charlie and I were apart I received flowers from him, the house looked like a florist's. The perfume was delightful as it filled every room in the house with the eternal essence of our dirty love, refreshing the memories of the many happy days and nights that we had shared.

Having had two weeks without Charlie, July was here, and I had missed him so very much, but that was life, a life we had to accept for now. I now had time on my hands as the build in London was slightly delayed, but at last Friday came I was overly excited to see Charlie's car pulling into the maternity unit car park. It was not hard to miss the gleaming, sleek, and expensive black sports car that stood out from the rest. As the heavy roar of the engine shuddered through me, waving erratically he smiled that special intoxicating smile, the smile that was so full of love, taking my breath away. I smiled back, relieved that he had kept his promise to be here with me, to share this special moment.

Our kisses said hello, along with all the I love you's I had missed. Charlie's hands were now resting on my bump, excited to be reunited with us both as we kissed again our hello's. I could tell from that beaming smile that he was elated, excited, and delighted that we were going to know the sex of our baby. I was so nervous, Charlie held my hand reassuringly as he said *I love you both*.

We were called in almost immediately. I was shaking with excitement holding onto the ring that hung patiently on my necklace for reassurance as Charlie continued to hold my other hand. The nurse was calm, lovely and made us feel very at ease, suddenly I had a thought Helen would have had a scan by now, did he know what they were having? He hadn't said, but it was not my business... but it made me think if he had been so excited at Helen's scan or when they were told the sex of their baby, again another mystery, another part of the puzzle. We looked at the screen, it was clear to see, *a girl* Charlie beamed, at last we had some news to both smile about, we were having a daughter, *a little girl Lizzy*. Charlie then squeezed my hand so tight.

We walked back to the car wrapped in each other's arms, but today we were both lost for words, totally speechless at the stunning news we had just received, knowing this was just the start of another amazing journey in our lives. Smiling uncontrollably, my face was hurting as I continued to smile, reflecting back the smiles that I was receiving from Charlie.

I fumbled around in my bag to find the paperwork with the date on and it read the 23rd of December. She would be here for Christmas. *What an amazing present, Lizzy how special, totally special.* We kissed again kisses of delight, my body now trembling with fear as reality hit me full on that I might now be a single mum. Suddenly I felt very scared and alone, although Charlie was right by my side. I once again felt like I had the weight of the world on my shoulders that felt so heavy as I was still not able to plan the perfect family life.

Do you have to go back tonight Charlie? I held my breath in anticipation, waiting to be rebuffed again by Charlie's answer, thinking Helen would rule once again this weekend. Before he had the chance to answer I begged him to stay. He smiled then hesitated, I grabbed his hand, *please Charlie.* I waited patiently for his reply. *Stay with me Charlie. Lizzy are you sure?* It felt like we were kids again, needing permission to love each other after all these years, bringing back hidden memories of the Christmas when Charlie had waited shivering outside for my parents to go to bed before making his appearance on that very cold, but special winter's night.

Charlie arrived later in the evening. Hearing his car roar onto the drive I excitedly let him in, instantly taking him by the hand and leading him straight to my room. I kissed him hello, he smiled, delighted that at last he was here with me, to be back in each other's arms for now, back in this house with me again all those years on from that late autumn afternoon when I lead him upstairs to seduce me in my old bedroom.

I want to show you something Charlie. I led him by the hand to the next room, our baby's nursery. On opening the door tears filled his eyes, his reaction was so emotional it stunned me, Charlie the cool, calm character with a reputation that was still clinging to him, was now stunned into silence by our forthcoming arrival, *Lizzy it's beautiful.*

We returned to my room and laid on my bed, our arms wrapped each other in glorious love. I couldn't contain my sexual desires any longer, I was in need of his dirty love tonight. I kissed him with a lingering passion, whispering thousands of I love you's, Charlie returned the words that I loved to hear, confirming again tonight his undying love for me.

I undid his shirt slowly and sexily, delivering Lizzy kisses on every button as I continued to kiss him, peppering him in lost kisses in a bid to make up for two weeks without his dirty love. Kneeling over him I pulled my t-shirt over my head sharply to reveal my swollen breasts, heavy with love for him. My baby belly was now visible to us both. I unzipped my jeans to unveil a delightful round bundle of pure love. Charlie smiled contently as I wriggled free of them. I was commando today, something I knew he loved as I laid naked his eyes took a journey following my curvaceous contours, admiring our baby bump, he seemed transfixed by it and I had to admit it was such a beautiful, round complete ball of baby.

His fingers then slipped eagerly in to my ever demanding naked pussy that was begging Charlie for more, so with that he applied more pressure allowing his fingers to dance delightfully with my pussy, as I moaned so loudly, my moaning now encouraging Charlie to love me harder.

Charlie withdrew his fingers, rubbing my nipples with my juice that was warm and fresh. His lips were now locked onto my nipples, sucking them hard with a renewed vigour. *That tastes so fucking good Lizzy.* So good he did it again, smearing my juice onto my nipples that were huge, full, and so hard to the delight of Charlie.

Charlie straddled over me again, his cock was wet with beads of pearly juice. *Lizzy I'm going to love you hard.* He caressed my nipples, squeezing them hard and making me moan deeply. I then without shame demanded him to just do it, to fuck me hard and long.

My legs were now draped over his arms, my legs totally relaxed as he thrust his cock lovingly and gently, but I demanded yet again to be loved much harder, a bit rougher, so with that the pressure built and we were riding it. His cock seemed much bigger tonight, more swollen and extremely hard as thrust after thrust, dirty love was delivered to my naked pussy. Charlie's firm gaze was fixed on my porcelain face. *Bloody hell Lizzy you're so very, very beautiful, you adorable bitch. You're fucking every bit my little whore, my gorgeous Lizzy.*

Charlie and I then laid together totally exhausted on my bed, my hand was resting on Charlie's chest, feeling him breathing. I then moved closer to kiss him. *I love you Charlie, I love you so very much, but we do need to talk about what will happen in the future.* He then kissed his fingers, placing them over my mouth. Let's not talk about it now Lizzy. Once again Charlie denied me of any commitment, keeping his plans to himself, leaving me no closer to what would be our future, if there would be any future.

After a peaceful night we awoke late. I nudged Charlie, whispering *come on sleepy head.* As I kissed him my smile showed I was delighted that we had spent another night together. Grinning now and blushing repeatedly, Charlie had now noticed my amusement. *Lizzy what is it?* I smiled at him. *Your car, it's parked on the drive.* Dad will have put two and two together, Charlie smiled reminding me of how naughty I was.

I'll freshen up Lizzy. I smiled. *Charlie, come back to bed, I have plans for you.* I then pulled him back into my arms, smothering him in fresh early morning kisses, then much to his surprise I led him by the hand, up the old staircase to my old beloved bedroom to capture memories of that glorious autumn day when Charlie seduced me right here. Charlie's eyes travelled around my old bedroom, he too was taking in the warmth we created here.

We laid on my little old, rickety bed, embracing the perfect love we had created throughout the years. Suddenly memories turned to passion, explosions of passionate aromas now sparked throughout my old bedroom, demanding again that he fucked me right here, right now and today I wasn't going to be disappointed. I moaned continually during this unexpected early lunchtime love session, wanting to receive every bit of his huge cock that thrust inside me repeatedly as he delivered so much warm, fresh juice, *Lizzy, Lizzy you naughty girl.* With that he peppered my body in warm kisses on his way over my body to love me once again as I allowed his tongue to make love to my naked pussy that was now shedding juice onto his lips.

We laid together embraced in love on my little old bed and it felt right, so very right and for the first time in a long time I did not feel the slightest bit guilty about anything, including Helen, Dave, even dad that now knew I was not alone this weekend.

We finally got up, I made coffee and took it into the garden. Charlie popped back into the house, it seemed as if he was gone ages so I went to look for him and as I crept in, he was stood by the nursery door still, quiet and motionless. *Charlie.* He turned to me sobbing, *Charlie what's wrong?* His hand was now reaching for mine, *I love you Lizzy, I don't know what to do.* I held him close, knowing full well he must be terrified as he had two babies on the way within weeks of each other, a wife and then me, his demanding dirty lover to keep happy.

Taking his hand I led him back to the garden where we sat reminiscing about all the happy hours we had spent there in the garden, the fields, and the woods. I thought maybe now it was time for some hard talking as things needed to be dealt with and not swept under the carpet, something Charlie was very good at, but as I looked at him once again he looked so pained at the prospect that we both would have to make some heartbreakingly difficult choices in the coming weeks and months ahead if this was going to work for us both.

My hand was now holding his, hesitating to utter the words that needed answers. *Charlie it's not fair for me to expect to share you, your life, your business, your wife, and your baby all back in Wales.* This was going to be an agonising conversation, full of sadness, a sadness that I had made possible once again as now the storm was so bitterly tormented and full of epic thunder, crippling lightning, and a torrent of rain.

We both knew that he could not keep us all happy. Holding his hand I repeated my words, *it's your call Charlie, I will make no demands of you only that you see your daughter as often as possible, that's all.* Yet again I took another step in making things easier for him, allowing him to have his cake and eat it too and by me doing that he would never have to make any commitment to me, never having to make his final choice, leaving our lives again hanging by a tiny thread.

He buried his head into his hands once again, *Lizzy I love you and our baby. Charlie, you have Helen and your baby in Cardiff,* my voice was slightly raised. At this point I was trying to push him into facing up to his responsibilities to us all. *I know Lizzy, but. But what Charlie? Tell me... I don't love her, I don't love Helen. We don't share what we have Lizzy. It's always been about you, my girl, my Lizzy.* Charlie kissed my hand that was now trembling with fear as I thought I was pushing him too hard to make an agonising choice.

Charlie looked awful. I felt for him, the triangle now impossible to deal with once again. I left Charlie wandering around in the garden, hoping that he could reflect on happier times spent here in this love capsule of a garden while I made us a very late lunch and more strong coffee, giving him time to clear his head, to try and put things in order, if that was at all possible at the moment.

I returned to the garden with lunch and strong coffee, we talked at ease yet again. I knew Charlie would now have to make some hard choices and soon, if we were to have any chance of a family life, knowing that in the next few months he would be tested to the limits with choices that would be agonising to make and I seemed to be making things easier for him, by doing that I was allowing him to have the best of us both. Suddenly I felt the need to seek some comfort from the ring on my necklace, my fingers intertwined with the ring.

Charlie's cocky smile had returned to his face again and he was now holding my hand. *Princess, remember when we used to sit in that tree house for hours and hours, sitting in the freezing cold wrapped up against the elements.* I smiled, nodding my recollection of the wonderful times we shared. *Dad had built it for me when I was about three years old and I had spent endless hours playing in it, it had been my sanctuary on many occasions.* Now unused, Charlie thought it would be a good idea to visit it once again. I giggled at his idea as I watched him climb up the wonky ladder that was broken in places before reaching the little house. *Lizzy join me.* Charlie then helped me into the tree house and once again it did not fail to reward me with delightful memories that I instantly adored. We spent all afternoon sat in the tree house, allowing us to escape the mental torture that was hard to deal with. We laughed delightedly to all the emotions and muted memories that we were now recalling. I told him about the fairies that had once graced this garden, dancing with me just where the garden met the fields. Looking at me he did a somewhat sideways grin, not believing in such fairy-tale rubbish as he called it, and it led me to wonder if I would ever dance with them again or if I even danced with them at all. Was I dreaming? Lost in my own little world all those years ago when everything was so perfect, so vibrant with no heartache, no violent and terrifying storms, nothing to blur and mar my unblemished early years.

It wasn't long before our conversation took us back to our baby. *Have you thought about names Lizzy?* Charlie was keeping the mood light for now, so excitedly I suggested we made a list of names for our new daughter, Charlie beamed. *Lizzy, what a great idea.*

We moved down from what was now a somewhat uncomfortable tree house. Charlie sat writing for ages. I was completely at a loss as we swapped paper, Charlie looked at me as my paper just contained just masses of question marks and kisses as I wanted Charlie to name her. *Lizzy.* Charlie questioned my lack of names, *sorry I just can't think Charlie.* He seemed amused by my blank expression, screwing up his nose while trying hard not to smile, making me blush again.

I started to read the list of names that Charlie had written, suddenly tears again blurred my vision as I choked back my reaction. I could not speak as I read what he had written. *What Lizzy? Charlie this is perfect, perfect for our little girl… Daisy, Charlie its beautiful, so beautiful.* Charlie's list only contained one name spelt out in capital letters and stamped with his approval as her name was adorned by hearts and a kiss.

Daisy Stevens.

We both thought it was a beautiful name for her as Daisy's had played such a very important meaningful part in our lives over the years, starting with a simple, but beautiful daisy chain made by Charlie for me on that chilly, but sunny March afternoon and then a plastic daisy shaped ring from a Christmas cracker that now proved so meaningful in our lives, driving our virginal love though the early years right up until now.

Charlie bent down, kissing and talking to my tummy as he once again outlined my bump with his fingertips. *Daisy, you're going to be a beautiful girl just like your mummy, I love you both so much, I promise I will never let you down.* Hard sentiments that now I demanded he keep while placing his hand firmly on my tummy letting him feel the enormous love that now embraced us. *Daisy Elizabeth Stevens, perfect. Elizabeth after my beautiful mum Lizzy, it's beautiful.*

After managing to compose ourselves we continued to enjoy the sunshine that now projected a pretty light into the garden. We walked hand in hand, recalling little memories that sparked a vivid kaleidoscope of the many moments we had created right here together.

Charlie now left me alone to spend the rest of the late afternoon and early evening in the garden deep in thought of how things would work out for us long term which was so hard to predict as the future was on hold for now. Settling back on my sun lounger I gazed around the garden as the light danced across the lawn casting its glow further away into the fields and the woods beyond, making everything look so innocent as once again my thoughts took me back to my youth, to the carefree days that were so full of laughter, fun and freedom. A far cry from today as life seemed so very complicated and overcrowded.

A sudden shiver ran down through my body leaving it paralysed. I could feel mum around me, out of the corner of my eye. I was convinced that I saw her, smelling the beautiful perfume from the roses that filled this garden with a sweet, vibrant aroma. I blinked again to recall the vision, but she had gone, my mind alas was playing tricks on me, or was she really here as now I could smell her perfume. My body now embraced by mum, once again all made possible by this enchanting garden that never failed to thrill, excite, and deliver the most perfect memories and now enriching my life with mum's presence.

Charlie had returned to keep me company a while longer, it was cooler now as the sun was just going down, but it was a really lovely summer evening to complete the day. We continued to sit in the garden, watching the evening drama unfold in the woods as the wildlife frolicked in the late sunshine.

Charlie stayed for another hour or so, holding hands as he talked about nothing else apart from Daisy, his excitement was so hard to hide, his beaming smile contagious, but still he managed to avoid any solid commitment as we played cat and mouse. Charlie was eager to change the subject if it raised its head.

Finally we kissed a tender loving goodnight. Charlie's hands caressed my porcelain face as he peppered kisses over my skin, leaving soggy patches which made me giggle, kissing my tits through the fabric of my t-shirt, kissing our beautiful bump as he smiled his cocky trademark smile.

Lizzy meet me in the morning before I go back to Cardiff, meet me at the old shed. How romantic, a Sunday morning visit that would undoubtedly lead to some much needed dirty love that the shed would allow us to share.

As Charlie left me alone, my happiness was deflated as the demons again raged in my head, crushing all my happiness. In the back of my mind

I knew it would end in tears for someone, it was inevitable as it could not be this easy to have it all.

How could it work? I knew it was going to be hard for Charlie as he was the one that the pressure would be on now, although we both felt the pressure and I remained sure Helen felt it too, with Charlie sloping off every few days for weekends and nights out, maybe she knew deep down, maybe it worked for her and maybe she liked it that way, but I knew that this would not work for me long term as the arrangement we had made was only to be a temporary one until Charlie had made his final choice, and time now was not on his side, the clock was ticking, and only Charlie could stop the time.

With the start of a new day I was now taking yet another trip down memory lane visiting the old shed, back to share its charm and its memories that were locked into its grubby walls and what a story it could tell. Charlie was already there, waiting for me like always and like his cocky smile it never failed to disappoint me. *Princess, you're looking so baby perfect.* He held me close, his kisses were hard against my lips. *Lizzy I love being here.* I had to agree, it was so special to be reunited with old memories just where we had left them, untouched and lining up ready for us again to recall.

We sat on our little makeshift bed, no one had been here since us and that was so very long ago. It still had that old dank, musty smell about it, complete with huge dark cobwebs that were home to the biggest spiders I had ever seen. Nothing had changed, but this remained special for so many reasons only known to us.

We talked about Daisy, our future, his life, my life, the list was endless and It was fair to say it was far from being boring, but now once again it terrified me as I could only see an uncertain future for us all, as once again Charlie made no commitment. Charlie's hands were now firmly on my tummy, the feeling that it gave me embraced my heart, that he loved her so much already, his love for us without doubt was uncompromising.

Charlie was going back to Cardiff today and I was not sure when I would see him again, if ever. He now had some very hard, agonising decisions to make for himself and for the two ladies and two babies in his life, so we made the most of our time together, allowing us to love our beautiful bump, without interruption, for now.

We said a very sad and tearful goodbye. I hated it, I hated the devastating pull that it had on my heart as he was returning to his life with Helen to share her bed instead of mine, to share things that we should have been sharing and once again my bitter jealousy and resentment of Helen came into play.

He got down on his knees, kissing my belly, his face crippled with not only pain, but something else was distorting his cocky smile today. My facial expression was now questioning his distress and he then handed me an envelope it had Daisy's name written on it. *Put it in her special box for when she is older Lizzy.*

Never forget I love you Lizzy. Once again tears were flowing down my saddened face as I walked away. It was always me to leave first, but today I turned around to admire Charlie's cocky smile, calling back *I love you Charlie Stevens* which made him smile even more.

As I walked back home clutching the letter for Daisy, wondering what Charlie had written and more so why if he was going to be part of her life could he not tell her everything that he had written in the letter? Again, something else that did not add up, like everything else.

Back home Dad was sat in the garden enjoying the late afternoon sunshine so we sat together and chatted over afternoon tea and cakes which made me smile, thinking how civilised and very British this was. Excitedly I told him I had wonderful news, I beamed. *It's a girl. Lizzy that's wonderful. We are going to call her Daisy Elizabeth. We,* dad questioned. *Yes dad,* knowing full well he knew Charlie had been here all weekend which made my cheeks glow as I tried hard to hide my blushes. Dad was delighted, but said nothing more in return.

Monday morning came just like every other day, my mind was wandering to Cardiff, to London, to Charlie, and Daisy of course. Dad suddenly appeared in the garden carrying a very big bouquet which again was wrapped in delicate pink tissue and cellophane, this brought me back to the here and now. *They are for you Lizzy.* I knew immediately who they were from, a note inside which read... *Thank you for giving me Daisy, our lives are now complete Lizzy,* followed by millions of little kisses and accompanied once again by the haunting and very taunting initials that seemed to be written so frequently and almost casually by Charlie, but was our life complete, I had the baby I craved growing inside me. I had a fabulous job, a loving home in which to bring Daisy into, but I didn't have the missing link.

His words I felt today couldn't be more wrong, knowing that this was just the start of what I knew would be a violent and at times a turbulent journey as we both had a huge mountain to climb which with those negative thoughts I grasped impatiently with the ring that hung on my necklace.

I left the flowers in the garden on the old cast iron table so that I could admire them and as I did I drifted once again into my thoughts that now never failed to play tricks on me, casting devastating reminders of mum, my baby I so tragically lost, the aggressive beatings from Dave along with the vile, unfounded sexual assault from Charlie's father. My thoughts also led me to the love triangle that pulled Charlie's love in two impossible directions, but I was forever embraced by the wonderful, powerful dirty love Charlie and I shared, all of my thoughts now marred by one huge imposing dark cloud that remained my constant nightmare, Charlie's secret mysterious life, the life he was leading that I was never going to be part of, not now, not ever and that terrified me knowing Charlie still remained tight lipped about his reputation fuelled life.

The next morning the post arrived, my completed details for London were all signed and sealed, that would almost take me up to maternity leave. In fact, right up to almost giving birth. My hotel was also booked and it looked extremely posh, very up market in a swanky part of London, a part of London I didn't know. My travel would be by a driver every day between the hotel and the site, a luxury that I had not expected. I was once again looking forward to what London held for me, knowing it would give me some freedom from prying eyes, the odd looks and ongoing whispering, but it would also come with sadness being so far away from Charlie.

I opened the other letter that looked very important, wrapped in a brown envelope it was from the solicitor, the house had been sold. The prison cell was now in someone else's hands, ready to also chain them into a life of absolute torture and pain as the house had no soul, no warmth and certainly no charm, a time in my life that certainly held no happy memories, only long-lasting earth-shattering ugly memories that managed to cast evil over my tender years when all the time all I wanted was to be loved and seduced by someone else, not the evil, vile, undermining and unloving man I married. Jolting my thoughts to something more positive for a change, I would now change my name back to my maiden name to rid me of the farcical surname I had carried with me for far too long, to rid myself of the burden of a surname that had brought nothing but misery, hatred, and violence, so I instantly started the process. I would be Miss

Elizabeth Peters once again, the name I would be forever proud to support, now staggered as to why it hadn't crossed my mind until today…

Charlie rang every day at least twice, in the morning to say hello and in the evening to say goodnight. On the odd occasion he seemed very distracted and slightly lost for any conversation, but I missed the special skin on skin contact. I missed his day to day company, his cocky smile, his infectious laughter and of course his dirty love that was never in short supply and on demand when I needed it, which led to negative thoughts, wondering if he and Helen were now playing happy families with me out of Charlie's daily life, leaving him with time on his hands, time that he would have spent with me. Now those times, the cosy nights in, the cosy nights out, trips to the cabin for special occasions, that might be now spent with Helen, or was there someone else that had filled my shoes? I had to forget the negative thoughts or it would drive me mad.

The nursery was now finished, it was very pretty and the white fluffy carpet completed the beautiful cosy room that was now fit for our very own princess, complete with a few of my old, treasured toys from my early years and of course my old cot and the huge teddy bear that Charlie had bought for her which today prompted tears that were hard to hide. As beautiful as it was, it would still remain so painful until Charlie was here, allowing us to be a complete family if ever that day arrived. At this moment it seemed like a million miles away as did Charlie, it felt like we were on opposite sides of the world rather than opposite sides of the country and now with Helen having my share of him every day made it worse, as my resentment of what they shared grew bigger every day, making my bitterness grow increasingly.

For now I placed the letter Charlie had given for Daisy next to the teddy for safe keeping. The reasons why he wrote it remained a mystery, but it was his letter to his little girl, and I had no right to pry.

Monday came and I was excited as to what laid ahead as I embarked on my new and very exciting posting, starting my new, but temporary life in London. I was a little worried to say the least, but I was looking forward to being in London again as it held fantastic memories for me and Charlie, knowing I had already given London a little piece of my heart.

Charlie rang while I was on the train to wish me luck which was nice of him, he promised we would talk more throughout the week knowing there would be many tears shed with the lonely nights that I would spend alone, as now the distance was even greater, leaving an even bigger gap in our lives.

CHAPTER 27

A car met me at the station and drove me to the hotel, my driver was called Mr Green, but I was to call him G. He was a Londoner, born and breed, so was able to give me great tips on places to go and things to do on my days off.

On my arrival I was shown to my office. It was much larger than Cardiff and very nice, very modern, light and airy, instantly my gaze was drawn to a vase of flowers on my desk and shocked they were daisies, maybe it was just coincidence. Suddenly my office was buzzing with voices that now distracted me away from the flowers that were so beautiful. The site officer introduced himself and as we talked we headed off for a site brief, complete with my hardhat. I was greeted by an army of contractors, far more than Cardiff, it was going to be very hard to keep up with them all.

I introduced myself, giving a short brief about me and my plans for this build as thousands of eyes were now fixed on my every word. A few seemed to be fixed on more than my words, feeling their gaze traveling over my curvy body, inspecting me from top to toe, but I chose to ignore the looks that I had become used to while in Wales, knowing it was all just a little bit of fun for some of them. Coffee was at last served and I managed to chat to some of them for a short time, but names, well there were so many to remember.

Walking back to my office alone with my thoughts, I heard a voice calling... *Lizzy*, followed by a whistle. Thinking I was already being eyed by one of the many builders on site taking a chance to chat me up on my first day, thinking I was hearing things, I turned around. My breath was now being taken away by this unexpected reunion. *Charlie*, I gasped. I threw my arms around him, needing to delight my senses that craved him, his arms were so firm as he held me tenderly, making sure we were both OK. I gasped in disbelief knowing nothing not even Helen or hundreds of miles could keep us apart. I returned a smile that contained my constant and everlasting dirty love for him, my body now rigid in disbelief that Charlie was here in London.

The flowers Charlie. Yes Lizzy, from me. He pulled me back into his arms again, peppering my lips in endless kisses, smudging my highly painted lips with a burning desire before forcing his tongue into my mouth, working his tongue seductively into my throat.

Where are you staying tonight Charlie? I questioned with not only words, but my expression. Charlie smiled, *with you I hope Lizzy. What, in my room? Yes Lizzy, with you in your room, in your bed for two whole weeks of us Lizzy.* I was now so overjoyed by this unexpected visitor knowing I was going to enjoy theses two weeks that would be filled with dirty love.

Not wanting to be parted from Charlie's seductive kisses I brushed my hand over his, knowing we both had work to do so I headed to my office, not before I had stolen another kiss, to be rewarded by Charlie's hand brushing against my thigh, gliding over my toned thighs. Charlie once again beamed his trademark smile that never failed to deliver.

I looked at the daisy's that had now sent a sweet aroma rippling throughout my office. I tried hard to concentrate on the mountain of paperwork that was staring at me, ready to topple of my desk at any moment, but my mind was drifting, smiling to myself thinking how lucky I was to have Charlie here, knowing we were going to share some much needed dirty love.

At 6pm my car was waiting for me and G drove me back to the hotel. I was looking forward to staying in the very posh, up market and lavish hotel that was to be my temporary home for the next however many weeks that I would be here. An hour later and Charlie was stood at the door beaming his adorable smile. I threw my arms around him, overjoyed we were together again. *Lizzy I have missed you, missed you and Daisy so much.* His hands were now firmly on my tummy as he whispered *I love you both.* Our kisses were long, powerful, and hard. We were now lovers once again, never wanting to replace old kisses for new ones. My body quivered as Charlie continued to shower me in passionate kisses, letting his tongue seduce my mouth for the second time today, that only added pace to my sexual desires, all of which had Charlie's name on.

Now with the bath ready we were both fully naked again, eager to spend our time together, eager to love each other. Charlie was looking at me smiling. *What?* I asked. *Your belly, it's beautiful Lizzy, it's perfect.* I had not really noticed until now how round my bump really was.

I knew it would not be long until I could not hide it anymore, but I was proud and wanted to show it off to let everyone know I was going to have Charlie's baby, knowing it would be a shock for some people and a disappointment to others, bringing my name into shame once more along with Charlie's, knowing people would point and wag their fingers in disbelief, allowing us both to hear the muted whispers.

I was going to love having him here with me for now, even if it was only for a couple of weeks, but we would embrace these unexpected days. We were both suddenly jolted from a perfect and most intimate moment by his phone ringing loudly, but instead of answering it he ended the call without comment. I looked at him puzzled and then it rang again. Charlie now seemed on edge, fidgeting, trying to hide his frustration. You better get it Charlie. He hesitated again and ended the call abruptly which once again aroused my constant suspicions. Charlie smiled at me wanting desperately to change the subject so I knew not to ask questions, knowing that I would not receive any answers.

We were both starving so we headed out and found a really cosy little Italian restaurant close to the hotel, ideal for me when hunger struck or if I was in need of a late night feast.

While walking back to the hotel Charlie's phone rang again, he reluctantly answered. It was Helen, so I walked on ahead leaving him to talk to her without me in the background to distract him. The call was short and I could tell Charlie was not happy, but he made no comment, although his face was once again eaten up with pain or was it guilt? This wasn't helping the mood tonight. We walked the rest of the way back to the hotel in silence, lost for words, neither of us knowing what to say as Helen yet again was managing to come between us, spoiling our time which frustrated me.

Back at the hotel we both seemed more relaxed and ready for a much needed night together as we both tried to blot out the unwanted and very unwelcome interruption from Helen and the mysterious calls received this evening. The kisses exploded into lost passion; this was what I needed. *Lizzy, come here you amazingly sexy lady.* Both of us were now in the grip of what was our dirty love as he pushed me firmly against the door in a frenzy of passion, his body heavy against mine, his kisses burning my lips as I moaned loudly, demanding hard love. Charlie then stepped back to admire my naked body, his gaze firmly fixed. *Christ Lizzy, you have the most suckable nipples.* They were now standing rigidly to attention, ready for the delicious lips that peppered them in deliciously sweet kisses. Charlie was sucking them hard, making me moan uncontrollably, his rough love now started to take hold. His lips met mine as our tongues were exploring, each other's mouth once again on the most seductive journey that thrilled mine, leaving me breathless, leaving my body begging for more as he pulled me onto the bed before straddling my legs. Charlie's cock was standing to my attention, upright, solid and rigid with dirty love as I ran my nails up and down its stem. *Lizzy you fucking whore, my whore.* I dug my nails in a little harder, knowing he loved it as he begged for more, knowing I would without doubt fulfil his sexual desires.

Charlie was moaning with pleasure, begging me for more. *Make me explode all over your beautiful tits.* I rubbed him harder to the deep moaning that Charlie was making. *You bitch Lizzy, you beautiful whore.* He was wanting me to have his juice that was now smeared all over my tits, glistening in the candlelight that graced our room. Charlie licked his juice free from my tits to share it with me as he so often did, his tongue forced deep into my throat and around my mouth so that I received the full taste of our intense dirty love.

Without hesitation I begged him to love my naked pussy, his head lowered and was now firmly nestled between my smooth thighs, my juice drenched pussy demanding the attention of Charlie's tongue, his lips clenching my clit as I moaned delightedly, encouraging him to never stop. I turned onto all fours to allow Charlie's cock to take full control, thrust after thrust I begged for it harder, and I was not disappointed.

Dawn was here in the blink of an eye, the alarm was ringing loudly. All I wanted to do was to stay in bed all day today with Charlie, but we both had to be on site early so I grabbed coffee and croissants on the way to the office and ate it in the car as I chatted to Mr Green who now insisted I called him by his first name which was George or G, as he would become known to me with great affection.

The rest of the week passed smoothly, Charlie and I shared my bed all week, treating me to some very powerful dirty love to keep my appetite at bay as my cravings for Charlie and his body were now increasing.

It was so nice, at last we felt like a proper couple, a very pregnant couple. If only it was to continue this way, but nothing could be this simple, nothing could be this easy or this special, as Helen seemed to be coming between us more now than ever with her endless phone calls that seemed to intrude on our time, every evening without fail, but she would have him to herself all too soon.

It was now Friday and Charlie was going back to Cardiff, back to Helen and back to her bed for the weekend while I was staying here in London alone once again, and as always I found it hard to accept. We said our loving goodbyes, sharing long sexy lingering kisses and like always thousands of I love you's were followed by my constant stream of tears that again stained my porcelain face in bitter resentment for Helen. I suddenly blinked and Charlie's silhouette had vanished into the distance. I was wanting him to stay a while longer, just another kiss, just another I love you; everything was now just another this and another that.

I felt alone as I laid on the bed, sobbing into my pillow and feeling very sorry for myself. I made plans to go sightseeing over the weekend, to set myself free from the four walls that surrounded me, not wanting to dwell on my unknown future and certainly not wanting to dwell on what was happening back in Wales as the love tug-of-war was relentless. My nightly visitors were rampaging again, jostling amongst themselves, the tormenting voices hard to deal with as I tossed and turned, wanting to rid them from my dreams, but my torment was not over tonight as now the female vision was nudging and jostling her way to the front, wanting me to know she was here with her arms folded, her face stern and cold, a vision that had now awoken me from my sleep. My sheets were flooded in wet, cold fluid, my body terrified again frozen by her presents... but who was she? Why was she so intent on spoiling my dreams? With my night's sleep broken I made coffee, lying awake most of the night shrouded by negative thoughts to what the future would now hold.

With a new day unfolding I found myself once again walking around Regents Park, allowing myself to get lost in my thoughts once more. It was nice to sit and be alone with my thoughts, trying to sort things out in my head. I sat on a bench overlooking the lake while letting my hands rest on my expanding tummy, reassuring me I was not alone which made me smile, but my thoughts were that I was going to be a single mum, bringing Daisy up as a single parent alone, but I was happy with that, and it did not fill me with the terrifying panic I thought it might.

I did not want to make Charlie choose, but for some reason I felt like Helen was going to have Charlie all to herself, to continue to play happy families in Wales and I would be the victim once again, leaving me to live my life with a magnitude of lifetime scars and tattoos that I had collected on my journey in a bid to have it all.

Whatever his decision, one of us would be delivered a devastating blow that would have such a heart-breaking effect on all our lives in one way or another, now and in the future, as we would never be free from the continual turmoil that our dirty love would cause us all.

Sunday morning came, I laid in bed while I listened to all our favourite love songs that constantly played in the background. A lazy late breakfast was ordered, croissants and coffee delivered to my room along with the Sunday papers that I read while taking a long luxurious bubble bath.

Oxford street awaited me today as I needed new clothes. My jeans were getting a little tight and once again it gave me time to reflect on my life and the future as I browsed around the shops, taking in the sights and the aromas that London had to offer and I wanted to embrace it all, the intoxicating smell of the underground, the heavy, pungent smell of fumes that filled the summer air, along with the chaotic noise that made this city so captivating, combined with the heavy thud of thousands of feet that pummelled the pavements daily.

On returning to the hotel I went straight to my room. I was surprised to see the room full of flowers and presents with Charlie sat on the bed waiting, his smile so full of sunshine. I gasped, *Lizzy I thought I would surprise you. Charlie.* I wrapped my arms around him. *You have certainly surprised me, look at all these flowers, are there any left in London?* Charlie smiled. *I love you, I love you so much Lizzy.* He then handed me more gifts, expensive gifts.

I started to cry, panicked by my fragile state, as my emotions were becoming fraught with a constant worry about the future, my future, Daisy's future, and Charlie's too. *Lizzy, Lizzy, Lizzy don't cry.* He held me in his arms, kissing away the tears that now once again stained my porcelain face as my body continued to quiver under the strain of our dirty love, knowing full well that Charlie could not keep our secret a secret for much longer, as time was running out and with nowhere to hide the reality was now biting hard.

My eyes flirted with his throughout dinner. Charlie was now fully aware that I wanted and needed some serious dirty love as my desire for his body was yet again impossible to ignore. I was becoming like a woman possessed and on a mission to be seduced by him every minute of the day.

I put this down to being pregnant, but when I thought about it I always had been like it, craving his love, his dirty love and everything that went with it. I even secretly craved his reputation that made him all the more mysterious, dark and in a strange way romantic and seductive.

On returning to the hotel our bedroom smelt beautiful, full of the most amazing perfume from the flowers that filled the room, complete with every vase from the hotel reception.

We kissed intently, letting our tongues revolve in each other's mouths, slipping nicely into the back of our throats for a little more seduction. Charlie whispered his need to fuck me as he kissed my long flowing silky hair, smothering it in love. He was feeling horny, and I was not objecting as I knew my sexual appetite and demands would be heard and taken care of.

Unzipping my dress I begged him to fuck me hard. I loved him being in control and taking the lead. He let my clothes fall to the floor, discarded eagerly as there was no need for neat piles of clothes tonight. I felt his huge, throbbing erection through his jeans as he laid me on the bed. As I watched him strip his clothes off I had to admit his body was very toned and lean, a body I wanted all for myself as I was not prepared to share for much longer, this temporary arrangement was coming to a close and now not for renewal.

He peppered warm sensual kisses across my body, paying extra attention to my tits which always seemed to fascinate him as he could command my nipples attention instantly, making them swell up into perfect pink love bumps, perfect for sucking and of course our baby bump got the delightful kisses I desired.

His tongue was now working around my big solid nipples that felt enormous tonight, Charlie's mouth took full control to suck my bulbous nipples lovingly. *Charlie*, I moaned loudly as his tongue glided down over our baby bump to find my naked freshly waxed pussy that was demanding to be loved by his tongue and I was not disappointed as his head was now firmly buried between my thighs, I could feel his teeth softly biting my pussy lips.

He then turned me onto all fours, his huge throbbing cock was begging to fuck my ever-demanding pussy. *I want to fuck you Lizzy and fuck you hard*. His words were powerful, encouraging to my repeated demands for more dirty love.

His cock was huge and cascading juice ready to give me so much dirty love as he rode me gently, filling my pussy to the maximum before increasing the pace, continuing to deliver the hard dirty love that I had grown to love. Charlie thrusted a little more, forcing our juices to mingle together as I moaned for more.

Charlie was once again on a mission to love my pussy with his tongue, his lips smeared with fresh warm juice, ready for the seduction that my mouth would create, leaving my tongue coated in juice that Charlie smeared around my mouth, leaving my lips bathed with tantalising juice.

Relaxed and satisfied we laid next to each other naked, proud to show off my baby body that now complimented my curves that Charlie had always admired, as a teenage boy and now as a man. The week continued and Charlie seemed slightly on edge while constantly receiving calls from god knows who and from Helen, some of which he ignored which must have only fuelled her suspicions even more, and in return it allowed me to resent her more.

I was going home to Wiltshire at the weekend to see dad, and Charlie was returning to Cardiff and to Helen. It was once again going to be a sad day as Charlie's two weeks here were over and Helen now would have him all to herself, day in day out, no slipping away for cosy nights with me, no endless evenings of passion that would spill over into sex fuelled all night love sessions.

Friday arrived and we both agreed that we would stay on Friday night to have a beautiful dinner together, to celebrate the wonderful two weeks we had managed to share here in London, knowing to this day I still remained his bit on the side, his whore, his bitch, his tart and at this moment in time it seemed as if it would remain that way as there was no visible commitment from Charlie, which I found very irritating as time was passing us by and would become more difficult for him to make his choice as Helen I felt sure would be commanding his attention daily.

Back at the hotel the conversation turned to babies. Helen and us, it was apparent things were getting very complicated now as he had to keep her and me happy with both of us pregnant. The strain of what seemed a million miles away, with him and I on separate sides of the country was in itself hard enough to deal with and now with the extra pressure, would he be able to cope with the increasing demands both Helen and I would make on him, physically and mentally? Charlie had confessed to me that he and Helen slept in separate rooms and didn't make love anymore, but I did have my doubts about that as why would Charlie not just leave, but if it was true then I was very pleased that at last I had sole use of Charlie's dirty love.

Alarm bells continued to ring loudly though, what was keeping him in Wales? It wasn't work as he could work anywhere and now he had admitted that he and Helen did not share a bed, but there was still something he was reluctant to discuss with me, his mysterious, secret life that bubbled away quietly inside me allowing my suspicions to grow, imagining all sorts of things that made no sense at all.

As we held hands I felt the time was right to talk. *Charlie, I have been thinking what will happen when I give birth to Daisy, I would love you to be with me.* He looked at me puzzled. *Lizzy I want that more than anything princess and I will be there, I helped make her I will be there with you.* I wondered if he had said the same to Helen. Relaxed now by Charlie's pledge to be at the birth to welcome Daisy into our world, a world that I hoped now would be without regret and without the constant battle every day to have Charlie in our lives forever.

Saturday morning came all too quickly. We caught the tube to the station, ready for the long and lonely journeys home that would separate us once again. Charlie held me close, showering me with kisses, whispering I love you's that filled the station with warmth. He then held my hands, kissing them both. *I will see you both very soon Lizzy.* We had said an emotional goodbye, I cried all the way as I walked down the platform, Charlie stood watching me walk the lonely walk. I turned around and was instantly nailed to the platform, my body frozen in some sort of rigid spasm, I felt helpless, but I managed to smile through my tears as I was now engulfed in emotions that were so overpowering, choking me with an emotion that terrified my fragile body, knowing Charlie was going back to Cardiff, back to Helen whom I feared would fight with his emotions, that would take its toll on our dirty love and that would once again leave me alone to dwell on my future as the victim I thought I would become. Charlie blew me more kisses, shouting *I want them all back and more Lizzy.* This brought a smile to my face as I boarded the train, but my smile was short lived as now I feared I may never see Charlie again.

After a fraught journey that had somehow allowed me a snatched preview to at last read the warning labels that were printed inside every piece of clothing that Charlie wore. They all read *handle with care, keep away from fire*, I was fearing now that I was about to get burnt, scorched by Charlie's love. At last I was home, back to the sanctuary I still called home, knowing I was free to roam the house and garden, to set myself free from the love tug-of-war and the daily torment and anguish it brought me. I was now absorbed in my thoughts and wondered if I should never return to London, but I would miss it and I was determined to see the build finished and I wanted to embrace more of London so that I could take a little more love from the vibrant city to keep for myself, as I now craved to inhale it personality, its charm and above all its love.

Monday morning arrived by an eye watering 4am alarm call and I was back to London on the early train, napping all the way throughout the journey. My car was waiting for me, and G was on good form, having taken the trouble to get me some breakfast as he knew I would be starving. He then took me straight to the site, ready to start the new week on a positive note. My work was planned for the week with meetings booked every day.

Charlie and I chatted at every opportunity; morning, noon and especially at night, when my needs for him hit an all-time high, possibly the time I missed him the most knowing I had to sleep without the strength of this arms to enrich my sleep, shielding me from the nightly invasion that had now become a terrifying habit.

The next few weeks flew by, and the weeks seemed to blend into one so I had now planned on staying in London every weekend until I had finished at the site, this would be less demanding on me, avoiding having to travel back and forth from the pretty Wiltshire village to London every weekend.

Friday morning was here once more. I handed my keys over the reception desk and the porter handed me a letter. To my total surprise it was from Charlie, it read, *in London on Friday fancy some us time? Call me.* I stood shocked and amazed, instantly I rang his phone, just hearing his voice made me smile. *Charlie yes, a huge yes*, I screamed down the phone startling everyone around me, especially the snooty nosed lady that stood beside me turning her nose up at my obvious outburst of delight.

I was in desperate need for some very dirty love. *Lizzy I will see you tonight.* I was now overjoyed that he was coming to see us once again, leaving me to wonder what he had told Helen he was doing, nagging thoughts again returned in my head to intrude on my happiness.

With the day now over G whisked me back to the hotel in a desperate bid to beat the rush hour traffic. I didn't want to be late for the arrival of my long awaited visitor and suddenly I heard a knock at the door and at last room service was about to be served. It was Charlie, delighted, I threw my arms around him, showering him in sexy, long Lizzy kisses as Charlie returned them, smudging my newly applied bright ruby-red lipstick in the process.

Princess you look great. His hands were now exploring my ever expanding baby bump, his cocky smile adorable, knowing he had missed me as much as I had missed him. Charlie's kisses were so sensual on my skin as he peppered kisses on my neck that sent sensual shivers down my spine, exploring again the romance of the ring that tonight he once again seduced with his lips, before returning to my gaze.

Neither of us had eaten, so a lavish room service was ordered and delivered; the perfect setting for us to talk, free to be us, to relax for a while without the stress of everyday life that now seemed a constant threat to my long term happiness.

Charlie's face was clearly reflecting his thoughts and I could see he was in love with us both, beyond any doubt, just like he always had been, but now his actions and words were very grown up and very serious, but with a tone that was laced in sadness as his head was once again resting in his hands, the cracks were appearing which Charlie seemed to brush aside. He then looked at me with his big brown eyes, reassuring me that everything would be alright, while smiling the boyish cocky smile I loved, whispering his intention to fuck me that night, like every night when we were lucky enough to be together which made me blush.

We loved the closeness of our relationship, it was without doubt very powerful and reflected in our kisses, allowing our tongues to make mad passionate dirty love as they always did, revolving powerfully, filling each other's mouths with never ending love.

His big, huge cock was full of juice, ready to please and satisfy my increasingly demanding pussy. *Charlie, fuck me. Lizzy, tell me what you want me to fuck; your pussy, your mouth, or your tits?* I blushed at his comments, *just fuck me hard Charlie.* He smiled back, *Lizzy you dirty little whore.*

My mouth then tightened over his rigid cock to allow him the pleasure of my lips as I sucked him hard, my tongue was exploring his huge

THE BROKEN DAISY CHAIN

bulb like helmet that was already cascading warm juice on to my lips. My tongue was now getting the full taste of fresh juice that continued to flow into my throat as Charlie moaned, wanting more. *Princess you dirty whore, my princess whore, suck it fucking hard Lizzy.* So not to disappoint him, I continued to suck the massive cock that was filling my mouth full of wonderful juice that now coated my throat.

He then helped himself to my wet naked pussy that was so delighted by the sensation that Charlie's tongue was creating, as my legs were now draped over his arms ready for some serious dirty loving. His cock continued to dribble with beautiful moist juice as my pussy became increasingly wet in anticipation of being fucked hard by Charlie, his thrusting was hard and with a little aggression as I continued to moan, demanding Charlie to fuck me harder so with more pressure Charlie thrust it all the way, allowing my pussy to receive every sensual thrust.

I felt pressure again as his cock continued to thrust much harder now, he kept the pressure on thrusting his cock further into my purring pussy and once again his juice engulfed my pussy with dirty love. Charlie slowly withdrew his throbbing cock after giving me every last bit of his juice that I was delighted to have received. I was then treated to the ultimate sensual pleasure as Charlie's tongue was making dirty love with my pussy. I moaned for more, knowing I was receiving some very powerful dirty love.

I woke early to watch Charlie sleeping, wishing I could wake up with him every day. He looked so contented, but I knew he must be going through such emotion hell. I stroked his hair gently as he awoke, smiling his trademark smile. *Morning Lizzy you gorgeous sexy lady.* He held my naked body in his arms, running his fingers gently over my curves, exciting my nipples that stood to morning attention, ready for closer inspection as we were showering each other in sensual kisses. Charlie peppered my belly in kisses, letting his huge tongue revolve around my belly button, both of us were now desperate for some early morning dirty love. As Charlie fucked my pussy hard on my command, once again my demanding sexual desires were taken care of.

With the early morning love now over, we stepped out from the hotel into the warm sunshine that bathed the streets of London, both looking forward to spending uninterrupted us time in Regent's Park where we remained free to be us. Suddenly my peace was shattered by Charlie's phone ringing loudly. He thought it was switched off and with that he answered it without any hesitation.

It was Helen, his face turned white as his hands started to shake. I heard him say OK as he then ended the call. *Lizzy, I have to go back to Wales.* My facial expression was one again of disbelief. *I'm so sorry Lizzy.* Charlie reached for my hand which I instantly brushed away, not wanting his hand in mine that day.

CHAPTER 28

Helen thinks she's gone into very premature labour, she's on her way to hospital. I'm so sorry Lizzy. His face was once again saddened as he kissed me goodbye, then he was gone. I then wondered if I would get the same reaction if I needed him in an emergency... God I was so bitter! My thoughts were so spiteful, this was not me, this was getting a habit, where had the real Lizzy gone?

I was alone again, feeling deflated that I was the one left on my own, abandoned once again. I felt hurt and not for the first time in our long on-off love affair. I wished for that split second when Helen called that his phone had been off but then was angry at myself for even thinking that. I hated myself for my vile thoughts.

I was now so bitter, how could we continue like this? It could only work for either her or for me. I had now made my mind up, something would now have to change and that would mean hard choices for Charlie to make as I was fed up with being second best, or that's how I felt. I was now eaten up with extreme jealousy and overriding bitterness, clutching violently at the ring on my necklace, almost snapping it free from the chain in anger, wanting to express my bitter frustration.

I went to Regents Park as planned, but now on my own. I walked for what seemed a very long time. Needing to rest I sat on the bench alone, reaching for the ring that hung on my necklace, twiddling with it repeatedly. Again, my thoughts were with Charlie and how they both were feeling. I prayed for them all, what a heart-breaking time. I hated myself for being so selfish, it was never my intention to be this bitter, but once again it was all born out of falling in love with the boy with a reputation, that had married somebody else.

I watched couples holding hands and in love, families having fun in the warm sunshine, everyone just being normal except for me, as heartache raged on within me. I just wanted to scream, letting free my pent up frustration, casting the relentless storm over London, letting it rage throughout the streets, lashing its cargo against the windows and doors of houses that lined every street, to let everyone know my ongoing torment.

Saturday came and went in a whisper, but I had loved my day in the park, free to be me, to enjoy the beautiful sunshine that brushed my skin leaving it glowing, showering me in glorious kisses that made my skin tingle.

When back at the hotel I reflected on the day, a day that had been filled with so many emotions, some hard to deal with and some that had made me smile. Every emotion contained my love of Charlie, as he remained one of the two reasons why every breath I took was for either him or for Daisy.

I slept with my emotions running wild in my mind, taking me on many multi-coloured journeys, sprinkling them with some delightful memories, but some that were tainted with appalling sadness, allowing me to relive the many nightmares that I had endured along the way, with haunting voices that tonight we're so loud, complete with vile images that sparked nothing but hatred, a hatred that was all mine.

Sunday was here and surprisingly I felt refreshed, amazingly so much so after the restless night that seemed never-ending. Now at a loss to know what to do with my time for the day I took the train to Brighton, somewhere I had never been, and It was beautiful, busy with family's having a great day out. I watched so many couples in love, holding hands, wrapped in each other's arms, something that just jumped out at me at every corner, every street in every park and then there was me. I sat alone again with my thoughts, allowing the sun to pepper my tender skin in warm kisses, wondering if I should now accept one or two of the endless requests I received daily from some of the builders that were constantly asking me out for dinner, lunch, the theatre, the cinema etc. My company was in demand, but it was reserved for Charlie who put me on the back burner when the time was right for him. Thinking again about all those casual dates, maybe that was what I needed, a fun free time for me, but I wasn't thinking of me, I was thinking of Charlie and the damage it would do to our relationship, but our relationship was today in tatters, holding on by a tiny thread.

I managed to get lost in my memories which enlivened such vivid times that Charlie and I had shared, such beautiful dirty love either in London or Wales, even going back to the very first time we made love together in the beautiful village barn, something Helen could never take away from me, as it was mine and not for sharing.

Monday morning and it was back to the old familiar routine and somewhat mandating with paperwork and meetings, but It kept me busy, allowing my mind a much needed rest from the daily torture and uncertain future I felt I was to face.

The day went well, but I felt shattered, and I was relieved to be back at the hotel as I just wanted to have a hot bath and relax. My phone rang while I was searching my bag for my keys that always managed to settle into the corner of my bag, it was Charlie.

How are you Lizzy? The line fell silent, I was lost for words. A lump of emotion had started to choke me. *Lizzy I love you both, Lizzy talk to me.* Silence reigned again at my end of the phone. *Talk to me Lizzy.* I sobbed through the mass of tears that I now could not hide. *I just miss you so much Charlie.*

I was now crying uncontrollably, my body shaking as I slammed the phone against the wall, wanting to shatter it into millions of pieces. Tonight there was no goodnight or air blown kisses, Charlie did not even bother to call me back what the hell was going on? This was not the way I had planned it; this was not the way to continue our dirty love affair. My heart started to break into millions of tiny pieces, crying myself to sleep to block out the torment for now, but I knew it would rear its ugly head again once I awoke, even sleep could not shield me from the constant terror that never allowed my mind to be free, not even for a split second.

Having composed myself and applying layers of makeup to mask my tear stained face, I headed to the office early to get a good start. G was waiting for me with steaming hot coffee, my head was splitting, my eyes red raw from crying all night. I looked a mess and nothing like the real Lizzy. I sat in my office alone, my heart was drained of love which should have been overflowing, a feeling I hated. My world felt like it was collapsing around me as the dark clouds had started to gather once again, ready for the storm that was already clouding every positive thought, replacing them for negative ones.

The front gate rang through. *There is a personal delivery for you Lizzy, I will send them through.* It was a delivery of flowers, a huge box of chocolates and a teddy bear with a note attached which read, *Lizzy wait for me I love you both, I never wanted to hurt you, I never want to be without you, H L F.*

Today I didn't feel like I wanted to wait for him any longer, wishing I had taken up the endless offers of dates in Wales, along with all the offers

I received daily here in London, as waiting for him was all I had done all my life and now I was beyond fed up with it, confirming today my fears that I could not cope with this arrangement any longer. I knew a tough road lay ahead for both of us as the massive storm clouds now swirled violently overhead.

As the day wore on my mind was working overtime, hating myself for being a total bitch, wondering why I was being so bloody mean to him. I hated myself and felt very ashamed of my thoughts, knowing I could never forgive myself. I hadn't even asked how Helen was, or if she had given birth, I hated myself.

My thoughts now led me to think that I should be on my own, to leave Charlie and Helen alone to live their lives, to allow the storm to pass which would allow me to step back from being his bit on the side, his bitch, his tart, and his dirty secret. To free myself from the shackles that still gripped my heart with an intense lock that kept me his lifetime hostage.

I sat yawning with every breath of stale air within the office, exhausted from thinking negative thoughts. 5.30pm and my phone was ringing, it was Charlie. Taking a deep sharp intake of breath I asked about Helen. He hesitated. *Yes Lizzy, Helen is resting in hospital it was a false alarm, but the doctors want to keep her in for a few days.* I then abruptly thanked him for the beautiful flowers and presents, something that I felt did not make up for the lack of commitment from him.

I will see you very soon Lizzy I promise. I snapped at him angered once again by promises that as soon as he made them they seemed to melt into iridescent puddles, but there was only one promise I needed him to commit to, but it was never forthcoming and at that moment I received yet another invitation to go to dinner with a very handsome and much younger builder, but I again declined his offer.

The week rolled on and my head and heart were still weighed down by the future I was now facing. Would I be alone to raise Daisy? Would Charlie commit to being in our lives long term? So much uncertainty now hung in the balance, uncertainty was something I hated.

On returning to the hotel I felt shattered mentally from over thinking our teetering relationship. As I collected my key the porter said *Lizzy I have a parcel for you.* I was not expecting anything, so a surprise awaited me. I took the parcel to my room; it was from Charlie with a naughty note attached. *Lizzy for you to use when I am not around having fun, but not too much fun, this is not my replacement, I repeat not my replacement.* I could not help but giggle tonight at his comment.

I opened the box, I gasped at the gift that was now staring at me, a huge pink vibrator filled the box, my eyes were popping out of my head at the sheer size of gift Charlie had sent me and all I could do was just imagine him smiling his wicked, cocky and infectious smile. I smiled, knowing he was probably smiling so much it hurt and at that very moment Charlie rang, chuckling down the phone. *Lizzy did you get your special present?* I blushed repeatedly; my face was now glowing with a vibrant red sheen.

Yes Charlie. My voice sounded somewhat distant and casual as it echoed through the phone back to Wales. *Lizzy, is everything OK.* I was silent again. *Lizzy talk to me. I'm fine Charlie*, it's just been one of those weeks that I want to forget. *Have I upset you with the present? No Charlie. Lizzy, I hate hearing you so down. I'm fine Charlie.* On that night it felt like I had almost lost interest in Charlie's love and that terrified me.

I love you Lizzy, I'm so sorry I have put you through hell. My head had now become numb as his apologies kept rolling out of his mouth like they were on repeat. *Charlie, please don't worry.* I quickly changed the subject; I did not want to get bogged down now with the torrid love triangle tug of war thing that I hated even more now and with that he must have sensed my growing unhappiness. Neither of us knew what to say, the situation we were in was now so overpowering, I could see no way out other than to go our separate ways and tonight like many nights and days recently I reached for the ring that hung on my necklace, needing something other than comfort as I constantly twiddled it, tightening it with my finger until it was so tight.

I was so damn unhappy. For the first time in our long relationship I felt flat, miserable and sad, every emotion allowed the tears to flow by the bucket. I must have fallen asleep as it was very late when I awoke, my phone had been switched to silent and I was annoyed with myself that I had missed six calls from Charlie, but maybe now he had got the message that I was hurting and that I needed him as well. At 6am the bloody alarm was ringing once again repeatedly, having wrestled all night long with images I wished I could forget, that left me deprived of sleep. I was due on site at 7.15am. I remained feeling flat from yesterday, but I needed to pick myself up to be back In control of my feelings, after all I had so much to look forward to even if Charlie would never be part of my life. I would cope as a single mum, so hot, strong coffee was needed to start my day and plenty of it.

The day wore on and I thought I should ring Charlie, but if he thought anything about me he would make the call that I so desperately needed to receive. At 6pm it was time to head back to the hotel for yet another deeply lonely evening, alone to dwell on my life, as the single mum that I would become in only a few weeks.

I had a bath and for the first time in months I had a large glass of wine, knowing full well it was not good for me, I wallowed once again in self-pity, not being able to see any positive outcome. I was saddened by my selfishness, I did not like who I was becoming, leaving again the real Lizzy in the background to be shrouded in bitter anguish.

I laid on the bed in my undies, drifting into my thoughts that seemed to only contain one other person other than me and that was Charlie. It seemed my life just totally revolved around him, I was suddenly brought back from thoughts of my traumatic life by my phone ringing. It had made me jump, it was Charlie. I wanted to ignore it, but I couldn't.

Lizzy I miss you; I miss you so much. I did not comment, he was the one who needed to do all the talking tonight as I just wanted to listen to his apologies, to hear him attempt to make things right, *Princess I know I have hurt you so much, tell me how to put things right.* With a cool and casual tone to my voice I replied. *Charlie, only you can do the right thing.* Once again the line was silent from Charlie, I knew instantly that this was not working. I could hear him breathing deeply, his pain apparent, but he continued to hesitate, not saying the words that would tonight reignite my fire to fall in love with him again.

I don't know what to do Lizzy. I snapped, my patience was running out, *well I can't tell you Charlie, just call me when you know.* I then slammed the phone down out of bitter spite, determined to ruin or to salvage our love. On reeling from my actions I realised this was so not like us, being separated by miles was now intruding on our relationship, maybe I was spoilt in Wales seeing him every day, but now with us so far apart the agony was apparent and so very hard to deal with day to day.

Distance was never going to be easy for either of us and I suppose it was harder for me as I was alone in a big city which that at this moment I found so very lonely as I heard London's mellow breathing tonight, but I needed to turn the volume to silent, to allow me to hear fully the impending storm that was now breaking and gathering speed, pounding hard with violent clashes of lightning, loud booming thunder followed by a heavy burst of ice cold rain as the lightning sparked vivid emotions that ran through my body, leaving me shivering with terrifying fear as I sat alone waiting for the storm to blow over, but tonight once again I couldn't help but wonder where the real Lizzy had hidden, as this was not me.

I sobbed fresh tears of resentment into my pillow, tears of pain that now haunted me every day. I was beginning to hate myself so much, so with a reluctance I picked up the phone to call Charlie back, instantly his words were *Lizzy I love you*. Repeating them over and over again, *I love you too Charlie*. I could feel myself getting emotional again, my mouth crippled and dry as the words that I wanted to say were muted by my terrifying sadness, unsure of whether we could continue our lifetime love affair that now ruled my everyday life, my dreams and my nightmares all challenged by my love for him.

I heard him take a deep breath. I felt his frustration as I continued to cry tears that now could not be kissed away. I was getting hysterical with emotion as I was desperate for him to fully understand what I was feeling and how being apart was impacting on my ability to cope without him and to cope being pregnant.

With my emotions now under control, Charlie and I talked a little more and suddenly things felt a lot clearer as the storm had lifted allowing me to smile, at last Lizzy had returned, even though I thought it would be short lived.

Charlie begged me to use the vibrator and to allow him to talk me through the entire love fuelled sex session that was to follow. *Lizzy you beautiful whore, my beautiful whore.* I was, but I was not finished yet as I needed Charlie once again, begging him for a repeat of the sex session we had just adored. Charlie was not objecting in the slightest and was more than eager to talk me through yet another beautiful dirty love session with my new and much needed present.

Now after almost two hours of tears, emotions and two sex fuelled love sessions we seemed to have put things slightly right, for now at least. We were at opposite sides of the country so it was always going to be hard, harder than I had ever imagined it would be.

We said goodnight, followed by beautiful I love you's. Charlie promised he would call every day to catch up, but once again his promises seemed to fade as soon as he had made them. Promises were never Charlie's strong point, along with his ability to cover his mysterious tracks, to smoke screen his private life, but it was his love that kept my attention.

Autumn was here in the blink of an eye, and I had not been home for a while and missed my walks in the garden to escape freely back into the past. I missed walking through the house, finding hidden emotions that just waited patiently to be found, but I had decided to stay in London to the end, to enjoy the little bit of time that I had left to embrace it, to breath in the unique aroma that was London, and I was happy to take everything London wanted to give me.

Friday 6pm at last and G was waiting to drive me back to the hotel for yet another lonely night. I felt tired, fat and so very unattractive with swollen ankles and a huge belly that was so stunningly beautiful, full, and very round. I was desperate for a bath and a sex fuelled catch up with Charlie.

As I arrived back at the hotel I collected my keys and headed for the lift. *Lizzy let me get that for you*, a familiar voice said, as I turned around it was Charlie. I threw my arms around him, screeching loudly as I had not seen him for so long, not believing he was here at last. I sobbed uncontrollably as it was so good to see him.

Don't cry Lizzy I'm here now. He kissed away the tears until my smile retuned, *you look great Lizzy*. His hands were now on my expanding bump, Charlie was smiling as he admired the immense size of my bump. *You look very pregnant Lizzy, but so very beautifully pregnant and extremely sexy.*

Now reunited, Charlie ran a bubble bath for us, to have some us time at the end of a very stressful and emotional few weeks for us both, a time that I wanted to forget, never wanting to repeat as a repeat would undoubtedly ruin forever what we were fighting for and against.

My vibrator was on the top of the shelf unit in the bathroom. On seeing it, Charlie gave me a sideways smile. *I see you have used it Lizzy. He* nodded towards the unit. *Charlie you know I have.* I smiled, blushing like a naughty teenager. Charlie reached out for the vibrator, desperate for us to enjoy dirty loving together as he teased my painted lips, seducing my mouth before teasing my naked pussy with the bulbous throbbing tip, with our bath time love session over we then took our love to the bedroom.

Pulling back my flowing hair, he looked at me with his deep, dark brown eyes that never failed to delight me. *I'm so sorry Lizzy, I promise I will never upset you again my beautiful Lizzy.* Again he was making promises that needed action and tonight I was not sure if he could keep those promises, but I was expecting a massive change and I was sure he knew it too, knowing this was the time for change in a bid to make us both happy, but one person would become the victim in this love triangle, sadly I was already wearing the badge.

Bringing me back to the here and now Charlie kissed my lips gently before kissing my neck with such sensitive and sensual kisses, his breath seducing the ring on my necklace.

His finger was now running over my tits, teasing, pleasing, and arousing my nipples that stood to his attention, begging to be sucked and I was not disappointed as I was promised some hard dirty love tonight.

Charles fingers danced delightfully over my curves, allowing his tongue to revolve around my belly button, peppering wet kisses on my belly. Charlie now admired my naked pussy for the second time tonight, this time his tongue took control, exciting my clit as he enjoyed the taste of my fresh, warm juice that was coating his tongue, leaving me moaning for more.

I was moaning with every firm and intense thrust that Charlie made, before being replaced by his huge tongue that glided between my thighs for the ultimate satisfaction. I begged again for Charlie to share the taste we had created, his lips smeared with juice. His kisses were passionate, letting his tongue glide over mine, making them tingle with some much needed excitement, smudging my nearly painted lips.

His cock then filled my mouth with force into my throat, encouraging his moaning to become gritty and intense as his body tensed up with passion.

Exhausted, we slumped back onto the bed, inhaling the aroma of the freshly laundered sheets, feeling safe in each other's arms with all the feelings of love that came flooding back for us both, wave after wave of extreme love flooded over us. It was lovely to have him here, to feel like a little family even if it was going to be short lived.

We woke relaxed after a peaceful night thankful that I had not received my habitual nightly visitors, allowing me a full uninterrupted sleep. Charlie leant over and kissed my porcelain face. His kisses were light, but so sexy and full of passion. *I have a little surprise today Lizzy.* My face lit up, I was excited that Charlie had done something without being prompted, my startled expression made him laugh hysterically. *Lizzy it's a nice surprise.* He continued smiling from ear to ear. *I have booked photo session for us. Charlie, what time? This morning Lizzy, but.* I knew it, yet another but, *but what Charlie?* My tone was once again sharp, laced with annoyance that seemed a regular occurrence these days. I held my breath, waiting for Charlie to reply. *I have to go back to Wales Lizzy.* I glared at him, *Wales?* My heart sank again as he was going back to her and their life, leaving me alone again, leaving me struggling to understand what the hell was happening in our relationship, having to share him was bearing heavy on my fragile body, something would have to give and that was now all down to Charlie, but Helen needed him too at this most precious time and I was being so selfish.

Composed from my outburst and with the storm having dodged us on this occasion, we arrived at the studio. The photographer was fantastic as we posed together and separate. I had some taken to show off our bump, some of the two of us together and some of Charlie and I naked to the waist, but covering the parts I wanted to cover, some in colour and some in monotone.

As we left the studio it was such a beautiful day, the sun was peppering us in warm kisses, we then enjoyed a cosy lunch together near Regent's Park, wishing he could have stayed with me tonight and not having to go back to Helen as our time always seemed rushed now, and somewhat compromised due to him leading a reputation fuelled double life.

Lunch was over, I had dragged it out as long as possible as I ordered more coffee in a bid to have him here with me a little longer. Sadly that time was up as he called a cab to take him to the station and back to Helen.

We once again said our loving goodbyes, complete with loads of I love you's, complete with my never-ending tears that seemed all too familiar these days. It seemed like we were forever saying the same things repeatedly, but now more often even to the stage that it seemed like a bad habit that we could not break free from.

Speak soon Lizzy. Squeezing my face with his hands, puckering my lips ready for his kisses, suddenly with that wicked smile he was gone, leaving me alone again and alone with my thoughts that would not let my mind rest. Something did not add up or was my mind once again over thinking? I wish I knew, but only time would tell and only then I might get all the answers that I needed; good, or bad so I had to brace myself for the collision course that was imminent.

The next week went by really quickly with the build taking shape I loved it. I loved being in London, it had a soul which had got deep into my skin, leaving me wanting more of what London gave me. It was vibrant with heavy pungent aromas that filled the air with a zest of intoxicating energy that emerged from every street, along with the hustle and bustle of everyday vibrating and echoing through the vast sprawl of this city.

I had thought I would stay in London until the end of the build, but I was missing dad, it would be lovely to see him this weekend, to be able to do a bit more to the nursery. As I had nothing planned it make sense to go home, maybe it would help clear my head from all the negative thoughts that were now like demons that trampled all over me, pounding my fragile body in yet more pain.

I had not heard much from Charlie. So much for his promise to call more often, but I knew he was busy, and I had to accept that, so with no word from Charlie in a few days I caught the early Saturday morning train back home to my Wiltshire roots to relax. Day by day my bump now seemed to get bigger, my belly expanding into a huge ball, a ball of baby which I loved and that was now admired by so many.

I walked in the garden for hours, alone, recalling thousands of memories each one made me smile, every memory was so easy to capture, to relive and to embrace as all the wonderful long warm days that I spent in the tree house as a little girl with my dolls that now would be a haven for Daisy to enjoy, just like I had done on so many occasions and I could not wait to see her doing just the same. This house would embrace her, cherish her, and allow her the freedom to be a child, to enjoy her childhood. Day by day it seemed more likely that it would be just her and I alone to face the future, as Charlie had still not made any firm commitment to us and again not having heard from him this weekend refuelled my ongoing thoughts that he would stay in Wales to live a life that he had carved for himself.

Monday morning came all too soon and I took the very early train back to London. G was there to meet me as normal; he knew I would want coffee and it was waiting for me complete with a warm croissant. He was a true gentleman who I would miss so much. We had formed such a wonderful and firm friendship and one I wanted to continue once my contract had expired.

The company had booked an end-of-build party in a large posh hotel in central London and was booked for two weeks' time. I had noticed that Charlie's name was on the list accompanied by a plus one, was he bringing Helen to London? My heart sank, how could he do something that stupid and that cruel? My hopes were now dashed that he would not be spending the weekend with me when he knew full well my dreams and hopes for the future. Sadly he had now finally made his intentions clear, but I would wait to see if he would tell me, but like on so many occasions he would hide behind his smile, content in hiding his secrets a while longer leaving me to dangle on a thread that was now about to snap.

Charlie rang later that evening, reluctantly I answered. He must have known by my tone that I was not in the mood for small talk tonight. I wanted to mention the guest list, to ask him out right, but I declined not wanting to hear the truth. My enthusiasm was now at an all time low and Charlie had responded wanting to know why I was so quiet, but I managed to brush it over saying I was tired, but all I wanted was him here with me, to feel his skin on mine, to smell his aroma that always lingered on my sheets. I loved to talk to him, but hated the sad goodbyes that always followed, and tonight was no different.

I will see you soon Lizzy I promise you and until I do, keep loving our baby. Lots of kisses followed as they always did, but tonight was as if he had to snatch a quick few minutes to call me, but I had to accept it, as hard as it was.

No sooner than when I had put the phone down there was a knock at the door and on answering Charlie was stood there with a grin that swept across his rugged face. I was stunned to see him, wanting to slap his face for putting me through yet more hell. Now lost for words, disbelieving my eyes I gasped at the vision that was stood at my door with something hidden behind his back while feasting his hungry eyes over my expanding curves. I pulled him into the bedroom, peppering him in long awaited kisses before the surprise was delivered, our photographs. We sat unwrapping the album, the photos were so absolutely stunning. I sat with tears in my eyes and a huge grin on my face as they were beyond perfect. The black and white photos were mine and Charlie's favourite, I loved the one of us naked to the waist and Charlie holding our bump, we both loved it.

Such a precious photo album, a keepsake for our beautiful daughter Daisy. Most of the photos would get framed and hung in the nursery, beautiful reminders of the journey to bring her into our lives. My negativity was swept aside for now until the next wave of the storm was delivered, and it would be without fail, which tonight lead me again to wonder why the hell was I putting up with this temporary arrangement. I clung again to the ring on my necklace while Charlie ran us a beautiful sweet smelling bubble bath so that we could have the perfect us time, but was it, things seemed different or was it my imagination getting the better of me? Or was it that I craved a night of full sleep? Sleep that was uninterrupted by shrill and vile voices, stagnant images and still the muted cry of my baby far in the distance.

I glanced at Charlie as his eyes met mine, instantly I knew tonight we were going to enjoy some serious dirty loving, something so powerful I could not contain my smile, which delighted him as he retuned me a smile bigger and much bolder than ever.

With my legs now over his, my pussy was as ever demanding to be loved, commanding Charlie's attention. *Princess your pussy looks good enough to eat.* So with a delighted expression I whispered, *then why don't you Charlie?* I blushed continually at my dirty comment.

He was now kneeling over me so that I could be intimate with his love fuelled cock as he begged me to love him hard. *Love me hard you dirty whore, my beautiful dirty whore.*

My moaning was so very loud now as I demanded him to love me. *Love your little whore Charlie.* His eyes fixed onto my expression, watching me as my pussy exploded with loving juices, all made possible by Charlie.

I was now demanding more of him, demanding what I craved and what was mine, now on a mission to have my desires and cravings satisfied, continually wanting more if his dirty love and he like always was not objecting.

I straddled over Charlie, teasing his cock, watching it grow big and extremely hard. He held my gyrating hips gently as I let my body ride him uncontrollably hard. Charlie just let me take control, to love his solid cock the way I wanted to love it. With my juice now clinging to his huge cock, his warm, fresh juice filled my pussy that I continued to demand daily, that had now become my passion, my dirty unforgiving habit. We laid together breathless from our dirty sex session that left us both satisfied, this could never be taken away from us by Helen or anyone else, but sadly once again he was leaving me in the morning on the early train back to Cardiff, back to the life I was not part of and never would be, but it never stopped, the tight grip of his chains that still held me his lifetime hostage, the chains I never wanted to be released from and never would, regardless of what the future held.

I awoke early, kissing him sweetly with Lizzy kisses, waking him from a perfect night's sleep. He always awoke smiling, pulling me into his arms. *Princess, you're a very sexy lady.* He smiled the cocky smile I loved.

He then climbed over me, his body naked against mine as passion was filling the air, our dirty love was overflowing, allowing us to make dirty love at dawn, which always seemed so tender, pure, and fresh, just like the new day that was about to unfold.

His kisses peppered my body, over our baby bump, stopping to tell Daisy he loved her, outlining my curves with his fingertips that always made my body go rigid, before his gaze once again met mine. *I love you both and never forget it Lizzy.* He squeezed my hand for the reassurance I needed to get me through the forthcoming days until he was back here in London. I will call tonight, and we can have some us time. He smiled that smile, I knew exactly what that meant so with long lingering kisses, lots of I love you's, he was gone again.

I hated seeing him go, seeing him walk away, walking back to her, Helen, and his life in Wales. I really resented that he was going back to Helen, to play happy family's in Wales, leaving me to brood over my life, my future and all the other negative and unwelcome thoughts that might spring into my mind and I knew full well they would.

I hated feeling so bitter, I never thought it would be like this, but it showed me what love does to you when you're having a relationship with a married man. It was always going to hurt, it was always going to be hard, I knew it would be, but I still went head long into it, but I loved Charlie so much I should have realised that I would always be the bit on the side, the tart, the whore and the bitch with a demanding dirty love that was only ever intended for Charlie.

I missed Charlie so much, needing to feel his body naked next to mine as we slept together, to have the skin-on-skin contact that I found extremely sexy, to feel his lips firm on mine that reassured me of his dirty continuing love, to share everything that we did and so naturally, but I continued to feel like second best and I suppose I always would as long as he was with Helen.

I needed his dirty love, his loving and his tender touch just to feel safe, wanted, needed and above all else to feel like the only one he loved, the only one he ever wanted to be with.

At that moment he rang, hearing his voice made me very excited. *Princess, how are you both? Charlie, I was just thinking about you.* Charlie sounded preoccupied once again, the signs so easy to detect now, he was silent, *Charlie what's wrong?... It's Helen again... What?* I snapped... his hesitation again petrified me. I have a son, he was born today, weeks early, but OK. I was stunned into silence, my mouth was so dry, my words muffled as I congratulated him.

I composed myself through my silent tears. Charlie seemed somewhat relieved after sharing his news. We chatted for a while, then long kisses and

I love you's followed, neither of us wanted to say the final goodbye as we lingered just to avoid saying the words I hated to hear at the end of every conversation we had, knowing that again tonight I would fight with the nightmares that would be sure to panic me until the dawn broke, releasing me from their almighty grip.

I was now worried that his loyalties may stay firmly in Cardiff, the realisation that I might have lost him again to Helen as now they had another bond to bring them close together again, would he even turn up for the party? Would I be alone again? This was agony, how long would I grant Charlie to continue to lead his somewhat perfect yet double life? I couldn't continue this relationship much longer, I was calling time and very soon, now with my mind made up, it was either Helen or me.

I had to wait eight long days and even longer nights until Charlie and I would be reunited. It felt like a lifetime away, but it gave me breathing space to mull over my thoughts, making it easier in some ways to make the decisions that I should have made months ago, decisions that were hard to make, but needed to be made and followed through.

The next few days went by, I was kept very busy at work with an ever growing pile of paperwork and an even bigger expanding tummy, vast tits, and swollen feet. Everything seemed to be growing bigger every day, even my appetite for Charlie, along with everything else as I munched my way through endless packets of biscuits, bags of crisps and bars of yummy chocolate.

At last it was the day of the party, and I was extremely excited as I could not wait to see Charlie. I got goose bumps every time I thought of him, hopefully he was going to be here tonight with me, in our bed, to allow us some serious dirty loving that I constantly craved, as my ongoing habit seemed to escalate when we were apart.

But would things be the same now that he was a father? Knowing his little boy would depend on him, as would Helen having had an early, traumatic premature birth. Their lives were turned upside down, leaving me to wonder why I was being so very selfish.

Life once again seemed to be so very complicated, but it was my own stupidity, my love for a bad-boy that had led me to a life which on one hand was extreme happiness and on the other such bitter unhappiness. I finished work at four, returning to the hotel as I waddled into reception to collect my keys. The porter nodded to his left and said, *You have a visitor.*

I turned around, to my delight it was Charlie, much to my surprise he had bothered to turn up.

    I was so glad to see him. *Princess, let me look at you my darling Lizzy.* He held my arms outstretched. *You're looking so… So what Charlie? So very pregnant Lizzy. You're looking very sexy princess*, he smiled that unforgettable and cocky smile which made me smile uncontrollably as it was so infectious, my fears now deflated, he was at last here.

We kissed our hello's, drenching each other in love and long awaited kisses that were so overdue. We went up to our room to have some privacy, away from the invasion of others who seemed baffled by my overwhelming display of love for Charlie as if they knew we were lovers, that I was the bit on the side, the tart who kept the bed warm for his sporadic visits, the whore who was happy to be his hostage, but I didn't care or had I lost all my self-respect?

We held each other close, both of us looking forward to making up for lost time as we got ready for the party. Charlie looked so handsome tonight; I was so proud to be seen with him, just as I had been all those years ago that brought back the same proud, seductive feelings that sent waves of tingling love through my entire body.

He wore black trousers, a white shirt and very posh sexy flip flops, he looked gorgeous and as I kissed his neck I was treated to the most sensual aroma that was Charlie. To compliment his look I wore a black short and very tight cocktail dress and high heels, my bump very visible, but a beautiful ball of adorable baby, even if I said it myself. *Wow princess, you look very sexy.* Charlie held my arms outstretched for his maximum pleasure.

    A special surprise was waiting to take us to the party, G was outside, complete with a stunning white limo and dressed in a very smart grey chauffeurs uniform complete with cap. He had done all this for me, I was once again overcome with emotion as it was so very special. On arrival at the very luxurious hotel, G helped me out from the limo, making me feel so very important, making me feel like the true lady he always said I was.

CHAPTER 29

After 4 hours of partying and dancing we were ready for some us time back in our hotel room, at last we were now alone. Charlie pulled me close to him, kissing my neck, peppering my skin in tingling kisses that burnt my delicate skin with burning passion. *Lizzy you looked so sexy tonight, so very sexy. I was proud to be with you and so proud to show you off as my girl, my Lizzy, my adorable lifetime Lizzy.*

His kisses were once again so tender and loving peppering my face, leading me into the bathroom, wanting us to relax in a long hot bubble bath. Candlelight flickered throughout the bathroom as he ran the bath, filling it with sweet smelling soft bubbles. It felt so good as he put his hands on my belly. Charlie looked so serious, his expression was worrying me, panicking my fragile body.

Lizzy you know how much I love you. My voice was questioning, as my heart missed beats in anticipation of the words that Charlie was about to deliver, words that I felt I was not going to like. I took a huge intake of air that instantly took me back to the night when Charlie dealt me a fateful blow, the night he told me he was leaving for Wales.

I want to make it permanent with you Lizzy. I'm going to leave Helen. I have tried, really tried for the baby, but it's not working, my heart and soul are with you. A lump hit my throat, was he now saying what I thought he was saying? *Charlie are you sure you want to leave Helen and you're son?* I repeated again, *are you sure Charlie?* His expression was so serious.

I can't love both of you, I don't love Helen. He was holding his head cupped in his hands, a look I had seen many times before when the going got tough. *I only have love for you, it's always been you. I have never been made to face up to what I really wanted until now and it's you, it's always been you Lizzy, my girl from school, my schoolboy dream.*

I was in shock as I could not believe what I was hearing, at last a commitment from Charlie. *You must be sure it's what you want Charlie,*

346

your son he's so tiny and Helen, she needs you. Lizzy, I have given it all my thoughts and every time they come back to you, time after time it's you, the love of my life, it's always been you, always my Lizzy, always my princess and always my girl, you're all I have ever wanted and now we are going to have Daisy it's complete, the chains we made are now complete Lizzy.

Finally the words that I wanted to hear, but his words seemed hard to digest after all this time of wanting him solely for myself, but that time was now and my lifetime dream was about to become a reality, but how could Charlie just walk away from them? I felt uneasy knowing I had torn his loyalties in two different directions, my heart seemed to break for Helen in a roundabout way, thinking would Charlie be happy in his choice? Leaving me to wonder if he would ever leave me that way when something better came into his life, a younger, much prettier model, knowing he was never short of female attention even when we were out in public.

I had to free myself from my unguarded and negative thoughts as tonight Charlie had yet again taken my breath away by this amazing powerful news, the news I had craved. I was delighted that it was me he wanted, leaving Helen to fade into the background, but knowing full well she wouldn't give Charlie up without a fight... why would she? With that in mind I braced myself for what lay ahead in the next few weeks.

With the water now going cold Charlie grabbed the towels leading me back to our bed, wrapping his arms around me. Tonight I felt like the luckiest girl in the world, but I knew my happiness would come with a hefty price tag, so with that in mind I braced myself for the storm that knew would be mine, a storm so violent it would test my strength to the limits.

Charlie's fingers now danced over my curves in long flowing strokes. *I could eat you Lizzy.* I looked at him with my steely sexy green eyes and said, *then why don't you Charlie?* He looked at me smiling naughtily, the smile that I still found so amazingly seductive, his love tonight roared louder than the menacing echoes of his vile fathers voice, so tonight I knew I would sleep without interruption. Charlie kissed my left shoulder gently, allowing his teeth to nibble my upper arm, his fingers then slid down over my skin that now glowed with an incredible love, reaching my nipples as he commanded them to stand to his attention. Charlie continued to let his fingers dance down over my curves, meeting my naked pussy that purred delightedly in anticipation for some dirty love, he gently rubbed his fingers along my pussy.

His moaning was again gritty and deep as he was loving our amazing dirty love. Charlie's tongue was once again locked onto my clit as I firmly wedged his head between my thighs, only letting him free from my thighs to return to my lips for kisses, repeating his actions over and over again, thrilling my senses to the limits, delivering my constant desires.

I then sat on his legs finding his huge, hard cock that was so firm and solid, thrusting it firmly into my mouth, letting my tongue tease his full helmet, showering it with dirty kisses, listening to him moan. *You dirty bitch, suck it Lizzy, suck it fucking hard.* I held his balls, squeezing them hard, sucking him with a beautiful passion. His juice was now filling my mouth, drenching my throat with juice fresh from his cock that now trickled from my lips that Charlie passionately kissed away.

I laid on my back now demanding to be loved by Charlie as he loved my pussy, groaning with passionate excitement that triggered wave after wave of pent up dirty love to rocket through my body.

Charlie, I whispered, *I love you fucking me Charlie. Lizzy, my beautiful Lizzy.* Charlie's cock was once again stiff and solid as he began to screw me hard, allowing more of the dirty love I craved.

Now slumped back on the bed we laid together smiling once again uncontrollably. Charles fingers were still delicately stroking my arm as we cradled each other, my hand resting on his chest. *We are good together aren't we Lizzy? Yes we are Charlie.* There has never ever been any doubt about that, but I questioned him again. *Charlie, did you mean what you said about you Daisy and me?*

Squeezing my hand tightly, *I meant every word Lizzy, my mind is made up. I should have done this years ago, I should have married you all those years back, but stupidly I let you marry someone else, something you know I have regretted every day of my life.*

As we kissed each other goodnight we were both delighted that we now had a future that was set in stone for us to enjoy or would it really be that simple? Were we on a collision course for yet another roller-coaster of events that I would have no control over leaving me once again cold and unloved?

We woke up late and had a very late breakfast together. Charlie wanted to do something special today so there was only one place that would be perfect and it had to be Regent's Park with the late autumn sun warm on our skin, perfect for a walk with the only man who made me truly happy in bed and out of it, now loving the freedom to hold hands without worry, to share kisses that were not important to anyone else other than us, to make each other smile so much it would send our faces into spasms of delightful pain.

It was still warm with the smell of autumn all around us as we looked a little closer, the blackberries had started forming in the hedgerows, the leaves were starting to change colour. Families were having fun, enjoying the last of the late sunshine before autumn turned instantly to winter, claiming its icy grip on London and the rest of the country once again.

We walked hand in hand talking about us, Daisy, and our future as a family. I was totally loving the thought of becoming a family for the very first time in my life and It felt so right, at long last I imagined myself having the life I had only dreamt about.

We managed to find a very pretty spot that had been warmed for us by the sun as it was secluded by trees and shrubs that nestled comfortably next to the lake. Charlie turned to me, holding my hand as he got down on one knee. *Lizzy I want to marry you*. Not even hesitating to think about my answer, I replied. *Yes Charlie, yes, yes, of course yes*. We both had tears in our eyes, blurring the beautiful setting that surrounded us, but he was still married to Helen, so my dream to be his bride was again on hold.

We sat sharing kisses, both delighted with our news, completely unaware of everyone around us in the most perfect place I knew of in London which had now completely taken my breath away, steeling yet more of my heart.

The sun was starting to disappear behind the London skyline leaving a real chill in the air, but still it remained so perfect in its ability to embrace me, to allow me to fall even deeper in love with it as I continued to inhale its pungent aroma's that mingled from one street into the next.

What a fantastic day we had shared, finishing with a very romantic dinner in our cosy restaurant with the mood much lighter. I was now free from the love triangle that had continually haunted me, but I worried as Charlie had to break the news to Helen that he was leaving and that was going to be traumatic for both of them.

Charlie looked at me with an expression in his eyes that held a hidden life that I was never going to be ever part of and that still worried me even now and my thoughts were that it always would, but I had been seduced by Charlie's reputation all those years ago and even today it still seduced me.

Exhausted from a day of delightful turmoil and a passionate dirty love session, we said goodnight knowing that tomorrow was going to be a tough day as Charlie was returning to Wales, back to end his marriage, but I feared that Helen might tighten her grip on him and I that would become a victim once again of his somewhat selfish love and not the hostage I longed to be my entire life, but Charlie could not go on lying, leading a double life with me that was now leaving a trail of deception and above all hatred behind him.

Stepping out from the hotel after a night of torrential rain the sky was alight with stunning rainbows, bring with it a warmth of love to take into our future, but I knew full well that yet more storms would undoubtedly be coming my way to cloud my dreams.

We said our sad goodbyes, sharing plenty of our long loving kisses that never failed to delight my senses, but today as usual they left my heart empty as I stood alone watching him walk away. I began to seek the comfort from the ring that hung lovingly from my necklace which still remained a mystery to me as my fingers outlined the raised pattern that surrounded it letting it take me on yet another journey.

I could now hear his voice raised, taking me away from my brief journey. *See you very soon princess and never forget I love you both very much.* Those words yet again threw my thoughts into a downward spiral of what he was keeping from me, the life that I was sure that was ruled by his reputation, a life that was dark and cold.

We waved until out of sight, the loneliness now flooded over me once again like an ice cold wind that left me shivering in its wake, needing Charlie's warm loving arms around me to protect me. I was now alone with only the city lights for company which tonight were cold and empty from any form of love, so once again I reached for what had become my comfort on so many occasions. I twiddled again just minutes after the last time with the ring that bore a secret, a secret that I may never know.

Charlie rang as promised, but instantly I could feel the pain in his trembling voice, knowing he would be devastated by the choice he had made. He was then silent from words; I knew it would be unbelievably painful and again I felt it was my fault that had led him to have to make the heart-breaking choice.

We said goodnight with muffled I love you's hoping that tomorrow things would maybe look a little brighter as being at the cute cabin he had space to clear his mind, to put things in order, for now anyway. Charlie and I chatted all week, excited that we would now see each other at the weekend, to build our future as a family.

Friday was here already, my part of the vast build was finished and I said a sad farewell to London and for all the love it had given me, leaving once again a little part of my heart here in this vibrant city, ready to collect when the time was right.

G was waiting outside to drive me on our final journey together, it had been wonderful to have him as my driver for my somewhat short time in London, we formed a great bond and a forever friendship, sadly it was time to say goodbye to him and a very emotional one as he waited with me on the platform, not wanting me to be alone, to share our friendship just a little longer, but I would never forget Mr Green, aka G.

Being back in familiar surroundings I took a long lingering walk around the house, soaking up the memories that were always waiting for me behind every door, but my bedroom held the best most secret memories and today was no different. As I gazed out of my old bedroom window it wasn't long before I was once again treated to my very own living landscape that never failed to delight me.

After lunch I took a very deep breath as I told dad about Charlie. I told him about everything, hoping desperately he would understand that I would need to move to find a family home for us, his facial expression shocked and saddened by my words.

Dad took a sharp intake of breath. *Lizzy, you don't need to move. We can sort out the extension for you all, your mum and I were going to develop the garage but we never got around to it somehow. Charlie could even have an office if he needs one. What a great idea dad, are you sure that would work for you? Yes this will be yours and your sisters one day anyway.*

I could not wait to see and tell Charlie the brilliant news. Dad drew a simple plan on the back of a cereal packet of what he thought would make a perfect place for us all, the plan he drew was the kitchen and sitting room at the front, keeping the bedrooms and bathroom as they were now and if Charlie wanted an office we could build up, putting in a playroom for Daisy.

Charlie arrived on Saturday morning. I was so excited to see him, but nervous at the same time. We held each other tight, kissing our hellos, he held my hand tightly, both of us relieved that we had made the final commitment. This was it, we were together forever, or were we? Only time would tell as my nagging doubts still clouded even my positive thoughts with a deep, ugly, dark mist that seemed to get much darker and much more uglier as the weeks were now turning into months.

Dad greeted Charlie with a very warm welcome and firm hand shake, reminding Charlie that he was watching him. I smiled to myself, knowing dad was comfortable with Charlie moving in and as we sat in the lounge Charlie and dad looked relaxed and comfortable together as they sat talking about the plans. Charlie said he would build it and I would fund it. Things really did seem like they were taking shape at last.

Dad looked tired so Charlie and I then went out for a long walk into the woods giving dad some time alone. Charlie and I talked at ease, thrilled that we would be a proper family at last and in our own little home, knowing that Daisy would now grow up in the very house that I did and I hoped she would grow to love it just as much, to create her very own dreams and to chase the many rainbows that awaited her.

We talked about Charlie's work, he said he would work in Wales from Monday morning to Thursday night and be home for three days every week. He would continue to stay at the cabin for three nights while continuing to build up his business.

Now happy and content with the future, whatever it held for us we would embrace it, as we had so much to look forward to; Daisy, our new home and just being together after all these long, painful, and demanding years that had tested our resolve to the limits and in my mind would continue to challenge us, even now when we thought we had it all.

Our walk took us to the old shed, Charlie had to push hard with some force to open the door as we had not been there for a while and neither had anyone else. I had hoped in a strange way that others would have loved it the way we did, used it the way we had done over the years.

Suddenly I took in the intoxicating aroma that had now reached my nostrils, now panicked by the memories of this little shed. I felt our world could not be this perfect, my mind was in constant fear that we were never meant to be this happy as now it all seemed too good to be true. I kept asking myself that question over and over again, how could something be this perfect? This was putting more doubts into my over crowded mind, wondering why I still had so many doubts.

We sat reminiscing about all the many times we had visited the little shed and three of the many occasions stood out for me; that special Christmas where we snuggled up under the stars on such a bitterly cold night, the special night before my wedding that gave me the strength I so needed to take into my married life, and the day after when Charlie had come back for me all those years ago calling my name below my bedroom window while he stood in the pouring rain. All these memories were still vivid in my mind as I recalled them again to tantalise my senses.

So with memories now flooding back we firmly closed the door behind us once again on the little shed, promising we would return. As Charlie fought again to close the old door his wallet fell from his pocket, falling open. I gasped, as I could not believe what I was seeing, a photo of a very glamorous, beautiful woman looked back at me. It was her, the vision that had felt she was welcome to intrude on my dreams turning them into nightly terrors, it was Charlie's wife... Suddenly he grabbed the wallet, trying to stuff it back into his pocket, not wanting me to focus any longer on the photograph.

My expression was dark as I glared at him. *Lizzy, sorry I should have removed it.* He reached for my hand. *Lizzy please. Don't Charlie.* I snatched my hand away in total disbelief that he had a photo of her still in his wallet... I screamed at him, *I thought it was over Charlie?! It is Lizzy. Well explain why you have it or more to the point, why it's not my photo?* Suddenly he ripped the photo from his wallet ripping it into shreds, discarding the fragments into the icy breeze. His expression weakened by my outburst, wiping the smile from his face.

Lizzy do you believe me now? I looked down at the fragmented, discarded photo, *I'm so sorry Lizzy.*

I felt sick at my outburst, wanting the ground to swallow me, embarrassed at my ability to be a such bitch, but on the other hand she had haunted me for weeks with her nightly appearance, scowling at me, muted from words, leaving me drenched in a pool of cold unwelcome liquid as I shivered and lay terrified.

Charlie pulled me into his arms, desperately trying to reassure me it was me, his girl, the girl that he wanted, kissing away my tears that had now smudged my makeup. There was the realisation that Helen was not giving up the fight just yet, but I had to forget her, put her out of my mind, she was nothing to me.

We walked back home, the conversation muted and lacking any love. I apologised again, I hated myself today, how could I be so nasty?... Charlie had now given up everything for me, but seeing the photograph had cast yet more suspicion which lead to negative thoughts once again, but I had to set them free if we were to embrace the future together, our future.

Back home we relaxed over dinner. Charlie and dad were both on good form and seemed to be getting along really well considering dad's view of Charlie's colourful past and the reputation he carried.

We enjoyed our time in the bath together that night as I craved our lives to be like this always, but again the nagging doubts remained in my head that were now crippling my perfect dream to have it all.

We slipped back to our bedroom with dirty love on our minds to share some us time in our bed, in our home, which felt so right for so many reasons, both of us knowing that we had paid the price during the long and unforgiving 15 years, that we had endured to now have a chance at what we should have had all those innocent years ago when our love was so very virginal, undemanding and so uncomplicated.

Making love was a combination of old and new as we relived the past, rekindling the first magical heady days of our dirty love that was fresh and new as we explored each other's bodies, fumbling to find ourselves and now, 15 years on, I was Charlie's bitch, his whore with demanding cravings that Charlie loved to satisfy and tonight was no different as I begged loudly for more.

Monday morning came all too soon, and Charlie went back to Cardiff for the week. I would miss him desperately, but I knew he was going to be back on Thursday night so I spent some of my day walking in the garden that now had a carpet of freshly fallen leaves in magnificent colours that awoke muted memories, glorious golds, burnt orange, sumptuous amber's and every shade of brown, mixed together forming a delightful picture that just came alive as I walked through them scrunching under foot as the breeze would whirl and spin around in the garden, lifting the leaves until they formed neat piles that just needed to be jumped in and scattered around once more.

Thursday night was here at last. I waited patiently for Charlie's car to drive into sight. On hearing the roar of the engine my heart seemed to beat even faster.

After a lovely supper we had time to relax, enjoying each other's company again, so bathed and ready for bed we laid skin on skin.

Charlie leant over pulling my hair gently to one side. *Princess, my darling Lizzy.* He peppered my skin in warm kisses that I just adored, I kissed his neck and again I was treated to his sensual aroma.

He kissed my lips, my neck, my tits, and my belly. Every part of my body received the Charlie kisses that peppered me in a sea of love, that allowed wave after wave of foaming love to take me on yet another journey.

Charlie gently put my legs over his so that I was more comfortable, as I was so heavily pregnant it meant that he could love me for total satisfaction, delivering all the dirty love that I constantly craved and demanded repeatedly.

Charlie's solid cock thrust gently and softly, making my pussy purr with delight and always wanting more dirty love. *Lizzy your horny bitch.* His moaning was gritty and loud as I felt the pressure build. I now had every bit of his huge, throbbing cock loving my pussy, drenching it in dirty love as he rode me harder, obeying my commands that I lovingly and now constantly made on him.

His cock always remained very hard for a long time after he had loved me and I found that very sexy as it gave me time to love him a little more, letting my lips firmly clasp around his cock. Both his hands held my head to allow him to thrust his cock repeatedly hard into the back of my throat, peppering my mouth with yet more warm juice.

My mouth was now free from Charlie's huge erection, my lips were now smeared with juice that I longed to share with him as our lips met, our kisses now so beautiful as Charlie's tongue revolved around my mouth finding the juice that was his.

Friday morning arrived and we headed to the hospital, I was very nervous, almost scared. My tummy was in knots as I could smell in the air the pungent fear in the ward from the expectant parents with the terrifying sounds of pain that echoed throughout the ward and along the sterile corridors as parents waited for their special gift to be delivered. Charlie reassured me as the midwife called us in. Charlie held my hand, again reassuringly as she examined me, poking and prodding my expansive tummy that now looked like a huge pink balloon, ready to pop.

CHAPTER 30

The midwife asked us about our birthing plan, we looked at each other blankly and it quickly became apparent we didn't have one, but I knew I wanted a natural birth, as calm and quiet as possible with Charlie by my side to help deliver Daisy and to cut her cord, so now with a simple birthing plan in place fingers crossed she would be on time. We left the hospital with some sort of relief written across our faces.

We both managed a very relaxing weekend, going for walks along the river and to the woods, loving every minute of us time. This was the way I had imagined our life to be like, making dirty love at every possible moment, after all we were free to make love without any guilt now, having weathered every life-changing storm possible.

December was now well and truly here and it was so bitterly cold. The long winter nights were beginning to bite with frosty days and an icy cold wind that howled throughout the house, shaking the old window frames that once again enlivened my memories of the years gone by.

I tried to get as much rest as possible, to take regular walks, to eat well and make dirty love with Charlie as often as we wanted. How could he love me looking like this? My tummy was expanding close to bursting, my tits swollen with milk and my baggy clothes.

Charlie came home late on Thursday nights to spend more time with me and now with only a week to go we excitedly went and bought the most beautiful Christmas tree. Charlie knew how much I loved Christmas and this Christmas we would receive a very special gift that would change our lives forever, enhancing it dramatically every day.

We spent all Saturday afternoon decorating the oversized spruce. I had one very special decoration to add to the tree which I placed in pride of place, my glass snow flake, the snow flake Charlie gave me all those years ago. Charlie gasped as I unwrapped the delicate decoration from its pretty pink tissue paper. *You still have it Lizzy.* He looked surprised. *Yes Charlie, every year.* I glanced at him smiling. *No Christmas tree would ever be complete without it.*

As we relaxed all evening with the fire glowing, a Christmas aroma filled the lounge with the intoxicating smell of the Christmas tree with its fresh, clean perfume that filled my senses with such sweet memories, mixed with the smell of the open fire it made for a very cosy feel as we sat and wrote Christmas cards, wrapped presents, all ready before Daisy came into our world to change our lives completely.

My baby bump was gloriously huge now, but so stunningly beautiful, a full round ball of baby, our baby, that we had lovingly made together. With only days to go I felt so uncomfortable. It was the 21st of December, Charlie and I had said our goodnights and it wasn't long after midnight when I was awoken with niggling twinges, but never the less I was panicked by the reality that Daisy was on her way, just like Father Christmas to bring us a gift, a beautiful gift of our little girl.

It was 5am and I could not get comfortable, so I walked around the garden in the freezing cold. The sun had not yet risen, I was wrapped up in a huge fluffy blanket wearing my pyjamas, a heavy coat, and boots, hoping that it might help, but still feeling like I was going to pop at any time. The pains in my back were increasing, Charlie was now insisting he walked around the garden with me, talking about the garden and its ability even on this cold, dark morning to embrace us, to always finding old memories to enliven our senses.

Charlie suggested we left immediately for the hospital, but there was something I had to do as I wanted to revisit my old bedroom to once again just stand at the window for a second, to recall again precious memories that I had left there, to recall on a day like this. The sun had just broke, casting a watery, winter glow into the woods as every tree was bathed in a glorious winter beauty, so beautiful that it transported me back to the days when Charlie and I would love to walk hand in hand on these sorts of days. Suddenly a cold shiver ran through me as I could smell mum's perfume before something brushed against me, leaving a hazy mist at my bedroom door, disbelieving this special moment. I rubbed my eyes for clarity, but the vision wasn't her, but a haunting vision remained by my side, as I felt her cold breath against my skin something that today scared me, Helen was here, but why? I left my bedroom at haste, leaving the past behind me on hearing Charlie's repeated requests that we needed to leave as he paced up and down the hallway.

On arrival at the hospital Charlie held my hand, reassuring me everything would fine as I was admitted to the ward and told I was in the first stage of labour. Music now filled the sterile cubical, music that we had played so often while making love, he had unbeknown to me made a special recording for us to help me relax during labour. I smiled at him lovingly as he had done that for me, so the midwife dimmed the lights as the music played softly and with Charlie by my side, I had everything I needed.

The pain was bearable for now and as the hours ticked by the pain increased. I now knew what all those expectant parents were feeling on the day we came to look around this very ward, as we both were feeling it now as the aroma of fear hung pungently heavy in the air with echoes of spine chilling pain that shuddered at every door.

Now hours later after excruciating pain, excitement and fear, we held at long last our very own bundle of joy. Charlie and I were parents to Daisy, our beautiful Daisy. Suddenly the clinically cold room and corridors fell silent from fearful voices and terrifying echoes, being replaced by joyous smiles, happiness and above all, love.

Daisy was born at 10.20pm on the 22nd December. The midwife congratulated us as she smiled. Daisy was now wrapped in a silky soft white blanket and handed to me for the most amazing cuddle, the feeling of love for her was so over whelming as wave after wave of something so powerful was transported through my body. There was never going to be a feeling like it, only a mother could experience this feeling of overwhelming love, knowing she was so adorable, born out of the most fabulous lifetime of love and we wanted her to know that, it was important to us both.

I looked to Charlie once again. He looked so proud, so very proud, his smile was beaming, his adorable smile radiating from every wall in the room. He was besotted with her as he could not take his gaze away from her.

We both just gazed at her, she was so perfect. Her button nose, her dark hair, her pale silky white skin, she was everything that I had imagined her to be like and more.

The midwife was back briefly breaking us from such a peaceful moment to weigh Daisy, 6 pounds and 6oz, perfect, complete with brown eyes, just like her daddy. She then gave Daisy back to me, we were then left again to love each other, to bond with our delightful daughter, Charlie leant over. *Princess, you are beautiful, you were fantastic.*

He put his arms around me whispering, *I love you both so much*. With Daisy now sound asleep it left Charlie and I deep in unforgettable love, amazed by the beauty of our daughter.

We all feel asleep for a couple of hours before Daisy woke again, sharing lots of cuddles that left us both not wanting to be parted from her for a second, as we were besotted with her. I stroked her pure, soft skin, inhaling her aroma while I touched her silky dark hair.

The morning broke into a beautiful crisp winter's day, uncovering a frosty landscape that I adored. A cold and frosty start with a watery sunshine which would enrich the landscape, enriching our lives that were today filled with beauty.

Back home, fresh from being discharged from the maternity ward, dad was overcome with emotion. His tears were hard to hide as he whispered through his emotions. *Mum would have loved her.* Who wouldn't love her? She was perfect and deliciously beautiful, her little fingers wrapped themselves around mine, leaving us all cocooned in a perfect circle of love that embraced us all.

Charlie then pulled me close to him. *Princess I love you and Daisy, I never want you to forget it Lizzy.* His smile was so perfect, but I feared the smile once again was hiding a secret, a secret so huge that was now so out of control that he would never want to share it.

With milk still seeping from my nipples, my hair a mess, no makeup to paint my porcelain face, I looked a mess. How could he find me attractive, when I knew he was never short of female attention? However, it was me he wanted, whether I was dressed to thrill, slouching around in jeans or like now, having just given birth.

Daisy was sound asleep in her pretty white crib, Charlie and I were laying in each other's arms with the room made so calm by the dimmed lights that were now so perfect for sleep. We kissed Daisy goodnight, Charlie stroked my back to help me relax and drift into sleep that I hoped would not be filled with unwelcome visitors and vile distractions.

Daisy slept well, allowing us some much needed sleep from the journey we had all been on to get here then we were up again, delighted to be having endless cuddles. God she was beautiful, her dark hair, her big brown eyes with a pale perfect skin that was so soft as I gently rolled my fingertips over the skin on her face, every bit of her was truly perfect.

Christmas Eve was now here and what a difference it was from last year when I had experienced a very lonely Christmas as Dave preferred the pub to any Christmas celebrations that I was part of. The endless rows that were followed by endless verbal abuse that just spewed from his mouth undermining my attempts to make Christmas special, knowing full well he knew just how much I adored Christmas and all that went with it, the Christmas tree, the Christmas decorations, the winter landscape, the snow, the holly, the Christmas church service and the lavish Christmas celebrations at home, well, mum and dad's house, but now this year was completely different, I was surrounded by love.

Daisy and I had a couple of hours on our own, the feelings were incredibly moving, far beyond my dreams. I never thought it would have been this powerful as the feeling of unconditional love just kept sweeping over me. I took Daisy up to my old room, both of us wrapped in a blanket as we stood in the window admiring the winter wonderland that awaited both of us. I was again suddenly transported on a journey into a winter wonderland from the past when I was a child, building snowman in the garden, using carrots for noses and lumps of coal for eyes, wrapping an old tatty scarf around him to keep him warm, I smiled to myself at these amazing memories.

A sudden interruption made me jump, Charlie was stood in the door way, smiling at us both. His cocky smile was bouncing around my old bedroom as he brought me back to the here and now. I gazed at Daisy hoping that one day she would be as gifted as I was to stand here and recall so many treasured memories that would take her on many whirlwind journeys that would leave her waiting in excited anticipation for the next journey to begin, that would enliven her senses, creating a journal of vivid memories for her to share or keep for herself to build her dreams.

On entering the lounge the fire was casting a heavenly glow, combined with the lights from the Christmas tree that twinkled like tiny stars, this was a very magical time for us all. I was suddenly taken away from the pretty picture of the lounge as the doorbell rang. I answered it to find a lady stood shivering on the door step, hidden behind the mass of delightful flowers that she was holding. They were for Daisy, the card read, *to my darling daughter Daisy thank you for being mine, I love you so much.* Sentiments which today made me cry, it was so moving. I left Charlie cuddling Daisy while I had a bath and changed into some nice new clothes in an attempt to feel a little more like me and as I walked into the lounge Charlie looked stunned, his expression caressing my body while his gaze seduced me. *Lizzy you look amazing.* I blushed at his comments that left dad raising his eyebrows with embarrassment, but smiling to himself as he made his way to the kitchen.

Charlie kissed me and whispered into my neck. *If you had not just given birth I would fuck you right now Lizzy.* He smiled that cocky reputation fuelled smile that made me blush again repeatedly, just like it had done right from when I was his virgin when unbeknown to me he moulded me to be his girl, the girl that fell in love with him like no other could.

We all said goodnight and headed to bed. I felt so tired, but that was to be expected. I laid in bed with Charlie sleeping peacefully by my side, but I was restless as my mind kept wandering back to last Christmas when we never expected to have an earth shattering year like this which contained every emotion and had tested us all to the limits, with monumental highs and earth shattering lows.

Daisy awoke soon after midnight. Charlie went and made us some hot strong coffee and sat beside me on our bed. *Merry Christmas Lizzy.* Charlie looked pre-occupied, his expression was hiding a sadness, one I had seen on many occasions that caused me to wonder why. *Charlie, some thing's bothering you. I'm fine Lizzy.* He looked so sad as I moved my hand to his to reassure him.

He then blurted out. *It's my sons first Christmas and I won't be there to see him Lizzy.* I gulped with emotion, trying hard to hold back the tears that I needed to shed for him and for them, knowing I was the cause tonight of his distress, having to choose his wife or his life time love.

He said he would ring Helen over Christmas and arrange to see his son. I was pleased for him, he needed to see him, they needed each other, it was important that Charlie had contact with his son, to build a father and son relationship and I was never going to stand in his way.

I changed Daisy, putting her to my swollen breasts, she was a hungry girl and feeding on demand that seemed to work. My other breast was drenched with milk as Charlie watched in total amazement. Our bond as mother and daughter was already a strong one, just like me and my mum. Again emotions of mum washed over me as I fought back my tears again, trying to hide my sadness from Charlie.

It was Christmas morning and as I looked out of the window I was treated again to my very own winter wonderland that was spectacular. It was frosty and cold with a watery sunshine that I loved. Looking up at the sky I thought it might snow and how magical that would be, but today I needed to seek the company of my old bedroom window, so I crept away making my way upstairs to my old bedroom, leaving the door slightly ajar.

Suddenly, I felt a very icy chill escaping from my room, an eerie chill that took my breath away, an aroma was fixed in my nostrils, mum's perfume. It was her perfume, she was here in my bedroom, a grey watery misty shadow glided across the floor, I stood motionless and still. Suddenly the door slammed shut, shuddering along the landing, making me jump back to the here and now. Confused by the surprise visit I headed back to the comfort of Charlie's arms and once again I reached for the ring on my necklace, not believing mum was here, but knowing full well she always would be.

With Daisy still asleep, Charlie and I sat and had some us time. Charlie whispered while clutching my hand. *I have a little something for you Lizzy, Happy Christmas princess.* He then handed me a little wooden box with H L F initials scratched in the lid, the same initials as on the ring, but why? What did they mean? I opened the box with care, gasping as I did. A beautiful eternity ring adorned the box, it was absolutely perfect. Charlie kissed the ring before placing it on my finger, whispering *I love you* as he did, followed by kisses that were so perfect as now another ring graced my finger.

Daisy was still fast asleep so Charlie and I took the opportunity to walk in the garden on this perfect crisp Christmas Day afternoon to admire the beauty of the winter landscape that looked like a scene from a Christmas card and right on queue the church bells rang out, calling everyone to the Christmas late afternoon service. Taking in the powerful toll I looked up to the sky that was now laden with grey heavy clouds waiting to shed the snow they carried, the ice cold wind was stinging my face, my eyes were blurred by frozen tears as I remembered mum and how she would have loved Daisy.

I started to shiver, Charlie had noticed my tears, knowing full well the reason for shedding them as he squeezed my hand allowing me to freely shed my emotions on the sleeve of his coat before I headed back into the warmth of the house.

Charlie remained in the garden for a while longer to make the call he so needed to make. I left him alone as I was sure he would need some privacy while I made us some much needed hot chocolate, complete with some delicious chocolates that G had given me on my departure from London.

As we all sat in the lounge we had a lovely Christmas afternoon, all four of us, lots of cuddles and kisses as we all enjoyed our hot chocolate sat in front of the roaring fire that crackled and sparked shards of glowing white flames, spitting them onto the hearth.

Christmas rolled on and winter gathered pace as bitter winds swept in across the open landscape bringing snow with it, covering the fields in a blanket of glorious snow that just glistened in the watery sunlight. Even in the evening the moonlight cast a light over it that was so stunning as it reinvigorated my senses.

It was the beginning of January and Charlie returned to work in Cardiff leaving Daisy and I alone. The winter was setting in hard now, I was once again on my own and alone with my thoughts that would sometimes overpower me, leading me down the darkest of paths in search of answers.

I missed Charlie during the week, but he rang every day to see how we all were, he missed us, I knew that, but sometimes he seemed distant, silent, and somewhat pre occupied, leading me to yet again question in my mind the reason why as I worried if this was all too much for him.

Could he be missing Helen? I knew he missed his son. Was the traveling to and from Cardiff too much for him? Was life with me not what he thought it would be? So many questions that all needed answers, my thoughts were escalating, bombarding me with every negative thought possible.

I took a much needed visit to my old bedroom to seek the sanctuary of my bedroom window in a bid to find some answers, but this window today like every day sadly could not explain Charlie's unhappiness, along with his worrying silences which were now so regular. Again my mind was in a whirl as I remained terrified that his mysterious, private life was yet again playing a huge part in his life that was without doubt intruding on our perfect family life together.

The window allowed me to take a journey back to the tree house, as there I had created my many dreams of a perfect life. How I loved those days when the summer sunshine was never-ending, the evening sun warm and mellow, complimented in full by the aroma of the garden, the delicate perfume of roses and lavender.

As I walked out of the bedroom I caught a glimpse of myself in the mirror, my body was slowly getting back to normal, and my shape was returning. I was now back to the slim, but curvy Lizzy that Charlie adored beyond doubt. Charlie was due home this weekend, so excitedly I waited for Thursday to arrive, knowing we would again share lots of special kisses, not just for me but for Daisy too.

I ran out to meet him, throwing my arms around him as he swept me into his powerful arms that filled my body with such love, that sent all my negative thoughts to the back of my mind, for now at least.

Charlie and I spent a long and lazy weekend with Daisy, just enjoying some much needed us time. I caught glimpses of Charlie over the weekend looking pre occupied, his face crippled and tense, but still I hesitated to ask why as I remained terrified of the answers I might get, but it was just as terrifying not getting any answers.

February was here in the blink of an eye. Charlie called every day, but I still remained unconvinced that all was normal in Charlie's life. He always seemed distant on the phone or was it me? I was still very confused by his unhappiness and reluctance to confide in me.

Charlie was due home tonight and I could not wait to see him. I had the all-clear to resume a normal dirty sex life and I wanted to make it special for him this weekend, hoping it might help the tension I knew he was feeling.

He got back late on Thursday afternoon, I was elated to see him as he kissed us both with kisses that were always perfect, smiling his trademark smile. *You both look fantastic princess.* Charlie sat cuddling Daisy with her little fingers wrapped lovingly around his.

With Daisy fast asleep and back in her crib I took Charlie's hand, leading him into the bathroom where I was tonight going to seduce him. Beautiful soft bubbles filled the bath, along with the candles that flickered and reflected off every wall. It looked so nice and very romantic. We slipped into the bath, sharing kisses like lovers again, slowly our tongues revolved around each other's mouths with ease. *Princess, I have missed you, my very beautiful whore.* That's what I was planning to be tonight and for the rest of our lives, exclusively his whore.

He touched me gently and I closed my eyes as it felt so good, so gentle, but I was needing a little rough dirty sex tonight and I was going to get it as now the eye contact between us was commanding dirty love and lots of it.

Charlie's wet fingers slid along my pussy lips, now naked of course, just the way Charlie loved it. My moaning encouraged his fingers to slide further into my pussy, something I had missed so much, I had missed his gentle dirty sex that was mine.

We continued to kiss; our emotions were on a high. Charlie's eyes were so beautifully brown as he continued to flirt with mine. *Princess, let's take this into the bedroom.* Now wrapped in towels that felt so warm and soft on our skin Charlie then laid me on the bed, allowing him to admire my body again, now free from my baby body that we had both adored. I was back to my slim, but curvy self.

His kisses were hard, long, and intense as he continued to pepper my body in delicate kisses, rolling his tongue gently over my naked nipples, making them stand to attention. His fingertips travelled over my curves, tracing the outline that sent shivers of delight down my spine. I was now moaning with such passion as Charlie straddled me, his fingers caressing my nipples that were still leaking milk that I demanded he sucked and as he did I begged for more.

I'm going to love you hard princess. His cock was now ready to please my demanding pussy once again, his cock was massive and desperately wanting the Lizzy love and kisses. I moved on to all fours prepared for the cock that was going to fill my pussy with so much dirty love tonight. *You dirty bitch Lizzy.* My pussy was now drenched and purring with delight for Charlie's cock, sliding his huge erection along my lips, making me take a huge intake of breath. Once again my breath had been taken away by Charlie's dirty love, my moaning was now so loud, as again I begged for more dirty love.

Having moved positions Charlie's hands were now working my hip as I gyrated on him. The wanting was so apparent between us, as the pressure was building we were both about to explode, my pussy now filled with warm, fresh juice from Charlie's huge cock that still begged my pussy for more.

His cock was still huge, still filled with more juice, more dirty love for us both to enjoy and I was going to have it all as Charlie stood in front of me, his massive cock now filled my mouth as my lips were tightly clasped over his throbbing purple helmet as he continued to thrust it hard, watching me indulge my sexual appetite. Charlie's hands then held my head firmly to receive every bit of his solid cock that was now peppering my throat, coating my tongue with yet more fresh, warm juice.

Charlie continued to thrust every bit of his cock into my throat, not stopping, not allowing me to take a breath, giving me every bit of the dirty love I craved, his juice now smeared on my lips, Charlie's moaning loud and full of dirty love.

Our lips then met again as Charlie's tongue revolved around my mouth, pleasuring my sexual desires to the full. Charlie then lowered his head, delightedly he found my pussy that so needed his ultimate dirty love tonight and as always I was not disappointed, as Charlie's tongue made sure of that.

You beautiful dirty whore princess. I blushed as I knew full well that I was never going to stop being his whore, his bitch and most of all, his princess.

The weekend went by, but we had managed lots of dirty love this weekend leaving us once again dirty lovers, but we both seemed restless, something was bothering us both, maybe it was because we were new to the parent game or was something else simmering beneath the surface? Sadly, before we knew it, Charlie was back in Cardiff working and the weather had turned incredibly cold, bitter winds bombarded us every day, as the snow just kept on falling.

The garden looked stunning, now covered in a thick blanket of frozen snow that just sparkled in the watery sunshine, but I needed a better view of this magnificent landscape, so I headed up to my old bedroom and again I was transported to a place I loved. My emotions were now saturated by the most precious memories I could recall, flashing through my mind, taking a beautiful winter journey which I loved, all made possible by this bedroom in this house. I stared out of the window which seemed to always allow me to escape back to my childhood, to my teenage years and now as a woman to fulfil all my yesterday dreams which flooded my senses with emotional delights and aromas that I had forgotten, with voices that had evaded me for so long now echoing gracefully in my mind and with colours that gave me such a vivid, spectacular kaleidoscope of forgotten images, yesterday's glorious days.

My room had not changed in all these years since I left it on that fateful day, the day of my wedding, a past memory I did not want to dwell on or recall for so many reasons, so I remained delighted that this window never allowed me to recall the disastrous married life I so sadly was forced to endure and the pain I went through in order to end it.

Posters that had now faded still hung clinging to the walls with sticky tape that had now gone brown with age, but still made me smile as I recalled each and every one of the baby-faced idols that graced the walls.

Suddenly I was brought back from my vivid journey into the past by Charlie, as he was now home and stood in my old bedroom door watching me recalling the past, watching me flirting with the pop idols in the many posters, memories were forming an orderly queue that today was never-ending.

I squealed with delight as I peppered him in Lizzy kisses. Charlie was now going to be on hand every day to build the extension. As the days went by he seemed to settle in and happy to be at home with Daisy and I, although at times he seemed very pre occupied, on edge, even with his phone in melt down, but he said nothing as my thoughts were again led into uncertainty about the life he was leading outside of our relationship, a life I was never allowed to be part of, that was shrouded in mystery and a secrecy that filled my mind like a dark fog not being able to see clearly the obvious, terrifying torment that was facing Charlie.

I knew something was wrong. I knew it was not money, me, our home life, or our amazingly dirty love, so what was it? I had to find out, because if I didn't I felt sure it would wreck our lives, that were now so perfect, well almost.

The extension was going well, Charlie was doing a great job, even on days like this when the winds blew in from the east. It was time for lunch, dad was out all day so the house was empty and with Daisy asleep having a much needed afternoon nap, I was in desperate need of some dirty love, so with that firmly on my mind I ran us a naughty bath, filled with delicate bubbles. I called Charlie in, leading him to the bathroom as I wanted to seduce him right now, at this very moment. *Lizzy*, he gasped, it's mid-afternoon you naughty girl, the builders will be wondering where I am.

I didn't care, I wanted and needed his dirty loving and I was going to have it. Charlie was now naked and his cock was standing to my attention, just the way I loved it; full, hard, and stiff with dirty juice for my pussy that was now demanding his love constantly every day, to quench my appetite for Charlie's dirty love.

Charlie kissed my neck. I felt his fingertips find my rigid nipples that just begged to be sucked, hard and long.

Relaxed now and Charlie's toe was naughtily playing with my pussy lips. I closed my eyes as I enjoyed the dirty sensation he was creating, his eyes now flirted with mine, I felt like the naughty virginal schoolgirl he had fallen deeply in love with all those years ago.

We made our way back to our bed for some very serious dirty sex. His cock was now wanting to embrace the demands of my purring pussy. The pressure built, I felt Charlie's cock loving my pussy completely and to the limits. Charlie's kisses were seductive, sensual, and dirty, as was his moaning. *Your pussy, it's so fucking loveable princess, so very fucking lovable.*

After loving my pussy it was time to love my mouth, so with my lips tightly over his huge cock it received the Lizzy loving and I was rewarded with Charlie's warm, fresh juice coating my throat. Charlie firmly held my head for maximum pleasure, his juice was now smeared across my lips ready for Charlie's kisses.

My thighs now tightly gripped Charlie's head while his lips locked onto my clit in a bid to deliver the ultimate dirty sex, as now he was licking my juice drenched Pussy, leaving his juice coated kisses peppered over my thighs.

Our lunch time sex session had lasted almost two hours and I was loving the fact I could have all the dirty love I craved on demand day or night, which made me smile contentedly.

Feeling satisfied, Charlie went back to work and as he walked out of the door. He grabbed my hand, pulling me into his arms, his grip firm around my waist whispering, *I have not finished with you yet Lizzy.* I blushed as he smiled his addictive, powerful smile.

Knowing that our addictive dirty love would be ours again tonight and every other night we shared a bed, I was never going to object.

Friday afternoon came and Charlie was heading back to Cardiff for the weekend to see his son, a weekend that I dreaded for myself, but I was pleased that Helen had given her approval for Charlie to see his son, a visit that was long overdue. Suddenly, he pulled me into his arms, his kisses peppered my face, which always made me smile. *I love you both, never forget you're my girls, my forever girls, my beautiful Princesses,* but once again he looked pre occupied, something was so seriously wrong and again my mind had all those reoccurring thoughts that behind his smile lay a tormented, mysterious and a very private life about to splinter into thousands of fragments.

Charlie was now sat in his car, his expression was terrifying as he slumped against the steering wheel, his hands holding his head. He started the engine and sat motionless, statue like, hesitating before looking back at us, waving to us both, his fake smile fully on show that masked a story that taunted and traumatised me, flashing before my eyes this afternoon was every image that haunted my hours of darkness.

We waved our emotional goodbyes, his smiles today left me cold and empty as I remained tormented by the life I was convinced he was leading back in Wales. Today Charlie didn't leave me in a cocoon of dirty love that had always embraced me, delighted me, and kept me as hostage, he left me flat, alone, cold, and unhappy.

Daisy and I wanted for nothing, we had money, Charlie had money and lots of it, as he was always lavishing us both with expensive gifts. Every time he came home he was laden with gifts, but my concerns were now that he spent a lot of time on the phone, his muted expression crippled his face that once only held the trademark smile that I adored, but I put that down to work, or maybe it was because he was about to spend another long awaited weekend with his son. Having Helen in the background was not going to be easy and as I panicked for him my shaking hand reached for the ring on my necklace. I twiddled with it, almost snapping the chain again in a bid for answers.

Maybe I should have forced the questions, demanded answers as now my mind suffered with the many nagging doubts that had left me in utter turmoil, never finding a solution to my ever growing suspicions.

Princess never forget I love you were Charlie's last words as he left again for Wales, words that now echoed in my head and repeated over and over again, with his haunting words that now terrified me, knowing he was in some sort of trouble.

I sat while feeding Daisy thinking about what Charlie had not said that afternoon, rather than what he did say. It was now terrifying me, leaving me petrified, seeing Helen's vision pacing backwards and forwards, her gaze fixed on mine with her arms folded, her emotions stagnant, her beautiful long blond hair, her sapphire blue eyes burning bright and of course her slim silhouette which made her stance even more powerful, but I could hear the roar from her muted words, the roar that was building into the most violent of storms and it was heading my way once again.

CHAPTER 31

I spent the weekend relaxing with Daisy, singing her songs, and pulling silly faces to make her smile and giggle. Her little cheeks would puff up like little balls that would turn bright red with laughter, leaving her breathless with chuckles.

Charlie was due back on Sunday night, but he hadn't rung me over the weekend which was a little odd and again sent my mind into working overtime. Why had he not called? Why had he not bothered? Did he really not care about us anymore? Especially Daisy.

It was 7pm Sunday evening and he was not back; I was worried, extremely worried. I rang him again and again, his phone was not in service, what the hell was happening? Again I was left alone, scared, helpless, and menaced by unwanted visions and voices that now were queuing to tell me it was all my fault, my misspent youth, my so called innocence following a dream that would end in terrifying pain.

I started to panic, what if he had an accident? What if, what if he had resumed his relationship with Helen? Dad was concerned, I could see it in his eyes, I could feel the hurt he was feeling for Daisy and me.

Charlie did not come home that night or any night that week, nor that month. I worried that I should have reported him missing, to have called the police or should have gone to Wales in a desperate bid to find him myself, my head was spinning out of control with what I should have done, but didn't. Maybe I was too afraid to learn the truth, not knowing was probably less painful.

I was so damn mad with him and so very angry. At that moment I wished I had not told him about Daisy; I should have kept her all to myself, making a life for her and me away from the torment that seemed to follow me around, sticking to me like glue, wanting me to repay at any cost my stupidity.

Tonight like most nights I laid awake going over and over every scenario in my head, playing it out in multi colour what had lead us to this stage in our lives. I heard the rain crashing against the window and that was my only company, wave after wave of torrential cold rain lashed every pain of glass, pounding rain that seemed so loud, but even its noise could not stop the vile images and unwelcome voices that seemed louder than the storm that now ravaged the pretty Wiltshire village I still called home.

I awoke with a startle, terrified by haunting dreams, vile images leaving me cold. Suddenly I was overcome with hate for him, a hate that I never thought I could feel for Charlie as once again my life spiralled and dark days followed. Some days it was hard for me to cope, I had a young baby with my lifetime lover who had promised the world, that now had managed to deliver nothing, breaking every piece of my heart again and not for the first time, knowing now why so many people had told me he was not worthy of my love and affection, I should have listened.

With my head spinning I walked around the garden with Daisy in my arms for comfort. As tears laden my eyes I looked at Daisy, our perfect Daisy. I was at a loss to know why, or for what reason Charlie felt like abandoning us, discarding us, leaving us to pick up every splintered piece, leaving my hands blood stained with wounds of discarded love.

Now in the blink of an eye spring was here at last. I loved watching the garden burst into life with succulent colours springing up throughout the garden, vibrant yellows, perfect pink, lipstick red, passionate purples with the odd glimpse of dazzling white.

I would sit on the big wooden swing with Daisy on my lap for hours on end wishing the hours to just disappear while I remained lost in heartache and pain, my fragile body aching for Charlie, aching for his arms to hold me tight, aching for his lips to kiss mine and to hear him tell me he loved me.

I was worried so much so that I called the people and all the contractors that might know him or know where he was, but nothing, no one had heard from him, or seen him. I even phoned G to find out if he was in London, sadly G knew nothing, but invited us to stay with the family in London, to have a break back in the city that had stolen my heart which was kind of him, but I declined for now.

I never thought it would be like this, it was extremely hard to deal with. Daisy was missing him so much as she would constantly look around the bedroom and the lounge hoping to see him or to hear his voice. She deserved better, so much better.

Dad did not seem surprised, but I knew he was worried. I think he had a rough opinion about Charlie, but no one knew him like me or so

I thought until now, maybe I didn't know him at all? Maybe he was a stranger that I had fallen in love with? But if he was a stranger then he had still managed to seduce me.

In the weeks following I tried hard to come to terms with the fact that he was not coming back and finding myself in a dark and very lonely place, constantly worrying about Charlie, knowing in the back of my mind it had to be serious.

My heart and soul were now aching for him as my body continued to crave some dirty love by the only man that could deliver my much needed desires. My head said forget him, but how the hell could I? That would never happen as my heart would not let me, the chains would never free me from the hostage I had become all those years ago, chains that now cut so deep, bleeding open wounds that tattooed my skin. Maybe I should not have been surprised? I had been told on so many occasions that he was trouble, his reputation even then, way back in the early stages of our love worried me, but it had seduced me, being young and easily impressed by his cocky attitude, by his ability to make it so easy to fall so easily in love with him.

Once again I was in desperate need to relive some beautiful memories as I looked across the fields into the woods willing them to take me on a journey, any journey far from the here and now and I did not have to wait long as glorious voices and aromas filled my senses as I travelled back in time, to a beautiful time in my life.

Suddenly a cold shrill embraced me. Mum was here in my old bedroom, smiling at me, her perfume awakening my senses as I reached out to touch her, wanting desperately to hold her hand, but suddenly and to my utter shock my bedroom door slammed closed, making me jump back to the here and now. I couldn't smell mum's perfume now, she was gone, my tears were blinding my vision in disbelief, but yet again mum's vision had been replaced by Helen's. I screamed at her, picking up a trinket box from my window sill, throwing it violently at her in a bid to smash her unwelcome vision. The trinket box smashed into the door with force, causing Helens vision to dissolve across the floor. Before I was able to breathe a sigh of relief I was for now alone, to capture my memories as today they were not for sharing.

My life and dreams were once again destroyed by Charlie who promised me everything repeatedly, promising me that my childhood dreams would be a reality only to snatch them away from me, leaving my body fragile and now terrified of my future and Daisy's too.

I wanted Daisy to have her daddy here to see her take the first steps, say her first words and to comfort her when she cut her first tooth, to go to her first ballet lessons and going to buy her first pair of shoes, things he would miss if he did not return and return quick with answers that I so desperately needed to hear.

I constantly went over and over everything, still nothing made any sense as I continued beating myself up every day with so many what ifs. I needed answers and those answers needed to come from Charlie and not the necklace that I constantly seemed to reach for in these trying days.

Daisy and I grew increasingly close. I was now her mum, her dad, her everything. I would never allow her to go without love. I wanted her to have an amazing childhood just like I did, to attend the local school, to have the freedom to explore her surroundings, to go on adventures into the woods, ride her bike for miles, to run across the fields, to chase rainbows and to be able to recall her precious childhood just like I could.

As the days rolled by, all blurring into one, I put all my effort into bringing up Daisy as a single mum, to make her childhood amazing. The Summer was now here, Daisy had started to really develop well, she loved being in the garden with me as much as possible, she was delightfully perfect with her dark hair hung in little ringlets framing the beautiful pale skin of her face, her eyes the deepest brown and now the sun had given her a beautiful rosy glow. She was picture perfect and with that I took lots of pictures so that if Charlie ever came back into our lives... How stupid could I be, I knew deep down he was never coming home, but I needed to keep the hope alive so that we could show him our adventures, big and small, but all so very important to us both, creating memories together to share later in our lives.

It was now only three months ago that we said a normal goodbye to Charlie, waving and blowing kisses, but now I knew it wasn't just a normal goodbye on that cold Friday afternoon and nothing if I was honest had changed for me. I loved him deeply and always would, but this was so difficult to digest as I constantly relived his words on that fateful Friday, hoping it might trigger something in my muddled mind to shed some light on his whereabouts.

I kept a diary to help me express exactly how I felt. I expressed myself with no holding back, all the good things as well as the bad, so on those really difficult days I would return to my old bedroom to stare out of the window, to chase those rainbows and dreams that were still so vivid in my memory, recalling my memories of mum, Charlie and everything that was my little world that was now feeling desperately empty, cold, and lifeless.

Not a day passed that I did not think of him, cried for him, worried for him, prayed for him and on the odd occasion I would fantasise about him, especially when I was in the bath as that was our favourite place, the place we always could have what we called our time, that would always lead us to expressing our dirty love for each other.

I used the vibrator when I felt the need, but now it was not the same without him, it never would be, as our dirty love needed both of us in the same room to embrace us both, to fill us both full of the most amazing love that we had created together.

Daisy was passing milestones day by day, growing up so fast she was a great comfort to me without Charlie, as every day she became more like him. Her brown eyes and huge smile a legacy passed on from her daddy, a daddy she may never get to know as it was obvious he was not coming home to the princesses that he promised we were daily.

Friends asked me out, but I declined again and again as my life was on hold for now, but on hold for what? Why was I waiting? It seemed like I had been waiting for my life to revolve again around something that would never happen while Charlie was absent from my life.

I went into my shell, allowing it to became my protection against the outside world and all it could throw at me, but once again the overriding feeling was that I felt cheated out of Charlie's love, his lifetime of love that we both committed to, but his commitment had been short lived as now he had chosen to break his part of the commitment, breaking it into millions of pieces, discarding our love just like he had chosen to do all those years ago, but this was different, huge in comparison.

I started to think about Helen and Charlie's son. I wanted to contact her, but I didn't know if it was the right thing to do. Would it be too upsetting for me and for her as I wanted Daisy to know her step brother, and Charlie knew that as we had talked about it so often, promising both of them that they would be in each other's lives.

Once again I wondered about Helen as she had chosen to enter my world on frequent occasions without any invitation, but now thankfully her vision had diminished since my violent outburst along with many of my nightly visitors.

The weeks just flew by, and Daisy was now crawling and talking in her own way, her little mumbled sounds and gurgles were so cute. Charlie was missing so much, milestones that could never be replaced, all these precious memories that he would never be able to recall. I was hurt for Daisy especially.

I went out for lots of walks to all the places Charlie and I used to visit, just to rekindle all the wonderful memories we shared, the intimate times, the sad times and all the times that were ours and that I hoped we would share again, as there had been so many and all of them to treasure. I was going to make sure Daisy knew how special our love had been and still was.

While taking Daisy out for her daily walk I met much to my surprise Charlie's grandmother. I avoided the pleasantries and was direct and to the point as I asked her if she knew where Charlie was. She seemed surprised that I asked and uneasy about my questions as I repeated them, hesitating while she looked constantly at Daisy who smiled back at her the trademark smile that was Charlie's, wondering to myself if Daisy was a secret to everyone. Daisy had been conceived through such an amazing love and a very special love that I shared with her grandson, and she knew that I loved him and that I had always been besotted by him since I was a fifteen year old virgin, that I had let him take freely away from me.

Still she looked at me blankly, still not wanting to divert her eyes away from Daisy, before looking back at me her focus now on my necklace. Her glare was almost burning the my delicate skin. I asked her if she knew Daisy was Charlie's daughter. She looked at me blankly, *no I didn't know about her, I'm sorry Lizzy. I don't see him at all now, I thought he was in Wales working.* I started to cry. *Lizzy I'm sorry, I did not want to upset you.* I was annoyed with myself that I had let her into Daisy's life, even if it was briefly. I said my goodbyes and left, glaring at her in a bid to make her feel something, some compassion for Daisy at least, but nothing was forthcoming.

I got home and fed Daisy, showering her in all my sloppy kisses. Thank god I had her, as while I had her, I had a lifeline to Charlie, even if it was a small lifeline, but I hated myself for the love I still held for him. I should now hate him, obliterate him from our lives for good, but still I held him in my heart that remained heavy with dirty and overwhelming love for him.

With my mind now made up I was going to call Helen tomorrow, as I had to know if he was with her playing happy families, but even if he wasn't I intended to tell her everything from being his mistress, to having his baby, she was going to hear it all, even if it meant there would be a war of words.

After a night of tossing and turning I was on a mission to find answers as I started to search for Helen's telephone number, in the hope it would still be the same one. I searched high and low finding her number on a tiny scrap of paper in the bottom of my bag.

I was still so sad as my heart broke a little more every day. I remained bitter that he had left us so casually, I felt like we had been discarded and it felt at times like Helen was having the last laugh, maybe they were back together, or maybe Charlie had yet another princess that demanded his full attention. My mind worked overtime to fill in the blanks, but now there were far too many blanks to fill in.

I plucked up the courage and strength for Daisy's sake to make the call, so I dialled the number I never thought I would dial. Suddenly a voice answered, my mouth once again so dry as I blurted out the name that now seemed to choke me.

Hello, can I speak to Charlie Stevens please? My voice was harsh and impatient with a stressful and blunt edge. *I'm afraid he does not work from this number anymore.* She asked me who I was, I had no problem in telling her my name. *It's Lizzy.* The silence at the other end of the phone was deafening, I listened to her silence. *Lizzy!* I screamed at her; my voice was now quivering as I repeated my name. I asked about Charlie, still silence ruled at the other end of the phone as I continued freely to tell her about my sordid dirty love affair with her husband, telling her that I had been his whore, his bitch and his tart, sleeping with him on every occasion we could get. She obviously did not like my outburst as with that she slammed the phone down and suddenly I heard the roar of the storm gathering pace once again. Reeling from my verbal outburst, I felt sick at my ability to speak to someone like that, I hated myself that I had now ruined any chance of finding the answers I so needed. I didn't know what to do next, at a loss to know what to do for the best, it seemed that I needed to do more to find him, as this was not fair on Daisy, but I had spent too much time waiting for him over the years and now I was not prepared to wait anymore, or was I?

How would Daisy grow up without a daddy? How would I tell her? What would I tell her? Charlie had yet again managed to spoil this amazing time in our lives that we should have shared as a family, but that now had been wrecked and once again wrecked by him and his selfish reputation.

I was so totally devastated for Daisy, knowing Charlie would miss her fist day at school, her first sports day, her first boyfriend, her first disco her first of everything.

This was not how we planned it, this should have been a beautiful, amazing time in our lives, to cherish watching Daisy grow, watching her chase rainbows, to see her creating her very own dreams.

I thought I should go to Cardiff to go back to the cabin to see if it held any clues about Charlie's mysterious disappearance. I had a key and it would be nice to go back to let it seduce me again, to allow myself to enjoy a little more of its beauty, but what if I found something I didn't like? What if he was with someone that had replaced me? What if? What if? My mind was playing silly tricks, in utter turmoil once again, but the cabin could hold all the clues that might shed some light on Charlie's mysterious life that was still shrouded in a dark veil, casting a cold unwelcome interference in our lives, but on reflection now was not the best time to take the long journey, so I put it to the back of my mind, but only for now as I knew my thoughts would be drawn to taking the journey I so dreaded.

I continued to write in my diary every day, I wrote about my feelings and what they meant to me, almost lashing out with every word I wrote, holding the pen so tight almost tearing the paper. I was astounded by the deeply sad comments that I wrote, most of which were heart-breaking to read, but all had been written from my heart, deep feelings that reflected every last living nightmare that I endured on a daily basis, tears now stained the paper I wrote on, smudging the words I had written, tears that splashed from the paper onto my already love-torn skin, leaving yet more open wounds and bare tattoos.

Breaking from the relentless torture for now dad and I bought two Christmas trees, one for the main lounge and one for my lounge. I spent all day on Saturday decorating them. Daisy was delighted to play with the decorations and all the tissue paper that they were wrapped in.

My glass snowflake took pride of place as it always had done and as I stared at it I caught a reflection beaming back at me. The reflection was Charlie, his face was now everywhere I looked within this house, along with the garden that continued to ignite sparks that had Charlie's name engraved on.

I then ran myself a lovely bubble bath with candles that flickered in the background as I relaxed having my time, a time when as always my thoughts drifted to Charlie, wondering if he was thinking of us as much as I was thinking about him. I thought about him every day, but the evenings were the hardest to deal with and tonight was just one of them, a time when I needed Charlie's dirty love.

The 22nd came and it was our beautiful Daisy's first birthday. I signed her card from mummy and daddy, drenching it with kisses. Daisy received masses of presents and cards, her little face was beaming as she was only interested in playing with the wrapping paper. She would scrunch it up into shapes, trying to throw them, her infectious laugh would just make me smile.

I was making a memory box for Daisy so all her cards would be wrapped in pink shiny ribbons and then put in the box until the time was right to let her unwrap it, along with the letter Charlie had written.

Christmas came and went in a blink of an eye, every day tarnished with hatred, but laced with an overwhelming heartache that was at times so hard to cope with, but Daisy remained my focus the reason to carry on, regardless of the tarnished past Charlie led.

It snowed heavily for two weeks, almost cutting the sleepy Wiltshire village off from the outside world. Daisy and I would play in the snow, both of us in wellington boots, Daisy's were pink with flowers, her scarf and hat matched. She looked adorable and as the snow fell around us she would try to catch each snow flake in her hands. Her face would be so disappointed as they melted and disappeared before her pretty little eyes.

Just watching her enjoy the snow reminded me of Charlie and I, as we loved days like these when he would be constantly kissing my frozen lips, warming my ice cold hands in his, but now they were just memories from my past, nothing more as he now had made sure of that, putting all our wonderful memories into jeopardy.

New year was approaching and my new contract would arrive soon, I was petrified to think I would have to leave Daisy with child minders, not knowing how far apart we would be and that was agony for me.

By mid-January Daisy took her first steps, unaided, what a proud moment. My only wish was that Charlie could have shared this triumphant moment, to celebrate yet another milestone that could never be replaced. It was the last day of January and my contract laid on the doormat ready for my signature so with my hands shaking I opened the massive envelope to reveal my next development schedule and placement,

Scotland. Scotland jumped off the paper, it was a world away from the here and now, away from the sleepy Wiltshire village we had always called home, the placement was 16 weeks, 16 weeks of child care and 16 weeks away from Daisy, dad, and the safety of home. Without hesitation I dismissed the request for my signature, knowing I would never leave Daisy, I couldn't.

Daisy was only tiny, she would miss me, as I would miss her, and I was not prepared to leave her. I had made my choice from the minute I saw the location; I was not going to take the contract in Scotland. Daisy was my priority, and she was so much more important so I rang the office and told them my decision, they were disappointed, but fully understood my reasons.

I started to think about going to Cardiff for a weekend with Daisy, knowing full well it would be emotional, knowing I would once again be seduced by the journey, but my mind was now completely clear and it was what I needed to do so I made the emotional journey, retracing the steps up to the cabin. I was now so very nervous at what I might find, but I had to do something as my emotions and thoughts were endless, now as I turned into the lane the cute cabin looked unloved, cold in its appearance and so very neglected.

I struggled to get the key in the lock as my hands were shaking violently. I suddenly managed to force the door open as piles of unopened post jammed the door. I managed to squeeze in with Daisy and it was instantly apparent Charlie had not been here for a very long time.

I lit the fire for some heat as I sorted through the post, it seemed like there was nothing really to shed any light on Charlie's whereabouts, bank statements with no entries or withdrawals, but a huge amount of money laden his account that made me even more suspicious. Maybe he had left the country and gone abroad to live? To hide away from us, from something or someone, this was total torture for me.

I checked all the drawers for some sort of clue to his mysterious life and as I did, to my surprise I found some of my underwear that I had left here to use when we spent our loving weekends together, when Charlie could slip away to spend quality time with me, his tart, his bitch, his whore, and his forever love. Daisy had fallen asleep in my arms, the fire was now so mellow, capturing the full beauty. I closed my eyes, allowing the cute cabin to seduce me once again and I freely let it, absorbing the love that I had left here and recalling the love Charlie and I had made here.

Feeling exasperated Daisy and I went to bed and on awaking I was treated yet again to vivid memories of our dirty love affair that we had shared here together. I was loving the intimacy once again that this cabin allowed me to recall.

Daisy and I took a visit to Cardiff. There was one place I needed to visit for old times' sake, to just sit in the window once more to watch people scurrying around, to just people watch as I drank my hot chocolate once again in this delightful cafe.

Now back at home and with the spring months approaching I had made my mind up to get out more and to enjoy life, after all I was free to do as I pleased, to let myself break free from the heavy chains that continued to embrace me as Charlie's hostage, so I called a few friends and we set a date for a girly night out.

My figure was back to normal and I looked good, even if I said it myself, so with an excuse now to go shopping I bought new clothes that hugged me in all the right places, knowing full well it was all done in a bid to retaliate against Charlie, to indulge myself in anything to blot out my continuing misery of a lonely life without the dirty love I craved.

Saturday evening came, I got ready and as I looked in the mirror I was delighted at my reflection, but as I looked closer Helen stood steely faced in the background, blemishing my image as she snarled at me. I glared back and as I did her image faded, but I had to admit I still found her image terrifying.

I knew Charlie would have adored my new lean, toned body and how he would have loved to seduce me, but my body was now on offer for someone else to enjoy, for someone else to admire. My bitterness once again was rearing its ugly head, but I just shrugged it off, a new Lizzy was being created, but I was never going to like her as I would and had already grown to dislike her.

Dad kissed me goodbye, squeezing my hand. *Lizzy you have a lovely evening and try to forget about things just for a while.* I smiled, if only it was that easy. I grabbed my bag and again I checked my phone just in case Charlie had called, but not this evening or any other evening.

I felt a little nervous to be going out again after all this time, checking every minute that Charlie had not tried to call me, checking my phone that had now become such a habit, but it gave me a little hope to cling to, just like the ring that still hung on my necklace.

Meeting up with the girls, some of which I hadn't seen in years, was a great distraction from my ongoing torment, but it still felt very odd as it had been so long since I had been out alone, but we had a lovely evening, all us girls together, catching up with the here and now and continuing to relive our childhoods that all of us agreed were fantastic.

We all seemed to be the centre of attention as blokes attempted to chat us all up which made me feel excited, knowing that I could still attract male attention, but I could never allow myself the intimacy with anyone other than Charlie as no one else could deliver my constant cravings and my sexual desires, my body was his and it always had been, but even more so now.

The girls had arranged more nights out, but I declined as I felt it unfair to bog them down with my heartache, as Charlie was my only conversation apart from Daisy. I was not interested in meeting blokes, hearing their false and somewhat cheesy chat up lines. Charlie was the only man I ever wanted and constantly craved, but he had filled my heart to the limit with constant heartache so there was never going to be any room left for anyone else, my mind and heart were now overcrowded.

Back to my sanctuary I laid on the bed, my mind wandering, thinking about Charlie and where he was and if he was thinking of us as much as we were thinking about him, but sadly only he could answer that, knowing that I had to do a tremendous amount of soul searching and It was not going to be easy. I thought I would go to Cardiff again soon to stay a little longer and tidy up the cabin to make it a little get away for Daisy and I, thinking it might help me get through this utter nightmare seemed would never get any better.

I must have fallen asleep as it was the middle of the night when I awoke, still in my clothes and still clutching my phone waiting for the elusive call that would set my world alight again. I got myself into bed for much needed sleep, allowing me to shut out all the demons for now that continued to march heavily in my head every day, but I knew the demons from my waking moments would be replaced by my nightly terrors of vile images and haunting voices that invaded my dreams.

The spring days rolled into summer days, I loved all the seasons as each one brought back such evocative senses, each of them different, but each one involved the man I loved so much, that sparked muted emotions, so there was only one place I could really digest the perfect memories and that was at my old bedroom window. As I stood there today instantly I could hear the rush of the breeze in the trees that flanked the fields, hearing them calling Charlie's name as they swayed gracefully, allowing me to hear his name clearly, but I wanted more today so I opened the window wide to take in its full beauty and I wasn't disappointed, I never was.

CHAPTER 32

The months went by, and I loved and adored being a mum. We were passing huge milestones that Charlie and I should have experienced together. I took as many photos as possible to record the delightful days we spent together, but alone without the one person we both would have adored to have been part of our photographs that now would be Charlie's only access to Daisy's enchanting childhood.

Now 4 years on and Daisy was about to start at the local village school, my little girl was growing up so very fast, but her innocent childhood was something I adored and wanted her to embrace.

The September day finally came when I had to say goodbye to her at the school gate, she looked so little compared to the other kids, now dressed in her little uniform, a blue skirt, white crisp blouse, and blue cardigan complete with her school bag and straw hat. She looked so cute, adorably cute now with her little black patent shoes that just sparkled in the September sunlight...

I left her, I left her in a big class with kids she didn't know. I sobbed all the way home and worried about her every minute of the day as I wandered from room to room not knowing what to do with my time. I headed again to my old bedroom for some much needed company, and I looked out of the window, my mind was drenched in glorious memories that enriched my life every day, emotions that were sometimes so cruel and raw, bringing tears to my eyes, blurring the vision of my lifetime of memories. The trees that flanked the fields were now turning colour, breaking away from the vibrant greens to more subdued colours, mixed with glorious ambers and russet reds.

At last it was 3pm, time to collect my world from the school gates as I was craving to hear her talk about her first day at school, another monumental day for us that I captured on camera that Charlie had so sadly missed by his inability to keep his promises that now were laced in a cocktail of spiteful bitterness. I wanted Daisy to grow up knowing that she would have to work hard to enable her to achieve great things and to enjoy a great social life, just like I had done which allowed me back into my school day memories when I was a virgin, embracing everything that had now become the most treasured gifts, recalling every emotion of which there had been plenty.

I stood alone at the gate of the school fifteen minutes before Daisy was due out and I saw her eagerly waiting at the door to the playground waving to me, beaming her adorable smile, before she came running out. *Mummy, mummy*. I picked her up in my arms, spinning her around as tears drenched my face. I peppered her in kisses, blowing raspberries onto her neck that made her squeal.

This was a day that Charlie should have been here, to see her on her first day at school, and to say the least I was bitterly disappointed for her. I looked around the little playground seeing all the other dads enjoying being part of this wonderful experience, I felt agonisingly sad for Daisy, but she never questioned his absence.

Weeks later and out of the blue the headteacher approached me about an office job at the school. I was thrilled when I managed to secure the job on a part time basis as it suited me perfectly and I loved it as I was never far away from Daisy every day, to watch her grow into a little mini me.

The following years just flew by, and I had come to terms with the fact that Charlie was not coming home, not now, not ever. We were once again alone, just Daisy and I as I thought we would be at some stage and now my instincts were correct.

Daisy was nearing her last few weeks at junior school, where on earth had the time gone? She was nearly 11 years old. We often talked about Charlie, especially when we sat either in the garden or snuggled up together in the old tree house where I would tell her stories about her daddy and how much love we had for each other, convincing her he had gone to live and work abroad. Her eyes would light up when I mentioned his name and I would watch her nose wrinkle up with laughter when I told her about the funny things that Charlie did, like the night he waited outside in the freezing cold, waiting for mum and dad to go to bed. I explained the mystery ring, I wanted her to know all about Charlie so I showed her letters, cards and photographs that I had kept and treasured for moments like this, our amazing story and lifetime of love, a love that I never questioned until now, all these years on.

The summer months were great, and I took Daisy abroad on holiday. It was fantastic, warm and sunny, the perfect place to relax together, even to let my mind relax from the daily torment that still raged on, never allowing me the freedom from torment.

We also went to Cardiff for a few little breaks to the cute cabin that we now called our second home. It was just what I needed and for Daisy to be able to feel a little bit of Charlie around us. We would walk in the woods that surrounded the cabin, embracing yet more memories that Charlie and I had created there. School term now was just around the corner and Daisy's new school was mine and Charlie's old secondary school, which I hoped Daisy would love and embrace just like I had done all those years ago, the very school in which I fell in love with a boy who had a seductive and very secret reputation that still to this very day I didn't know why, a boy who with the most incredible cocky smile and that called me his princess every day.

I hoped Daisy would do well; I knew she would as she was very talented. She loved art, photography, and all things creative. Nothing would be too much effort for her, she had an amazing yearning to learn and to absorb life. She loved everyone without judgement, without prejudice and with a love that rubbed off on everyone that she came into contact with. She was a delightful girl with a very bright and positive future ahead of her, just as her end of junior school report said.

The day came and Daisy was stood in her new uniform. She really did look just like me, so much like me I found it so hard to hide my tears as my dream wish was that Charlie could have seen her today, as she embarked on her journey into the big wide world of teenage life. Daisy met her friends at the end of the road, they all walked together to the bus stop just like I had done all those delightful years ago.

I wanted her to have a great school and social life, wanting her to be aware of everything that I was not at her age, to be able to talk openly about anything and everything, something that was never possible for me.

As the years past us by my love for Charlie remained strong in my heart and would continue forever, my heart could never let that love go as I had to hold on to it forever with all the strength I had left as one day we might be reunited.

Daisy was now 16 and so grown up with a very wise and firm level head, knowing her own mind and having her head firmly screwed on, having decided that a career in art or photography was what she wanted to do. Dad was always on hand to help her, to give her advice should she ask for it. They loved being together as they had a real bond, they would talk for hours. Dad would talk to her about mum and sometimes even about Charlie although his conversation remained cold when he mentioned Charlie's name.

A few weeks later and results day arrived. I was a nervous wreck, my hands clammy and cold, Daisy seemed very calm considering. All of us prayed that she would do well, we knew she had worked and studied so hard she deserved a great set of results.

We had to wait for the postman to do his round on his faithful red and blue bicycle that seemed to take forever, particularly today, knowing his unforgettable and somewhat tattered blue bag would be brimming with eagerly awaited results. I looked back again on memories; it seemed like a lifetime ago when I was in labour waiting for Daisy to come into our lives and now we were all waiting again, but this time for her future to be delivered.

It was a long wait as I paced the living room floor backwards and forwards, strangling the necklace that hung around my neck, feeling the chain cutting ever deeper into my porcelain skin. I twiddled it over and over again, so needing the comfort of my bedroom window I stood for a few moments to once again be transported, to capture the many emotions that still waited patiently to be found.

Suddenly I heard Daisy calling me, her voice was raised with sheer excitement, at last the long awaited envelope slipped through the letter box. We all stood starring at the letter that lay alone on the door mat, all of us totally silent, totally still, and motionless.

Daisy opened the pristine white envelope while dad and I held our breath in anticipation for the big reveal. We could all hear her breathing as the room was so silent and we could clearly see her hands that were shaking as she struggled to get the envelope open.

I watched her face, she was so incredibly petit and so stunningly beautiful, her face then lit up. *I've done it mum! I've done it grandad!* She was screeching as she jumped up and down with sheer delight and joy. *Daisy that's fantastic news.* Once again I struggled to hold my emotions back as the tears of joy blurred my eyes, feeling the emotional lump in my throat that almost choked me.

Daisy looked up from her amazing results smiling her trademark smile that had Charlie written all over it. *Dad would be proud of me mum wouldn't he?* I nodded, *yes Daisy very proud of you.* The lump still stuck in my throat as I held back the tears I so wanted to shed, but they would have to wait until I was alone. Daisy then read the college details with a trembling, but very happy voice. *London mum, it's London.* I gasped, holding my breath until Daisy had finished her eloquent words. *Daisy that's fantastic.* We then hugged each other with sheer delight.

Taking myself into the garden to come to terms with Daisy's exciting news I stood at the open view that led me into the woods, allowing my mind to wander as I captured more delightful dreams that I now wanted so desperately to share with Charlie so I climbed up into the very old tree house that had become very rickety with age. Instantly I heard his voice, allowing it to dance with me, to seduce me and to wrap me in a cocoon, remembering we had sat here on that beautiful summer's day, the day he named our baby, our little girl. I could hear his voice clearly as now I could feel his warm breath on my skin. I took in his aroma that was heavy in the air, what a delightful moment.

The days that followed I had some thoughts that Daisy and I could both live and work in London. Daisy seemed comfortable and somewhat excited with my proposal. *That would allow me to invest my time in my photography, really put my heart and soul into it, even do more courses and get a job to fund our move.* I had money put aside and dad wanted to invest money for Daisy.

One evening after our supper dad called Daisy and myself into the lounge. We felt like naughty girls about to be told off, Daisy giggled all the way down the hall. I tried hard to keep a straight face which seemed to make her giggle even more.

We stood in front of dad who looked very serious with his hands behind his back. Daisy was still holding her breath, trying to hide her giggles from dad as I nudged her to stop. *I have something for you both, Daisy this is for you to help you through collage.* He handed her a large white envelope, Daisy opened it and as she did she gasped, her face was stunned. *Grandad this is too much. No Daisy it's yours and you will need it, you have worked very hard it's my way of saying well done, I am so very proud of you.*

Daisy kissed her grandad then turned to me showing me the cheque dad had written, I gasped *Daisy, Dad. Lizzy say nothing please.* Dad then handed me an envelope. *And this is for you Lizzy, to help you get a home for you and Daisy.* I opened it, holding my breath. *Dad, I can't take this. Lizzy, I want you to have it, put it as a deposit on a little place for you both I know it won't get you far, but it's a start.*

The days rolled by, and we planned to the letter our new life in London. It was going to be very exciting and very special, another new adventure, just Daisy and I. We were like two peas in a pod, so alike in many ways as we both loved photography and art. Daisy remained my mini me, but she did have such a lot of Charlie's qualities and nature about her.

Daisy and I went to London for a week to visit the college in which would become her future. Daisy was so excited as she walked around, impressed that she had made it by putting in the extra study time to be rewarded by this amazing opportunity. I knew she would fit in here perfectly, to embrace it and everything that London would challenger her with and it would.

We also searched for somewhere to live and to look for work for me. I knew I had a little time to find somewhere to work as I had a cushion of money to fall back on what with the money I had saved over the years and now with dad's help we could afford somewhere nice to live.

I wanted Daisy to join me in a visit to Charlie's and mine most favourite place, Regents Park, the most romantic place I knew. We both loved London, it had so much to offer. I told her about the lovely moments Charlie and I shared here, she also fell in love with it instantly, allowing itself to wrap us both in its own very unique blanket of love.

We had decided to buy a flat, it seemed the best thing to do, we would rent for a while so that we could search for the perfect home, a place that we would never want to leave, to call it home. We found a nice cosy flat in north London, a great place to rent. It was pleasant with lots of open green spaces, shops, cinema, cafés and a good social life, lots for Daisy and I to get involved with, but for me Charlie remained my every waking moment and that would continue here in London as I was not ready to let him go free, not just yet anyway.

We would miss dad, village life and the house in which both Daisy and I had grown up in, with all its treasured memories that I would again recall, but the big wider world was out there calling us both to board yet another roller-coaster, at the start of a new and refreshing journey. Daisy and I would thrive on our new adventure, we were going to take every opportunity that London would give us, to embrace it.

We were ready to embrace life in the big smoke and everything that went with it, maybe it was what I needed to get on with my life, to put Charlie and his love behind me, I knew deep down that would never happen because if I were totally honest I still loved him passionately.

Luckily, I had managed to get a few interviews lined up, but out of the blue the old company that I worked for in Cardiff and London got in touch. They wanted someone in the office to be based in the heart of London working Monday to Friday, I accepted without hesitation, it was so perfect for me.

I had worked hard to get here, bringing up Daisy alone without her daddy in our lives. Not that I would have changed any bit of Daisy's wonderful life, as I was so proud of her, proud that Charlie and I made her from the most incredible dirty love, and she knew that as we often talked about him. I wanted her to know all about him, I kept nothing from her, well almost, but she knew I would always love her daddy endlessly.

The move was only two weeks away, then suddenly as if I blinked the day had come. Daisy and I were on our own in north London, I was now in my early 40s and once again full of life. I wanted to embrace the London life that I had fallen in love with all those years ago.

I was going to love it here and I knew Daisy would without any doubt, it had captured my heart, giving me back something I had missed for so long. I took a long deep breath, taking in London's unique aroma, listening to the love that echoed through the street in which we now called home.

The flat now looked so cosy and warm, surrounded by all our treasures that we loved, Daisy's artwork on show and my photography hung well in the flat although we were only here temporarily we wanted it to feel like home.

Now a few days on and by luck while out walking getting to know the area we found a beautiful flat to buy. It was a large old Victorian conversion in a sleepy street lined with leafy trees not far from the hustle and bustle of the lovely North London town where we already called home.

The flat had a large lounge with a high ceiling and a huge bay window that overlooked the park. The kitchen was huge, great for entertaining. My large table would sit nicely in the centre of the room in a very commanding position, along with the old tin vase from the cabin that I would fill with flowers, another reminder of my darling Charlie. There were three great size bedrooms, all with private bathrooms and an added room for me to use as a studio.

We were very excited and had already planned where things would go, it seemed like we had already moved in, so luckily our offer was accepted, and we would be able to move very shortly as things seemed to move so fast here in London.

The following week Daisy was due to start her new college, so we had a few girly days out, seeing what North London had to offer, soaking it all up. The fantastic atmosphere that seemed to embrace this pretty North London town.

In the blink of an eye Monday came and Daisy was off to college to start her new venture and she was taking it all in her stride, her excitement very apparent as she closed the door behind her embarking on a new adventure.

I sat in the kitchen drinking my coffee, flicking through the paper worrying about her all day, trying to take my mind off how she was feeling, but I knew she would be fine as her head was firmly screwed on. She had become very wise to the world, being very polite and well-spoken she knew what she wanted and she was going all out to get it.

I popped out and sat in a little cafe on the main high street, people watching. My thoughts were never far away from Charlie as always. All these years on he was forever in my thoughts and would be forever and deep down I wanted it to stay that way as I still continued to cling on to our dirty love and to his mysterious past, even if it was hanging by only a tiny, frayed thread now.

I left the little cafe, heading back home to wait for Daisy to return. I wanted to be in when she got home, eager to hear about her first day and again I was taken back to her very first day at school, I was then feeling the same emotions all these years on. Suddenly I heard the door close. *Mum,* she called from the hall. *Daisy, how was it?* I didn't really need to ask, I could see it written clearly across her face, her smile was delightful and instantly told me exactly how it went as her smile was uncontrollable.

She had met some great friends and I knew Daisy and her new found friends would form her social life in the coming weeks, months and years that lay ahead, friends from all over London and beyond, friendships that would last a lifetime.

London was going to give us both a great life and we would not change that for the world, not now. It was now late September and beautifully warm, the trees were changing colour as autumn was now just around the corner, reminding me once again of the natural beauty that came with every season.

The weekend was over and before I knew it I was on the tube heading to my office in central London which took about 30 minutes on a good day. London had so much that I loved; the sights, the smells and all the wonderful cultures I loved, the smell of the tube, it had something that made my senses go wild.

I wore a suit; my high heels complete with brief case. I still had it, as I received many flattering glances, even a few eye-to-eye glances that made me blush as I sat tugging at my skirt, not wanting to witness the ongoing flirtatious looks from my fellow male travellers on this early morning commute.

Some of the office staff were going out at the weekend and asked if I wanted to join them. *Come on Lizzy, please say you'll come.* Encouraging me with every breath to take my next step to embrace London, to take all what this vibrant city could offer me.

I accepted without hesitation as I wanted and needed to once again embrace this vast city and take all I could from it. We were meeting for drinks, the pub was packed allowing a great atmosphere to sweep thought it and I was loving it, knowing I could let my hair down with ease, something I had not felt in a very long time. It was for me like a breath of fresh air where no one really knew me, so there was no finger pointing, no whispering and no one to say I told you so. This was my new life now and I was going to do all I could to embrace it, putting yesterday behind me, letting the past drift slowly back into yesterday's shadows.

On my way home, having had a wonderful night out, I crept in quietly not to wake Daisy. I knew she was home as her shoes lay in a heap in the hall just where she had kicked them off, something that always managed to make me smile as that was exactly what I used to do.

Sunday morning I got up really late, Daisy was still in bed so I crept around trying not to make too much noise. Sitting with my coffee I made a few calls, to dad, my sister and to catch up with G, who was delighted that I was once again in London.

The next few months went by and it was leading up to Christmas and Daisy's birthday and we still did not have a moving date for our stunning new home, but I was agitated at the fact we would not move until the new year now so we collected a Christmas tree for the lounge and decorated it. It looked amazing and very beautiful, adorned with our most treasured decoration the snowflake. It would not have been Christmas without it and as we decorated it warm cherished memories flooded back, every one of them special in its own delightful way, but one Christmas remained the most special and that was the Christmas Charlie and I spent together, as a family with our new born daughter, cocooned in a bubble of love, a bubble I thought would never be broken.

Daisy and I were going to spend Christmas Day together and a traditional day was called for so that was what we would have. Turkey, Christmas pudding, mistletoe and even a stunning garland of holly and ivy to grace the front door, complete with a large red velvet bow.

The office was having a get together at the weekend, a pre-Christmas party. I excitedly said I would go, but tonight I felt anxious once again as I tugged at the necklace, wanting some sort of comfort and reassurance, tracing again the raised intricate pattern with my fingertips.

As I got ready I felt like the real Lizzy for the first time in a long time. I now looked like me again and it felt good, so dressed in a short black mini dress and killer heals, Lizzy was back, this time in total control, ready to put Charlie to the back of my mind, where I should have put him a very long time ago.

We were meeting for a meal and then on to the club in Camden to dance the night away into the early hours, knowing full well it was going to be a fabulous evening. The atmosphere would be created by wonderful people just wanting to have a brilliant evening.

On the way out of the club for some reason I was distracted by a bloke, he was one of the door security team, there was something about him. He stood talking with three other men, there was just something that I could not put my finger on, maybe it was the wine, after all I was feeling a little tipsy. Or maybe I was craving the attention of male company again as it had been a long time since I had been in the company of a man, a very long time in fact, but the Lizzy who loved life was back, so it should not have surprised me that my craving for male company was now once again on my mind, knowing I had not slept with anyone since Charlie.

Christmas now was approaching fast, and London was buzzing with people socialising and I was having my fair share as I was never without an invitation to drinks, to a show, to dinner, the list was endless, but I declined each and every one, as Charlie still ruled my unforgiving fragile and still vulnerable heart.

Daisy and I both embraced the very busy time leading up to Christmas. I now had two weeks holiday and Daisy had finished college for three weeks. Her diary was overflowing with invitations and today, Christmas Eve was no different. Daisy was out today with her friends, shopping and doing the normal girly stuff.

I sat alone with my coffee and read the local paper, there was so much going on in this little town in North London. I felt relaxed here, this was now my home and London was intent on giving me back something that was missing from my life.

Christmas Day in London and what a difference from Christmas in the sleepy Wiltshire village that now seemed a million miles away, but one that held my heart, Daisy and I were going to attend the Christmas service in the local church and it was beautiful as we sang along to the wonderful hymns that echoed delightfully through the church. Then it was back home for lunch and an afternoon on the sofa as we munched our way through a large box of extremely decadent chocolates, drinking mulled wine and watching the television, snuggled up together, some things would never change and this was one of them.

Christmas came and went. I went back to see dad for a few days and it felt good to be back, but it allowed once again my thoughts to revolve around Charlie as he had been so much a part of my life here in this little remote Wiltshire village that I used to call home, that now seemed so very small in comparison to the North London town where I now lived, and was to now be my forever home.

I spent a little time in the garden that I loved so much, letting it freely seduce me with every emotion as I stood in the freezing cold, feeling icily cold flakes of snow to hit my skin, letting myself slip back to so many treasured and much loved memories, but it was so cold as I shivered to keep warm, wishing there were two strong arms wrapped around me, as there had been on many occasions in the past.

I returned to my old bedroom that I had missed so much to now once again step back in time to capture my winter memories, as one by one they sprang into my vision. Snowflakes that glistened, trees that were laden with snow, the family of deer that would invade the garden looking for food and winter watery sunshine that enhanced the landscape that I adored.

I was suddenly aware I was not alone as I glanced back at the mirror, startled to see Helen's vision once again glaring at me. Her vision was somewhat hazy, but it was her; cold, steely faced and menacing, but why did she still feel need to still haunt me? I diverted my gaze, before slamming the bedroom door behind me, leaving her alone in my room.

Relieved to be back in London we had now at last received a date for the move and we were so excited, no more living out of boxes and not being able to properly unpack, it would be nice to be settled in our new home.

Back to work and I had been asked out for a drink, so I thought I would go. He was nice, a good looking bloke. We got on well, he liked the things I liked, but he wasn't Charlie. There was no spark, no flame, it was dull. We didn't even exchange kisses at the end of the evening, he wasn't the man that I craved, so I did not see him again. He probably thought the same about me which lead me to wonder if there was ever going to be a man who could live up to my very high expectations.

The new year was off to a great start, my job was going very well and to our delight we made the move into our new stunning home, and it was amazing. Daisy was blissfully happy with so many new found friends to enhance and enrich her life daily.

I walked regularly in Regents Park and every time I was there I thought of nothing else but Charlie, reliving all our many walks, our conversations and above all being totally in love with each other. I now walked alone and in complete silence, but I was still in love with a man that had broken my heart repeatedly, who had stolen my soul and my virginity, wanting it for his own and now all these years later I was still his hostage.

Work had organised another night out, I said I would go although I really had to make a great effort as I struggled to find the right outfit, but I did and I looked good. As I looked in the mirror my reflection was one I liked and not clouded by images that I wanted to forget.

CHAPTER 33

I arrived early at the restaurant and not everyone had arrived so while we waited we all chatted about family, children, work, and life in general, knowing full well mine was still on hold and exclusively for one person, wondering why after the monumental and terrifying heartache he had managed to cause me, but was it his fault or mine for falling in love with him so readily?

We once again had tickets for the club in Camden, that was very exciting, it had a soul and a very unique feel about it which I seemed to have become very addicted to with its aroma that just invaded my nostrils, taking me on a wild exciting journey.

On arriving at the club it was very busy and we had to wait to go in. As we got nearer to the door my senses once again sprang into action, the same bloke caught my eye. It was the bloke that I had seen on the last occasion I was here, who the hell was he and why was I so intrigued by him?

As I got nearer to the door I was stunned, blinking repeatedly as a cold and somewhat sensual and chilled breeze kissed my neck. Now I was transfixed on him with intrigue, suddenly he turned around, allowing me to see the clear vision. There was no doubt the vision was one from my past, suddenly I broke out into an ice cold sweat, his eyes also transfixed on me, we could not take our eyes off each other. My legs suddenly felt like they were stuck to the pavement beneath me that now I wished would swallow me up from the impending meeting that was about to change my life once again. Hearing the thunderstorm gathering pace, roaring throughout the streets of London with nowhere to hide, the noise was terrifying as I waited for the unpleasant cargo that the dark and unwelcome storm was carrying to be unleashed.

He smiled, I burst into floods of heavy uncontrollable tears. My colleagues were concerned and distressed at my sudden anxiety, I told them I was fine and that I would catch them up later as they all made their way into the club without me, leaving me in bits and alone on the cold London pavement. I stood motionless and still trying to catch my breath that had suddenly been taken away from me again, now not knowing what to say or what to do. I just stood shaking, dazed by this unexpected face from the past that had haunted me, seduced me and broke my fragile body into so many splinted shards for so many long, lonely and painful years.

The next thing I knew he was holding my hand, leading me to one side away from the increasing growing crowd that were waiting to go into the club as they jostled and edged a little closer to the door. *Lizzy, Lizzy, Lizzy you look stunning.* I pulled my cream coat together, stumbling to button it up, not wanting his eyes to feast once again on my body. I could not answer him, I was speechless. He had taken my breath completely away with his adorable and still cocky smile that had evaded my senses for all these years.

He leaned forward to kiss me. Suddenly I regained my thoughts as I moved away abruptly. How dare he? How dare he be so fucking casual about it and to call me his princess? I was so bloody angry, wanting the earth to swallow me up. *Lizzy, we need to talk.* He was right, but we needed to talk years ago as now it all seemed far too little and far too late.

How's Daisy, Lizzy? I now wanted to slap his face hard, wanting to lash out, to let him feel what real pain felt like, because it had been him that had scarred and tattooed my body in unrelenting pain since we shared our first unforgettable kisses.

I stood speechless, not having echoed one word. I was speechless that he had not bothered or tried to find us. *Lizzy, please talk to me* he begged, repeating his words that reeled around in my mind like an out of control tornado.

Still my words were muted as I had been stunned into silence. *Lizzy, talk to me please.* I couldn't, I was so hurt, it hurt so much that he was here in London and that he had made a new life for himself while Daisy and I did not know where he was or even if he was alive. Had he even given us any thought? I was overcome by so many emotions that continued to shudder through my body, mixed with overwhelming love at the same time.

He looked down at my hand that he was still holding, his smile beamed across his rugged face as my daisy ring was still on my finger after all this time. Damn it, Damn it, as I pulled my hand away sharply not wanting him to admire my ongoing commitment to him. His gaze then took a journey to my neck, his gaze firmly fixed on the ring, I wanted to rip it from my body, to throw it at him. A familiar voice now entered into my dilemma, it was my mum, her voice commanding my attention as I diverted my gaze back to Charlie. *Walk away Lizzy, walk away, and walk free.* I shook my head in disbelief that I was here tonight, surrounded by strangers, but it was two of the people who I treasured the most that pulled me in two different directions tonight. *Lizzy, Lizzy.* Charlie was now squeezing my hand even tighter as mum's voice had now faded, having made her feelings felt. I was shaking with rage now, how dare he spoil my London life, my life for once was back on track since he left us all those years ago. Then of course there was Daisy, had he even given her a moment's thought? Why had he not come to find us, to claim what was always going to be his? He knew my body, soul and love all belonged to him, it always had done, damn him! He still had that look, the look that I found so very attractive. Damn him! *Lizzy lets go somewhere and talk, tell me about Daisy, tell me about you.*

My face was now eaten up with rage and pain, my voice raised by anger. *No not now, not here, not ever... I can't Charlie! Please Lizzy.* I started to walk away, somewhat shakily. My legs felt so heavy like they were weighed down by heavy chains. *Lizzy wait, please wait.*

Charlie had managed to get a slight grip on my wrist, I wriggled to free myself, screaming at him to let me go. His grip tightened again, people were now starting to stare and to point fingers on hearing my raised, anguished, and whimpering voice.

My face was now wet with tears of anger and of pain that was rocketing across and through my body, leaving me weak and again leaving my body fragile, open to every emotion that wanted to invade it, scarring my already heavily tattered and torn skin, tattooing again any virgin skin that was not already marked by love, by hatred, by sadness and now anger.

Let's meet up on Sunday, tomorrow Lizzy please... I stood glaring at him. *No, it's too late now Charlie.* Snapping my sharp reply, *it's far too late for small talk. Please Lizzy, please say you will.* The air was now heavy and pungent with anticipation of my reply as London took a sharp intake of breath, holding it until I could stop myself from choking on words that were now muted, words that I just wanted to scream at him, wounding him with words that would scar his skin in long lasting spiteful blood stained graffiti.

As I glared at him I thought about Daisy and what she would have wanted, what we both wanted, but I knew deep down I wanted Charlie's dirty love just once more. Stupid me, selfish me, why was I being so stupid when I wanted to start a new uncomplicated life for myself here in London. I had it all mapped out, a good job, a lovely home, men queuing up wanting to date me, to treat me to the delights and the finer things in life that were on offer here in the big smoke and of course the reason I was here in the first place, Daisy.

With my head in a constant whirl I gave in, I gave in yet again when I should have retracted his desperate plea to be reunited. *Yes, OK*, I snapped, I was still so annoyed with him. *Where Lizzy? Regents Park, 11am and don't let me down again Charlie as this is the last time, the final time.* I wagged my finger at him, making sure he knew I wasn't going to be led astray by his lies and false promises. For once in my life I took the higher ground, not to be walked over ever again.

I looked at his face, it was now numb with pain as my words were hard, harsh and bitter and for good reason. Charlie once again tried pulling me into his arms, allowing me to inhale his aroma just for a split second but I hurriedly pulled away. *Lizzy please. No Charlie I can't.* I turned and walked away, not looking back as I needed to prove to him that I was strong, much stronger now. I went home so bloody annoyed, upset, angry, cross, and hurt by every emotion you could think of, and I was feeling it tonight as my body remained tense and somewhat rigid at times. On reaching the front door I felt relieved to at last be embraced by the comfort of home. I slammed the door shut, throwing my keys across the oak table out of sheer frustration.

I struggled to sleep, restless in my ability to think straight, constantly seeing Charlie's rugged face in my mind as I tried to come to terms that he was back in my life, but for how long? Well that was going to be my decision now depending on the answers I so needed to hear, and that I would demand.

After a restless night Sunday morning came at last and I made my way to Regents Park dressed in my jeans, boots, and leather jacket, dressed to impress to show him what he had missed and what was on offer for any other man to have and to my amazement there were many who had made advances, wanting my attention daily.

A chill hung in the late winter sunshine, but it was very beautiful. Suddenly I saw him stood waiting for me. Mum's voice once again entered into my mind echoing in my head, telling me to turn and walk away, walk away to avoid yet more agonising heartache that would undoubtedly follow. With doubts now invading my mind I paused for a while, just to catch my breath, wanting to be deliberately late today, to show him what it felt like to be left waiting, so I lingered a little longer.

As I walked ever closer to him, the chilling voice in my head got louder and louder repeating words that I knew I should listen to, but once again I declined as my heart continued to rule my head, just like it always had done and today was not going to be any different, but this was going to be a huge life-changing meeting for one of us at least.

I felt very nervous as I approached him, my heart was pounding. My mouth felt so dry, my body was tense from terrifying pain, not wanting to be seduced by his love that would for sure overpower me. After all, it had been a very long time. Suddenly he saw me, now I was unable to turn around, unable to hide, he smiled that cocky smile that I had loved for so long, it was one of the things I loved about him the most as it was so intoxicating.

Holding my hand, he tried to kiss me, I pulled away sharply, but as I did I was once again treated to his aroma that delighted my senses, throwing me off guard, taking me by surprise and leading me into a false sense of security, allowing my vulnerability to bubble to the surface.

Once again he tried to kiss me, I pulled away again. He must have been so unaware of my feelings and what he had put us both through for all those lost years, the constant worry about what people thought, the mind churning hours I spent believing he was coming home and then the earth shattering devastation when I realised he wasn't smashing my world apart by his selfish behaviour.

I needed him to explain all those lost years and why he hadn't bothered to find me if I was the love of his life that he had always claimed I was, and that I always had been, so there was now so many questions that swirled around in my mind, all seemed to fight for priority.

We sat on a bench and as we did he tried to hold my hand again, I snatched it away. *Lizzy don't.* I glared at him with a vile and cold lingering stare, letting him know that I was extremely upset, hurt, my heart destroyed by him and not for the first time as he had built up a habit of breaking my heart, but this time he had smashed it into millions of pieces.

His beautiful brown eyes being so deep were inciting me once again to reignite our dirty love, something that now terrified me as it had done all those years ago when I was a virgin and when Charlie had taken me his hostage leaving me fragile and even more now.

Lizzy, how's Daisy? A lump hit my throat as I fought back my emotions. Sadly, I was not able to contain myself as I cried uncontrollably. *She's beautiful, she's talented and a very exceptional girl.* My voice was reflecting my absolute love for her, but laced in bitterness with every word I spoke. *She is everything you could want and wish for in a daughter Charlie.*

Charlie's voice somewhat muted Lizzy. *I'm so sorry, I know I have hurt you and Daisy beyond belief, I hate myself for that and I always will.* I said nothing as I sat rigid on the harsh wooden bench wanting to hear it all from him, to hear how he would cover up all the long and very lonely years that I suspected would be based on lies and more lies. I could smell and see the fear he held in his eyes and in his facial expression.

He squeezed my hand; his brown eyes were now clouded by a watery glaze. *Lizzy let me explain.* I took a sharp intake of breath. *Well that's why we are here Charlie*, I said sharply and as he looked at me. He seemed genuinely sadden and hurt.

He rested his head in his hands with the burden that was so obviously heavy for him to bear, his voice shallow and almost timid. I knew it would be hard for him, but this was the moment for honesty, for Daisy's sake. He held my hand once again, he was shaking now knowing he had to tell me what was behind his selfish stupidity and the lies that hide his mysterious, dark, and secret life that once seduced me.

I could see him fighting with his emotions as he began to splutter the words I needed to hear. *I got in with some very bad men Lizzy, I did some really stupid stuff that led me to a life I hated, a crime driven life that I wanted to end, but couldn't. I could not find a way out as it kept creeping up on me, I was desperate to escape from that life, to lead a normal life. I thought you knew I had a reputation Lizzy.* I looked at him knowing full well his reputation had seduced me. I nodded, but I was never aware of the full extent of his reputation.

It got so bad there was no going back and like a fool I just went along with it, it was a dark time for me Lizzy. I wanted you and Daisy so much, I wanted only the best for you both. To cut a long story short, it started before I went to Wales. My reputation was already tarnished, I was repeatedly in trouble and the outcome all those years later was that I was sent to prison for a few years and when it was time for my release I could not face you, I was so scared to contact you fearing you would have fallen out of love with me and been appalled by my actions knowing I was a convicted criminal.

As I listened to Charlie's admission I was amazed that he had managed to keep such a terrifying, mysterious life so secret, such a huge and frightening secret from me. He glanced over, *Lizzy I felt sick at what I had done, the man I was, I was weak, and I hated myself for everything I put you through and still do. I never stopped thinking about you and Daisy, you were both in my thoughts every day without fail and it was the thought of you both that got me through such a dark time in my life. I suppose you could say I paid the price, but I know it cost you and Daisy so much more. I'm so sorry Lizzy, I can never repay my stupidity.*

Composing himself again he continued to explain. *I then found myself in London getting work where I could get on with life and not very well either, living hand to mouth, just hanging on by a thread living day to day. You and Daisy were constantly in my thoughts and it was a burden on my heart that I could not tell you princess. I never wanted to hurt you; you must know that.*

I blurted out, my tongue twisted with spiteful and bitter anger now desperate to have my say. *Well you did, and it still does Charlie, it always will. It's been hell for me, watching my dad go through hell, seeing Daisy grow up without her daddy, the list goes on Charlie.*

He looked at me, squeezing my hand for added reassurance. I knew full well he was telling the truth and telling me he was sorry, but it wasn't making it any easier to take in, as everything he was telling me just seemed a blur, muddied in my mind wishing I could make sense of it all, again my torment leads me to clutch the ring on my necklace.

Princess I loved you then and seeing you now, my god Lizzy I love you still. I could feel my heart melting, but my head was spinning with justified anger, the tension hung heavy in the air here in Regent's Park. *Lizzy, I will do all I can to make it up to Daisy and you.* I looked at him dazed by his attitude that was still so bloody casual. *Charlie,* I snapped, *a few I'm sorry's won't do it and I don't ever see that it will.* What right did he think he had to assume that he would once again be part of our lives, only to wreck it again and again with his stupidity. *I stood by your side Charlie, I even walked in your shadows but I didn't walk away from you. This is madness Charlie I don't know why I even agreed to come here today.*

I felt his hand embracing mine, *Lizzy I know you're angry with me right now, please tell me how I can put it right. Charlie, I have been angry with you for all the years you missed after Daisy was born, this is just the tip of the iceberg and I don't know what, if anything can make it right.*

Can we talk more please Lizzy, for Daisy. Charlie, how dare you! Lizzy, please. I beg you Lizzy please. Charlie looked petrified as he begged for me to hear his desperate plea, I looked at him and in a strange way I felt sorry for him, I knew I shouldn't but stupid me once again falling for the Charlie charm.

We sat in the cafe on a sumptuous old and somewhat battered sofa and talked over some hot, very strong coffee. I asked where he worked, lived and if he was married, if he saw his son and Helen. *Lizzy, slow down.* Holding my hand once again I was loving the feeling it was giving me to have his hands embracing mine after all these lost years, his dazzling gaze never leaving mine, seducing me once again with everything that was him.

I work here in London, building, earning a crust, that's why I do weekend work at the clubs for extra money. I live in east London in a small grubby bedsit, but it's a roof over my head and I am not married, I have no lady in my life, only one that is constantly in my thoughts she was my first love, her name is Lizzy, I call her my princess. I burst out crying, unable to contain my tears any longer. *Lizzy, don't, I am so sorry. I hate seeing and hearing you cry.*

I was annoyed with myself that I had allowed Charlie the pleasure of my tears, but they needed to be shed as emotions were once again at an all-time high for both of us. I desperately wanted to hide my emotions from everyone around us clearly witnessing my distress.

He held my hand once again, so gently and loving the fact I still wore his rings. He smiled again looking at my hand, he then touched my porcelain painted face, tracing the outline with such a delicate touch that sent ice cold shivers down my spine as I remembered fondly how I used to love him doing just that.

I pulled back, afraid of my actions that now were just simmering away, ready to explode with pent up emotion as I continued to look at Charlie. There was still a ruggedness about him, a charm which I loved and adored.

I repeated my question about his life wanting to know more. *Well Lizzy, I divorced Helen and I don't see Andrew, Helen has never allowed me to see him. I know Charlie, I spoke to Helen a little while after you left. I did all I could to find you, I called everyone that might know where you were.*

What can I say Lizzy? My Love for you has never left my heart and it never will, I could tell you that for the rest of my life, nothing has changed,

I love you Lizzy. Charlie looked at me with those stunning brown eyes. *Tell me about you Lizzy.* I had to compose myself as I knew my words would be emotional. *Daisy is always my priority; she always has been and will continue to be so.* The tone in my voice was making it clear everything was now on my terms.

My life when you left was pure hell Charlie, it was like hell on earth not knowing where you were or what might have happened to you, I cried for you every night and every day, more so I cried for Daisy not having her daddy in her life, to have you there when she crossed every milestone, to have you there when she cried, when she smiled and when she needed you.

His reaction was one of devastation that had just hit him full on, maybe that was what he needed to be told, direct and to the point, just what impact his leaving had on us.

He pulled me close to him, I cried on his chest, beating it with my fist out of pure frustration. He whispered *Lizzy let it all out.* I hit his chest again with my fist, hard and with impact, repeating my muted words. I want to hate you I really want to hate you; I do hate you Charlie.

I cried so much as Charlie was still holding me and once again I was treated to the aroma of him which I had loved and it had not changed, it still provoked my senses and today was no different. *Princess, look at me.* He lifted my fragile face which was now smothered in tears of agony.

Changing the subject he started to ask me questions that I knew he would ask at some point during our heated conversation. *Are you married Lizzy? No Charlie.* His expression clearly one of shock. *What, you mean never? No Charlie, never.* He smiled as his eyes lit up. *No Charlie, you're not getting it, I have not been out with anyone or been intimate with any other man since you.* He looked shocked at my revaluation. *Princess, you mean you did that for me.* I glared at him, snapping at his reply. *No Charlie, I did it for me, to keep my eternal everlasting dirty love for you, but I bloody well wish I hadn't now, I wish I had slept with all the men that had asked me out and there have been plenty that would have wanted to have what I kept exclusively for you Charlie.* His face once again crippled by my words.

Back all those years ago people said you were trouble, a heart-breaker and how right they were. I sounded so bitter, but then I was, and I had a every right to feel bitter for all the years that I had endured without his love.

And you Charlie? A couple of one night stands, but no one has ever been bothered about me and I can't blame them either. I had to agree with him, if only out of sheer spite and anger. I smiled at him. *God Lizzy you're so beautiful.* He then moved closer and kissed my hand, I hoped deep down that he would not want to let it go as it was lovely to have that feeling once again, the feeling that no other man could give me or that I would want to receive.

Are you here for the weekend? I smiled at him, I couldn't help but giggle, he really did have no idea. *No Charlie, we live here, we live in north London and have done for some time.* Stunned into silence, he spluttered. *Lizzy you both live here? What? I can't believe that.* Well, *I'm working here and Daisy lives with me.* He looked so totally shocked, his face was pale with amazement. *What, my girls here? Here in London? Yes, right under your nose Charlie, London is our home now.* Charlie was now gasping from my revaluation, his face stunned by my ongoing stories and vibrant tales about Daisy and myself.

What's Daisy doing? I looked at him, my eyes bathed in tears that I was now trying to hold back. *You will be so proud of her Charlie. She's has a great career ahead of her, she's a great artist with a huge talent, she's at collage now and is hopefully going to university. Lizzy, my Daisy all grown up.* I could now see his pride in his smile that beamed throughout this vast sprawling park and beyond into the streets of London that today smiled with him, but also held its breath, just like I did, knowing Charlie's track record.

Charlie, I have some photos if you would like to see them. He started to sob as his hands were holding his head again. He seemed panicked now as he was about to see his little girl for the first time in a very long time even if it was in photographs, *Lizzy can I?*

I took the pictures out of my bag and passed them to Charlie, his expression was of deep and terrifying sadness, his smile instantly wiped from his rugged, sun kissed face as he looked lovingly at the photographs now with his hands shaking, his expression terrified me.

I started with her first day at school, his emotion apparent as he was so overcome. I could see the love and pain that swept across his face, crippling his ability to smile. *Lizzy she is beautiful, she has you written all over her.* Yes she is a mini me, *everyone says so, she has a zest for love and for life, a passion that is so radiant and powerful.*

I then passed him the latest photograph. He looked at it, stunned, his body rigid and tense. *My god Lizzy what have I done? I don't deserve to see these beautiful pictures of a truly beautiful girl that I have let down so badly, she is a credit to you Lizzy.* I nodded in full agreement with him knowing without doubt I had done my best.

His head was now resting in his hands once again. I was relieved, pleased in a strange sort of way that he was feeling so bad, hoping now that this really made him realise just what he had lost, memories that he was never part of. Years that could never be replaced, but I loved him still, I loved him so much the feelings I knew I would feel, the feeling that would not go away, not now, not ever. I was so scared that I would allow freely Charlie's love to seduce me again, my emotions were running wild, clashing together like some out of control thunder storm, but I was not about to allow Charlie the pleasure to know my true feelings.

Lizzy let me take you out for supper. Sorry Charlie I need to get back to Daisy. My tone was now casual, not wanting to allow him a way in to seduce me, I had to be in control. *Charlie, she will be worried. Then stay a little longer, please let's talk more.* I hesitated, *I'm not sure Charlie. Please Lizzy.* His hand met mine again, sending my body wild with pent up emotion.

We had talked for a while longer and suddenly the daylight was fading, it was getting dark. Charlie wanted to take me home. As much as I wanted him to I had to talk to Daisy, so I declined gracefully as this was all very soon for me, like a whirlwind spinning around, sweeping my feet from beneath me, not allowing me to take a breath of fresh air and not for the first time.

We kissed so passionately as our lips met again for the first time in years. My lips experiencing fireworks, multi-coloured fireworks, with magnificent rockets that exploded again as Charlie's tongue once more seduced my mouth, with kisses that were now smudging my painted lips, burning my soul with the power of his love. The kisses were so passionate, just as I remembered them, but that now left me falling in love once again for the third time and I could tell Charlie was feeling it to, whispering into my hair, *Princess I have never stopped loving you, I loved you then and I love you now Lizzy.* I melted with love, just as I did all those years ago, wishing I was once again a virgin to allow him that pleasure to take it away from me again.

Can I see you again Lizzy. I hesitated to reply, *I don't know Charlie, I can't allow myself to get close to you again, I can't be hurt again Charlie. Please Princess, I have changed. Please Lizzy, I beg you.* As he looked at me his eyes were once again hungry for my love, a look that left me weak as I once again became vulnerable to Charlie's love.

Reluctantly I gave him my number and he promised to call me, but I was not going to hold my breath as I had been promised the earth and more, given false promises that had been broken more than once and taking my heart with it, shredding it into fine fragments that had been left discarded.

He pulled me back into his arms, his body tender against mine allowing the feeling of the eternal dirty love sweep throughout my body, leaving me a quivering mess, leaving me wanting more, much more. *I have missed you Lizzy, I have missed loving you.*

I smiled, not wanting to give away my true feelings. I needed time to absorb what was happening, but I knew full well we would be lovers again. It was written years ago, tattooed on everything we touched, tattooed across not only my body, but Charlie's too, but were we once again to board a journey that would once again be on a collision course for yet more heart-breaking moments? Again, today our history was about to be rewritten here in London…

I could not resist the passion that was now apparent between us once again. My heart was now overruling my head, not thinking things through yet again, hearing my mother's words clearly. *Walk away Lizzy, walk away,* but I chose to ignore her wise words, blurting my words. *Why don't you come over for the weekend Charlie? We can then talk properly as Daisy is away for the weekend.*

He gasped at my invitation; his cocky stature was back on show as I placed my hand on his. *Charlie I want you to.* He smiled that stomach churning smile, he knew I needed desperately to be loved by him once again, to feel his passion, to feel the sensitivity between us, to share again what was us, his face beamed knowing we would be lovers again, sharing some very dirty and intense love once more.

The week went on and I said nothing to Daisy as she was so excited about her weekend away with friends, to be going out celebrating, creating memories that London would never deny her.

Charlie called endlessly during the week which was nice, I loved hearing his voice, I also received the most glorious and elaborate bouquets, all wrapped in pink tissue and pink cellophane. Some things would never change and that was one of them, along with messages that ended as always with the taunting initials that were so familiar… H L F. The powerful aroma was stunning, allowing me to take many journeys that included Charlie once more, but these gestures were just a drop in the ocean, I needed more, much more from him if this had any chance of working.

Friday came and I desperately wanted to look nice for Charlie, to show him what he had missed, but more importantly we needed to talk as there were still lots of hard questions that needed to be asked and I needed answers, truthful answers.

Charlie turned up at 7pm, his smile instantly took my breath away and as he kissed me, I kissed him back with kisses that were warm and long. My body and soul were begging to be loved and loved by Charlie. *You look great Lizzy.* I felt his hand gently brush against my thigh. *Come in Charlie you can put your bag in the bedroom.* He questioned, *in your room Lizzy? Yes Charlie, my room.* My reply was very casual, making me blush. He smiled, I blushed again, he smiled back leaving me giggling like a nervous school girl. I could see Charlie's eyes traveling around on a mission to capture the lifestyle that myself and Daisy had created here in London. *Lizzy, you have a lovely home. Yes, we like it Charlie.*

Now relaxed we sat on my huge sumptuous, comfy sofa while supper was cooking. Our eyes were never far away from each other's gaze, flirting with a hungry passion, dancing with raw emotion. Our relationship still had such evocative sparks and fireworks that now seemed to be sending a vivid wave of pent up emotions between us.

My eyes were now fully entangled with Charlie's, his brown eyes that again tonight managed to seduce me as I continued to allow his eyes to flirt deeply with mine. His ability to seduce me was fully on display again tonight, his aroma very powerful.

We talked over supper, small talk really, skirting around the much bigger conversation we needed to have, but knowing full well he was deeply sorry for his stupidity and reluctantly. I had started to forgive him, already knowing it was possibly the next mistake I would make, the impact of which could end in disaster.

With supper finished we sat drinking wine together, relaxed to be in each other's company once again. Charlie looked at me. *Lizzy, I have been utterly stupid. Can you ever forgive me?* I looked at him, wanting desperately to say the words of forgiveness he wanted to hear, but I declined him for now that luxury as I needed him to prove that to me, that he was sorry, not by words, but by his actions.

He put his arm around me, allowing my body to sink into his warm love, something that I had missed and craved so much. *Lizzy I love you. I love you so much and I will prove to you that I'm a changed man.*

Foolishly words just fell from my mouth, I was unable to contain my emotions, spluttering my words of love, *I love you Charlie.* Instantly hating myself, instantly wanting to retract my words of love. *Nothing has changed for me Charlie, my love for you remains unchanged, but it's hard for me Charlie, you do understand that don't you? Yes Lizzy, I can't start to understand and imagine the earth shattering hurt I have caused you and Daisy.*

You never will Charlie, you can never imagine. He looked somewhat shocked by my remarks, but he knew it was time for hard words as I was never going to sugar coat the excruciating pain that he had caused us both.

I showed him some of Daisy's artwork that was in her folder. *God, she's very talented Lizzy, our little girl did all this?* Charlie was now sat with his head resting in his hands, once again looking so ashamed. *Lizzy I can't believe I have done this to you, I hate myself, it was never meant to be like this, all I ever wanted was to love you both.*

I was now about to take control, my cravings were now out of control as I took his hand and led him to the bathroom, slamming the pristine white door with my foot firmly behind us, just letting him know that seduction was heavy on my mind. I ran us an indulgent bubble bath and lit candles, just like we did way back and again loving intimate memories flooded back, engulfing us in a tidal wave of love.

While the bath filled I invited him to unzipped my black dress, slowly letting it fall to the floor to reveal my black stockings and suspenders. I felt the cold tingling down my spine, making my nipples stand to Charlie's attention. He held my arms outstretched. *Lizzy, my Lizzy your stunning, your tits so fucking perfect.* I now knew we were back, dirty lovers once again and I was not ashamed to be in his company, not ashamed to be his whore once more. Silence now filled the air as there was no need for words.

I could feel the sexual tension between us, again gathering pace with a renewed freshness, but we were loving it. Charlie looked into my eyes that now demanded his undivided attention, commanding some much needed dirty love.

I removed his shirt, letting it fall lovingly on top of my dress, his eyes were exploring my partly naked curvy body that once again begged for his attention.

His chest was still very firm and tense, his body lean, he looked older of course and more rugged. His skin was weathered and his head shaven, but still he remained so very sexy, I hated to admit that I still found him very arousing to every one of my senses that he continued to seduce.

Charlie's fingertips traced the outline of my porcelain painted face, never taking his gaze away from mine. Our eyes were demanding an intimacy that was so long overdue. He undid my bra, my breasts still very full and firm. *Lizzy your tits, they are stunning.* I felt his gaze burning into my skin, my nipples huge and standing to Charlie's attention once again as he touched them tenderly with his fingertips just to make sure that he had the same desired affect that he always had. He was now kissing my neck, arousing my sexual desires before seducing again the ring that I still wore on my necklace, allowing me the beauty of his aroma as I inhaled deeply filling my nostrils with the tantalising aroma that was Charlie.

I unzipped his jeans and they too fell to the floor and I was not surprised to see that he was commando, his cock was still fucking huge and stiff with a dirty desire and love, so tonight it was all mine, completely mine, ready for the sex fuelled dirty love session that was about to unfold, that would take us into the early hours of tomorrow.

Both of us were in a frenzy of desire to share and rekindle our dirty love. I never thought I could feel like this ever again, I knew we had true love and this time it had to be forever as anything less would not be enough, it never could be.

Once in the bath Charlie teased my pussy, naked of course and it felt amazing once again, made possible by Charlie as his ability to deliver all the dirty love I adored. I smiled. *You still love a naked pussy then Charlie?* I blushed repeatedly, with the water getting cold Charlie suggested we continue our dirty love, our sex fuelled reunion somewhere more comfortable, so we made our way to the bedroom to continue this amazing love that we were making. I sat on the edge of the bed, Charlie's cock was now level with my mouth, it felt great to be loving him again. He held my head firmly but gently, letting his rigid cock ride my mouth until it was in my throat. His cock was tense and about to make dirty love to my mouth, feeling it peppering my throat with delightful tasting juice that Charlie yearned to share. As his mouth then met mine we shared the warm, fresh juice, our tongues dancing a very intimate dance that was ours and always had been. Charlie continued to allow his tongue to seduce my mouth.

Lizzy my darling little whore. His moaning was intense as he laid me gently back on the bed, straddling over me, his tongue rigid as he teased my newly waxed pussy. My pussy was demanding more as his tongue found my clit, sending me wild with passion, but it was just the start.

He then kissed my lips gently, preparing me for a night of dirty love as our tongues revolved intensely around each other's mouths. Seduction was at an all-time high, but was I ready to embrace Charlie's love again after all the lost and lonely years? But I needed his love tonight.

Charlie then straddled over my naked body, his cock once again level with my mouth as I clenched it firmly between my lips allowing him to ride my mouth hard, allowing him to thrust into my throat again and again, peppering more juice over my tongue ready to share with him.

His cock was now free from my mouth to tease and love my pussy as he slid his huge love filled cock so gently into my pussy, but with an intense power, a power that brought back such evocative memories. With my legs now wrapped around his neck, his cock was now completely and fully loving my pussy to the limits. He was now riding me hard as I commanded hard, raw passion that filled my bedroom tonight. It almost felt like I had reverted back to being a virgin, allowing for the second time to allow Charlie that pleasure. His cock was now thrusting so hard again, making me screech with passion, allowing his cock that continued to love my pussy. *Lizzy you bitch, let me fuck you harder.* I remained relaxed; how could I ever refuse?

We were completely riding it, both of us moaning so loudly as I continued to demand it rough and hard, repeating my commands for some very hard, very dirty love, knowing full well that my demands were being taken care of. *Lizzy you want it rough, you dirty whore.*

Suddenly Charlie forced and thrust much harder, making me scream out. I grasped the pillow beneath my neck with both hands as his cock filled my pussy, just like it always did, but this was very intense, his cock so rigid, solid, and so full of juice for me. Charlie's riding was so very hard and powerful now and I was loving it, his moaning was deep and gritty, his breathing was hard.

Suddenly Charlie's head was firmly gripped between my thighs, his tongue was on a mission to seduce my beautiful naked pussy again, his lips locked on to my clit sending me wild with extreme passion and dirty love, making me scream out repeating his name over and over again as Charlie still gripped my clit. My demands for more now echoed from every wall in my bedroom, a bedroom that was now made for lovers, long lost lovers.

With our out of control sex fuelled dirty love over for now, we laid back in each other's arms to catch our breath, neither of us moving or saying a word. Both of us were caught up in the perfect moment, Charlie looked at me. *I love you Lizzy; I love you so much.* He stroked my face that was for now without pain and sadness. *Lizzy, I would love to meet Daisy soon.* I gulped, I knew he would ask that question at some point and that point came sooner than I had anticipated. I hesitated with my reply. *Yes you can but not yet, it's too soon Charlie.* He looked a little disappointed, but these were my terms now, our love was also on my terms as that was the way it was going to be, the way it had to be.

We kissed an amazing goodnight, glancing at the clock it was way after three am, our incredible love session had lasted hours, now falling asleep once again wrapped in each other's arms which now felt so natural and so very normal, but would I remain this contented for the foreseeable future? Only time would tell, but I was content tonight having received the most incredible dirty passion.

We awoke early on Saturday morning needing to celebrate once again our dirty reunion. I opened the bubbly while serving a delightful breakfast for us to share, I still could not believe we were lovers again. Charlie's smile was still so cocky and intoxicating and as I looked at him I craved to be loved again and Charlie was not complaining as we enjoyed some early morning dirty love, untamed and out of control, fuelled by a long separation.

As we sat in bed together after an unexpected, but very enjoyable dirty early morning loving Charlie suggested that we should go and have some special time together today. I agreed we should, and I knew the very place to take him.

Now it was my turn to show off my sleek lipstick red sports car. Charlie seemed very impressed, as I drove I could not help but smile knowing Charlie was here with me and not giving his dirty love to anyone else and that now he never would. I was going to make sure of that, our dirty love now something to celebrate, having found each other again, fate had yet again played a part in us being reunited.

At last we arrived at Daisy's art college, some of Daisy's art was on display and I thought Charlie would love to see it. I knew it would be emotional, but thought it might help him to realise what a talent she held. He was without doubt shocked, but so very proud, while we walked around admiring her work. It was totally apparent he was so proud of her as his smile was even more wider today and as Charlie looked at me his eyes were full of tears. *I'm so proud of her, so totally proud of what a talented girl she is Lizzy, what an amazing little lady she has become.* He squeezed my hand, I knew he had really enjoyed this little preview of her work with a sneak preview into her life and the special young lady she had become.

Suddenly Charlie's eyes were diverted for a split second by a small group of boys about Daisy's age who were also admiring and chatting about all the artwork on display. A mixed culture of boys, some with accents that were familiar to us both, as the Welsh accent seemed to echo loudly throughout the huge open hall. *Charlie what is it? Nothing Lizzy.* He then continued to talk about Daisy, but I could tell that on hearing them all chatting in the group something had triggered emotions, obviously jousting emotions within Charlie.

That evening we found a cosy little place for our supper and to talk more, as talking had to be key if our rekindled relationship was going to work, we both knew that so now there were to be no secrets, no lies just totally honesty.

On returning back to my flat Charlie asked about meeting Daisy again. I had to make sure he would be in our lives or Daisy's life forever, I had to know if I trusted him not to go off again leaving me to pick up the pieces, destroying our lives again, knowing that this was his last chance to prove himself beyond his words.

But then he loved me before and promised me everything, but failed to deliver his promises on so many occasions, so talk was always going to be cheap as far as I was concerned, leaving me with a lot of thinking to do because this would have a huge impact on Daisy and myself in the coming months and years ahead.

Relaxed, we talked at ease until very late as we snuggled up on my huge, comfy sofa, embracing our dirty love once again. Charlie's arm was around me as we continued to reminisce, bringing back such provocative memories that sparked so many wonderful emotions.

I could feel that Charlie and I were falling in love again and what could be better, as life again seemed to be complete. My only hope was that it would stay that way forever, but the future was never going to be that simple to predict as storms had started to gather far away in the distance, ready to cloud our future, if we had a future.

It was now 2am, lying in bed we both had to admit it was so wonderful to be together again and sharing our dirty love, our special love, rekindled from a chance meeting. Even Charlie had to admit that fate was playing its hand again in our relationship, as it had done on so many occasions in the past.

Now London was on my list of places to love and share Charlie's love, just like the pretty Wiltshire village I still adored, along with Wales, the place that had seduced my soul on that bitterly cold January afternoon.

We woke on Sunday morning and the love was so apparent between us, it filled every room with renewed love, complete with the aroma of Charlie that still sent cold shivers down my spine, spilling over into a war of untamed passion. I took control, taking Charlie on a wild and extreme sex fuelled hour of passion that left us both breathless.

Now showered and ready for the day ahead, I made us a fabulous lunch to enjoy together, complete with an expensive bottle of wine that G had bought me for Christmas. We continued flirting over lunch, Charlie continued his never-ending ability to make me blush, his eyes full of dirty love, hungry for my love. Suddenly he brushed eagerly our empty lunchtime dishes to one side before lifting me on to the huge solid oak kitchen table, peppering my lips in seductive kisses. *Lizzy*, he moaned and in a frenzy of dirty passion he had stripped me naked, my body begging to be loved here and now as I lay on the huge table. Charlie's body was now free from clothes also, our clothes lay in an unruly heap on the kitchen floor just where they fell, now with my naked body aroused by him I was treated to an unexpected early afternoon of dirty seduction complete with dirty love, as we loved the intimacy allowing us to express our pent up passions. My mouth was now loving his huge, throbbing cock.

My pussy was treated to the ultimate dirty love by Charlie's tongue, as his head was once again buried between my thighs and locked firm as I demanded more, allowing my juice to coat his lips as we continued our dirty love all the afternoon, making ourselves more comfortable on my sofa, determined to satisfy both our demanding sexual desires.

Sadly now our afternoon of dirty love was over, embracing each other in passionate kisses, not wanting to let each other go. Needing to treat my senses to Charlie's aroma again I kissed his neck, my desires were growing again, surging through my body. He knew I was feeling once again aroused so with that he scooped me up in his arms and took me to bed for yet another hour or so of dirty love.

With both of us now completely exhausted from our powerful, demanding dirty afternoon of passion, we kissed our goodbyes and whispered our I love you's, not wanting the kisses and I love you's to end, replacing one kiss for another, neither of us prepared to let go. We both knew what we now had could be amazing, but it would need absolute commitment from us both, my commitment was never in any doubt it never had been.

I pulled Charlie back into the lounge, throwing his bag into the hallway, I wasn't finished with him just yet. My sexual desires were out of control as we made passionate love again on my sofa. *Lizzy, Lizzy, Lizzy, you naughty lady!* His smile was beaming, leaving my blushes burning my checks.

So now with heavy hesitation I kissed him goodbye, never wanting him to leave, passionate kisses followed. Charlie's hand was holding mine until I closed the heavy front door behind him, my body was heavy with love once again for Charlie.

Daisy came home around 7pm excited and upbeat about her weekend. I could tell that her weekend was enjoyable from the look on her beautiful face. *It's been amazing mum, I loved it.* Excitedly she wanted to know if I had managed to see her artwork. Taking a huge breath, replying in a shaky voice, blushing in the process, *Yes I did and it was wonderful Daisy, absolutely fabulous.* Now was the right time to tell her, my voice was low, wondering if I would stumble on my words, if my admission would send me into floods of tears. I took a deep breath, *I had someone with me who loved it to Daisy.*

Her eyes lit up, her smile dazzling. *Who mum? Is grandad, is he here? No Daisy.* With that I took yet another deep breath, stumbling with my words that seemed to be muddled tonight. London held its breath in anticipation for such an unbelievable reunion. *Your dad. My dad? Yes Daisy, your dad.* Her facial expression was now crippled by a pain, a pain that was of sheer joy, disbelief shone in her eyes as I felt her hold her breath, not believing my words that now seemed all too good to be true. Her panic was on full show as she started to cry. *My dad, my dad mum. Yes Daisy, he loved your work, he is so proud of you and is desperate to see you if you would like that.* Her face was of disbelief, not knowing what to say, to either smile or cry, her tears an endorsement that she needed to meet him so

I held her little petite frame so tight, knowing this was monumental for her, watching her face go through so many stages of emotion.

With both our emotions stable I looked at her. *Shall I call him Daisy and you can talk to him if you want to. Can I mum?* Daisy was so excited and overcome with emotion, tears now once again replaced her smiles for now, I knew Charlie would be very emotional.

I dialled his number and passed the phone to a very excited Daisy who was shaking, my emotions were in tatters as I awaited both their reactions. *It's ringing mum*, she said excitedly, her tears were now replaced with a smile that was so addictive just like her daddy's.

Hello, Charlie Stevens. Daisy's face was a picture, she was silent, stunned, her breath taken away for a split second. *It's me dad, Daisy.* Silence filled the other end as I heard Charlie take a very deep breath as tonight he heard his daughters voice for the first time. *Hello darling, how are you?* My eyes were now blinded with tears as I fought back my emotions. I could tell by Charlie's voice that he too had been engulfed by emotion. *I'm fine dad, how are you? Oh Daisy, so much better now I have spoken to you.* I heard a real passion in his sexy voice tonight, a passion that I was delighted to hear. *Daisy I will see you soon I promise.* Silence now ruled both ends of the phone, both of them obviously overwhelmed by this unexpected and astonishing reunion.

Suddenly Daisy blurted out, *can you come now dad?* Daisy was desperate to meet him and get to know him. I held my breath, *yes I can come now.* Daisy glanced over, wanting my approval. I nodded my head, *mum said yes.* I smiled, *I'm on my way Daisy.* Charlie knew this was his final chance to be a dad, a proper no messing about dad. I had given him a lifeline yet again and if he messed up then there would not be another chance.

We were all so excited, Daisy was about to meet her dad, the father she never knew. This was a life-changing moment as we waited, pacing the hall for which seemed a lifetime, but then I suppose it was for her, my little Daisy.

The doorbell rang 30 minutes later. I looked at Daisy's pretty, young, petit face that was bursting with smiles. I smiled, brushing my hand over hers, *are you ready Daisy?* She was so excited as I let him in through the hallway door with Daisy in the lounge.

Charlie looked so happy. Daisy then suddenly appeared in the doorway to the hall, unable to contain herself, throwing her trembling arms around Charlie's neck. He picked her up and spun her around, we were all in tears but tears of happiness and love as they just stood looking at each other. *Daisy you're so beautiful, just like your mum.*

He then kissed her gently on her forehead and as he held both her hands he apologised over and over again for being an idiot and promising her that things would be different now and that he would never let her and I down, but again I still felt his words were cheap concerning his ongoing promises. *Dad I don't care, you're here now and that's what matters.* She was right, he was here and that was the most important thing.

I left them to talk and get to know each other, they looked so natural together. I could see the love in Charlie's brown eyes as he was now transfixed on her delicate face, her dark hair framing her petit features. Charlie was transfixed on her every word that I knew took his breath away, his smile was now full of pride as he listened to her talk freely and comfortably about her work, her new found friends, living here in London, me, her hopes and dreams for the future.

Our lounge was now full of father and daughter laughter, priceless and precious love filled the air, surrounding us in a blanket of silky, soft love. I could not get a word in edge ways, but I was so pleased for them and for us, delighted to be a family at last, the family I never thought at one point we would become.

I heard Charlie talk about me which sent a cold shiver through me, he talked about me with passion, telling Daisy about how he had fallen in love with me, his schoolboy dream, his first and only love and his never-ending love for us both. It was so very moving, maybe he had changed and turned the corner. It was getting late, and we all had a busy week ahead. Daisy and Charlie hugged each other and kissed each other goodnight and I could tell Daisy didn't want him to leave and the feeling was mutual, I too wanted him for my own again tonight, but that would have to wait.

They both had smiles larger than life itself, as we all did. Showing Charlie to the door he kissed me goodnight and whispered *I love you so much Lizzy.* He gently let his hand stroke my porcelain face, caressing my neck before smothering it in seductive kisses. I felt his hand glide over my breast, reaching inside my silk blouse. *Charlie* I moaned. He had begun to seduce my body again, I smiled, *Charlie Stevens...* I kissed him goodnight, smothering him in kisses, literally having to force him out of the door. We both smiled, knowing our dirty love was bubbling away under the surface as Charlie and I stole yet another kiss goodnight. He held my hand

and said *thank you so much for giving me another chance to be Daisy's dad.* I nodded; he knew by my expression it was his last chance.

We said goodnight over and over again, neither of us wanting to be parted. I wanted him to stay and give me some rough dirty love tonight, but that was not fair on Daisy, it had been a great weekend, so many powerful emotions that had embraced us this weekend that would undoubtedly have a lasting effect on us all.

Daisy talked about her dad at every opportunity, dad this dad that, it was so very heart warming, hoping desperately that Charlie would keep his promise and not let her down in any shape or form, because he would never get another chance, I would make sure of that.

Mid-week came and Daisy and Charlie went out for a pizza together. Charlie brought her home and Daisy went straight to bed as she had an early start, so she kissed her dad goodnight, her loving smile still so contagious. Charlie and I sat together on my comfy sofa, snuggled up while drinking our coffee, but sadly we had to say goodnight. Charlie was coming to stay again at the weekend, and I was desperate to share my bed with him again, but for now my desires would have to wait.

Friday came and Charlie was over at 7pm, I was so excited to see him. Daisy had already planned a night out with friends, and she would be back on Saturday morning, so Charlie and I had the evening to ourselves to enjoy us, so while I made us a lovely supper Charlie poured the wine, our eyes never far from each other's gaze as the flirting was too obvious to hide, fully on display, like some out of control mating ritual.

I had sorted all the photo albums out so while I cooked, Charlie sat on the old sofa looking through them, stopping for a while to gaze at Daisy's milestones, running his finger over the shining silhouettes that adorned the pages of the old albums in a desperate bid to recreate in some way possible, those lost and precious moments once again, moments that I had recorded for this very special and somewhat unexpected moment. *These are wonderful princess; did you take these? Yes Charlie, most of them.*

Tears raged within his eye now, realising just what he had missed. He looked away for a second from the precious albums. *What a fool I have been, how can you ever forgive me Lizzy? Charlie, you're here now and we love you so very much.* Rapidly, and without any thought I then asked him to move in with us. *Charlie lets be a proper family*. He looked at me surprised, by my somewhat casual request.

Instantly he smiled that sexy smile, hesitating a reply. I looked at him bemused while he smiled, keeping me in suspense, nodding his approval. *I would love that very much, but Lizzy is it too soon?* I questioned him firstly with my eyes, then my facial expressions, then with a slightly raised voice, *Charlie, why not?*

Lizzy, Charlie pulled me into his arms, I smiled. *Just move in with us Charlie. Lizzy, my gorgeous Lizzy how can I refuse?*

Can I tell Daisy? Yes of course, give her a ring Charlie. Without hesitation Charlie rang her to tell her the much long awaited news. I heard her screech with delight as she screamed to all her friends that her dad was coming home. My tears were uncontrollable as I was totally overwhelmed by her reaction, as was Charlie.

With our future living arrangements made we spent a fantastic night celebrating our new life together, as we now had so much to celebrate so we did in true Charlie and Lizzy style. Charlie opened the bubbly while I ran us a bubble bath, hot and steamy as I was going to seduce Charlie with all my life tonight. Dressed to thrill I made my move, I took him by the hand complete with fizz and lead him to the bathroom.

Lizzy was back, the naughty Lizzy. With my dress covering the secret that I was wearing, I stripped Charlie naked, every piece of his clothing now laid on my bathroom floor, while I remained fully clothed adding to the ambience.

I kissed his firm, naked, lean body with the Lizzy kisses that were special and sensually all laced with love. Charlie was silent apart from the odd moans of passion. I was now on my knees, my mouth fully engaged with the most perfectly stiff, huge throbbing cock, as Charlie was receiving my love and I knew it by his moaning that was now very deep, as his cock slipped perfectly into my throat.

Charlie then begged to strip me off, leaving me in just my secret that was my very sexy undies, complete with suspenders and killer heels. He held my arms outstretched. *Let me look at you Lizzy, stunning, fucking stunning, you beautiful whore, my beautiful whore.*

Back in my bedroom and the bubble bath was still full and now stone cold, unused, discarded for something more comfortable. Back to my huge bed I straddled over him, still in my underwear as his cock was standing to my attention full and erect, wanting to love my mouth again. *Charlie are you ready for some Lizzy loving? Princess you naughty girl.* His smile commanded my full attention. I took his cock, gently pulling the skin back tight as I thrust my mouth around its massive purple head and as I did, every bit of his body tensed up. I was sucking hard the cock that had made me a woman, that now filled my mouth. Charlie's breathing was hard, his moaning loud and very intense as he begged me to be his whore again tonight and I was never going to object.

My mouth moved to his as our tongues entwined, dancing the dance that was ours as Charlie could now taste his juice fresh from my lips, *Lizzy, Lizzy Lizzy.*

I let Charlie's cock dance with my pussy that was demanding to be loved hard and with that I received the full Charlie magic, hard and a little rough, but I was not complaining, I never would as he knew how to love me.

With Charlie's cock fully loving my pussy we made the most perfect dirty love, a love that had taken us throughout our lives and we still came back for more, repeating our eternal love.

Renewed passion followed as Charlie sucked my nipples, each one received the full pleasure of Charlie's lips that never failed to deliver.

He caressed my body with love that had been awakened once again, creating every sensual emotion that transported me back to the barn in which Charlie took my virginity allowing me to store the erotic senses that were now once again filling my body, as we made dirty love again, as tonight I needed some rough love that would burn my lips setting a fire raging within my body.

We laid in each other's arms, our lives for now were complete; we were blissfully happy at long last as our love had been reunited, but I was sure the storms that we had dodged for a while were sure to cast unwelcome clouds to mar this spirited reunion.

Saturday morning we awoke late, I made coffee and we sat in bed together just looking at each other and with smiles that said it all, wanting to pinch myself, wanting to make sure it was real and not a dream. He then leant over to kiss me again, smiling his wicked smile.

I put my coffee down and with that I once again made my intentions clear, that I needed his dirty love, and he was not objecting either as beautiful love followed. What a wonderful way to start the new day, taking us until lunch time to finish our dirty morning of love.

Charlie moved his things in over the following few weeks, reliving memories every day, finding hidden gems along the way, discovering little things about each other that we had forgotten, things we didn't know about each other.

Every evening during dinner we sat together around the huge oak table that was adorned as always by the pretty tin vase that always contained daisies, listening to Charlie tell stories to Daisy about the early days when we fell in love, telling her that it was love at first sight as our eyes met while waiting for our next lesson to start, telling her about our winter adventures into the woods, about the little cafe in which we spent so many glorious hours listening to the old and battered jukebox playing everyone's favourite songs, the little shed that was always freezing whatever time of the year that continued cobwebs that always made me shudder along with the spiders, telling her about the many Christmas memories that we cherished daily, like walking around the garden in my pyjamas and boots, while I enjoyed the first stage of labour which always made Daisy giggle. All of Charlie's stories made my skin tingle with excitement as he described our love so passionately, leaving me holding my breath and keeping my fingers crossed that Charlie would not let slip the more sexual and sensual side of our relationship.

Daisy and I loved him being with us every day, we now felt like a proper family at long last. Charlie and I continued to make fabulous dirty love every day, sometimes twice a day; in the bath, on the sofa, in bed, anywhere if it allowed and if we were alone to share our exquisite love.

The next 12 months flew by, and we were in total love, and it showed. We didn't have to hide it from the world, to not have to be so secretive about our ongoing love, Charlie and I settled into domestic bliss, loving London and all it gave us, visiting all our favourite places, Regent's Park being the place I loved the most. I still worked in the city Monday to Friday and Charlie continued building, leaving us the weekends to cherish and enjoy together.

The summer months stayed gloriously warm, but always reminded me that autumn was not far away. Charlie and I remained stunned by our love, never taking it for granted, worshipping each other daily, but suddenly in the blink of an eye September came and the day had come for Daisy to go to university. My heart was heavy with sadness as I would miss the little girl I brought up alone, but now she was a beautiful young lady with a zest for life, a zest to learn and embrace her social life, to spread her wings far and wide on what I hoped would be an amazing journey.

With Daisy at university the flat felt so empty, but there were vast amount of memories that had already been made here, constantly made me smile daily, like not having to repeatedly fall over the vast amount of Daisy's shoes that were discarded and abandoned where she stepped out of them, reminding me that it was exactly the same thing as I did, leaving my discarded belongings in the wrong place for mum or dad to trip over or to pick up, smiling to myself that this was history repeating itself, knowing mum would be smiling, telling me I told you so as she so often did, telling me I would be saying the same things to my daughter all those years later.

Now I had Charlie all to myself, exclusively mine for now and forever the way it should have been all those long years ago when we were in the first throws of our lifetime of love, a love that was never meant for anyone else, but us.

I felt guilty that I was so happy and that others had suffered for me to enjoy the ultimate happiness, but I could not imagine my life any different now, but how could we be this happy? Was life about to give us yet another cruel beating? Would it decline us from having another chance to be the couple we were destined to be all those years ago when we committed to a lifetime of love with a plastic cracker ring, a ring in a shape of a daisy, something that shaped our lives giving us the ultimate and most precious gift of all and that was our beautiful daughter Daisy?

Why not us? We should be allowed to be happy at long last, as we had earned our happiness. After all, we had both paid the price of love, which still to this day remained priceless.

I told myself to enjoy the happiness, treasure the gift that we had been given, to unwrap everyday of our lives, so with that we toasted our new reignited dirty love, our new found dirty love, a love and a life brought back to the here and now with a renewed passion, our dirty love, and my constant desire.

Years had past of loving, craving, and desiring one man, Charlie. The boy who had stolen my heart, burnt my soul, stole my virginity and my love to keep it for himself, making me his hostage, never freeing me from the chains that had shackled me to him and that still did, knowing full well I would never want it any other way. We raised our glasses to him, to me, to us and to our future whatever it had in store for us.

Suddenly my mind slipped instantly into the past, recalling the catalogue of events that had led me to become so very vulnerable and that had challenged my most precious dreams, haunting me daily in a bid to have it all, seeking the love I craved at such a tender age, allowing my body to become someone's selfish trophy, firstly being misled by Paul only wanting to trap me for his pleasurable trophy, falling in love with Charlie and his seductive reputation, wanting nothing more than to be his girl, having to endure a heart-breaking miscarriage to endure the despair I brought on my parents, bringing sadness and grief into our warm and loving family home, for just a second to fall for the virginal charms of Charlie's younger brother, to then be sexually abused and battered by Charlie's vile father in their family home with no respect for his wife or family, to allow myself a sordid one night stand with Roger, completely out of spite for my unforgettable and unforgivable actions.

To enter into a marriage built on a farce with a man I didn't love, a marriage to someone that I hated and despised, a man that happily called me his wife when surrounded by his vile circle of friends on a rare night out that I was forced to endure, but who felt it was his right to batter and bruise me for being just that, tattooing my porcelain face in a rainbow of hatred created by his very own hands.

Having to cope with terrifying sadness on my mother's untimely death at such a tender age, along with the nightly ritual of haunting visions that left me weak and terrified, having to sleep repeatedly with the light on in my room at night for comfort and some sort of reassurance that was mostly in short supply. Hearing the harrowing and endless echoes of my baby crying far in the distance that left me helpless. The relentless shame I had brought into the family home, watching my mother and father fight back the tears of my shame, knowing I had disappointed them.

Seeing Charlie's wife enter into my world, seeing her foggy silhouette in my mirror, knowing she was watching me while I seduced her husband.

Dodging the storms that were relentless, hearing the unwelcome and terrifying words that were being echoed from every unwelcome nightly visitor that left me gasping for air as I lay awake in a cold pool of fluid, all of them promising yet more storms that would lash my already tormented, battered and beaten body, coating it in yet more gruesome tattoos for others to admire, sneer and jeer at and for good measure to finger point and say *we told you so Lizzy*. Then the ultimate challenge, to love my whole life the man that remained the only man I could ever love and that was Charlie Stevens which still remains to this day the cost of my love, the price I paid to have it all… but was it ever going to be enough?

I feared today that the past would come back to haunt and taunt not only me, but Charlie too, as the past held so many secrets, lies and betrayal, knowing Charlie had a very chequered past it may only be a matter of time until we were once again shrouded in dark and threatening sky's that would be littered with storm clouds ready to shed its evil cargo from both our pasts.

H.L.F.

Hope…Love…Forever.